Lessons from

Lessons from Hogwarts

Essays on the Pedagogy *of* Harry Potter

Edited by MARCIE PANUTSOS ROVAN *and* MELISSA WEHLER

McFarland & Company, Inc., Publishers
Jefferson, North Carolina

This book has undergone peer review

ALSO OF INTEREST AND FROM MCFARLAND

Girl of Steel: Essays on Television's Supergirl *and Fourth-Wave Feminism* (2020; edited by Melissa Wehler and Tim Rayborn

LIBRARY OF CONGRESS CATALOGUING-IN-PUBLICATION DATA

Names: Rovan, Marcie Panutsos, 1985– editor. | Wehler, Melissa, 1983– editor.
Title: Lessons from Hogwarts : essays on the pedagogy of Harry Potter / edited by Marcie Panutsos Rovan and Melissa Wehler.
Description: Jefferson, North Carolina : McFarland & Company, Inc., Publishers, 2020 | Includes bibliographical references and index.
Identifiers: LCCN 2020027112 | ISBN 9781476676807 (paperback ; acid-free paper ∞) | ISBN 9781476640273 (ebook)
Subjects: LCSH: Rowling, J. K.—Criticism and interpretation. | Rowling, J. K. Harry Potter series. | Education in literature. | Mentoring in literature.
Classification: LCC PR6068.O93 Z759 2020 | DDC 823/.914—dc23
LC record available at https://lccn.loc.gov/2020027112

BRITISH LIBRARY CATALOGUING DATA ARE AVAILABLE

ISBN (print) 978-1-4766-7680-7
ISBN (ebook) 978-1-4766-4027-3

Front cover image © 2020 Shutterstock

Printed in the United States of America

McFarland & Company, Inc., Publishers
  Box 611, Jefferson, North Carolina 28640
  www.mcfarlandpub.com

Dedicated to my favorite muggles:
Aaron, Matilda, and Lucy.
M.P.R.

～

Dedicated to Cillian B.W. Vickless,
my most powerful work of magic.
M.W.

Table of Contents

Introduction

Making Magic in the Classroom:
An Introduction to Pedagogy at Hogwarts

Marcie Panutsos Rovan
and Melissa Wehler

Before she was a renowned children's author, J.K. Rowling was an educator. Rowling taught English as a foreign language in Portugal, then trained as an educator in Edinburgh. While writing the *Harry Potter* series, she taught French part-time in Edinburgh. Rowling's educational background left an indelible mark on her books, which focus not only on magic but on magical education. Hogwarts, the central location of the series, is first and foremost a boarding school. Most of the characters within the text are either students or professors. While numerous scholars have looked at the series' relationship to other boarding school stories or considered how the series can be used in the classroom, there has been little focused analysis of the educational theories and practices depicted within the walls of Hogwarts.

Since its publication, the series has inspired scholars to analyze its engagement with gender, its relationship to mythology and fairy tales, and its literary and historical influences. Scholars have examined the impact that the books have had on popular culture, children's literacy, and children's literature. Collections have considered the series as a way of exploring various disciplines, such as politics, philosophy, religion, ethics, and psychology, among other fields. In her introduction to *Critical Insights: The Harry Potter Series*, M. Katherine Grimes outlines the many ways in which the *Harry Potter* texts can provide useful subject matter for almost any course curriculum and identifies specific texts that could be used in various fields. Collections like Valerie Estelle Frankel's *Teaching with Harry Potter* and Catherine Belcher and Becky Stephenson's *Teaching Harry Potter* provide a wealth of information on this topic. Yet, lost in all this scholarship has been a serious engagement with the way the series portrays education and teaching.

Several scholars have provided individual critiques of the educational pedagogy of the *Harry Potter* series. Renée Dickinson and Elisabeth Rose Gruner both argue that most learning at Hogwarts is self-directed and occurs outside of the classroom. Mary Black and Marilyn Eisenwine similarly explore the importance of critical thinking and problem solving within the Hogwarts curriculum. Lisa Hopkins echoes this theme in arguing that learning at Hogwarts "must always be acquired slowly, painfully, and over a period of time" (3). Charles Elster extends this argument to demonstrate how the series relies on "inquiry based learning" (204) that distinguishes classroom learning from "real learning." Elster notes that the adults often conceal important knowledge from the students at Hogwarts. Kathryn McDaniel uses Professor Binns as a negative example to argue in favor of effective lecturing strategies. Other scholars, such as Andrea Bixler, Melissa C. Johnson, and Jennifer Conn examine the failures and successes of individual instructors with a focus on specific strategies, such as metacognition (Bixler), skillful questioning and constructive feedback (Conn), cooperative learning and inclusivity (Johnson), and active learning (all three). Dickinson examines the failures of Hogwarts' instructors to scaffold learning and move students to higher levels of Bloom's taxonomy.

The existing research on this topic is a useful starting point for any discussion of educational pedagogy within the series. However, its scope is limited, and many of the articles focus more on the evaluation of individual instructors rather than providing a sustained look at the educational culture of Hogwarts. *Lessons from Hogwarts* aims to enrich this conversation by providing a sustained look at pedagogy and praxis within the book series. The essays in this collection address a broad range of educational topics, building on the foundation established by the existing scholarship to provide a more in-depth look at the educational philosophies present within Hogwarts School of Witchcraft and Wizardry. All the essays use pedagogy as the lens to discuss the *Harry Potter* series. Some authors choose a social sciences approach while others use literary analysis to examine education practices in the series. This collection is aimed at educators interested in seeing a popular application of pedagogy theories and strategies as well as *Harry Potter* scholars who are invested in a unique analysis of the teachers and students at Hogwarts.

Methodology in Context

In assembling this collection of essays, we examine various pedagogical approaches and educational concerns depicted in the *Harry Potter* series to see what the books can teach us about the nature of teaching. The collection analyzes the *Harry Potter* series by using many of the methods and concepts common in the Scholarship of Teaching and Learning (SoTL). As a body of research, SoTL emphasizes using reflection to systematically analyze teaching, employ evidence-based practices to assess that teaching, and report those findings to improve the learning experience of students. Kathleen McKinney defines SoTL as the "systematic study of teaching and/or learning and the public sharing and review of such work through presentations, performance, or publications" (39). Similarly, Peter Felten defines five principles of good practice for SoTL. According to Felten, SoTL inquiry must be "focused on student learning," "grounded in context," "methodologically sound," "conducted in partnership with students," and "appropriately public" (122). This collection uses many of these same techniques and applies them to literary artifacts in order to examine the ways that teaching practices are represented in literature. For instance, several essays in the collection employ comparative analysis and case studies—two SoTL methods—as the organizing principle for their literary analysis and criticism. Applying SoTL methods to literary artifacts in this way creates connections between two seemingly disparate fields of study and contributes to our understanding of both literature and pedagogy. In addition to using SoTL methods, all of the essays examine a core concept within that body of research. These include learner-centered pedagogy, active learning, peer tutoring, and mentorship. By using these concepts to frame their literary analysis, the authors in the collection demonstrate the possibilities for using SoTL in a transdisciplinary way. These approaches allow us to unpack literary representations and understand them as part of popular narratives around teaching and learning.

The *Harry Potter* series incorporates many common tropes about teachers in popular culture, and many of the professors themselves initially appear to be archetypes: the bumbling but well-meaning teacher (Hagrid); the stern but kind-hearted matron (McGonagall); the mysterious, all-knowing, but often aloof professor (Dumbledore); the constantly unsure, seemingly long-term substitute (Quirrell); the fire-and-brimstone teacher (Snape); the street-smart, practitioner rebel (Crouch-as-Moody); the boring professor (Binns); the unqualified teacher (Trelawney); and the inspiring, *Dead Poet's Society*–style educator (Lupin). Some of these professors exist solely as stock characters, unable to transcend their stereotypical depictions, and their pedagogy reflects this lack of development. For others, however, readers are given a more extensive look at their classroom practices and develop a more nuanced understanding of their characters. When we examine the pedagogy of these characters, what we learn is that Rowling uses these stereotypes from popular culture as an entry point to help readers understand that teachers and teaching go beyond what we see in the classroom and that what we do see in the classroom is informed by what happens beyond those walls. Pedagogy, in other words, is the product of training and expertise, yes, but also of character, history, life experience, and relationships. By examining teaching and teachers within the walls of Hogwarts, we can gain a look "behind the curtain" of education.

Section and Essay Summaries

The essays in the collection have been organized thematically around the specific element of pedagogy they examine, including learning environments, approaches to teaching and learning, and mentoring relationships. This organizational structure contextualizes the individual essays and creates a dialogue among the essays in order to provide a cohesive examination of teaching and learning throughout the series.

In "Rooms of Requirement: Environments for Learning," authors explore different learning spaces at Hogwarts and the ways these spaces impact teaching and learning. In "The Role of Academic Librarians in Student Learning: A Comparative Analysis of the Hogwarts Librarian and Muggle Academic Librarians," Samantha Bise uses the outdated practices of Madam Pince to explore the evolution of library and information science and the central role of research within the *Harry Potter* series. In Marcie Panutsos Rovan's essay, "Dumbledore's Army: A Case for Peer Tutoring," the author looks at Dumbledore's Army within the context of writing center pedagogy to argue for the necessity of a "third space" for student learning. In "Neville Longbottom and the Multifarious Learning Environment: Inclusivity and Reciprocity at Hogwarts," Emma Louise Barlow and Alice Loda explore the various classroom-based and non–classroom-based learning experiences of the character Neville Longbottom to discuss attitudes and pedagogical approaches towards inclusivity within Hogwarts. Concluding this section, Brynn Fitzsimmons and Addison Lucchi examine the pedagogical implications of the Hogwarts houses in terms of both learning and teaching styles and learner-centered pedagogy in "Teaching Wizarding Houses: Hogwarts' Case for a Learner-Centered Pedagogy."

The next section, "Sorting Out Approaches to Teaching and Learning," explores specific theoretical approaches to teaching and learning to unpack the pedagogy in the series. In "Composition Pedagogy as Defense Against the Dark Arts," Rachelle A.C. Joplin considers differing approaches (theoretical, practical, and integrated) in Defense Against the Dark Arts (DADA) classes in terms of pedagogical approaches to composition instruction. Jessica L. Tinklenberg explores the wide range of active learning strategies employed to differing degrees and varying results by Hogwarts faculty in "Active Learning Pedagogy at Hogwarts." Tara Moore's essay, "Sorted on the First Day: A Hogwarts Guide to Extinguishing Growth Mindset and Instilling Fixed Ideas of the Self," takes a critical view of the Hogwarts house system and how both the Sorting and instructor feedback create a fixed mindset that is only occasionally offset by an emphasis on effort and growth. Finally, Laurie Johnson and Carl Niekerk examine classroom power dynamics in Dolores Umbridge's Defense Against the Dark Arts classroom within the history of totalitarian pedagogy in their essay, "Fascism in the Classroom in *Harry Potter and the Order of the Phoenix*," to explore the political implications of different pedagogical approaches.

The collection's final section, "Fantastic Mentors and Where (Not) to Find Them," analyzes effective and ineffective mentoring relationships throughout the series to unpack the impact of these relationships on both the students and the mentors. Lee Anna Maynard explores Harry's evolution into the role of educator and how he draws on positive and negative role models to focus Dumbledore's Army (the D.A.) on student-centered experiential learning in "Defending Against the Dark Arts: Harry's Path from Pupil to Professor in *The Order of the Phoenix*." Next, Mary Reding argues that multiple mentorship is necessary for initiation into wizarding pedagogical space and explores the array of mentors who guide Harry through liminal spaces throughout his education in "Harry Potter's Pedagogical Paradigm: Multiple Mentors Maketh the Man." In their essay, "The Good, the Bad, the Toxic: Using Muggle-Borns as a Lens for the First-Generation-Student Experience with Mentorship," Jamie L.H. Goodall and Kerry Spencer examine appropriate and inappropriate mentor/mentee relationships within Hogwarts to provide guidance for first-generation students and the faculty who wish to mentor them. The section concludes with "The Fractured Pedagogy of Care: How Hogwarts' Teachers (Don't) Demonstrate Self-Care" by Jen McConnel, which considers ways in which Hogwarts professors demonstrate a pedagogy of care (to varying degrees of success) that consistently neglects self-care.

Pedagogy Beyond Hogwarts

Rowling's *Pottermore* provides context on only 19 Hogwarts professors who teach during Harry's educational career at Hogwarts on its "Professors" page: Albus Dumbledore, Minerva McGonagall, Severus Snape, Dolores Umbridge, Sybill Trelawney, Quirinus Quirrell, Pomona Sprout, Filius Flitick, Professor Binns, Gilderoy Lockhart, Remus Lupin, Rubeus Hagrid, Horace Slughorn, Barty Crouch, Jr. (as Mad-Eye Moody), Charity Burbage, Firenze, Alecto Carrow, Amycus Carrow, and Professor Kettleburn. In addition to these, the books mention a few others: Aurora Sinistra, Septima Vector, Wilhelmina Grubbly-Plank, and Madam Hooch among them. However, many of these instructors (Quirrell, Hooch, Burbage, Sinistra, Vector, Kettleburn, and the Carrows) are never (or hardly ever) shown in the classroom, so there is little available information on their teaching pedagogy or praxis. This leaves about 14 professors for whom a sustained analysis of pedagogy is possible. Among these, a few clearly rise to the forefront of discussions of teaching: Dumbledore, McGonagall, Snape, Umbridge, Lupin, Hagrid, and Crouch-as-Moody. Because of this, many of the essays in this collection focus on these same central figures; however, the authors within these pages have varied perspectives on the teaching approaches at Hogwarts. Thus, while several essays may hold Dumbledore up as a paradigm of effective teaching, others use him as a negative example. Even where the authors agree on a professor's effectiveness, they are still analyzing that teaching effectiveness through different lenses such as mentoring, librarianship, active learning, and growth-mindset, among others. Our goal is to provide diverse perspectives that can help educators hone their craft and help others think more critically about the quality of education at Hogwarts, specifically, and the way education is represented in popular culture more broadly.

WORKS CITED

Belcher, Catherine L., and Becky Herr Stephenson. *Teaching Harry Potter*. Palgrave Macmillan, 2011.

Bixler, Andrea. "What We Muggles Can Learn About Teaching from Hogwarts." *The Clearing House*, vol. 84, no. 2, 2011, pp. 75–79.

Black, Mary S., and Marilyn J. Eisenwine. "Education of the Young Harry Potter: Socialization and Schooling for Wizards." *The Educational Forum*, vol. 66, no. 1, 2001, pp. 32–37.

Conn, Jennifer L. "What Can Clinical Teachers Learn from *Harry Potter and the Philosopher's Stone?*" *Medical Education*, vol. 36, 2002, pp. 1176–81.

Dickinson, Renée. "Harry Potter Pedagogy: What We Learn About Teaching and Learning." *The Clearing House*, vol. 79, no. 6, 2006, pp. 240–244.

Elster, Charles. "The Seeker of Secrets: Images of Learning, Knowing, and Schooling." *Harry Potter's World: Multidisciplinary Critical Perspectives*, edited by Elizabeth E. Heilman, Taylor and Francis, 2003, pp. 203–220.

Felten, Peter. "Principles of Good Practice in SoTL." *Teaching & Learning Inquiry: The ISSOTL Journal*, vol. 1, no 1, 2013, pp. 121–125. www.jstor.org/stable/10.2979/teachlearninqu.1.1.121?seq=1#metadata_info_tab_contents.

Frankel, Valerie Estelle. *Teaching with Harry Potter: Essays on Classroom Wizardry from Elementary School to College*. McFarland, 2013.

Grimes, M. Katherine. "On J.K. Rowling's Harry Potter Series." *Critical Insights: The Harry Potter Series*, edited by Lana A. Whited and M. Katherine Grimes, Salem Press, 2015, pp. 3–16.

Gruner, Elisabeth R. "Teach the Children: Education and Knowledge in Recent Fantasy." *Children's Literature*, vol. 37, 2009, pp. 216–235.

Hopkins, Lisa. "Harry Potter and the Acquisition of Knowledge." *Reading Harry Potter: Critical Essays*, edited by Giselle Liza Anatol, Praeger, 2003, pp. 3–34.

Johnson, Melissa C. "Wands or Quills? Lessons in Pedagogy from Harry Potter." *The CEA Forum*, vol. 44, no. 2, 2015, pp. 75–91.

McDaniel, Kathryn. "Harry Potter and the Ghost Teacher: Resurrecting the Lost Art of Lecturing." *The History Teacher*, vol. 43, no. 2, 2010, pp. 289–95.
McKinney, Kathleen. *Enhancing Learning Through the Scholarship of Teaching and Learning: The Challenges and Joys of Juggling*, Jossey-Bass, 2007, pp. 122.

Rooms of Requirement
Environments for Learning

The Role of Academic Librarians in Student Learning

A Comparative Analysis of the Hogwarts Librarian and Muggle Academic Librarians

SAMANTHA BISE

Madam Irma Pince—witch and librarian at Hogwarts School of Witchcraft and Wizardry—is an unhelpful librarian who is not present throughout the storyline, despite the many times Hogwarts students utilize the library's resources to conduct academic and personal research. Her commitment to protecting her library's books best aligns with the outdated values of ancient libraries, and she fails to adapt to the evolving needs of her school's community and the greater library and information science profession. The series is set during the 1990s—a time when the practices and values of librarians had already evolved into a more accessible model. The values of academic librarians changed to include protecting their collections, providing equitable access to information and resources, teaching information literacy to their campus communities, helping students evaluate sources, and working against censorship efforts to preserve democracy. Madam Pince displays a strong resistance to these expanding responsibilities, even as Lord Voldemort rises to power, but various other characters throughout the saga make up for the librarian's failure to adapt to modern professional standards.

The Evolution of Libraries

A library in its most basic form is a repository of records and artifacts. The practice of collecting, organizing, and protecting these records to preserve history and human knowledge is known as the academic discipline of library and information science, a discipline within which Madam Pince works. This practice of storing and managing records to preserve knowledge is a defining mark of a civilization, so the concept of libraries is almost as old as civilizations themselves. As civilizations and the needs of communities become more complex, these repositories and practices continue to evolve. Madam Pince, however, has not adapted according to the needs of the community she serves.

Ancient libraries valued protection, like Madam Pince, because records and artifacts were seen as a valuable commodity to guard. Historical records indicate that ancient libraries date back to the 21st century BCE, when the clay tablets existed ("Library"). Clay tablets, like all forms of ancient writing, were difficult and time-consuming to replicate. As a result, collections of these rare records were valuable and protected. Madam Pince's practices in librarianship reflect the philosophy of ancient libraries. For example, in *Order of the Phoenix*, Ginny Weasley brings Harry Potter a chocolate egg for Easter, and Madam Pince immediately notices the chocolate as a danger to her books (*OotP* 655–56). She approaches Ginny and Harry in a fury and forces the two students to stop what they are doing and leave the library by casting a spell that makes Harry's possessions attack the students on their way out (*OotP* 656). This incident demonstrates that the Hogwarts Librarian values protecting her collection above all.

As a librarian, Madam Pince should realize that a collection is only valuable if it is accessible to members of the community. In the centuries to follow the first clay tablets, the ability to more easily replicate records and the demand for access to information increased. The Library of Alexandria, one of the most notable libraries in history, grew to a cataloged collection of about 700,000 scrolls, and a branch library was created to accommodate this growth ("Library"). The primary focus of libraries expanded to include both protecting collections and providing access to information. However, when there is an increase in access to information, there is an increase in political concern. The Library of Alexandria was a casualty of enemy fire during an Egyptian civil war around 48 BCE, and the branch location was purposely destroyed in the 4th century by those in power as a display of control and an attempt to censor alternative ideas when Christianity became the only recognized religion of the empire ("Library—The History"). Libraries and other organizations dedicated to the preservation of information have been created, destroyed, and rebuilt repeatedly throughout history, proving that information and knowledge have power. Destroying or limiting access to recorded knowledge is an effort by those in power to control a population, and Madam Pince's efforts to restrict access to her library's collection contribute to this injustice.

The famous burning of the Library of Alexandria occurred because the people in power knew an uninformed population is the easiest to control. Madam Pince does not burn the Hogwarts library, but her practices, unapproachability, and tendency to chase students out of the library create similar destruction to the access of valuable information. Restricting this access hinders the learning process of the Hogwarts students and does not align with the best practices of modern Muggle academic librarians seeking to help foster a learning environment for their students.

Censorship and Libraries

Censorship goes beyond the removal of unwanted books from a collection and includes the process of selecting what items are accessible to a community. Censorship can be committed both intentionally and unintentionally, and all limitations and restrictions to information can be considered forms of censorship. Librarians are responsible for deciding what books and resources are available to their communities, and therefore must be intentional about not contributing to the censorship of a community while making professional decisions. In an effort to avoid censoring a community, libraries create collection development policies and procedures to follow when making decisions about what resources to include in their collections. Often these policies are directly related to an institution's mission. The mission of Hogwarts is to educate young witches and wizards, so each resource at the Hogwarts library should be accessible to students to directly benefit their learning. Madam Pince's passive contributions to the censorship of the Hogwarts community lead to academic frustrations for her students and arguably contribute to Voldemort's growing power over the magical community.

Although libraries have been destroyed violently in the past to support the agenda of those seeking power, censorship can happen more subtly and be equally as damaging. As displayed in *Order of the Phoenix*, the Hogwarts community finds itself under the control of the Ministry of Magic and Cornelius Fudge, rather than the obvious enemy: Voldemort. The Ministry of Magic attempts to control information and silence the truth by discrediting Harry Potter and Professor Dumbledore (*OotP*). The *Daily Prophet* claims that Harry is spreading lies about the return of the Dark Lord because he enjoys the fame and attention, and the news source attempts to ruin Professor Dumbledore's reputation by stating that his old age is affecting his mind (*OotP*). This news source is under the direct influence of the Ministry of Magic and is contributing to censorship.

These censorship efforts are equally as dangerous to a community as the burning of books during wartime. When a community begins to use information passively, they are in danger of losing fundamental freedoms that keep a democracy in place. As seen in the *Order of the Phoenix* storyline, bureaucracies bend towards self-preservation and often operate out of fear. The Ministry of Magic acts out of fear by silencing and discrediting valuable voices in the wizarding world, ultimately helping Voldemort rise to power as the community fails to unite against a common threat. With access to dangerous information, like Harry's experience witnessing Voldemort first-hand, Hogwarts and the greater wizarding world would have had the knowledge necessary to begin preparing for Voldemort's return. Instead, they struggled to increase public awareness of the truth. Librarians strive to protect the intellectual freedoms of their communities by resisting all forms of censorship, but Madam Pince's passivity in her role as an information professional contributes to these bureaucratic censorship efforts.

In *Order of the Phoenix*, the Ministry of Magic continues to censor the magical world by giving Dolores Umbridge the power to decide what information the Hogwarts community can access. One of her new responsibilities at Hogwarts is to teach Defense Against the Dark Arts (*OotP*). Umbridge refuses to participate in any process of inquiry in her classroom, restricts lessons rooted in defensive magic, and promotes theory over practice (*OotP*). Restricting the content students are able to question in the classroom not only hinders their growth mindset, but also prevents Hogwarts students from obtaining the knowledge and skills they need to help defeat Voldemort and protect the rights of the greater wizarding world. Umbridge's censorship efforts are the most dangerous, because she is convinced that her efforts are contributing to the safety of the community. Current philosophies of librarianship have evolved to understand that all forms of censorship—no matter how well intended—are an infringement on a society's freedom and power. No amount of ignorance equates to the safety of a community. Although Umbridge may have ultimately found a way to control the Hogwarts library's collection and policies, Madam Pince should have promoted the library as a third learning space where students could find answers to their suppressed questions. Madam Pince had a larger role to play during Umbridge's reign and censorship of her school, but she failed in this mission.

Readers see the subtle censorship efforts of the Ministry of Magic when the ministry attempts to discredit members of the Hogwarts community and sends Umbridge to control the school, but the censorship efforts become more obvious when Umbridge bans *The Quibbler* in one of her Educational Decrees (*OotP*). *The Quibbler* has a controversial interview with Harry Potter, and Umbridge will do anything to keep the Hogwarts community from reading this issue (*OotP*). An informed public is difficult to control, so Umbridge attempts to ban this publication in response to her fear of losing control over the school. As Hermione points out, however, banning something makes it more desirable, so students still manage to find the interview published in *The Quibbler.* Banning information does not make it inaccessible, and these kinds of censorship efforts can often backfire.

As Umbridge demonstrates, bureaucracies and policies censor a community in the same way that book burning does. Madam Pince's library collection policies also work against the anti-censorship efforts of many modern librarians. The Restricted Section of the Hogwarts library has disturbed many academic librarians. Elizabeth A. Richardson and Sarah Wagner discuss the Restricted Section as "the most outward display of limitations and censorship in the Hogwarts library" (10), and the authors claim that labeling items as restricted does not actually discourage students from attempting to access the materials. In *Sorcerer's Stone*, Harry, Hermione, and Ron are in the library researching Nicolas Flamel (*SS* 198). When Madam Pince sees Harry getting close to the restricted section, she makes him leave by "brandish[ing] a feather duster at him" (*SS* 198) instead of offering her expertise to help the students find what they are looking for. Later, Harry wears his Invisibility Cloak to sneak into the Restricted Section (*SS* 205–07). Creating and maintaining a restricted section of items is censorship at its core— giving somebody the power to decide what information the public is able to access.

Often, libraries are subject to power dynamics and policies that go beyond the control of librarians. For example, after Headmaster Albus Dumbledore discovers that Tom Riddle learned about black magic from library books, Dumbledore removes all the Horcrux books from the library collection (*DH*). Dumbledore has only the best of intentions when making this decision, but this is an unjust response to the problem. The information that led Voldemort to kill people is the same information Harry Potter and his friends need to defeat Voldemort in the end. Censoring this information for future generations causes more problems than it solves. A more effective response would have been for Dumbledore to work with Madam Pince to create a plan to educate students about how to be responsible users of information.

Information can be dangerous, but censoring information has been proven more dangerous throughout history and throughout the *Harry Potter* series. Information is often censored by those in power who are reacting to fear and also by those who have noble intentions. Both forms of censorship are equally as damaging to a community and a democracy. Libraries play a vital role in working against all censorship efforts, and the best way to avoid information being used to cause harm is to educate students on the power information has. Librarians are in a unique position on campuses to be able to teach students about these complicated issues.

Librarians Become Educators

Hogwarts students, like other members of academic communities, require access to information and resources to learn. As a result, many schools have placed their libraries in central locations on their campuses and in their buildings to make the services and resources more accessible to students, faculty, and staff. As academic libraries become a focal point for academic communities, the roles of librarians expand to include educational responsibilities. The American Library Association (ALA) began to provide leadership and direction in the best practices of the library and information science profession across the country in 1876. Three years later, ALA's political reach began to expand when it was "incorporated under the laws ... of Massachusetts" ("History—About ALA"). In the century to follow, ALA helped libraries across the nation create book mobiles, provided books to deployed members of the military, began diverse round tables and committees to promote equitable access to information, and established The Office for Intellectual Freedom ("History—About ALA"). Within one hundred years, libraries became an organized force dedicated to providing equitable access to information, educational resources, and research services to people of all backgrounds, education levels, and socioeconomic statuses. In the *Harry Potter* series, Madam Pince serves a diverse community of students, but unsuccessfully offers the resources and services that the profession strives towards.

Madam Pince fails to meet many of the profession's standards, and her approach to her role as the librarian of Hogwarts is an inaccurate depiction of what present-day academic librarians offer to their campus community. ALA outlines the professional responsibilities of library professionals in their Code of Ethics. Library professionals should not only provide "equitable service" and "equitable access," but also commit to offering "courteous responses to all requests" ("Professional Ethics"). The descriptions of Madam Pince throughout the series demonstrate her disrespectful and unapproachable tendencies towards students using the library. In her debut scene, she is found "brandish[ing] a feather duster" at Harry and telling him to "get out" (*SS* 198). In *Chamber of Secrets*, readers get the first physical description of the librarian—a "thin, irritable woman who looked like an underfed vulture" (*CoS* 163). We continue to see examples of her irritable characteristics throughout the rest of the books. For example, when Harry is searching for a way to survive under water for the second task of the Triwizard Tournament, she is found rushing him out of the library at closing time despite his obvious anxiety (*GoF* 488). She is seen "breathing down the necks" of students (*OotP* 538), "prowling the shelves" (*H-BP* 305), and "lung[ing] at [a book] with a claw like hand" (*H-BP* 308). These images are uninviting and create barriers between a librarian and a student, ultimately causing harm to students' education. Students are less likely to ask for research support with these misguided perceptions of how a librarian helps them throughout their educational careers.

Academic librarians educate both in and out of the classroom, and librarians are often embedded into curriculum and provide formal instruction in courses. They provide one-on-one reference services to students seeking research support. However, stereotypical characters in popular media, like Madam Pince, make it difficult for librarians to be seen as helpful resources in a student's educational career. These stereotypes can make providing information literacy instruction and research reference services a challenge, as examined by academic librarians Nicole Pagowsky and Erica DeFrain. Through the academic lens of educational psychology, Pagowsky and DeFrain argue that instruction librarians, a concept dating back to the 1970s, are most successful when a librarian can be perceived as simultaneously "warm" and "competent" (2). Although these two traits can seem contradictory, educators often develop identities in the learning environment that allow them to be both a teacher and mentor for their students. Academic librarians, however, have to contend with stereotypes of characters in popular culture—like the irritable and unapproachable Hogwarts Librarian—inhibiting their efforts to educate their communities on the complex information landscape and the need for responsible research skills.

These stereotypes do not align with ALA's professional codes and standards for modern library professionals, which demonstrate the major shortcomings of Madam Pince. As a librarian, she should strive to be courteous to her campus community and provide access to her collection. Her practices have not evolved alongside the profession and the academic needs of students. In addition to preserving and providing access to records, academic librarians have further evolved to offer formal educational instruction on topics related to information literacy and research. Madam Pince, once again, fails to adapt and does not serve her campus community as needed.

Madam Pince's nonexistent role in the education of her students is not unique or new. Academics have been examining the evolving role of the librarian as an educator for decades. In 1998, Gary P. Radford challenged library and information science scholars to "rethink traditional notions of the library, librarian and, most importantly, library users" ("Flaubert" 616). Radford emphasizes the problems library professionals had in the 1980s and 1990s combatting library and librarian stereotypes present throughout literature: the "raised finger to the librarian's lip," the librarian's "strictness," and the "dusty volumes" ("Flaubert" 619). The stereotypes create a power dynamic between the practitioners responsible for keeping knowledge and the students seeking knowledge. Students, as seekers of knowledge, require academic librarians who are committed to working against stereotypes like those demonstrated by Madam Pince, and library workers continue to adapt to the information and educational needs of the communities they serve.

Librarians Help Students Evaluate Sources

Academic libraries, like that of Hogwarts, serve a unique community, so they have their own set of standards. The Association of College and Research Libraries (ACRL), a division of ALA founded in 1940 ("ACRL History"), leads academic libraries by providing standards and best practices for the profession. Among these standards is the Framework for Information Literacy for Higher Education, which was formally implemented by the ACRL board in January of 2016 ("Framework"). The framework presents guidelines for academic librarians who provide information literacy instruction for students. Some of these guidelines include teaching students about the need to evaluate the purpose and authority of information in all formats, teaching research as a nonlinear process of inquiry, and providing instruction and reference services to help educate students ("Framework")—all of which Madam Pince disregards.

One major concern for librarians who teach information literacy is how students are evaluating sources for credibility. The Hogwarts collection, although not digitized, is as diverse as the current information landscape. As formats of information began to progress—like online journals, digitized archival collections, social media, and websites—the library profession became more complex. Information became easier to create and more accessible to the public, creating an overabundance of information to navigate. Academic librarians found their campus communities in a world of rapid information evolution, and their roles expanded once again. Academic librarians became responsible for educating their campus communities on how to navigate the increasingly complex information landscape and mentoring their students throughout their education. Madam Pince's collection continues to be accessed without professional guidance or education.

Unlike modern Muggle academic librarians, Madam Pince fails to provide classroom instruction or reference services to help teach her students how to critique sources, determine their purpose, and evaluate them in all formats. Mary P. Freier, a librarian who researches depictions of librarians in mystery and detective fiction, claims that the irresponsible use of information by Hogwarts students has resulted in dangerous circumstances (Freier). She analyzes Ginny Weasley's initial reaction to trust the information coming from Tom Riddle's diary, a magical book and a Horcrux (*CoS*), resulting in the "entire school [being] in danger" because it "nearly takes her life in order to embody its piece of Voldemort's soul" (Freier 3) and ends up in the hands of Harry. Freier's analysis of the students' misplaced trust in the source faults Madam Pince and her lack of instruction efforts. If Madam Pince were to provide instruction that stressed the importance of understanding how a resource is created, Ginny Weasley and Harry may have been more likely to be critical of Tom Riddle's diary and less likely to end up alone with Lord Voldemort in the Chamber of Secrets (*CoS*).

In addition to students trusting dangerous sources, an underlying theme in the latter half of the series is the need to evaluate news sources. Rita Skeeter, journalist of the *Daily Prophet*, publishes embellished and misleading news stories surrounding Harry's participation in the Triwizard Tournament (*GoF*). After Harry witnesses the return of Lord Voldemort (*GoF* 643), the reports from news organizations divide the magical community into those who believe Harry's claim and those who do not (*OotP*). Madam Pince, as the information expert on campus, should work to help students understand the power dynamics and agendas often involved in the creation of information. The Ministry of Magic's fear of acknowledging Voldemort's return influences the news reports (*OotP*). Librarians should help students learn to be critical of these factors in order to be responsible users of information.

There is no shortage of examples of Hogwarts students using sources irresponsibly. In addition to Riddle's diary, Harry misuses a non-magical book—his annotated potions book, which formerly belonged to the Half-Blood Prince (*H-BP*). Despite Harry's previous experience with the diary and his growing curiosity, Harry does not investigate the author of the annotations (*H-BP*). He speculates on who the author may be but makes no effort to discover his identity. Making an intentional effort to discover who the author is would have changed the way Harry used the book as a source (*H-BP*), and a more competent librarian would teach students the complexities of giving sources credibility.

Research is a process in inquiry, meaning that evaluating sources and reading a text closely is an educational method. However, researching to find the answer to one question inherently raises additional questions and requires more research. This process of inquiry and close reading of a source is most present in *Deathly Hallows* when Harry, Hermione, and Ron are searching for the Horcruxes preserving pieces of Voldemort's soul (*DH*). The more information they have access to and the more they learn about the Horcruxes, the more questions they have. For example, Dumbledore leaves Hermione a first-edition copy of *The Tales of Beedle the Bard*, a children's book, in his will (*DH* 125–26). Hermione knows this is an important piece of information in their efforts to locate the Horcruxes but must read the source critically before ultimately understanding its purpose (*DH*). She eventually realizes the Deathly Hallows mark is in the book and connects it to a necklace worn by Luna Lovegood's father—Xenophilius Lovegood (*DH*). Understanding a source's purpose and relevance can take time and be frustrating for students. Fortunately, the Hogwarts students become comfortable with the nonlinear research process without the help of Madam Pince. Unlike academic librarians in the Muggle world, she fails to foster the important sense of curiosity in her students.

Educators need to meet students where they are in their learning process, and readers see evidence of this throughout the education of Hogwarts students. Renée Dickinson writes that classroom instruction plays only a minor role in the overall education of Hogwarts students, and many students guide their own learning experiences (240). She discusses the strengths and shortcomings of the pedagogy implemented at Hogwarts by arguing that it is questionable how much students can learn from their professors without having real-life experiences to supplement the course material (243). Students manage their own learning experiences, so having educators in supporting roles to help students outside of class is important. Madam Pince, as the librarian of Hogwarts, should be helping to fill this role. A librarian's expertise and contributions to education have the potential to help students locate and destroy Voldemort's Horcruxes (*DH*), evaluate news sources (*OotP*), and understand the authority of the author of the annotations in Harry's potions textbook (*H-BP*). However, Madam Pince fails to fulfill her duties.

Madam Pince's lack of teaching and providing educational support to her students contributes to the staggering stereotype of the modern librarian, and library and information science scholars are examining the real-world effects of these stereotypes. Pagowsky and Miriam Rigby are scholars in social psychology and anthropology who study the overlaps between these disciplines and librarianship. Pagowsky and Rigby analyze the impact of popular culture's librarian stereotypes on student learning by stating it is "nearly impossible for one to enter a completely unknown situation without expectations or some form of stereotype" (18). Many students have preconceived ideas of what a library and a librarian are, and many students come into college unaware that their librarians are research experts and educators dedicated to their successes. This decreases the likelihood of a student asking for research support and being exposed to credible information. At a school like Hogwarts, students need a librarian who is dedicated to teaching students how to think critically about the types of information they are working with.

Libraries and Democracy

Library professionals work to preserve records, provide access to information, combat censorship efforts, and help communities evaluate sources. These efforts all play a vital role in the preservation of democracy, and academic librarians understand the importance of these overlaps. As seen in the *Harry Potter* series, research skills have real-world applications for students and faculty. In addition to helping educate students to become more information literate, academic librarians are researchers who collaborate with their colleagues to produce scholarship and improve practice. ALA's Code of Ethics emphasizes how important it is for library professionals to "enhanc[e] [their] own knowledge" and contribute to academic scholarship ("Professional Ethics"). In contrast, in all of Dumbledore's research efforts, Madam Pince is not consulted once, demonstrating that she is not an engaged participant in the scholarship produced by Hogwarts faculty.

While Madam Pince is not present to help her community through their research processes throughout the series, research continues to play a dominant role. Harry, Hermione, and Ron utilize the library and its resources to research Nicolas Flamel and learn about the sorcerer's stone (*SS*), which leads to discovering that Lord Voldemort strives to achieve immortality through the stone. The library's resources and the ability to conduct research continue to aid the students when they research past cases of dangerous creatures who have been on trial in an effort to help Rubeus Hagrid prove to the Committee for the Disposal of Dangerous Creatures that Buckbeak, a hippogriff, is innocent (*PoA*). In both instances, Madam Pince is not available to help her campus with its research needs. Librarians, like most educators in higher education, are both practitioners and scholars, but Madam Pince does not successfully offer her students research support or contribute to their scholarly assignments at Hogwarts. After Lord Voldemort comes back (*GoF*), the need for relevant research becomes increasingly important. The librarian of Hogwarts should be perceived as an expert in information and research; therefore, she should be seen as a vital member of The Order of the Phoenix— a group created to fight Lord Voldemort's attempt to rise to power (*OotP*). An expert in research with a working knowledge of the complex power dynamics and access barriers to information would be a valuable addition to the group, but Madam Pince does not prove herself to be a valuable collaborator on campus.

Madam Pince should also participate in the research and scholarship that helps the magical community defeat Lord Voldemort. A librarian's ability to streamline research efforts would prove valuable to the Order of the Phoenix. Many professions have librarians on their team, including education, medicine, law, government, and business. Academic librarians contribute to scholarship related to pedagogy, digital research services, information access, communication and media, and more. Research drives practice, so librarians can serve and collaborate dynamically on many teams. Unfortunately, readers do not see evidence of this in Madam Pince.

The library profession continues to change rapidly, and stereotypical librarians in media like Madam Pince tend to resist change. David J. Staley and Kara J. Malenfant attempt to predict the future roles of academic librarians as the library and information science professions continue to evolve. In order to adapt, these practitioners conduct their own research to speculate on the changing best practices in the discipline (Staley and Malenfant). They have concluded that research and practice are necessary for success (Staley and Malenfant). Like the librarianship discipline, Madam Pince's community also sees a rapid need to research and learn in order to implement changes as Voldemort slowly tries to make his return.

Research plays a vital role in defeating Lord Voldemort, and there are many opportunities for Madam Pince to do her own research and to aid Harry, Hermione, and Ron in their research efforts throughout their academics and adventures at Hogwarts. Students' ability to conduct research will help them beyond their academics—to decide what leaders to vote for, to acknowledge when there is an unjust system in place, and to learn how to take action to improve injustices. Madam Pince should help her students understand the necessary research concepts vital to preserving the democratic process. Additionally, she should contribute to the conversations and efforts of the professionals in the wizarding world, including the Hogwarts teachers, who fight Voldemort's rise to power. Instead, Madam Pince remains uninvolved in the community's research and creates barriers for the students who ultimately save the wizarding world from a dictatorship.

Better Librarians Than Pince

The librarian identity has been culturally created over time, and librarian stereotypes continue to be represented in popular media and integrated into people's understanding of the library: librarians "cannot step outside of this discourse" (G. Radford and M. Radford 323). The collective perception of the role librarians play in education is lacking, and Madam Pince's failed methods to educate her students have been dismantled by many information literacy educators and scholars. Other characters throughout the *Harry Potter* storyline compensate for Madam Pince's nonexistent efforts to provide access and information literacy education to her campus community.

Hermione Granger is the most obvious character to be considered a librarian. She understands that research is a process rooted in inquiry and turns her research into action to learn and to solve problems. She says to Harry and Ron, "I think I've just understood something. I've got to go to the library" (*CoS* 255), implying that the more she understands, the more she needs to learn. Research requires building upon preexisting knowledge, which is difficult for many students and scholars. Hermione, however, has a vast knowledge of many topics, thanks to her ability to interact responsibly with information. Freier also analyzes the many instances where Hermione takes on the responsibility of connecting students with useful information. Freier claims that Hermione makes up for Madam Pince's shortcomings as a librarian by helping her classmates and being instrumental in the research that leads to the defeat of Lord Voldemort. She states that Hermione "interacts with the texts critically and evaluates all of the information given rather than simply accepting or dismissing the whole publication" (Freier 4). Hermione's curiosity and desire to share knowledge contributes to the learning of Hogwarts students in ways that Madam Pince does not.

Similarly, Rubeus Hagrid is an example of the ways academic librarians serve as mentors to their student populations. Teaching and mentorship coexist. Librarians are often in a unique position. They interact with students in a formal learning environment and are able to provide supplemental class instruction, but they do not have to grade student work. Librarians are in an ideal role to mentor students through their education, as is Hagrid. Many of the barriers that exist for instructors do not exist for Hagrid because Harry, Hermione, and Ron do not first encounter him as a teacher with any preconceived power dynamics in the classroom. Creating systems of support is considerably important for certain populations of students. For example, first-generation students face unique obstacles. Harry and Hermione, both students who were raised by Muggles, can be considered first-generation students. Access to resources and academic support matters for students in similar situations, and Madam Pince could play a bigger role in supporting these students. Instead, Hagrid fills this role. He advocates for Harry from the beginning when he takes Harry to Diagon Alley, despite the Dursley's vengeful reservations (*SS*). College librarians often find themselves advocating for students unfamiliar with the academic landscape—by helping students obtain campus employment, providing information about scholarship opportunities, and making college resources more accessible. Eventually, Hagrid begins to teach (*PoA*), and the students are more comfortable with him than they are with other instructors. Similarly, when academic librarians teach, the students who have already established a level of trust by interacting with librarians in an informal third learning space, like the library, are more comfortable when the librarian is offering instruction. Hagrid begins as an approachable and nonthreatening resource for students seeking support, like many academic librarians on college and university campuses.

While far less approachable, Professor Severus Snape also fulfills some of the librarian role. Slytherins have a negative reputation, but they are an ambitious and resourceful group. Their zealous nature means they are always striving to be better and contribute to a task. Librarians, too, are often striving to contribute to the goals of a learning community by serving in many roles on campus. Professor Snape's values are misunderstood, and most of his acts of loyalty and contributions go unnoticed by the students. However, he does attempt to teach Harry the art of Occlumency by volunteering his time outside of official coursework (*OotP*). Like the study and practice of Occlumency, research skills are often skills taught collaterally. Like Professor Snape, librarians help students learn these skills that will later be vital for their successes outside of formal classroom instruction. Professor Snape is a misunderstood character, but his contributions to Harry's success are similar to the roles academic librarians play in higher education to ultimately aid in the education of students and the improvement of their research skills. Educating students is a relatively recent addition to the academic library profession. Like Professor Snape's role at Hogwarts and in the war against Lord Voldemort, it takes time for many organizations to understand and adapt to a librarian's evolving use and value.

Finally, Albus Dumbledore, the Headmaster of Hogwarts and one of the best wizards in the magical world, demonstrates some of the principles of librarianship. Dickinson discusses the strengths of Dumbledore's educational approaches in Half-Blood Prince. Dumbledore begins to teach Harry about how Voldemort continues to survive through Horcruxes by explaining to Harry the process in which he learned about the Horcruxes' existence (*H-BP*). Librarians, too, are more concerned with teaching the research process than the product. Dumbledore's non-authoritative methods gain Harry's trust, which is vital for the learning process. Dickinson states that Dumbledore's "ability to admit when he has made mistakes and to explain why and how he made them" and his "trust and confidence in his students' abilities to learn and grow" make him a valuable educator (244). Academic librarians often educate students outside of classrooms, therefore having a less authoritative role to begin with in the student's learning process. Dumbledore is an example of how supplemental educational support benefits the learning processes of students.

Librarians as Plot Devices

Madam Irma Pince's primary character traits—her meanness and unapproachability—are not unique portrayals of a librarian's personality and demeanor as seen throughout popular media. The Hogwarts Librarian's character falls victim to a popular librarian stereotype, and this negative archetype of the profession fuels student expectations and increases their anxieties concerning interacting with librarians. As the creator of Madam Pince, J.K. Rowling has apologized for stereotyping the librarian ("J.K. Rowling at an Evening with Harry"). During the question and answer segment of a benefit fundraiser, Rowling stated that she "would like to apologize" and that her "get-out clause is always that if [the students] had a pleasant, helpful librarian, [her] plots would be gone" ("J.K. Rowling at Radio City"). Rowling admits that a good librarian would streamline the students' problems ("J.K. Rowling at Radio City"), so in defense of Madam Pince as a character, an unhelpful librarian with outdated practices may have been vital for the storyline.

Although Madam Pince's stereotypical traits helped drive the storyline, her outdated concern with protecting her books, rather than providing access to resources and information literacy instruction, causes her to miss many opportunities to support student learning. Education and research contribute to the preservation of democracy, as demonstrated by the defeat of Lord Voldemort, and Madam Pince should be on the frontlines of these efforts by educating students to become responsible users of information. She fails as a research expert and educator for her school, but there are other members of the wizarding world who do possess traits and values of a helpful academic librarian. These characters contribute to the academic success of the Hogwarts students and to the defeat of Voldemort in ways that Madam Pince, as a librarian, should. Instead, Madam Pince hinders students' academic and personal growth, rather than strengthening it.

Additionally, Madam Pince, like many librarians, is not present throughout the novels, contradicting the role academic librarians can and do play in learning environments. Modern academic librarians are integrated into every aspect of the current information landscape—from the acquisition and protection of sources, to providing access and educating scholars to be ethical users of information. Although the Hogwarts Librarian is not a central character throughout the storyline, the connections between research in student learning and in the defeat of Lord Voldemort outside of the classroom remain strong. Academic librarians are educators committed to helping students use information to be academically successful and to contribute responsibly to the democratic values of their communities.

WORKS CITED

"About ALA." *American Library Association*, www.ala.org/aboutala.

"ACRL History." *Association of College and Research Libraries*, www.ala.org/acrl/aboutacrl/history/history.

Dickinson, Renée. "Harry Potter Pedagogy: What We Learn About Teaching and Learning from J.K. Rowling." *The Clearing House: A Journal of Educational Strategies, Issues and Ideas*, vol. 79, no. 6, 2006, pp. 240–44, doi:10.3200/TCHS.79.6.240-244.

El-Abbadi, Mostafa. "Library of Alexandria: Ancient Library, Alexandria, Egypt. *Encyclopedia Britannica*, 27 Sept. 2018, Www.britannica.com/topic/Library-of-Alexandria.

"Framework for Information Literacy for Higher Education." *Association of College and Research Libraries*, 11 Jan. 2016, www.ala.org/acrl/standards/ilframework.

Freier, Mary P. "The Librarian in Rowling's Harry Potter Series." *Comparative Literature and Culture*, vol. 16, no. 3, 2014, pp. 1–9, doi:10.7771/1481-4374.2197.

"History—About ALA." *American Library Association*, www.ala.org/aboutala/history.

26   Rooms of Requirement: Environments for Learning

"JK Rowling at an Evening with Harry, Carrie & Garp-Q&A." *YouTube*, uploaded by InHono-rofRowling, 7 Jan. 2012, www.youtube.com/watch?v=tSdIwR3DEHI.

"J.K. Rowling at Radio City Music Hall—Part 2." *The Leaky Cauldron*, 2. Aug. 2006, www.the-leaky-cauldron.org/2007/07/29/jkrnycnight2/.

"Library." *The Columbia Encyclopedia*, 2018.

"Library—The History of Libraries." *Encyclopedia Britannica*, 12 May 2017, www.britannica.com/topic/library/The-history-of-libraries.

Pagowsky, Nicole, and Erica DeFrain. "Ice Ice Baby: Are Librarian Stereotypes Freezing Us Out of Instruction?" *In the Library with the Lead Pipe*, 2014, pp. 1–13, hdl.handle.net/10150/552910.

Pagowsky, Nicole, and Miriam Rigby. "Contextualizing Ourselves: The Identity Politics of the Librarian Stereotype." *The Librarian Stereotype: Deconstructing Perceptions and Presentations of Information Work*, edited by Nicole Pagowsky and Miriam Rigby, The Association of College and Research Libraries, 2014, pp. 1–37.

"Professional Ethics-Tools, Publications & Resources." *American Library Association*, 22 Jan. 2018, www.ala.org/tools/ethics.

Radford, Gary P. "Flaubert, Foucault, and the Bibliotheque Fantastique: Toward a Postmodern Epistemology for Library Science." *Library Trends*, vol. 46, no. 4, 1998, pp. 616–34, www.ideals.illinois.edu/bitstream/handle/2142/8181/librarytrendsv46i4d_opt.pdf.

Radford, Gary P., and Marie L. Radford. "Libraries, Librarians, and the Discourse of Fear." *Library Quarterly*, vol. 71, no. 3, 2001, pp. 299–329, www.jstor.org/stable/4309528.

Richardson, Elizabeth A., and Sarah Wagner. "Restricted Section: The Library as Presented in Harry Potter." *Edinboro Potterfest Ravenclaw Conference*, 2011, pp. 1–14, digitalcommons.kent.edu/libpubs/2.

Rowling, J.K. *Harry Potter and the Chamber of Secrets*. Scholastic, 1998.

_____. *Harry Potter and the Deathly Hallows*. Scholastic, 2007.

_____. *Harry Potter and the Goblet of Fire*. Scholastic, 2000.

_____. *Harry Potter and the Half-Blood Prince*. Scholastic, 2005.

_____. *Harry Potter and the Order of the Phoenix*. Scholastic, 2003.

_____. *Harry Potter and the Prisoner of Azkaban*. Scholastic, 1999.

_____. *Harry Potter and the Sorcerer's Stone*. Scholastic, 1998.

Staley, David J., and Kara Malenfant. "Futures Thinking for Academic Librarians: Higher Education in 2025." *Information Services & Use*, 2010, vol. 30, no. 1/2, pp. 57–90, doi: 10.3233/ISU-2010-0614.

Dumbledore's Army

A Case for Peer Tutoring

MARCIE PANUTSOS ROVAN

At Hogwarts School of Witchcraft and Wizardry, most formal learning takes place inside classroom spaces. While those spaces are often nontraditional, such as the outdoor classrooms for Care of Magical Creatures, flying lessons, and Herbology or the rooftop classroom for Astronomy, they are still formalized classroom spaces, where instruction is provided by an ostensibly qualified professor who has authority over the students and their grades. Learning also happens outside the classroom—often collaboratively— through dormitory conversations, library research, and real-life experiences. However, Hogwarts provides no officially sanctioned student services; there is nowhere for students to benefit from structured peer-to-peer tutoring. With Harry's illicit creation of Dumbledore's Army (the D.A.) in *Order of the Phoenix*, Rowling demonstrates the significance of this lack by showing the overwhelming benefits that peer tutoring can provide. An examination of Dumbledore's Army through the lens of writing center pedagogy illustrates the positive impact of peer-tutoring and the need for a "third space" for student learning at Hogwarts. Specifically, the D.A. makes an effective case for learning centers by showcasing the profound effect they can have on the students who participate in them.

The definitions and methodologies associated with writing centers can be easily applied to the ideology and activities of Dumbledore's Army in *Order of the Phoenix*. The D.A. is created in response to a specific educational need that is not being met in the traditional classroom. As the ministry has begun to interfere with education at Hogwarts, the new ministry-appointed professor of Defense Against the Dark Arts is actively preventing students from learning the subject. This is a problem both because their Ordinary Wizarding Level exams (O.W.L.s) will require the students to perform defensive spells and because growing threats from the outside world have made students desirous of being prepared for the threat outside the castle walls. In response to this need, the students decide to organize a "study group" of sorts, where they can learn advanced defensive magic collaboratively, outside of the classroom, under the guidance of a knowledgeable peer. Essentially, they are creating a learning center—one entirely run and coordinated by the students themselves. Understanding the defining theories of writing center pedagogy can help readers to recognize the role and function of this student-run center for learning and gain a better understanding of the services such sites can offer.

Writing Center Pedagogy

Writing center pedagogy often centers on questions of definition and the role of a writing or learning center within the university. Scholarship surrounding writing centers and their function in the university is far more prolific than studies of learning centers specifically; however, both function according to similar rationales. For the purposes of this discussion, the terms will be used interchangeably to refer to any center offering peer-to-peer tutoring. Writing centers are often defined by their role outside of the traditional learning structure. Eric Hobson argues that writing centers occupy "a unique pedagogical space" because they "provide tailored, one-to-one guidance" (166). In his seminal text, "The Idea of a Writing Center," Stephen North asserts that "a writing center can be there in a way that our regular classes cannot" because it allows students more time to work at their own pace and meets students wherever they are in the process (442). For these reasons, tutoring centers tend to be less ordered than a traditional classroom, as the D.A. meetings will demonstrate. Eric Hobson describes such centers as places of "frenetic activity" (167), and Angela Petit refers to the "chaotic day-to-day activities" that occur in such sites (113). Writing centers and other tutoring centers are largely defined in contrast to the traditional classroom space. Where classrooms are focused on the group, learning centers are focused on the individual. Where classrooms maintain order, learning centers embrace chaos; when two dozen young wizards are learning and practicing defensive skills at their own pace, such chaos is inevitable.

For this reason, learning centers can be considered a kind of third space in a university. Gloria Anzaldua defines the third space as "a site of transformation, the place where different perspectives come into conflict and where you question the basic ideas, tenets, and identities inherited from your family, your education, and your different cultures" (548–49). A third space is a place of resistance and re-formation, where one questions authority and gain new insight. This idea of the third space marks a productive metaphor for tutoring centers—a place where different ideas and perspectives come into contact. Indeed, both in the D.A. and in many learning centers, students seek help specifically because they are looking for a different perspective or approach to the subject matter. In applying the metaphor, Nancy Effinger Wilson and Kerri Fitzgerald argue that "a writing center could/should be—a metacognitive, flexible third space—a part of the university but also apart from it." In this perspective, the writing or learning center offers an alternative space that is outside the classroom but still a part of the institution. It is a place where learning is supported through collaboration and the exchange of ideas.

This emphasis on collaboration is central to the way such centers are conceived. Learning centers are sites of peer-to-peer tutoring, where knowledge is gained collaboratively and learning is more self-directed. North argues that in such sites, the tutor serves as a "participant-observer" ("Idea" 438) rather than a teacher, and Hobson emphasizes how centers replace "single authority figures" with "a community of learners" (171). In these centers, the tutor is not only teaching, but learning as well. The tutor and tutees work collaboratively to further their knowledge and abilities. Hobson further notes that such sites are beneficial because of "people's tendency to learn from each other when they desire to grasp difficult concepts or overcome common obstacles" (171). In his essay extolling the virtues of collaborative learning, Kenneth Bruffee observes that "students' work tended to improve when they got help from peers; peers offering help, furthermore, learned from the students they helped and from the activity of helping itself" (418). Like Hobson, Bruffee emphasizes the importance of peer learning, noting "we must acknowledge the fact that people have always learned from their peers" (428). Andrea Lunsford similarly praises collaborative learning; she observes that students indicate "their work in groups, their *collaboration*, was the most important and helpful part of their school experience" (5). Because collaboration and peer-to-peer learning are central to the educational process, peer-tutoring centers serve a vital role in learning institutions, a function that is severely lacking in the officially sanctioned educational hierarchy of Hogwarts.

One explanation for the importance of peer-to-peer learning has to do with the way these environments "reject traditional hierarchies" (Lunsford 6). With peer learning, there is less fear of judgment or reprisal. As North explains, "we are not the teacher. We did not assign the writing; we will not grade it" ("Idea" 442). This distance from authority allows for a different kind of relationship to develop between tutor and tutee; they are essentially equals. Because of this, they develop "more personal contact" (Petit 112) and are less hesitant to acknowledge their weaknesses or limitations. Students are often far more willing to admit to a peer when they are struggling and need help because they feel less judged. We can see this in students like Rowling's Neville Longbottom, who frequently reaches out to his peers for assistance while being too intimidated to ask professors for help in or after class.

This also means that students who visit learning centers are more motivated and ready to learn, a fact noted by both Hobson and North. Highlighting the difference between classroom learning and the more informal learning that takes place in learning centers, North asserts that "an hour of talk ... at the right time between the right people can be more valuable than a semester of mandatory class meetings when that timing isn't right" ("Revisiting" 16). Extrapolating from this, one can argue that motivation is essential to student learning. Students are best able to learn when they are ready and willing to seek help. Learning centers are unique in their ability to meet students at this point of need, or to borrow North's phrase "the conjunction of timing and motivation" ("Idea" 443). This allows learning centers to be far more student-centered than a traditional classroom can be; they can truly meet students where they are to support individualized and self-directed learning. As we will see with the D.A., students who are invested in their own learning are more likely to succeed.

Part of the unique function of learning centers results from their emphasis on individualized learning. A learning center or a group like the D.A. can focus on individual improvement without the need for a single student to keep pace with the rest of the group. In describing the student-centered approach of learning centers, North asserts that "in a writing center the object is to make sure that writers, and not necessarily their texts, are what get changed by instruction" ("Idea" 438). He elaborates, "any curriculum—any plan of action the tutor follows—is going to be student-centered in the strictest sense of that term. That is, it ... will begin from where the student is, and move where the student moves.... The result is what might be called a pedagogy of direct intervention" (North, "Idea" 439). While North is speaking specifically of writing centers, the concept applies to all tutoring centers. Students direct the sessions by explaining what they know, where they are, and with what they are struggling. With the tutor, they "assess current status" and "establish session goals" based on current need (Hobson 168). The learning in these spaces is individualized, in that it "reacts to each student's particular needs" (Hobson 169) and "can be varied with the learning style of the student" (George qtd. in Hobson 169). Instead of focusing on meeting the objectives for a particular class or lesson, learning centers focus on helping students understand whatever concepts they are struggling with. They are more focused on learning than on learning outcomes—on process rather than product.

Dumbledore's Army as Learning Center

The student-led D.A. demonstrates all of the key qualities of learning centers outlined in the prevailing scholarship. Emphasizing the function of the learning center or the D.A. as a third space, the D.A. meetings physically occur in a liminal space. Searching for a location where they can learn and practice defensive magic in secret, Harry learns of the existence of the Room of Requirement, a room that is called into existence only when needed and "is always equipped for the seeker's needs" (*OotP* 386–87), as Dobby explains. This room is itself both a part of the learning institution and outside of it. Many professors do not know of its existence, and those who do are not aware of its full potential or powers. Professor Trewlawney knows of it as a labyrinthine room to hide empty sherry bottles, and Professor Dumbledore has encountered it only as a room full of chamber pots that he was unable to locate again. As Dobby the house-elf explains, "Mostly people stumbles across it when they needs it, sir, but often they never finds it again, for they do not know that it is always there waiting to be called into service, sir" (*OotP* 387). It is unplottable, beyond the range of the Marauder's Map, and while it is in use, no one can get in unless they know exactly what they are looking for. It is literally a space that can only be found when there is a need for it. Within this liminal space, D.A. members encounter people and perspectives that would not be a part of their ordinary learning experience. Students from different years, houses, and backgrounds work together to improve their magical knowledge and abilities and prepare for the world beyond Hogwarts.

This peer-to-peer collaboration is central to learning within the D.A. just as it is within learning centers broadly conceived. Hogwarts is an institution where students are carefully segregated into their designated houses from day one. Although there are occasional opportunities to work with other houses in classes or compete against them in sporting events, inter-house collaboration is so rare that Hermione is alarmed when various D.A. members start to come over to the Gryffindor table to talk at breakfast one day. Reacting with frustration at their lack of discretion, she declares, "the idiots can't come over here now, it'll look really suspicious" (*OotP* 354). As students are separated into houses by their natural talents, skills and abilities (bravery, intellect, loyalty, and cunning) rather than the random assignments that are more common in British schools, this segregation seems deeply antithetical to the goals of an educational institution. The D.A. corrects this problem by providing a space where students from different houses can come together in a collaborative learning environment and benefit from the different perspectives and skills that each student brings. In this way, it is much like a learning center, where students from various majors and skill levels work together to gain knowledge and ability.

Harry takes on a leadership role within the D.A., but he serves as a peer mentor akin to the peer tutors in a traditional learning center. While he provides his classmates with guidance and instruction on the performance of different defensive spells, the bulk of the D.A. meetings consist of peer-to-peer practice. Students routinely break into pairs to practice spells and presumably learn how to do so more effectively from observing and interacting with their classmates. They participate of their own volition and are frequently reminded that they have the option of leaving if they are uninterested in a particular lesson. Harry's role is more of the "participant-observer" that North describes ("Idea" 438) than a traditional instructor, and the group clearly reflects Hobson's emphasis on "a community of learners" (171). Harry sets the agenda for each meeting, but most of the work is done by peer groups working together, with Harry circulating for guidance and offering encouragement.

The collaborative emphasis on this endeavor is clear from its origin. The group is Hermione's idea, but it is formed by mutual consent. Diverse students from across the campus gather to join because they are interested and "want to learn" (*OotP* 332). The group collectively determines who will lead the sessions, unanimously electing Harry as leader, and the members collaborate and vote on a name (*OotP* 391). Students come together not necessarily to learn from Harry, but to learn together and to learn from each other with Harry's guidance. They collaboratively determine the best times to meet and make decisions for the mutual welfare of the group. The group is democratic in origin and functions more as a collective endeavor than a traditional classroom.

Through this emphasis on collaboration and self-motivation, the D.A. demonstrates the learning center's focus on self-directed learning. The students who participate in the D.A. meetings are actively seeking an opportunity to improve their own learning. In the D.A. as in most learning centers, self-motivation is crucial to success, and individual progress sometimes directly reflects increased motivation. Progress is made by those who are willing and eager to do the work. This is clear from the students' response to a mass breakout of Death Eaters from Azkaban. Rowling notes, "all of them, even Zacharias Smith, had been spurred to work harder than ever by the news that ten more Death Eaters were now on the loose" (*OotP* 553), and those whose family members were counted among the victims of the escapees worked the hardest and showed the most progress.

Amongst the D.A. membership, there is one notable exception to this rule about self-motivation. Marietta Edgecombe is coerced into attending meetings by her friend Cho Chang, and as Cho acknowledges, "she doesn't really want to be here" (*OotP* 395). Consequently, Marietta actually demonstrates a convincing case for why learning centers are limited in their ability to help those who are not there by choice, such as students who have been sent to a center for remediation or are required to attend. Because her participation is not her own choice, she is not fully committed to this learning opportunity. As such, she does not have the same dedication to her learning, and she is ultimately responsible for the formal dissolution of the group, by selling it out to Professor Umbridge. Because she is not there of her own volition, she lacks the self-motivation required for nontraditional learning.

Beyond this question of motivation, the D.A. also promotes highly individualized learning experiences. Students start with whatever abilities or skills they have already acquired and work to improve upon those skills. Harry begins the first session by asking students to demonstrate a basic defensive spell in order to gauge individual skill-level. He then works with individual students to help them improve. Unlike a traditional classroom, there is no requirement for students to achieve certain learning outcomes or objectives in any given lesson, and those who do not succeed at the same level are not made to feel that they have failed in any way. Instead, there is an emphasis on the need for practice and a constant reminder that success with any specific task will not guarantee success in the real world.

The D.A. can only make the students better prepared to handle real-world challenges. This is best illustrated when Cho expresses her regret that Cedric could have survived if he'd had the same training (*OotP* 455). Harry assures her that Cedric was well-trained and explains that the tests they will face in the real world are not passed or failed based on knowledge or skill (*OotP* 455). The D.A.'s function is to improve the wizard the way that a writing center focuses on improving the writer; success or failure on a specific assignment or endeavor is not a direct measure of learning. As depressing as this may sound in the context of learning self-defense, it is an accurate representation of the goals of a learning center. If a student works hard and improves as a writer, that is a better measure of the center's success than whether or not the student achieves the grade or outcome he or she desires. The stakes of the D.A. are much higher than an academic learning center—literally life-or-death—but the approach is the same. A learning center can never guarantee a desirable outcome; it can only help students improve their abilities.

The D.A.'s Impact on Student Success

The success of the D.A. is not based on the ultimate survival rates of its members, but the willingness and ability of those members to fight against the dark forces that threaten their world. The group, like a learning center, motivates students to keep trying and keep improving. Rowling emphasizes this focus in the way that Harry reflects on the group's successes. In his evaluation of their performance, Harry focuses less on the achievement of particular skills and more on the progress that members have made. In the first meeting, Harry observes a gradual general improvement (*OotP* 394). By Christmas, he proudly reflects that all of the D.A. members "had made enormous progress" (*OotP* 454). The members improve as defenders against the dark arts, regardless of whether or not their personal defenses are ultimately successful in every encounter. In other words, the emphasis is on process and progress rather than product. No class or learning center can guarantee the students' survival in a chaotic and dangerous world; it can only ensure that they are better prepared when they leave than they were when they began. Though the stakes are clearly much higher here, this reflects the basic principles of a learning center. The center cannot prevent students from failing, it can only improve their chances of success.

If we conceive of Dumbledore's Army as a kind of learning center or peer-to-peer tutoring site, then an analysis of the effects of this group on its members makes a compelling case for the importance of such sites within learning institutions. In D.A. meetings, Harry constantly remarks on the progress of individual members, as well as the overall progress of the group. When Umbridge and her followers capture Harry and his friends, Neville, Ron, Ginny, and Luna are able to put their knowledge into practice and easily overcome their captors. As Harry races to the Ministry of Magic to fight the Death Eaters, he is accompanied by five D.A. members, all of whom are eager and willing "to do something real" (*OotP* 761). When the Death Eaters invade Hogwarts at the end of Harry's sixth year, it is those same D.A. members who engage in a deadly battle to protect the castle's occupants. In the same way that learning centers prepare students to be better writers in the real world, the D.A. prepares its members to face the threats and challenges of the real world. The classroom is not the primary focus of either group.

Ultimately, almost all of the members of the D.A. end up on the front lines in the war against Voldemort and his followers. Forced into hiding within the Room of Requirement, the D.A. members still put their lives at great risk sneaking around the castle to help the victims of the Death Eaters' injustice. When Harry, Ron, and Hermione arrive, the D.A. members eagerly volunteer to help them defeat the Dark Lord, asserting over Harry's objections, "We're his army.... Dumbledore's Army. We were all in it together" (*DH* 580). While other more experienced defenders against the dark arts are involved in the war, the D.A. members make the biggest impact; every one of Voldemort's Horcruxes is destroyed by a member of the D.A. (Harry, Ron, Hermione, and Neville), with the exception of those destroyed by Albus Dumbledore and Voldemort himself. This means that the D.A. is ultimately responsible for the fatal blows against Voldemort by destroying his links to immortality.

D.A. members are prominent in the Battle of Hogwarts, as well, with three of the students taking on Voldemort's most dangerous supporter, Bellatrix Lestrange, and several members actually coming to Harry's rescue when he does not have the strength to keep fighting the dementors. Indeed, the D.A. study sessions are directly referenced in this scene, as the tutees become the tutor and emphasize the collaborative nature of learning: "'That's right,' said Luna encouragingly, as if they were back in the Room of Requirement and this was simply spell practice for the D.A. 'That's right, Harry ... come on, think of something happy...' 'Something happy?' his voice cracked. 'We're all still here,' she whispered, 'we're still fighting. Come on, now...'" (*DH* 649). Here, Luna and the others use the knowledge they have gained under Harry's tutelage to help Harry remember how and why to keep fighting.

Neville Longbottom: Poster Child for Peer-to-Peer Learning

Perhaps more than any other, the case of Neville Longbottom provides a compelling argument for peer-to-peer learning and demonstrates the limitations of the traditional classroom. Neville is a student for whom traditional classroom learning does not seem to be working. Upon his arrival at Hogwarts, Neville already demonstrates the timidity and unease with authority that comes from a lifetime of casual bullying. Raised by his "formidable" grandmother (*PoA* 55), Neville is constantly reminded that he is failing to live up to his talented parents, heroic aurors (dark-wizard catchers) who were tortured into insanity for refusing to disclose information to Voldemort's followers. Neville is introduced as a forgetful, tearful, "nervous and jumpy" (*SS* 147), "poor, blundering" (*SS* 243) child who is an easy target for bullying both outside of and within the classroom. While Draco Malfoy and his friends torture Neville as a peer, Neville is also frequently bullied and insulted by Professor Snape, who goes beyond intimidation tactics to outright insults, calling the child an "Idiot boy!" (*SS* 139) for a mistake in his first potions lesson. This professorial bullying continues throughout Neville's career at Hogwarts, and Rowling directly connects Snape's intimidation with Neville's poor performance, noting: "Neville regularly went to pieces in Potions lessons; it was his worst subject, and his great fear of Professor Snape made things ten times worse" (*PoA* 125). At times, Neville is also insulted by an exasperated Professor McGonagall, and other professors demonstrate an expectation that he will fail (as when Trelawney "predicts" that he will break the tea cups and will be late to class). The only class at which Neville is successful is Herbology, which is taught by the far-from-intimidating Professor Sprout. Even before the D.A., Rowling makes it clear that Neville does not respond well to authority figures and is more likely to succeed with the help of his peers; Hermione regularly helps him to correct the mistakes he makes out of nerves and anxiety. In general, Neville is much more comfortable asking for help from his peers than his professors.

Neville's classroom anxiety extends beyond his negative experiences with Snape's bullying and intimidation. Neville seems equally uncomfortable with professors' praise or attempts at kindness. When Snape "warns" a new Defense Against the Dark Arts teacher, Professor Lupin, of Neville's ineptitude, Lupin responds with a confidence in Neville's abilities that makes Neville feel even more intimidated. When another new Defense Against the Dark Arts teacher invites Neville to his office for tea after a traumatic lesson, Rowling declares that "the prospect of tea with Moody" was even more frightening to Neville than witnessing the spell that destroyed his parent's sanity (*GoF* 218–219). Neville's self-doubt and discomfort with authority figures make it challenging for him to learn in a traditional classroom setting, where the fear of judgment and reprisal interferes with his ability to learn.

Despite his seemingly timid and meek character, however, Neville demonstrates early on that there are things for which he is willing to fight. In his first year, he "trie[s] to take on Crabbe and Goyle single-handed" in defense of a friend (*SS* 227), risks punishment to warn his friends of a trap, and stands up to those friends in defense of what he thinks is right. In his fifth year, he attempts to attack Draco Malfoy and his cronies for making jokes about mental illness. In all of these attempts, he proves ineffectual; however, his willingness to fight for what's right demonstrates his potential and motivation for learning defensive magic, given the right conditions for learning. In fact, Professor McGonagall openly acknowledges that Neville's only problem is a "'lack of confidence'" (*OotP* 257)—a problem with which peer tutoring is uniquely situated to help.

More than any other student in the D.A., Neville demonstrates the potentially transformative power of peer-to-peer learning. During his first D.A. lesson, he demonstrates immediate progress, successfully disarming Harry while practicing *Expelliarmus*. Neville is overjoyed by his success, as he had never been able to execute the spell properly before (*OotP* 393). After two months of D.A. meetings, "Neville had improved beyond all recognition" (*OotP* 454). He is able to successfully execute most of the spells they have learned, and even when he misses his target, "it was a much closer miss than usual" (*OotP* 454). This progress increases exponentially in the wake of the Azkaban breakout, when Neville learns that the woman who tortured his parents into insanity has escaped from prison. Rowling notes that in response to this news, Neville "barely spoke during D.A. meetings anymore, but worked relentlessly on every new jinx and counter-curse Harry taught them" (*OotP* 553). This increase in motivation and effort leads to tremendous progress.

As Harry observes: "He was improving so fast it was quite unnerving, and when Harry taught them the Shield Charm, a means of deflecting minor jinxes so that they rebounded upon the attacker, only Hermione mastered the charm faster than Neville" (*OotP* 553). Neville's remarkable progress demonstrates the positive impact of a nontraditional and self-directed learning environment. With an increase in motivation and the right opportunity for learning, Neville is able to learn more in a few months of D.A. meetings than he has learned in over four years of classroom education.

The importance of the learning environment on student success generally and Neville's success in particular is directly referenced when the fifth-year students sit for their O.W.L.s. Despite the high pressure and high stakes of the exams, simply being away from the stifling classroom atmosphere and intimidating faculty members seems to improve student performance. This is most notable during the Potions exams. With Snape absent, Rowling describes the students as being more comfortable, more relaxed, and more capable in the exam setting than they were in the classroom environment (*OotP* 716). Ultimately, Neville's exam scores, which arrive the following year, are higher than he had expected in most of his subjects. Though exams cannot truly measure the success of a learning center experience, Neville's ability to achieve Exceeds Expectations (the second highest mark) in his Defense Against the Darks Arts exam (*DH* 173–174) seems to be a direct reflection of the progress he has made in the D.A. meetings, as his prior classroom experiences did not result in similar academic success.

Beyond these standardized measures of academic success, however, Neville demonstrates the progress he has made through the D.A. more directly in the real-life situations that require defensive magic. When Ginny, Ron, and Hermione are captured by members of Umbridge's Inquisitorial Squad, Neville jumps to their defense. Although he also ends up captured, the entire group is able to escape by using the knowledge and skills they have gained from the D.A. Explaining how they overcame their captors, Ron mentions among their accomplishments that "'Neville brought off a really nice little Impediment Jinx'" (*OotP* 760). This is a substantial improvement from Neville's ineffectual attempts to support or defend his friends or himself in earlier fights with Malfoy and his cronies, where he ends up "out cold" in the hospital wing (*SS* 227) or with his legs jinxed together. Subsequently, Neville (along with Ginny and Luna), insists on accompanying the trio on their rescue mission to save Sirius from Voldemort. He declares, "this is the first chance we've had to do something real.... We want to help" (*OotP* 761). The confidence and determination Neville demonstrates in this moment reflect the transformations he has undergone through his participation in the D.A. No longer content with his experiences in the classroom or the D.A., Neville is ready to test his knowledge in the real world.

These transformations are even more apparent in the battle that follows at the Ministry of Magic. Whereas Neville previously could not hold his own in a fist fight, he is now able to survive an all-out battle with some of Voldemort's most skilled followers. He successfully disarms a Death Eater who is dueling with Harry (*OotP* 789), and he keeps on fighting until both his wand and his nose are broken. Even after he can no longer effectively defend himself, he remains determined and refuses to turn back. Ultimately, Neville and Harry are the last two D.A. members left standing in the battle. Although they are surrounded by the Death Eaters, Neville remains defiant despite Bellatrix's suggestion of torturing him to get Harry to surrender. When the Order of the Phoenix arrives and Harry is captured in the chaos, Neville comes to his defense: though he is "unable to articulate a spell" (*OotP* 802), he still finds a way to attack the Death Eater holding Harry, helping Harry to escape. In this first real-world test of his knowledge and skills, Neville demonstrates the tremendous progress that he has made through his involvement with the D.A.—both in terms of ability and in terms of self-confidence.

As a true mark of the D.A.'s significance, readers see that Neville's progress and growth do not end when the meetings cease. Neville is "most disappointed" (*HBP* 138) when Harry decides not to continue with the group, but he does not forget the lessons he's learned from it. The D.A. has inspired Neville with a confidence and self-motivation that set him on a path for lifelong learning, as the best learning centers will do. This is apparent as the threat from Voldemort and his supporters grows more ominous. At the end of their sixth year, Death Eaters invade Hogwarts, and it is Neville and Luna who respond to Hermione's summons for help as she, Ron, and Ginny try to defend the school in Harry and Dumbledore's absence. As they are battling the Death Eaters, Neville is the first to charge into danger, chasing the Death Eaters and ultimately running into the barrier they have erected behind them (*HBP* 620). Though he is less successful in this battle than the prior one, he demonstrates a greater courage and willingness to fight than any other student, and he is not deterred by his failure. Notably, the classroom learning experience is essentially unimproved after year 5. Professor Snape takes over Defense Against the Dark Arts in year 6, making it difficult for even Harry to progress much, and the subject is discontinued in year 7. Despite this, Neville continues to improve, building on the lessons he learned through the D.A.

Neville truly comes into his own in his final year at Hogwarts. When the Death Eaters take control of Hogwarts, Neville leads the resistance movement. He and the other D.A. members work to undermine the regime and defend the innocent. When he is reunited with Harry, Ron, and Hermione, Neville has clearly been transformed. He is no longer an awkward and timid child, but a battle-scarred warrior. Neville "dismisse[s] his injuries with a shake of his head" (*DH* 571) because each one reflects a moral triumph in his battle against the dark arts. When he cannot take physical action against the Death Eaters, he challenges them verbally—a lesson he learned from Harry through the D.A.: "The thing is, it helps when people stand up to them, it gives everyone hope. I used to notice that when you did it, Harry" (*DH* 574). In Harry's absence, Neville, Luna, and Ginny took over *de facto* leadership of the newly re-formed D.A. Under their leadership, the D.A. members have risked personal safety to resist the Dark Lord and his supporters, taking refuge in the Room of Requirement. However, after Ginny went into hiding with her family and Luna was captured, Neville took the lead. In a remarkable demonstration of the power of collaborative learning, the student who was initially the weakest has become the new mentor and leader of the learning group, "keeping it going" (*DH* 580) in Harry's absence.

In the final battle, Neville's learning progress is irrefutable. Neville is the first to break free from the spell Voldemort has cast over the crowd and the first to take a stand against the Death Eaters in the wake of Harry's presumed death. When Voldemort disables him and forces the flaming Sorting Hat onto his head, Neville again breaks free and pulls a sword from the hat. He immediately goes on the offensive, destroying Voldemort's final Horcrux and last link to immortality before diving back into battle. His experiences with the D.A. have helped him develop both the abilities and the character to become a successful defender against the dark arts in a way that his classroom experiences were never able to do. After four years of formal classroom education, Neville still considers himself a hopeless case, unlikely to pass most of his exams. After one year with the D.A., he is able to achieve success both academically and in real world tests of his knowledge and skill. Furthermore, the relationships forged through that year of collaborative learning help him to continue his educational journey. Neville evolves from considering himself "almost a squib" (*CoS* 185) to becoming the *de facto* leader of the anti–Voldemort resistance at Hogwarts.

Neville's remarkable growth over the final three years of his career at Hogwarts can be directly attributed to his involvement with the D.A. The group's emphasis on collaboration, self-motivation, and individualized learning provides a fertile ground for students like Neville to thrive. The. D.A. provides Hogwarts with a much needed third space for learning—an opportunity for collaboration and peer-to-peer tutoring that is sadly missing from the officially sanctioned learning opportunities. Out of necessity, Harry and his friends develop an unsanctioned learning center, and in less than a year of collaborative practice, the D.A. members learn more than they have learned in years of formal education.

Those of us who have been both classroom instructors and peer mentors know that some students learn best outside of the traditional classroom space.

A former educator herself, Rowling is likely aware of the limitations of a traditional classroom for students who learn differently, students who are intimidated by instructors, or students who simply need more individual attention. Removing the learning experience from the anxieties and evaluation of a traditional classroom allows students to focus on personal growth and development in a third space that is both a part of the institution and separate from it. As Rowling illustrates through Neville's transformation, this kind of peer-to-peer learning is essential for students who struggle with confidence in their abilities. Spaces like learning centers are necessary because they meet student needs in a way that classroom instruction cannot. Through the progress made by Neville and the other members of the D.A., Rowling demonstrates the vital role of third-space learning environments and makes an effective case for peer tutoring—for Muggles and wizards alike.

Works Cited

Anzaldua, Gloria. *Borderlands/La Frontera: The New Mestiza*. Aunt Lute, 1987.

Bruffee, Kenneth. "Collaborative Learning and the 'Conversation of Mankind.'" *Cross-Talk in Comp Theory: A Reader*. 2nd ed., edited by Victor Villanueva, NCTE, 2003, pp. 415–436.

Hemeter, Thomas. "The 'Smack of Difference': The Language of Writing Center Discourse." *The Writing Center Journal*, vol. 11, no. 1, 1990, pp. 35–48. *JSTOR*. www.jstor.org/stable/43442593.

Hobson, Eric H. "Writing Center Pedagogy." *A Guide to Composition Pedagogies*, edited by Gary Tate, Amy Rupiper, and Kurt Schick, Oxford UP, 2001, pp. 165–182.

Lunsford, Angela. "Collaboration, Control, and the Idea of a Writing Center." *The Writing Center Journal*, vol. 12, no. 1, 1991, pp. 3–10. *JSTOR*. www.jstor.org/stable/43441887.

North, Stephen. "The Idea of a Writing Center." *College English*, vol. 46, no. 5, 1984, pp. 433–446. *JSTOR*. doi: 10.2307/377047.

_____. "Revisiting 'The Idea of a Writing Center.'" *The Writing Center Journal*, vol. 15, no. 1, 1994, pp. 7–19. *JSTOR*, www.jstor.org/stable/43442606.

Petit, Angela. "The Writing Center as 'Purified Space': Competing Discourses and the Dangers of Definition." *The Writing Center Journal*, vol. 17, no. 2, 1997, pp. 111–122. *JSTOR*. www.jstor.org/stable/43442024.

Rowling, J.K. *Harry Potter and the Chamber of Secrets*. Scholastic, 1999.

_____. *Harry Potter and the Deathly Hallows*. Scholastic, 2007.

_____. *Harry Potter and the Goblet of Fire*. Scholastic, 2000.

_____. *Harry Potter and the Half-Blood Prince*. Scholastic, 2005.

_____. *Harry Potter and the Order of the Phoenix*. Scholastic, 2003.

_____. *Harry Potter and the Prisoner of Azkaban*. Scholastic, 1999.

_____. *Harry Potter and the Sorcerer's Stone*. Scholastic, 1997.

Wilson, Nancy Effinger, and Keri Fitzgerald. "Empathic Tutoring in the Third Space." *Writing Lab Newsletter*, vol. 37, no. 3/4, 2012. www.thefreelibrary.com/Empathic tutoring in the third space.-a0331080947.

Neville Longbottom and the Multifarious Learning Environment

Inclusivity and Reciprocity at Hogwarts

EMMA LOUISE BARLOW *and* ALICE LODA

J.K. Rowling's teaching expertise is an asset to her building of the fictional Hogwarts School of Witchcraft and Wizardry. This expertise emerges in her depictions of classroom practice and peer learning interactions, which have a significant impact on the dynamics of acquisition and dissemination of knowledge in the series. Her construction of teaching and learning dynamics is indubitably informed by reflections on teaching styles and student engagement, which were well disseminated before the publication of the series.[1] Peer relationships occur both within and, most significantly, beyond formal classroom settings. The informal learning spaces that abound at Hogwarts appear to be central for many characters and for one in particular: Neville Longbottom. These peer-led learning environments allow Neville to find his way towards reflectively constructing his learning and foreground his progressive path toward becoming the series' *quiet hero*. Neville's evolution and its implications offer a rich case study on the relational dynamics of learning.

As a place, Hogwarts has been the object of several analyses, targeting its significance on multiple levels: as an educational, social, and physical space (Sailer), as a narratological space that both furthers and mobilizes the genre of the public-school narrative (Mynott), and as a counterpoint to actual school systems, with a focus on methodologies and leadership (Bixler; Booth and Booth). Further studies have also mapped the significance of the school setting for the progressive maturing of the main characters, and Harry in particular (Mulholland). Scholarship has tended to focus less extensively, however, on other aspects of pedagogical action and "relational" education dynamics at Hogwarts. In particular, very limited literature exists regarding the gradual empowerment of secondary characters and the roles of peer-facilitation, peer-learning, and reciprocity in constructing knowledge. All these aspects are nonetheless vital in supporting the characters' paths towards adulthood and professional trajectories and are highly relevant to the diverse readership of the series.

In this essay, we aim to illuminate the aforementioned aspects through a focus on the progressive empowerment of Neville Longbottom and the related evolution of relational peer dynamics. We first introduce the significance and characteristics of Hogwarts as an educational space, focusing on classroom settings, active learning, and peer-learning dynamics. Next, we analyze Neville's characterization and his path at Hogwarts. We then interrogate the notions of inclusivity and reciprocity in light of two complementary and subtly intertwined spaces: the Hogwarts classroom, where Neville is extensively "othered," and the Hogwarts community of peer-learners, where he eventually finds opportunities for growth. Finally, we examine Neville's progressive trajectory towards self-awareness, which ultimately leads him to become an inspirational figure for his peers and to embody the role of the series' *quiet hero*. Ultimately, we argue that transformation through peer-learning and acknowledgment of different styles of learning are crucial components in Rowling's understanding of educational pedagogies and in the related progressive construction of both an inclusive learning environment and Neville's quiet heroism.

Context: Teaching and Learning at Hogwarts

Hogwarts is an educational institution that plays host to approximately fifteen active teachers at any given time, in accordance with the number of subjects offered (comprising the thirteen subjects taught by Professors, as well as flying lessons taught by Madam Hooch and apparition lessons taught by the Ministry of Magic employee, Wilkie Twycross). The range of pedagogical styles explicitly displayed in the series, however, is surprisingly limited. During the lessons that Harry attends (and to which we, as readers, are therefore privy), two particular teaching and learning approaches are represented and adopted to varying degrees: a practice-based one and a theory-based one.

Many classes, including Apparition, Care of Magical Creatures, Charms, Divination, Flying, Herbology, Potions, and Transfiguration, showcase practice-based and interactive educational methods. Etienne Wenger-Trayner, et al.

provides a theoretical grounding in practice-based education that can be applied here. In these classes, the cohort of amateur witches and wizards are allowed to test out new techniques in a controlled environment. Students are often invited to actively conduct experiments; they also appear to be comfortable asking questions during lessons conducted by Hagrid, Slughorn, and Trelawney, amongst others, and are even sometimes tacitly encouraged to do so (*PoA* 82; *GoF* 472; *H-BP* 177).

Practice-based activities at Hogwarts, wherein interactions occur more frequently, still display significant omissions from a strictly pedagogical perspective. During practice-based lessons, teachers demonstrate a particular skill to students or give them clear instructions to complete a task. Students are then often left to practice on their own, and thus carry out the work independently, sometimes in small groups. Although these activities give students space to interact and to co-construct their outputs based on initial teacher prompts, no particular attention is given to strategies for providing constructive and formative feedback or for guiding students towards progressively improving their skills, both vital stages in the learning cycle. John Hattie and Helen Timperley discuss the significance of generative feedback in teaching and learning practice. The crucial position of feedback in the context of active learning is also investigated by Linda Van den Bergh, Anje Ros, and Douwe Beijaard. These scholars offer an effective conceptualization of feedback as existing on a continuum with instructions; while the latter are clearly delineated in Hogwarts classrooms, the former is significantly less developed.

Teachers in Hogwarts' practice-based classrooms seem to be called on mostly to demonstrate and to inspire, rather than to guide students step-by-step towards learning outcomes. The instructor may also speak from an elevated or authoritative position. This is particularly apparent in Gilderoy Lockhart's classroom, wherein he hides his lack of preparation by constantly distancing himself from the task of imparting knowledge or skills and instead regaling students with tales (but no evidence) of his own magical talents and immense bravery, but it is also evident in the classrooms of more skilled teachers.

This "distant" and non-interactive approach tends to be radicalized in theory-based subjects. The one subject with a primarily theory-based design is History of Magic. The pedagogical approaches undertaken in other subjects, such as Arithmancy, Astronomy, Muggle Studies, and the Study of Ancient Runes, are almost impossible to classify as little or no space is given to the classroom experience of these subjects in the series. However, from Hermione's descriptions of and references to Arithmancy, Muggle Studies, and Ancient Runes at least, we might presume that these subjects are significantly theory-based. When entering the space of more theoretical subjects, the teacher-oriented nature of delivery increases and interactions diminish further, resulting in a significant impact on student engagement. We can observe this trajectory in Defense Against the Dark Arts (DADA), one of the most troubled teaching spaces at Hogwarts, where the high turnover of teachers impacts the linear development of the subject and students' in-class progression.

While often involving dangerous creature demonstrations and spell practice, DADA also sometimes involves theoretical aspects, developed most notably in Dolores Umbridge's lessons. This component becomes dominant when the Ministry of Magic forbids the use of defensive spells in the class, decreeing that "a theoretical knowledge [of defensive spells] will be more than sufficient" for students to successfully perform them in exams (*OotP* 243). This purely theoretical approach provokes an actual student revolt (*OotP* 227, 290–291). The young witches and wizards form a clandestine group in which they exercise their practical skills, necessary not only to pass their exams but also to survive in the dangerous political climate of the contemporary wizarding world. Theoretical learning in DADA is thus imbued with a negative association due to: the antiquated nature of most teaching styles; the perceived intimidating or disagreeable personality of some teachers; the parallel negation of a practical element in Umbridge's classes; and the consequent perception that theory alone has a limited impact on contingent matters and is unable to fulfill the students' need for immediate action.

As the series progresses, the work in classes becomes globally more difficult, and the theoretical component becomes more important and visible in a range of subjects. For instance, we are made aware that Harry needs to study the theory behind Summoning Charms due to his difficulties in mastering the charm (*GoF* 278), and that he lacks the theoretical knowledge necessary in Slughorn's Potions lesson on Golpalott's Third Law regarding the creation of antidotes (*H-BP* 351–353). It is only Hermione who possesses the necessary skills to produce an antidote in Slughorn's lesson and only due to her usual habit of having "swallowed the textbook" (*CoS* 72). Again, students do not react particularly well to this notable increase in theoretical learning, which is less than adequately supported by instructors. For example, in McGonagall's lessons in sixth year, "Harry barely understood half of what Professor McGonagall said to them these days; even Hermione had had to ask her to repeat instructions once or twice" (*H-BP* 205). The narrow space allocated to the explanation of the value of theoretical knowledge and to the effective combination of theory and practice results in a lack of student engagement and motivation. This leads to a subsequent search for further spaces for learning and interaction.

Surprisingly, in both practice- and theory-based classes, there is little movement of students and instructors around the classroom, and the learning space is organized hierarchically. This teacher-centered setting has been extensively challenged in scholarship. Studies on educational environments have acknowledged that the reorganization of the classroom space, especially with an interaction-centered approach, can positively impact productivity and enhance active learning.[2] The lack of concern for these dynamics may, in the case of Hogwarts, be motivated by narratological constraints. Nonetheless, this outdated organization of space weakens the effectiveness of in-class settings as a whole.

A further contextual aspect that deserves attention is the competitive nature of the Hogwarts teaching and learning environment. Students receive house points for achieving goals that tend to be reached through their own independent learning and performances or through their previous knowledge. The ability to expand and co-construct knowledge within the classroom space or within a productive teacher-student relationship seems to be far less valued, and no comprehensive attention is paid to teaching approaches that might maximize the outcomes of a highly diverse cohort in terms of skills and inclinations. For instance, teacher questions are frequently used to check background knowledge of the concept being demonstrated or explained and are very often answered by Hermione who is already "the best in [their] year" (*H-BP* 71). Therefore, such questions perform no pedagogical role for the rest of the cohort, which is relegated to the role of an almost silent spectator. This attitude fosters competition, while leaving a blank space in terms of the potential for collaborative and co-constructed in-class learning strategies.

Relying on students' diversified previous knowledge, and hence on their diversified contributions, is in fact an essential principle for active learning. Jeffrey Karpicke suggests that previous knowledge retrieval can be a generative actor in enhancing long-term meaningful and in-depth learning. Yet this method calls for the successive expansion of previous knowledge through prompt and progressive meaningful interaction and feedback within the learning environment. As previously mentioned, this second aspect seems to be significantly underexplored by Rowling in the formal classroom setting.

Students at Hogwarts demonstrate highly diverse learning styles and strategies. The widely disseminated framework delineated by Richard Felder and Linda Silverman identifies a series of twofold dimensions of learning: sensory and intuitive, visual and auditory, inductive and deductive, active and reflective, sequential and global. The active-reflective dimension is particularly relevant to the present discourse. According to Felder and Silverman, "[a]n 'active learner' is someone who feels more comfortable with, or is better at, active experimentation than reflective observation, and conversely for a reflective learner" (675). The school environment of Hogwarts seems to cater mostly to students who develop an active dimension in their learning, and less so for those who demonstrate a reflective learning style.

Given the limited diversity in teaching styles and approaches throughout the series, then, it is perhaps unsurprising that informal spaces of both in-depth self-reflection and peer-learning become key dynamic factors in student success, in particular for students with reflective learning styles such as Neville Longbottom. His learning happens most often within informal contexts, only surfacing occasionally in the classroom. Scholarship has stressed the importance of peer learning as an asset in the progressive building of students' knowledge (Topping et al.; Boud, Cohen, and Sampson). In this context, the notion of reciprocity is particularly significant, as interactions are rooted in continuous and mutual support. Reciprocity entails an acknowledgment of the crucial role of co-construction of knowledge in teaching and learning and professional scenarios: "Seeing you allows me to see myself differently and to explore variables we both use" (Fanselow 184, cited in Pressick-Kilborn and te Riele 62).

Peer learning experiences at Hogwarts are guided by a double set of needs. Students need personalized attention and mutual discussion in order to unpack teacher-explained concepts and demonstrations. Students are also driven by their own curiosity, and most importantly, their desire to effectively contribute to the wizarding community's fight against dark powers. As such, many peer-learning trajectories emerge, with certain characters proving particularly active in this space. Hermione can be considered a leading figure in this context, a champion of peer-facilitation. Students often rely on her support in the classroom, as evidenced by her instructions to Neville in Potions (*PoA* 97) and outside of lessons, too. She helps Harry and Ron with both essays (*OotP* 268) and more general homework tasks: "She would never let them copy ('How will you learn?'), but by asking her to read [their homework] through, they got the right answers anyway" (*PS* 134). Hermione's greatest strength lies in her background reading, which gives her an enormous advantage when aiding her peers, as she is often able to explain the theory behind the practical element that has been shown to the students in class. Evidently, when articulated concisely and in an accessible manner, the theoretical underpinnings of Hogwarts subjects need not be intimidating or disheartening. Hermione in turn receives support from her peers in the few areas where she does not excel. Ron teaches Hermione to play wizard's chess, and Ron and Harry note that her frequent losses were "very good for her" (*PS* 159). Hermione is also clearly comfortable asking Harry for help with her potion in Slughorn's first class, though she admittedly refuses to accept his help when she discovers that it will involve diverging from the "official" instructions (*H-BP* 184). Hermione's generosity, and her faith in reciprocity, is built progressively. Initially, she is described as an "insufferable know-it-all" (*PoA* 129) whose greatest fear (failure) is notably self-absorbed (*PoA* 234). Towards the end, she appears to be motivated by a new will to disseminate knowledge through sharing and receiving for the good of the community.

The famous trio of "conventional" heroes—Harry, Ron, and Hermione—represents a micro-peer community that is particularly productive in terms of its magical outcomes. The three frequently discuss interesting or difficult aspects of their lessons, demonstrating a reflective and collaborative intention. The passage of the three characters towards adulthood is marked by a growing friendship that represents an empowering tool, allowing them to share and improve their skills, thus proving that reciprocity is pivotal in their personal and professional paths.

On the contrary, the peer-learning space associated with Neville is a primarily negative one in the early books. This pattern is then significantly mobilized in the last three books, and undergoes a radical inversion by the end of the saga. The effects of Neville's involvement in peer engagement play a key role in the development of his character and the narrative as a whole. This attention to peer-learning demonstrates Rowling's concern for the diversified spaces of learning and different learning styles that characterize the cohort. Through a gradual yet deliberate emphasis on reciprocity in student learning interactions, the author is thus able to infuse the characters' learning with principles of inclusivity, which then move the inner mechanisms of the plot and come to profoundly characterize the pedagogy of the *Harry Potter* series.

Neville Longbottom as a Quiet Hero

Neville Longbottom is one of the least investigated yet most nuanced characters of the *Harry Potter* series. Despite a general lack of attention paid to the character, the few insightful analyses of Neville's role within the saga confirm his status as a pivotal figure. The shaping of Neville's character and its progression allow Rowling to significantly mobilize patterns of heroism and to design a path towards personal and professional empowerment that has the power to inspire a heterogeneous audience of readers.

Critiques of the *Harry Potter* series have addressed extensively the normative and heteronormative nature of Rowling's undertaking, in particular in relation to heroism (Pugh and Wallace). The series portrays Harry, a male protagonist with significant magical and emotional abilities, as the just leader who is predestined to save the world alone. Therefore, little space is allocated to the mobilization of either gender or diversity of skills and inclinations. Such a critical reading is essential and supports the positioning of the series within the realm of children's literature, while at the same time outlining the need for the queering of contemporary coming-of-age stories in order to infuse them with an increased sense of dynamicity and inclusivity. A diligent analysis of the narrative path undertaken by Neville Longbottom, however, may open a space in which to challenge aspects of the aforementioned normative heroism and may suggest a new avenue through which to queer this narrative and expand the discourse on inclusivity in the series. Neville is an imperfect hero, and as such, his authenticity and relatability present an opportunity to step outside the normative politics of identity at work in hero figures such as Harry.

Rather than following a path involving displays of spectacular courage and sensational skills from its beginning, Neville undertakes a quiet yet meaningful path from complete fear to total openness. This contributes to the illumination of both empowerment and reciprocity as active mechanisms not only in Neville's journey, but also in the advancement of the narrative. As he first appears within the Hogwarts cohort, Neville is more "non-hero" than "anti-hero." He never intentionally hurts his peers or acts maliciously, and he seems intent on slipping under the radar in and outside of lessons, rarely drawing unnecessary attention to himself. In line with his quiet personality, he appears in the first four books to be immersed in frequent attempts to hide himself, and thus gives himself little space for exploring or improving. Referring to himself as "almost a Squib" (*CoS* 139) and even a "nobody" (*OotP* 168), he is often described as having significant problems relating to organization, memory, and attention span, as well as issues following multi-step directions, a notable physical clumsiness, and a severe lack of confidence in his own magical abilities.

Neville is an introverted learner, extremely quiet during most classroom lessons and inclined to observation rather than to the practice or performance of his magical skills. This can be observed in the DADA lesson in which Lupin aids Neville through the process of facing a boggart (*PoA* 100–104). Lupin explains the process clearly and gives Neville both the necessary time to understand and process his instructions and the physical space to then successfully tackle the boggart. Using the widely disseminated Felder-Silverman model on teaching styles as a point of reference (678–679), he can easily be identified as a reflective learner. The classroom space, however, seems not to respond in full to the needs of reflective learners such as Neville, and caters more significantly to wizards who are keener to attempt newly acquired skills immediately and who thrive in an environment in which they are constantly and actively challenged. On the contrary, from the beginning of the series, Neville is severely stigmatized, particularly for his in-class performances: he experiences discrimination, condescension, and blaming from teachers and students alike. In internalizing these stigmas, often the only reaction available to him is silence. Indeed, it is for this reason that the sporadic early incidents in which Neville momentarily embodies self-confidence, standing up for himself and his friends (in fighting Crabbe and Goyle at a Quidditch match, *PS* 163–164) and for himself (in standing up to the trio before their fight for the Philosopher's Stone, *PS* 197–199), are so surprising; later, of course, it becomes evident that these are brief glimpses at Neville's potential for a more holistic self-confidence.

As the series progresses, Neville's standard response of silence and erasure is shown to be closely related to a constitutive lack of self-confidence, generated first and foremost by his family situation and treatment at the hands of his relatives. Neville is not an orphan, but he is unable to experience the love of his parents who were tortured into insanity by Voldemort's supporters (*GoF* 523–524; *OotP* 453–455; *H-BP* 139). Additionally, Neville grows up with an overbearing grandmother who (up until *Half-Blood Prince*) does not hesitate to demonstrate, even publicly, that she would have preferred a different kind of grandson, and who, far from accepting and encouraging his natural skills and inclinations, dwells instead on his struggles. As Jaime Feathers notes (3–5), the scene at St. Mungo's hospital where Neville's parents live visually epitomizes this pattern of unequal power: the small, silent, invisible Neville walks with his tall, loud, domineering grandmother, who, rather than nurturing her grandson in this difficult moment, bullies him instead. In particular, she denigrates his magical skills and harshly upbraids Neville in front of the trio for his decision not to confide in them about his parents' fate, incorrectly assuming that he is ashamed of them (*OotP* 453–455).

At Hogwarts, too, Neville is maltreated by teachers and peers alike. Even primarily "fair" characters, such as Hermione and Harry, sometimes distance themselves from him. For instance, his very first attempt to speak up, in which he challenges the trio to stop them from breaking the rules and losing points for Gryffindor, is instantly silenced by Hermione's Body-Bind charm (*PS* 197–199). The temporary petrification of Neville epitomizes the silencing of the character in his first incarnation. In the first four books, his peers make little effort to understand, include, or get to know him. Neville's reflective style and shy nature also seem incompatible with the competitive learning environments at Hogwarts. The time constraints for gaining skills do not seem to be adapted to his pace as a learner, and his aptitudes are thus undervalued. The trauma of bullying seems to torment him in almost every situation and his silence is often understood as surrender.

Overall, these patterns have a dual effect on the evolution of the character. On the one hand, they create a separation and "othering" of Neville, painful both for the character to experience and for the reader to witness. On the other hand, this "othering" is used by the author to demonstrate Neville's resilience. The reader witnesses his empowerment through the lens of a quiet achiever who learns from observation, listening, self-acceptance, and a progressive opening towards self-determination. In later developments, dynamics of peer-learning closely interest Neville's character. His opening up to the "other" strengthens his receptivity, whilst his ability to give becomes the key to his empowerment (just like Harry's ability to love). It is Neville's faith in reciprocity, despite his constant isolation, that characterizes his personal and educational growth.

If Harry is the indisputable hero from a narratological point of view, Neville provides a nuanced foil to this figure, qualifying as the *quiet hero* of the series. Many symmetries between the two characters justify this approximation. First, the Sorting Hat is unsure as to which Hogwarts house he should place each character in: the hesitation is between Gryffindor and Slytherin for Harry (*PS* 90–91) and between Gryffindor and Hufflepuff for Neville ("Hogwarts Students"). This detail is highly significant in the delineation of the characters. While the choice for Harry is substantially between the good (Gryffindor) and the bad (Slytherin), the choice for Neville is between courage (Gryffindor) and loyalty (Hufflepuff). Both characteristics are significant elements of his personality, the first remaining unrecognized by him for a long time, and the second, prefigured in the evolution of his name from Neville Puff (Rowling, "The Original Forty"), being the foundation on which he builds his progressive empowerment and self-awareness.

The specularity of the two characters is apparent in further aspects. Both Harry and Neville were born at the end of July in the same year, and both have parents who were members of the Order of the Phoenix and escaped Voldemort three times. Thus, either of them could have been "the one with the power to vanquish the Dark Lord" (*OotP* 741) mentioned in the prophecy. While it is Harry who is marked by Voldemort as his equal, and thus becomes the Chosen One tasked with defeating him, it is Neville who undergoes the greater struggle throughout the series. The aforementioned condition of Neville's parents is acknowledged by Alastor Moody as being worse than death itself (*OotP* 158). Harry would appear to agree: "[Harry] imagined how it must feel to have parents still living, but unable to recognise you. He often got sympathy from strangers for being an orphan, but … he thought that Neville deserved it more than he did" (*GoF* 527).

Moreover, Neville's grandmother is a dominating and controversial figure who belongs to the world of wizards and is loved by Neville; his initial perceived lack of magical ability is a cause of embarrassment to her, and so she simultaneously places great pressure on Neville to improve and extols skepticism about his ability to do so. Harry is tormented by his uncle, aunt, and cousin, who consistently mistreat him; yet Harry does not love them, nor does he expect any acknowledgment of love from them. On the contrary, Neville, though he dreads his grandmother's constant judgment and disappointment in the earlier books, still clearly loves her and appreciates her selfless efforts in caring for him in place of his parents. As such, there are many more nuances and conflicting tensions in his interactions with his family.

Over the course of *Order of the Phoenix*, the aforementioned patterns involving this character are mobilized, and Neville transforms himself into a new figure. This transformation relies on two mechanisms: the reciprocity of his relationship with his peers and a process of self-awareness. Both mechanisms acknowledge and value his reflective nature and inclinations and finally reveal the essence of Rowling's inclusive pedagogy.

Neville in the Classroom

Within the Hogwarts classroom at large, Neville is extensively bullied by teachers and is consistently "othered" due to his learning style and lack of self-confidence in his magical abilities. He is also explicitly described as a prisoner of his fears and his lack of practical skills. His fear of Snape, and Snape's targeted bullying of Neville in class, worsens his already abysmal skills in Potions and further weakens his confidence (*PoA* 95, 96, 100, 107). In a rare instance in which Neville is able to practice Potions without Snape present, the change in his countenance (and presumably his performance) is immediate (*OotP* 631).

Neville's treatment by teachers, and particularly by Snape, exacerbates his lack of self-confidence. While Snape's intimidation of Neville is the most blatant example of such teacher behavior, it is not the only instance. In one lesson, McGonagall berates Neville for accidentally transplanting his own ears onto a cactus but gives him no tools with which to improve his skills; the implication is that he should perhaps stop trying at all. Barty Crouch, Jr. (disguised as Alastor Moody), would appear to encourage Neville to volunteer information about the Cruciatus curse. However, as this curse was performed on Neville's parents by Crouch Jr. himself, this encouragement must be read as bullying of the worst kind, particularly given Neville's horrified reaction to seeing the curse performed (*GoF* 190).

This horror also translates to classroom situations more generally. In class, Neville is often terrified of being addressed at all, as evidenced by his reactions to teacher questions and by his general fear of potentially dangerous classroom situations (*PS* 109; *PoA* 80, 102). Neville's other particular physical and emotional characteristics are also played on by teachers. Trelawney, an incompetent teacher and Seer, relies on a talent for reading people. Likely noting Neville's physically clumsy deportment and nervous demeanor, she "predicts" his accident and advises him to select another cup from which to read his tea leaves after he has broken his first (*PoA* 81). She also plays on his forgetfulness by advising him to work hard to catch up as she has "seen" that he will be late to the next lesson (*PoA* 83). Trelawney makes these comments entirely at Neville's expense, as even more attention than usual is paid to Neville's blunders when they do occur, further damaging his self-confidence.

It is clear that this lack of self-confidence contributes to Neville's many unsuccessful educational experiences. The only area in which Neville seems to excel is Herbology, "which was easily his best subject" and the "only class in which Neville usually volunteered information" (*GoF* 189). His aptitude for Herbology seems to be a natural talent, rather than the result of any particular pedagogical approach. His innate skill in this area gives him a sense of pride, but his confidence does not translate to other subject areas. Indeed, in one of McGonagall's Transfiguration lessons, she cites his "lack of confidence" (*OotP* 232) as his main barrier to learning. Unfortunately, though, the level of confidence he acquires in order to pass his Transfiguration O.W.L. is not enough to sufficiently improve his skills in order to continue with the subject at N.E.W.T. level (*H-BP* 165). Lupin actively bolsters Neville's confidence in the classroom. However, his use of Neville as the primary demonstrator of the Riddikulus counter charm occurs in reaction to Snape's bullying of Neville immediately before the lesson, so it is unclear whether this confidence-building exercise would have occurred without this stimulus.

Due to the poor treatment from so many of his teachers, Neville understandably seeks both solace and help from his classroom peers. As per the early peer dynamics previously discussed, however, students who habitually lack the background knowledge needed to take equal part in interactions are initially excluded by the community. Such exclusion can be seen in Harry's desire to avoid Neville as a working partner if possible: "Harry's partner was Seamus Finnigan (which was a relief, because Neville had been trying to catch his eye)" (*PS* 126). This avoidance and exclusion continues until the point in which the ability to open up new spaces flourishes within the series. Inclusion in the peer-learner community comes about as a result of the co-occurrence of multiple factors: the need for a collective effort to beat dark forces, the general maturation of the cohort, and a singular effort towards self-determination undertaken by Neville within spaces of self-reflection.

Neville, Reciprocity and Empowerment

Neville obtains the self-confidence that has been lacking throughout his magical education outside the classroom and, in particular, within the context of Dumbledore's Army (the D.A.). The D.A. is a group of students who meet to improve their practical use of the defensive spells that have been banned from Umbridge's DADA classroom. Wishing to prepare themselves for the new and pressing dangers of a wizarding world in which Voldemort is again gaining power, these students practice both basic spells and more advanced magic in a peer-learning environment. During its two iterations, in *Order of the Phoenix* and *Deathly Hallows*, the group sees a succession of leading figures, although all students contribute to the co-construction of knowledge within the group.

Initially, Harry's prior experiences in dealing first-hand with life-threatening defensive situations sets him in good stead to take on the role of a facilitator within the group. The way in which Harry sets up this experience is inclusive and based on personalized approaches that take into consideration learner backgrounds, skill levels, styles, motivations, and paces. Moreover, the peer-learning structure provides a space for practicing in a comfortable and non-judgmental atmosphere. Distanced from adult dynamics of validation, students' receptivity to the co-construction of knowledge increases significantly.

Rowling provides significant detail surrounding strategies of peer-learning and co-construction of knowledge adopted within the D.A. Meetings progress according to a consistent pattern: Harry, taking into consideration the background knowledge of his peers, encourages them to divide themselves into pairs and practice a given spell on each other repeatedly. He then performs a series of dynamic actions, paying constant attention to the classroom space by walking around the group, correcting and making suggestions as he goes (*OotP* 349). Harry also provides the cohort with prompt and specific feedback and motivates the group by speaking to them in an encouraging manner while also indicating areas and strategies for improvement (*OotP* 349). These prompts illustrate the personalized, inclusive, and effective practice-based learning model that the D.A. meetings utilize.

This model, which fills the gaps in Hogwarts' pedagogies outlined above, includes clear provision of instructions by a peer-facilitator, meaningful organization of and movement within the class space, creation of a confidence-building environment, and provision of essential individual formative feedback. These aspects enhance inclusivity and promote reciprocity and cause a shift in focus towards the diversity of student skills and outcomes, which are now proficiently co-constructed. In evaluating his initial inclusive approach, Harry notes that "he had been right to suggest they practice the basics first" due to the "shoddy spellwork" he observes (*OotP* 348). In this moment, readers are left with the impression that this cohort of students will be working from a "clean slate" of sorts. They will be given the opportunity to fill in the gaps in their learning so far, building on those basics towards a deeper learning of old and new concepts.

Neville plays a vital role in this group and in fostering the aforementioned peer dynamics. His transformation within this narrative arc, from the familiar timid but untiring Neville of the earlier books to a student in possession of great confidence in his own magical abilities, allows him to contribute to his community and to later qualify as the series' *quiet hero*. In

Neville's sixth year, the D.A. disbands, and so we see little of Neville in learn-ing situations. *Deathly Hallows*, however, sees the fulfillment of Neville's learn-ing arc, in which he takes both the self-confidence and the magical skills garnered through his participation in the D.A. peer-learning environment and transforms himself from a peer-learner into a peer-facilitator. Hogwarts gives him a space to embrace this role when the school is taken over by Snape and a number of Death Eaters, rendering the majority of the staff powerless over their methods of teaching and of disciplining students (*DH* 461–462). With many of the teachers who failed Neville now indisposed and with a new body of ineffective and cruel teachers against whom many students wish to rebel, Neville is provided with a space in which to complete his transforma-tion.

While Harry, Ron and Hermione are absent from Hogwarts throughout *Deathly Hallows*, their classmates' learning experience continues without them. The trio hear of the exploits of D.A. members through various channels, learning that "Ginny, and probably Neville and Luna along with her, had been doing their best to continue Dumbledore's Army" and were keeping up a "constant, low-level of mutiny" against the new Headmaster Snape (*DH* 257). With the original trio absent, a new trio forms in its place in order to continue the peer-educational work of the D.A., and in this iteration, it is Neville who takes up the mantle of peer-facilitator.

When Neville meets with the original trio in the Hog's Head, he reveals that his "battered visage" (*DH* 460) is the result of the election of two Death Eaters as heads of student discipline. Ron berates Neville for his cavalier atti-tude towards provoking these disciplinarians, but as Neville himself says, "it helps when people stand up to them, it gives everyone hope. I used to notice that when you did it, Harry" (*DH* 462). Here, Neville directly demonstrates the way he has transformed his peer-learning within the original D.A. into a peer-facilitating strategy in order to instruct and organize a potentially larger cohort than Harry directed and to combat the actions of not just one teacher, but three.

Progressing with the narrative, it becomes clear that the new and direr educational situation at Hogwarts requires a greater heroism than was nec-essary during Harry's leadership of the D.A., and it is Neville who embraces this role. While Neville describes Luna, Ginny and himself as "sort of the leaders" of this cohort, he reveals that following the departure of Luna and Ginny from the school, he was left as the sole leader. During that time, the cohort "were still fighting, doing underground stuff" (*DH* 463). When the trio and Neville rejoin the new D.A., it is Neville who gives instructions to the group (*DH* 467–468). As the Battle of Hogwarts concludes, Neville refuses to join Voldemort, and indeed, incites the watching crowd to join him in cheering for Dumbledore's Army—notably, a crowd "whom Voldemort's silencing charms seemed unable to hold" (*DH* 586). In a precise mirroring of Hermione's Body-Bind attack on Neville in *Philosopher's Stone*, Voldemort then makes Neville "rigid and still," but this time, the empowered Neville "broke free of the Body-Bind Curse upon him" (*DH* 587) in an explicit refusal to be silenced any longer. Neville receives the ultimate encouragement from Harry when he is entrusted with the mission to kill the snake Nagini (Voldemort's penultimate Horcrux). Neville easily completes this task, solidifying his trajectory from self-doubt to self-confidence, from a student consistently mistreated and "othered" to a mentor who plays a pivotal role in saving the wizarding world. This trajectory finds an ultimate reciprocity in the Epilogue, in which we discover that Neville has become Professor of Herbology at Hogwarts (*DH* 606) and is thus able to continue to transmit both his inherent talent, and more importantly his hard-won skills in pedagogy, to his students.

The Power of Peers

Students' learning and their appreciation of any given class is significantly linked to the teacher's personality, and students' frustration with dated teacher-oriented approaches tends to emerge insistently throughout the *Harry Potter* series. Although "good" and "fair" teachers seem to play an important role in inspiring the cohort, they tend not to intervene directly in the development of student outcomes. They rarely provide constructive feedback, and they endorse the competitive nature of education at Hogwarts in both direct and indirect ways. This latter aspect does not facilitate the inclusion of students who rely on reflective learning styles or who need space and attention in their learning. This absence of nuance within the formal classroom space may be a result of narratological constraints; however, Rowling finds another way to highlight the importance of interaction, inclusivity, and reciprocity at Hogwarts, addressing these aspects more directly within dynamics of peer-learning and the co-construction of knowledge that occur in informal settings.

The character who evolves the most significantly within this educational space is Neville Longbottom. Bullied in class, significantly marginalized by teachers and peers, and generally misunderstood in the early books, Neville develops an incredible capacity for resilience on which he constructs his progressive empowerment. Dynamics of peer-learning facilitate this process of self-determination, building his self-confidence and nourishing his progressive empowerment. The moment in which Neville truly comes into his own, however, is the moment in which he becomes a peer-instructor and realizes that he is capable and, most importantly, able to give.

While Harry is viewed as the salvation of the wizarding community, Neville is just as significant in his role as a *quiet hero* who learns both alone and with others. Using his sensitivity and reflective personality, he is able to grow and embrace change. Eventually, through this process of growth and development, he is shown to possess a strength that is perhaps unmatched in any other character drawn by Rowling's pen. Neville's trajectory, so different from the traditional hero narrative explored through Harry's journey, poses to readers an alternative inspiration: he is proof that "quiet" does not equate to "powerless," and that where traditional pedagogical practices fail, there are always alternate models to turn to that offer every learner the opportunity to flourish.

NOTES

1. On this topic see for example Bonwell and Sutherland, who frame their investigation in the context of active learning. For a focus on both teacher and student approaches see Trigwell, Prosser, and Waterhouse.

2. See in particular Park and Choi on the evolution of educational environments and collaborative learning spaces; Lim, O'Halloran, and Podlasov on the relevance of movement in the classroom; and Parnell on lighting and classroom objects.

WORKS CITED

Bixler, Andrea. "What We Muggles Can Learn About Teaching from Hogwarts." *The Clearing House: A Journal of Educational Strategies, Issues and Ideas,* vol. 84, no. 2, 2011, pp. 75–79.

Bonwell, Charles C., and Tracey E. Sutherland. "The Active Learning Continuum: Choosing Activities to Engage Students in the Classroom." *New Directions for Teaching and Learning,* vol. 67, 1996, pp. 3–16.

Booth, Margaret Zoller, and Grace Marie Booth. "What American Schools Can Learn from Hogwarts School of Witchcraft and Wizardry." *The Phi Delta Kappan,* vol. 85, no. 4, 2003, pp. 310–315.

Boud, David, Ruth Cohen, and Jane Sampson, editors. *Peer Learning in Higher Education: Learning from and with Each Other.* Kogan Page, 2001.

"The Definitive Guide to the Order of the Phoenix and Dumbledore's Army." *Pottermore,* Wizarding World Publishing, www.pottermore.com/features/the-definitive-guide-to-the-order-of-the-phoenix-and-dumbledores-army-infographic.

Fanselow, John F. "'Let's See': Contrasting Conversations About Teaching." *Second Language Teacher Education,* edited by Jack C. Richards and David Nunan, Cambridge UP, 1990, pp. 182–197.

Feathers, Jaime. "The Unsung Hero of Harry Potter: Neville Longbottom." *Hog Creek Review: A Literary Journal of the Ohio State University at Lima,* 2013, pp. 1–10.

Felder, Richard M., and Linda K. Silverman. "Learning and Teaching Styles in Engineering Education." *Engineering Education,* vol. 78, no. 7, 1988, pp. 674–681.

Hattie, John, and Helen Timperley. "The Power of Feedback." *Review of Educational Research,* vol. 77, no. 1, 2007, pp. 81–112.

"Hogwarts Students Who Could Have Been Sorted Into Different Houses." *Pottermore,* Wizarding World Publishing, www.pottermore.com/features/hogwarts-students-who-could-have-been-sorted-into-different-houses.

Karpicke, Jeffrey D. "Retrieval-Based Learning: Active Retrieval Promotes Meaningful Learning." *Current Directions in Psychological Science,* vol. 21, no. 3, 2012, pp. 157–163.

Lim, F.V., K.L. O'Halloran, and A. Podlasov. "Spatial Pedagogy: Mapping Meanings in the

Use of Classroom Space." *Cambridge Journal of Education*, vol. 42, no. 2, 2012, pp. 235–251.

Mulholland, Neil, editor. *The Psychology of Harry Potter*. BenBella Books, 2007.

Mynott, Glen. "Harry Potter and the Public School Narrative." *New Review of Children's Literature and Librarianship*, vol. 5, no. 1, 1999, pp. 13–27.

Park, Elisa L., and Bo Keum Choi. "Transformation of Classroom Spaces: Traditional Versus Active Learning Classroom in Colleges." *Higher Education*, vol. 68, no. 5, 2014, pp. 749–771.

Parnell, Emily Caruso. "Making Space: Designing the Classroom Environment for Movement." *Physical & Health Education Journal*, vol. 78, no. 4, 2013, pp. 26–28.

Pressick-Kilborn, Kimberley, and Kitty te Riele. "Learning from Reciprocal Peer Observation: A Collaborative Self-Study." *Studying Teacher Education*, vol. 4, no. 1, 2008, pp. 61–75.

Pugh, Tison, and David L. Wallace. "Heteronormative Heroism and Queering the School Story in J.K. Rowling's Harry Potter Series." *Children's Literature Association Quarterly*, vol. 31, no. 3, 2006, pp. 260–281.

Rowling, J.K. *Harry Potter and the Chamber of Secrets*. Bloomsbury, 1998.

_____. *Harry Potter and the Deathly Hallows*. Bloomsbury, 2007.

_____. *Harry Potter and the Goblet of Fire*. Bloomsbury, 2000.

_____. *Harry Potter and the Half-Blood Prince*. Bloomsbury, 2005.

_____. *Harry Potter and the Order of the Phoenix*. Bloomsbury, 2003.

_____. *Harry Potter and the Philosopher's Stone*. Bloomsbury, 1997.

_____. *Harry Potter and the Prisoner of Azkaban*. Bloomsbury, 1999.

_____. "The Original Forty." *Pottermore*, Wizarding World Publishing, www.pottermore.com/writing-by-jk-rowling/the-original-forty.

Sailer, Kerstin. "The Spatial and Social Organisation of Teaching and Learning: The Case of Hogwarts School of Witchcraft and Wizardry." *Proceedings of the 10th International Space Syntax Symposium*, edited by Kayvan Karimi, et al., Space Syntax Laboratory, The Bartlett School of Architecture, University College London, 2015, pp. 34:1–34:17.

Topping, Keith, et al. *Effective Peer Learning: From Principles to Practical Implementation*. Routledge, 2017.

Trigwell, Keith, Michael Prosser, and Fiona Waterhouse. "Relations Between Teachers' Approaches to Teaching and Students' Approaches to Learning." *Higher Education*, vol. 37, no. 1, 1999, pp. 57–70.

Van den Bergh, Linda, et al. "Teacher Feedback During Active Learning: Current Practices in Primary Schools." *British Journal of Educational Psychology*, vol. 83, no. 2, 2013, pp. 341–362.

Wenger-Trayner, Etienne, et al. *Learning in Landscapes of Practice: Boundaries, Identity, and Knowledgeability in Practice-Based Learning*. Routledge, 2014.

Teaching Wizarding Houses

Hogwarts' Case for a
Learner-Centered Pedagogy

Brynn Fitzsimmons *and* Addison Lucchi

> I sort you into Houses
> Because that is what I'm for...
> ...Though I must fulfill my duty
> And must quarter every year
> Still I wonder whether sorting
> May not bring the end I fear.
> —J. K. Rowling, *Order of the Phoenix*, 206

While the four Hogwarts houses are often discussed in terms of the rivalries they create among students (and fans), they also represent different pedagogical and educational philosophies. The Sorting Hat groups students based on their values, but each house also implies a distinct set of learning preferences and styles, which in turn, inform teaching styles that correlate to each instructor's own Sorting. This essay will discuss the specific ways that the values of each of the four houses inform these distinct teaching and learning styles. As the Sorting Hat points out with respect to house values, strict delineations among houses can also lead to unhelpful pedagogical divisions among both students and teachers. These divisions are especially problematic since house placement can indicate learning style *tendencies* but cannot predict the ways in which *all* members of a given house will learn. The failure of Hogwarts professors to reach across the house learning style boundaries causes most of the pedagogical failures within the *Harry Potter* series. Both wizard and Muggle teachers can benefit from reexamining the Hogwarts classrooms, houses, and learning styles to better understand the diverse needs of all learners.

Although it would be easy—just as the Sorting Hat warned—to treat house divisions in this essay as four completely separate categories for learners and teachers, it is critical to understand that learning and teaching styles exist—for both wizards and muggles—on a continuum (Schweisfurth 263). This demands a pedagogy that centers on learners as individuals who may fall anywhere *among* categories rather than *into* just one of them. The divisions among learners are obvious, and which style a student tends toward often correlates to their house. For instance, students in Ravenclaw tend not to acquire knowledge in the same way as Hufflepuff students, nor do teachers from Gryffindor handle their class the same way as those from Slytherin. Some students learn best through intellectual challenge, others through a sense of adventure. Some learn best through a feeling of achievement, others through a sense of play. However, it is also true that not every member of a given house learns the same way; each student may be a blend of multiple learning styles, only some of which are typical of their house, or their learning style may not match their house assignment at all. Thus, for Hogwarts teachers—and teachers beyond those pages—to be effective, they must be able to navigate the diverse continuum on which their students learn.

As discussed more fully in *Learner-Centered Pedagogy: Principles and Practice,* teachers embodying a learner- or learning-centered pedagogy must consider their own biases, educational philosophies, and learning styles and adjust their instruction to reach all types of learners (Klipfel and Cook 2–15). Hogwarts teachers must not only attempt to cater to mixed-house classrooms of students with varying values and learning needs, but these instructors must also navigate their own house values and the effects of those values on their teaching styles and philosophies in order to be effective. In short, Hogwarts teachers must understand both themselves and their students in order to evaluate their instruction critically and make adjustments so that it is learner-centered rather than teacher-centered.

Learner-Centered Pedagogy

Education must prioritize authentic student learning—hence the need for a pedagogy centered on it. While learning is partially dependent on students, it is up to teachers to engage their students and discover what and how they need (and want) to learn. In this way, teachers act as facilitators of learning, and learning occurs as a partnership between teachers and students. Throughout the *Harry Potter* series, Rowling uses numerous examples of both effective instruction and ineffective instruction to, as Brian and Anna White have written, "teach us what it means to be a good teacher" (White and White 12). By comparing and contrasting examples of these varied teaching experiences, we can make informed conclusions about what it means to embody a learner-centered pedagogy.

A learner-centered pedagogy stems from an understanding of learning as both universal and personal. In their article on possibilities for learner-centered pedagogy, Elite Ben-Yosef and Limor Pinhasi-Vittorio explain that this pedagogy understands learning as universal in that "all people can learn, want to learn, and learn continuously" and as personal in that "learning is specific to each learner in context" (Ben-Yosef and Pinhasi-Vittorio 7). This means that in order to teach from a place of learner-centeredness, instructors must seek to know the unique learning needs and learning styles of students. Applying a learner-centered pedagogy involves two major components: authentic learning (analyzing learner needs) and resource provision (meeting those needs). Thus, teachers must first discover the learning styles, preferences, and needs of their students, then instruct them in a way that facilitates optimal learning.

Wizarding Houses and Learning Styles

The mixing of learning styles within houses and the mixing of houses within the classroom pose several pedagogical problems for teachers. First, having a classroom full of students with four different learning styles presents a formidable challenge to any teacher—a challenge which is further complicated by the teacher's own bias toward one of these houses/learning styles (based on their house affiliation). However, the pedagogical reality of teaching at Hogwarts—much like the real world—is far more complicated, because learners do *not* exist in four distinct learning categories. Learners exist, both in the wizarding world and the Muggle one, on a continuum among a variety of learning styles. Although their houses' core values often win out and confirm their official Sorting, student learning styles reflect less of a sense of four learning style boxes and more of a web interconnected among four distinct points—a continuum upon which the students of Hogwarts must learn and their professors must teach.

Gryffindor learners can best be compared to bodily kinesthetic learners. Kinesthetic learning, according to Gardner's theory, involves learning through doing—more specifically, learning by using "one's body in highly differentiated" ways (Gardner 206). Harry learns best when he is not just engaging his mind in learning, but also his body. The classes Harry most enjoys and excels in are those that involve significant activity, such as Defense Against the Dark Arts and Transfiguration. Harry frequently learns through experience—outside of the classroom—arguably more than he often learns within it. An example of this is when Harry effectively uses the Summoning Charm during his trial against the dragon in *The Goblet of Fire* after not being able to master the charm in class (347). Harry learns how to brew certain potions or cast specific spells by using them in this kind of active way; he learns how to conjure a Patronus by using it to protect himself in Quidditch and later to save his own life (and his friends) from the dementors (*PoA* 411).

Gryffindors are also inherently competitive learners; they thrive when given opportunities to use their learning in a competitive environment. Consider how Gryffindor students respond to activities such as Quidditch, the House Cup, and the Triwizard Tournament. Competitive activities bring out the best in Gryffindor-learners; competition helps them rally together all that they have learned and actively demonstrate it where it will have a perceived impact. In real-world classes, Gryffindor-type students are always itching to *do* in class, not just learn facts or theory. They are the students who care about learning most when it is actively making an impact. This type of learner appreciates active learning activities, which include gamified class models, role-playing, polls, or interactive discussion models such as jigsaw discussions.

Hufflepuff learners can be compared to those who have a high level of Gardner's musical or auditory intelligence. This type of learning is based on listening and experimentation. Whether it is learning through games, learning through sounds, or learning in collaboration with others, Hufflepuffs excel when they are able to connect their learning to engaging and relational activities. Helpful Hufflepuff-centric learning activities can include group projects, games or other team-based activities, and multimodal learning assignments or activities.

While Neville Longbottom is a Gryffindor, he falls far along the Hufflepuff spectrum of the learning continuum. This is clearly demonstrated by the ways Neville responds to encouragement and relational, project-based learning (*GoF* 220) and struggles with other forms of learning, such as in Potions (*SS* 139). Much of Neville's failure in Potions can likely be attributed to the constant belittling Snape provides rather than much needed encouragement (*PoA* 128). Neville is a prime example of how a rigid house structure can fail to fulfill students' learning needs. While understanding different learning styles is important, it is also vital for teachers to recognize that each individual student is unique, and that no student fits entirely into a single box (or house).

Another way to express the Hufflepuff learning style is to equate it to low-pressure learning. Hufflepuffs understand the value and importance of playing "with the subjects they are learning" (Yager 219). Hufflepuffs learn the most when they do not have to fear failure and can express themselves in diverse ways, such as through multimodal or non-traditional assignments. Neville, for example, excels at Herbology—a class that is incredibly low stakes and is also taught by Professor Sprout, a Hufflepuff (*GoF* 220). For Hufflepuffs, learning is all about collaboration; it is the relationship that Hufflepuffs value most in learning. To be truly engaged in the classroom, Hufflepuffs require collaborative, relationship-driven learning activities. Ideally, these activities should take place in a low-stress environment with some fun experiential learning thrown in.

Ravenclaw students, although they vary widely (consider Luna Lovegood as compared to Cho Chang), share a number of learner characteristics. Their house indicates what they value about learning—wisdom, or learning for its own sake. Ravenclaws learn best through words, either spoken or written (Gardner 78). This leads to their affinity for lecture- or theory-based learning that utilizes mainly linguistic-intelligence-based methods. Ravenclaw students tend to prefer traditionally academic assignments, such as reading and written work that allows them to synthesize theoretical and textual knowledge. This style shows itself in Luna's tendency to cling to obscure pieces of knowledge entirely for their own sake, as in her first introduction to Harry and his friends in *Order of the Phoenix* (193–94). However, Luna quickly reveals that her tendency to collect information the way Harry and Ron collect chocolate frog trading cards is useful. In fact, Luna's entire contribution to the plot of the series returns to her ability to listen—to exercise her linguistic learning style through both reading and hearing—and retain information that she can later recall, often to Harry's benefit. Her ability to recall and apply her knowledge of thestrals quickly, for example, allows her to suggest a solution to Harry's problem of how to get to the Ministry of Magic to rescue Sirius (*OotP* 762–63).

Ravenclaw learners are also more adept with abstract knowledge. Hermione, who learns like a Ravenclaw in spite of being a Gryffindor, is one of the few students to keep up with Professor Flitwick's (Head of Ravenclaw House) Charms course. Although predicated on the performance of the various charms, Flitwick's course relies heavily on the theoretical framework behind the charms' execution. Flitwick, although clearly a well-studied teacher, talks too quickly through Charms theories and historical context for most of his students to keep up. In an early lesson on levitation spells, Hermione is the first to be able to perform their charm perfectly (*SS* 170–71), because she has already read and grasped the concepts in her textbooks. This emphasis on abstract knowledge also shows up in other classes, including Transfiguration as well as Professor Binns' History of Magic, where, again, as Kathryn McDaniel notes, Hermione is far more successful than her Gryffindor-learner classmates (294). She can succeed because of her distinct linguistic learning style, which is demonstrated not only through her ability to comprehend and note-take through even the driest of lectures but also (to Ron and Harry's dismay) through her tendency to recite textbooks she has read for fun.

Slytherin, for all its bad reputation in the wizarding world and its Muggle fandom, has one of the most driven learning styles at Hogwarts. Rather than being motivated by some abstract concept of knowledge for its own sake or an idealistic sense of learning to achieve the greater good, Slytherins take an almost entirely utilitarian approach to learning. Consistently goal-oriented learners, Slytherins are the types of students professors have in mind when they try to get students to see beyond the test and into the future careers for which they will need their classroom knowledge. These achievement-driven students respond well to coursework that rewards them for applying classroom knowledge to their own individual goals. This includes activities such as project-based assignments (usually individual) and assignment prompts written collaboratively between teacher and student.

Readers see an example of a Slytherin learner perhaps most clearly with Draco. Draco starts off his time at Hogwarts with a very distinct sense of which subjects he values and which he does not, a division which only grows as he continues his studies and his path toward becoming a Death Eater. Classes such as Defense Against the Dark Arts and Potions successfully engage aspiring Death Eaters like Draco, who can easily tailor these courses to his own interests, while courses like Hagrid's Care of Magical Creatures are less engaging. Slytherins tend toward what Gardner calls a logical-mathematical learning style, one that concerns itself largely with "confrontation with the world of objects" (129). Although this utilitarian learning style favors students like Draco within certain courses (like Snape's Potions), Slytherins can quickly lose interest and their classroom performance may suffer if course content does not directly fulfill their utilitarian aims for learning.

Wizarding Houses and Teaching Styles

As with the learning styles of Hogwarts students, the teaching styles of Hogwarts professors are also influenced by houses. Each teaching style tends to cater to a specific style of learning. Marić and Sims explain that the key determiners of teaching style are controlled by one's experiences: "Available interpersonal interactions, available symbol referents via one's cultural tool kit, and identity organization … influences individual level experiences and characteristics—including a professor's teaching methods and how s/he relates to students" (52). Thus, a teacher's house affiliation would affect their teaching style. Teachers of each house philosophy can meet learners' authentic needs and facilitate optimal learning through utilizing varied methods of instruction.

Gryffindor teachers tend to employ active learning techniques and to apply learning directly to the impact it can create. Gryffindors respond most to referent power—the kind of power that, according to authors French and Raven, is generated when students identify with teachers and thus want to be like them and learn from them (266). Throughout the series, Dumbledore (the Gryffindor Headmaster) demonstrates learner-centeredness through his uncanny ability to know (or guess) precisely what his students need. Dumbledore empowers Harry, in particular, providing him with information, resources, and advice. Also, by allowing Harry frequent opportunities to learn through his own experiences, Dumbledore caters to Harry's Gryffindor need for active learning. Yet, despite Dumbledore's incredible ability to analyze and provide for the needs of Gryffindor students, he often fails to provide for the needs of students from other houses (especially Slytherins such as Draco, who needed the mentorship Harry received). Professor McGonagall, on the other hand, is a prime example of a teacher who treats all of her students equally, regardless of her identification or lack of identification with them. McGonagall's willingness to enforce punishment on members of her own house (*SS* 135) and her ability to recognize the strengths and weaknesses in her students (*SS* 151) demonstrate this learner-centered behavior. McGonagall is one of the few professors who is universally recognized for her teaching prowess by members of every house.

Professor Lupin, also a Gryffindor, exemplifies learner-centeredness through mastering the art of organizing class periods in a way that caters to the learning styles of all students. Lupin begins one of his most successful classes from a Slytherin-learner standpoint by asking his students to "please put all your books back in your bags. Today's will be practical lesson" (*PoA* 130). He then proceeds to instruct his students how to defeat boggarts through actually fighting them—thus capitalizing on his strength as a Gryffindor instructor and providing for Gryffindors' need for active learning (*PoA* 134). Lupin encourages Neville, who often struggles, by expressing confidence in his abilities—thus recognizing the Hufflepuff's need for encouragement and relational learning (*PoA* 132). Finally, he shares some theoretical information about boggarts, which allow Ravenclaws the opportunity to gain knowledge about a new creature and learn in a way that is efficacious for them (*PoA* 133). Through these diverse instructional methods, Lupin demonstrates a mastery of organizing class periods in a way that caters to every single learning style—not all at once, but one at a time in the same class period.

Through their style of instruction, Gryffindor teachers promote a hidden curriculum of risk-taking. Indeed, in his article on Dumbledore's pedagogy, Knutsen asks, "what kind of headmaster would reward his students for violating rules?" (204). The answer is, of course, a Gryffindor headmaster. Through the way Gryffindors teach (such as Lupin with the boggart), they model this kind of risk taking for their students and thus teach them that learning often requires an element of risk—sometimes, even failure.

Hufflepuff teachers are defined by their desire to engage their students relationally. For these highly relational instructors, creating fun, collaborative class periods is the goal. Professor Sprout is, perhaps, the prime example of a Hufflepuff instructor. It is under Sprout's encouraging and welcoming class environment that Neville Longbottom excels in Herbology. Perhaps Sprout's most demonstrative session is her lesson on Mandrakes in *Chamber of Secrets* (92–94). In this session, Sprout shares verbal information about the Mandrakes, allows the students to actively handle them, and discusses their practical use for healing Basilisk victims—all the while encouraging and motivating her students. Sprout's student-centeredness is apparent in her comment in *Half-Blood Prince,* when she states that "if a single pupil wants to come, then the school ought to remain open for that pupil" (627). Sprout, throughout the series, demonstrates care for each and every student, regardless of their house. She prioritizes her students over her own instructional strategies or professional priorities. Hufflepuff teachers like Sprout naturally utilize reward power by offering positive reinforcement to their students—whether that is through encouragements, gifts, or house points (French and Raven 263). Neville is the perfect example of a Hufflepuff-type learner who responds positively to reward power, such as when he responds to Lupin's encouraging words when facing the boggart and thus performs admirably in the lesson (*PoA* 132). Through the way Hufflepuffs teach, they promote a hidden curriculum of sincere care to their students.

Though Hagrid is a Gryffindor, he is also very far along the Hufflepuff-end of the learning continuum. Hagrid regularly interacts with his students (especially his favorite students) outside of class periods—even going so far as to invite them to tea (*SS* 135). Teachers with Hufflepuff tendencies, like Hagrid, believe that relationship is one of the most important aspects of instruction—both peer-to-peer and teacher-student. However, while this side of Hagrid's instruction caters to the learning needs of Hufflepuff students, his tendency towards dangerous and high-stress learning environments (such as interacting with Hippogriffs) does not. Unfortunately, once the exciting and dangerous activities are stripped away from his instruction, Hagrid's teaching becomes "extremely dull" so that "nobody really liked" it (*PoA* 142). Ultimately, it was Hagrid's aptitude towards experiential and relational learning that made his teaching most effective for students inclined towards those learning styles.

Professor Grubbly-Plank (who seems to be a Hufflepuff but whose house is not mentioned in the series), is overall a much more learner-centered teacher. While Harry, Ron, and Hermione are a bit biased due to their close friendship with Hagrid, Harry still admits that many students "preferred Professor Grubbly-Plank's lessons" and that "a very small, unbiased part of him knew that they had good reason" (*OotP* 442). In her lesson on bowtruckles,

Grubbly-Plank uses both lecture (describing how to recognize a bowtruckle lodge) and active-learning (examining actual bowtruckles) in a Hufflepuff-friendly, low-stress atmosphere (259). She even incorporates some fun experiential learning by having her students sketch the bowtruckles by hand (259).

Ravenclaw professors, such as Professor Flitwick and Professor Binns (who is not named by Rowling as a Ravenclaw but certainly appears as one), teach according to a hidden curriculum of resourcefulness. These instructors expect students to be able to utilize information once they are given it, without their having to set it in a particular context. This, of course, comes from Ravenclaw's emphasis on wisdom and wit—knowledge for its own sake, applied in clever and versatile ways. For the natural Ravenclaw learner, such as Hermione or Luna, the application of seemingly unrelated information to a given situation is a natural intellectual connection, and Ravenclaw professors tend to teach assuming this connection is present.

Professor Binns demonstrates how this focus on knowledge for its own sake can alienate students. Binns is, notes Megan Birch, "like his subject—a relic, old, outdated, out of touch with students, literally a ghost" (105). Even when confronted with questions from students about the practical implications of his knowledge about the Chamber of Secrets (which would apply to impact-driven Gryffindors concerned about the school, goal-driven Slytherins' desire for the power held in the Chamber, and Hufflepuffs concerned about their friends), he brushes over the issue (CoS 150–152). Binns could and should have used whatever parts of Hogwarts history or lore he needed to engage his students' interest in the subject, but he prefers to remain in his strictly factual, knowledge-as-its-own-end realm.

Similarly, Flitwick demonstrates the danger of an over-reliance on theory. Flitwick's direct instruction is informed by his broad theoretical base. In his attempt to impart to students the broader theoretical context of his subject, he often offers so much linguistically based information that the only students who can keep up with him are Ravenclaw-style learners. His spit-fire mode of giving information might work for Hermione (and it does—"It's Wing-gar-dium Levi-o-sa," she quickly and now, famously corrects her classmates [171], to the praise of Flitwick), but it is not helpful for kinesthetically oriented Gryffindor learners like Harry and Ron, for whom linguistic instruction for a hands-on skill is entirely unhelpful.

This inability (or unwillingness) to move beyond Ravenclaw-style teaching causes non–Ravenclaw students to perceive Ravenclaw teachers as less powerful in the classroom, since these teachers build their authority on expert power—a sense of power that, according to French and Raven, is derived from the professor's knowledge of their subject matter (155–56). This wisdom- and linguistic-oriented, theory-heavy pedagogical approach works for learners who gravitate naturally toward abstract ways of thinking, but offers few entry points for students who do not already possess a strong linguistic intelligence (Gardner 78) or who are not already interested in the subject matter of the course (although they might be interested in related material, even if that material is supposedly fictional).

For Slytherins, the goal-driven, utilitarian, logical-mathematical learning style creates a teacher who teaches logically, toward a utilitarian goal, from a position of legitimate or performed power in the classroom, as exemplified by the most famous Slytherin Hogwarts Professor: Severus Snape. Snape, Rowling notes, shares some characteristics of McGonagall's Gryffindor teaching style, such as "the gift of keeping a class silent without effort" (*SS* 137). However, unlike McGonagall, Snape commands this silence through a sense of legitimate rather than referent power—that is, while McGonagall commands respect by consistently demonstrating her expertise and perceptiveness in the classroom, Snape commands respect simply by being Snape.

Snape reflects Slytherin's learning style within the first few minutes of Harry's very first Potions class by revealing that he privileges salient information over theoretical: "I can teach you how to bottle fame, brew glory, even stopper death—if you aren't as big a bunch of dunderheads as I usually have to teach" (*SS* 137). Here, and throughout the series, Snape employs metacognition, which is an important part of pedagogy, but he wields it as a weapon rather than a learning tool (Johnson 82–3). This pedagogy makes sense when one considers Snape's house values, where metacognition—like all learning—is meant to serve an extra-curricular end. In the first lesson, Snape asks Harry a series of questions and then mocks him for not being able to give information about the Draught of Living Death, an antidote for most poisons, and alternative names for a plant used in potion-making (*SS* 138). Although Snape's behavior toward Harry (both here and throughout the series) has more complicated internal motivations, his demeaning of Harry here is outwardly based on the fact that Harry has not lived up to Slytherin's utilitarian purposes for learning. Because of Snape's Slytherin-centric teaching style and clear house bias, he is "disliked by everybody except the students from his own house" (*CoS* 77).

Horace Slughorn, another Slytherin professor, is likewise results-driven, reinforcing that the Slytherin teachers possess a hidden curriculum of utilitarian ambition. Slughorn consistently privileges students in whom he senses both ambition and the ability to help him fulfill his own ambition. This pedagogical value informs whom he praises in the classroom, which voices he privileges, and which information he is willing to impart—as is the case with Harry's struggle to glean information from Slughorn regarding Tom Riddle. Slytherin-tending learners, including Harry at certain points, do benefit from these values, but students who are not able to fully enter the Slytherin learning style find themselves disadvantaged in a Slytherin instructor's classroom. A

Slytherin teacher creating a sense of power based only on Slytherin's concept of legitimate power (French and Raven 153) will find that non–Slytherin students may fear them but are unlikely to respect them based simply on social conventions and rank. Slytherin learners such as Draco will accept established social structures of power (based on class, political position, education, etc.) even in the classroom in a way that other types of learners may not, especially since these structures tend to reinforce the Slytherin's historic dedication to an elitist approach to education.

Barriers to Adopting a Learner-Centered Pedagogy

Looking at these various examples of instruction for and by members of each house/learning style helps illuminate how teachers of each style can adapt their instruction to cater to the needs of all learners. However, while it is clear that learner-centered approaches to teaching are ideal for learners, there are many educators whose instruction does not, in fact, embody them. The *Harry Potter* texts illustrate some of the reasons why many teachers do not choose to teach from a place of learner-centeredness.

One major barrier to adopting a learner-centered pedagogy comes from the (understandable) focus on one's own career and/or learning and teaching preferences in the classroom. The clearest example of this downfall is, perhaps, Gilderoy Lockhart, the Ravenclaw professor for Defense Against the Dark Arts in *Chamber of Secrets*. Rowling directly identifies Lockhart as a Ravenclaw in her article about him on *Pottermore*. Lockhart, although valued mostly for his celebrity appearances, interestingly gains his stated reputation based on a number of scholarly publications, including the textbooks he requires Hogwarts students to purchase for his class. Like a true Ravenclaw, his reputation for knowledge precedes even his appearance at Hogwarts. In the fiasco with the Cornish pixies, Lockhart further seeks to push his own scholarly reputation: "Know only that no harm can befall you whilst I am here," [101]—under the guise of developing his house's ideal of resourcefulness by "see[ing] what you make of them" (*CoS* 102). Lockhart's hubris is demonstrated further in that he refuses to admit his own mistakes as a teacher such as when Snape disarms him during a practical demonstration of the "Expelliarmus" spell (190–191). All of this informs Ron's demonstrative statement that he has not learned anything from Lockhart's ego-based teaching "except not to set pixies loose" (*CoS* 251).

While most teachers would look at an example like Lockhart's and recoil, there are less extreme examples that perhaps ring true within more of our classrooms than we care to admit. For example, Trelawney dismisses students who do not fit her learning style in favor of enjoying her position of power/gatekeeper of knowledge in the classroom for the more successful students who stand in awe of her Divination skills (*PoA* 322). Because the series is necessarily limited to a Gryffindor viewpoint, Gryffindor teachers are often commented on in the most positive light, but even they fail to reach other students who value different aspects of learning. This is clear in the case of Barty Crouch, Jr., as Mad-Eye Moody, whose extreme emphasis on active learning delights the highly Gryffindor students yet simultaneously intimidates and distances learners high on other ends of the learning continuum— such as Hermione, who learns much like a Ravenclaw (see *GoF* 211–219).

What is interesting about many of the failures of teachers at Hogwarts is that the *majority* are done with the best of intentions by professors who are at least competent and oftentimes *excellent* in their fields. However, knowledge of one's field, while a component of excellence in teaching (Bain 15–20), does not in itself equate to pedagogical skill or effectiveness. The other characteristics of successful teachers are largely outward focused: good preparation, high but achievable expectations, feedback-oriented learning environment, and a habit of self-evaluation (Bain 15–20). Consequently, academic facility and even the ability to put that facility to use within the styles and values of one's house cannot make a successful teacher unless that teacher *also* chooses to move beyond their own preferences and personal achievements, meet students where they are, and tailor to *their* needs.

Interestingly, the first time teachers at Hogwarts are formally evaluated is under the influence of arguably the worst teacher in the history of Hogwarts: Dolores Umbridge. Umbridge's form of teacher evaluation undermines learning in the classroom (Dickinson 243) by destroying teacher ethos and agency and demoralizing students. However, throughout the rest of the series, there is a profound lack of *positive* evaluation of teachers and their pedagogy, whether by administration, peers, or the teachers themselves. Snape, for example, is not checked by administration or colleagues for his abusive treatment of students (Marić and Sims 49). Hagrid, good intentions aside, manages to cause his students physical harm (*PoA* 118–122). While this calls the nature of their administrative oversight into question, there is, perhaps, an equal problem that lies with the teachers themselves: they are not self-evaluating their teaching based on feedback (direct or indirect) from students, a critical component of successful pedagogy (Bain 8–9). This solicitation of feedback reinforces an environment where students feel like their voices matter to the teacher, which strengthens the bond between student and teacher. As Klipfel and Cook explain, "The way to establish an emotional bond with learners is for them to experience us as the kind of person who understands and accepts them for their authentic selves" (114). Before a teacher can accept, they must understand, and to understand, they must *ask*. Understanding the *subject* you teach your students does not equate to understanding your *students*. Only intentionally soliciting and gathering data and feedback from students can offer this understanding. For example, Hagrid's class would, perhaps, have gone quite differently if he had taken his interests into slightly less account than the interests of his students; many Muggle classrooms could take a lesson from his failures, too.

Application for Teachers

Though much can be learned through an analysis of the teaching and learning in Hogwarts, teachers adopting a learner-centered pedagogy might first consider focusing on: understanding each individual student, balancing student control of the classroom with necessary teacher control, and working toward a selfless teaching model. The following applications represent the most crucial mindset shifts when adopting a learner-centered pedagogy.

One of the most effective guards against limiting oneself to one's natural teaching style (informed by one's learning style) is to make an effort to understand each student individually, rather than assuming they all have the same needs, which often are assumed to be similar to the teacher's learning needs. This individualization in pedagogy becomes even more important when we consider that there are no sets of learning styles—whether those be four Hogwarts' houses or any other systematization—that can truly contain students. Such categories can be useful in giving teachers or students a reference point from which to begin getting to know the individual, but the reality is that every learner—be that a student or a teacher—exists on a spectrum somewhere in between the various learning types. Thus, it becomes imperative for a successful instructor to understand each student individually, as Klipfel and Cook discuss, and to listen to and understand students in each pedagogical encounter, even before attempting to correct or instruct a student (Bain 28–29). Teachers can accomplish this understanding by soliciting student feedback throughout the semester; making time to get to know students on an individual or small group basis; and providing opportunity for students to develop a sense of metacognition about their learning styles.

Showing a "real personal interest" in students' individual learner needs and unique learning goals can help stimulate their curiosity and unleash their potential (Rogers 136). McGonagall demonstrates this learner-centered pedagogy by taking the time to understand her students' unique learner needs and innate potential. Because of this, when she helps students prepare for O.W.L.s in *Order of the Phoenix*, she expresses confidence that all students—even Neville—can receive satisfactory scores (257). Starting from a belief in a student's innate ability, learner-centered teachers must then aim to discover and develop educational opportunities for that student's specific learning styles, working from an understanding of their goals, not just the teacher's (Bain 31–33). Lupin did this for both Neville and Harry in *Prisoner of Azkaban*, where he taught the lesson on the boggart completely differently based on their needs (*PoA* 130; 132–140; 155–56). Lupin, then, although working with learners who did not all share his Gryffindor learning or natural teaching style, was able to reach the students in his class with an effectiveness that led him to be termed "the best Defense Against the Dark Arts teacher we ever had" (*PoA* 170).

Teachers must recognize that students are entitled to a certain amount of autonomy and self-direction in their schooling—and, to maximize learning, students and teachers should work together to determine the course of learning. While "humans do have a knack of choosing precisely those things that are worst for them" (*SS* 297), teachers who determine that they know what students need better than the students know themselves often force students into learning activities and patterns that do not match their interests, authentic needs, or values (Bain 33–37). In order to let students partner in their learning, teachers might consider collaborating with students in writing certain portions of assignment prompts or syllabi; encouraging student direction of class discussion; and grading on progress rather than performance through revisable assignments when possible.

Certain instructors in the series, such as Snape, continually fail at partnering with their students and sharing control of the classroom. Snape refuses to respond to student attempts at directing class discussion, and he rebukes his students for correcting or criticizing his teaching (*PoA* 172). Conversely, Professor McGonagall demonstrates an exceptional ability to consider the needs of all types of learners and respond to their progress in unbiased ways (*SS* 135). She recognizes and respects strengths in all of her students (even when they do not see those strengths in themselves), evaluates students based on their individual progress (*SS* 151), and dedicates herself towards doing whatever it takes to help her students succeed in what interests them (*OotP* 665). In these ways, McGonagall epitomizes an instructor who balances teacher and student control, collaborating with her students and thus facilitating learning.

Ultimately, effective learner-centered instruction must be a selfless endeavor. Seeking to understand and provide for the diverse learning styles and needs of students requires tremendous effort on the part of the teacher. In spite of demanding schedules and their own career or personal priorities, learner-centered teachers must make time to invest mentally and emotionally in students both inside and outside the classroom. For example, when McGonagall advocated for Harry against the wishes of Umbridge (then administrator of Hogwarts), she sacrificed her own potential advancement for the sake of a student's growth (White and White 15). Similarly, when Lupin maintained the composure and confidence necessary to effectively teach his students, despite enduring initial disparaging comments, he selflessly focused on student learning rather than on his own reputation (*PoA* 131–132). Dumbledore, as an administrator, also modeled selflessness to Harry throughout the series, prioritizing Hogwarts' staff members and his students' growth over his own desires and ultimately, over his own life. Rather than maintaining the path of least resistance and greatest personal advancement, these teachers exemplified selfless behaviors in their instruction that reaped incredible benefits in terms of student success.

Learning Diversity in the Classroom

Ultimately, the variety of cases discussed in this essay demonstrate the vital need for a pedagogy that is centered on student learning. Just as Hogwarts students respond to pedagogical situations in different ways often based on their house, the way Muggle students achieve learning outcomes varies widely based on the individual learner's style, background, and attitude. Through recognizing the diverse needs of learners and seeking to meet those needs in the classroom, teachers can begin to help students of all learning styles succeed and grow. To succeed in learner-centered instruction, teachers must put away a pedagogy centered on their own instructional preferences and instead work intentionally toward a diverse pedagogy that helps all types of learners succeed. As this study of Hogwarts pedagogy has demonstrated, this process requires an enormous amount of effort and intentional growth on the part of the teacher, but it pays dividends in the positive effect it has on students.

This is not, however, to say that teaching from a place of learner-centeredness does not also greatly benefit teachers in the process. Learner-centered teaching creates a loop effect in which students engage and connect as learners, which in turn gives confidence and encouragement to the teacher, which makes the teacher more enthusiastic in teaching, and so on. Diane Wood and Betty Lou Whitford discuss the effect of learner-centered classrooms:

> The healthiest and most productive learning communities have the power to make teachers, as one fifth-grade teacher put it, "feel like they can see, hear, think, and act like true professionals." They imbue teachers with a sense of professional agency and responsibility; the teachers, in turn, create communities committed to and capable of making classrooms better places for students to learn [145].

Facilitating this type of learning environment, then, can create a rapport that not only leads to the mutual growth of students and teachers but also to the reciprocal teaching/learning experience that many teachers endeavor to foster in their classrooms. Teaching in a learner-centered way requires that teachers acknowledge their natural instructional tendencies and house/educational philosophies as well as their areas of weakness as pedagogues. If they are able to navigate these tensions, however, both they and their students will enjoy a challenging, stimulating educational experience.

Teachers, like students, exist on a continuum in terms of natural teaching and learning styles. As teachers begin to instruct in ways that cater to the needs of each learning style (or house), they will break down the divisions among the houses/learning styles. Such a pedagogy unites the strengths of a variety of teaching styles and curbs the inequality in the educational experience for students whose individual learning needs cannot be met by a single, teacher-centric approach. As the Sorting Hat says of Hogwarts and as we can say of the academy, "And we must unite inside her/Or we'll crumble from within" (*OotP* 207). Around what should a school unite, if not its learners?

WORKS CITED

Bain, Ken. *What the Best College Teachers Do.* Harvard UP, 2004.

Ben-Yosef, Elite, and Limor Pinhasi-Vittorio. "Possibilities Inherent in a Learning-Centered Pedagogy." *Encounter: Education for Meaning and Social Justice*, vol. 25, no. 4, 2012, pp. 1–19.

Birch, Megan L. "Schooling Harry Potter: Teaching and Learning, Power and Knowledge." *Critical Perspectives on Harry Potter*, edited by Elizabeth E. Heilman, Taylor & Francis Group, 2003, pp. 103–20.

Dickinson, Renée. "Harry Potter Pedagogy." *Clearing House*, vol. 79, no. 6, 2006, pp. 240–44.

French, John R.P., and Bertram Raven. "The Bases of Social Power." *Classics of Organization Theory,* edited by Shafritz, Jay M., J. Steven Ott, & Yong Suk Jang, Cengage Learning, 2016, pp. 251–260.

Gardner, Howard. *Frames of Mind: The Theory of Multiple Intelligences.* 10th anniversary ed., BasicBooks, 1993.

Johnson, Melissa Carol. "Wands or Quills? Lessons in Pedagogy from Harry Potter." *The CEA Forum*, vol. 44, no. 2, Dec. 2015, pp. 75–91.

Klipfel, Kevin M., and Dani Brecher Cook. *Learner-Centered Pedagogy: Principles and Practice.* ALA Editions—ALA, 2017.

Knutsen, Torbjorn L. "Dumbledore's Pedagogy." *Harry Potter and International Relations,* edited by Daniel H. Nexon and Iver B. Neumann, Rowman & Littlefield Publishers, Inc., 2006, pp. 197–212.

Marić, Jelena, and Jenn Sims. "Pedagogy of the Half-Blood Prince." *The Sociology of Harry Potter: Enchanting Essays on the Wizarding World,* edited by Jenn Sims, Zossima Press, 2012, pp. 46–57.

McDaniel, Kathryn N. "Harry Potter and the Ghost Teacher: Resurrecting the Lost Art of Lecturing." *History Teacher,* vol. 43, no. 2, 2010, pp. 289–295.

Rogers, Carl R. "Questions I Would Ask Myself If I Were a Teacher." *Education*, vol. 95, no. 2, 1974, pp. 134.

Rowling, J.K. "Gilderoy Lockhart." *Pottermore,* https://www.pottermore.com/writing-by-jk-rowling/gilderoy-lockhart.

_____. *Harry Potter and the Chamber of Secrets.* Arthur A. Levine Books, 1999.

_____. *Harry Potter and the Goblet of Fire.* Arthur A. Levine Books, 2000.

_____. *Harry Potter and the Half-Blood Prince.* Arthur A. Levine Books, 2005.

_____. *Harry Potter and the Order of the Phoenix*. Arthur A. Levine Books, 2003.

_____. *Harry Potter and the Prisoner of Azkaban*. Arthur A. Levine Books, 1999.

_____. *Harry Potter and the Sorcerer's Stone*. Arthur A. Levine Books, 1998.

Schweisfurth, Michele. "Learner-Centered Pedagogy: Towards a Post-2015 Agenda for Teaching and Learning." *International Journal of Educational Development*, vol. 40, Jan. 2015, pp. 259–66, doi:10.1016/j.ijedudev.2014.10.011.

White, Anna M., and Brian White. "Fantastic Teachers and Where to Find Them: Professional Development Through YA Literature." *Language Arts Journal of Michigan*, vol. 31, no. 2, 2016, pp. 12–19.

Wood, Diane R., and Betty Lou Whitford. *Teachers Learning in Community: Realities and Possibilities*. State University of New York Press, 2010.

Yager, Susan. "Something He Could Do Without Being Taught." *Honors, Play, and Harry Potter*, vol. 11, 2015, pp. 213–222.

Sorting Out Approaches to Teaching and Learning

Composition Pedagogy as Defense Against the Dark Arts

RACHELLE A.C. JOPLIN

> By means of words, inspired incantations serve as bringers-on of pleasure and takers-off of pain. For the incantation's power, communicating with the soul's opinion, enchants and persuades and changes it, by trickery.
> —Gorgias, Encomium of Helen

Rhetoric is magic; magic is rhetoric. The ancient Greek rhetorician Gorgias famously argued that "words are a drug that bewitch the soul." Using this lens, this essay examines the three main pedagogical approaches outlined within the Defense Against the Dark Arts (DADA) classes at Hogwarts and their relationships to composition instruction in today's universities. The methods used by Hogwarts professors reflect those used in composition instruction, such as: sacrificing practice to focus on theory, focusing extremely on practice due to immediate danger/need, or addressing relationships between actor and "text." Ultimately, I argue that creating a connection between rhetoric and magic, especially dark magic and DADA, can provide a fresh avenue for composition instructors to reach their students.

This essay addresses two major exclusions in the academic canon. First, the pedagogy of Hogwarts instructors is entirely undertheorized, as evidenced by this collection. The *Harry Potter* series is based firmly around the school experiences of the students. Therefore, the pedagogical aims and methods of the teachers are a worthwhile space for critical interaction. Second, most composition classrooms are woefully unaware of pop culture. Anecdotally, instructors who seek to implement pop culture in their classrooms, even in the humanities, tend to be scoffed at, seen as "trying too hard" or "being cool," when there are rich sources of pedagogical material both from the instructors in these books and from the books themselves. Last, rhetoric as magic has been a consistent opinion since ancient times; the original Dark Arts could be said to be rhetoric. This essay will present these ancient ideas with a new approach that will prove useful and illuminating in the modern university's composition classroom. Drawing a through line from ancient rhetoricians, Rowling's DADA teachers and the composition classroom can provoke a coming-together for the spheres of the academic and non-academic, the fandom and the ordinary, the fantasy and the reality.

Gorgias and Magic Is/as Rhetoric

The Gorgias quotation that opens this essay demonstrates the deep relationship Gorgias believed rhetoric had with magic. He begins with "inspired incantations," a clear reference to witchcraft and spellweaving. Gorgias uses this magical language to describe powerful, meaningful rhetoric; the type of rhetoric that he espoused moved people and decided fates. The two words themselves serve as important bookmarks of the relationship between rhetoric and magic. "Inspired" relies on the speaker having internal voice, agency, and desire to externalize; "incantation" evokes a particular image of spell-casting, of mystical power, and of a drive to change certain forces around the speaker. He continues to say these words "serve as bringers-on of pleasure and takers-off of pain" (Gorgias). Obviously, this is a speaker-centric view of rhetoric: some words/magic cause explicit and deep harm to the audience. However, Gorgias' point is that the incanting individual is, ultimately, seeking to enjoy pleasure and remove pain, however that is conceived by them. The DADA instructors use their pedagogical power in similar ways depending on their priorities and incantations. Dolores Umbridge has a very different, sinister idea of pleasure, one that invokes explicit pain on and implicit ignorance in her students. The version of incantations used by Barty Crouch, Jr., as Mad-Eye Moody, grants him pleasure by harming his students with the very magical knowledge he espouses. Remus Lupin, of course, understands his incantations to serve a pedagogical purpose that respects the power of magic/rhetoric.

Gorgias continues to say that the soul's opinion is changed by the incantation's power through "trickery." This trickery he refers to is the very nexus of rhetoric and the lynchpin of the magic/rhetoric dichotomy I draw here. Gorgias fundamentally believes that words have an ingrained mystical power that cannot be watered down or dismissed and that the power itself is untamed. Umbridge, "Moody," and Lupin enact this understanding in their pedagogical approaches throughout the novels. Umbridge fully acknowledges incantations of power; the darkest magic to her is knowledge of dark magic itself. She attempts to hide the rhetorical reality from her students through her own trickery. "Moody" is violently opposed to hiding that reality. He creates a classroom environment wherein his trickery is trauma: he controls the knowledge his students are aware of by incanting—real, but inappropriately applied—rhetorical violence. Lupin, however, invites his students to share in the trickery itself. He creates fellow rhetoricians by exposing the power dark magic has and inviting the students to shift it and change it with him. Lupin creates incanters by teaching the students to understand Gorgia's ultimate point: the real power of rhetoric is in the hand of the rhetorician.

In the same speech, Gorgias communicates the final building block of rhetorical theory for this essay: "words are a drug that bewitch the soul." His treatment of words and incantations is interchangeable here, as he establishes in the earlier quote: "by means of words, inspired incantations" (Gorgias). Words are the very nucleus of the concept of rhetorical agency, power, and transfer. Gorgias believes they are a drug, an external substance that significantly alters and even "bewitch[es]" the soul. Another use of mystical and witchy wordplay, this description lends itself to the analysis of DADA pedagogy. Umbridge is acutely aware that dark magic/rhetoric can bewitch the soul, and thus, she does not want her students to have that power. She attempts to hide it from them with her refusal to teach beyond theory. "Moody," of course, exposes the students directly to the bewitching elements of the drug dark magic, prompting the students to see trauma instead of useful knowledge. His attempt to educate becomes a side effect of this particular phenomenon: he bewitches his students into fear that they cannot process through. Lupin creates an environment where his students are empowered to become bewitchers. They understand words, creatures, and other manifestations of rhetoric as capable of immense power, and therefore can wield that power for their own protection and furtherment as scholars and "doers."

bell hooks' Collapsing Worlds and Eros

Lupin's embodiment of deep care for his students through his desire to teach them these complex and powerful concepts is tied to bell hook's *eros*. She asserts that *eros* is an essential component of teaching and connecting worlds. These worlds, while not explicitly connected by hooks to Gorgias' ideation of incantations and trickery, naturally correlate in this argument. Worlds are rhetorical: they are taught, created, destroyed, and linked by magic and the power of information. Hooks then describes the ideal classroom—subject matter omitted, tellingly—by discussing passion in *Teaching to Transgress*. She explains that the classroom collapses the contexts of the outside and inside worlds, due to the professors' ideal love for ideas—or *eros* (hooks

195). This linking of the outside world and the inside world of academia can be directly applied to the pedagogical foci of the DADA instructors at Hogwarts. Each of them allows linkages between the outside and inside world to varying degrees with concrete results on their students' experiences. Umbridge attempts to enforce ignorance of dark magic/rhetoric to disempower her students inside the classroom. "Moody" invites the entire dark world to enter his classroom, allowing fear to cloud an educational experience. Lupin links the ideas of *eros* and of collapsing worlds, as hooks intended. He allows his love for ideas and care for his students to influence the way he teaches dark magic/rhetoric, linking the outside and inside worlds carefully.

Lupin also brings to the forefront the concept of pleasure in teaching, or *eros*, that hooks claims we must embrace as a powerful teaching aid. That is not to say the other DADA instructors do not have ideas of pleasure in their teaching. It is clear Umbridge enjoys explicit bigotry, ignorance, and spreading misinformation in her classroom, as well as being openly abusive to Harry. "Moody" thinks he is providing pleasure in information: he arguably believes the students will have better, more pleasurable lives with the real world in sharp focus. However, it is Lupin that encompasses an *eros* of teaching in the most positive way. He seeks active relationships with his students, as opposed to all other DADA instructors, who would prefer to focus on their particular agendas for the course. Lupin takes pleasure in the act of teaching by engaging with his students as people and fellow magic-users, rather than simply as vessels for knowledge. His deep love of the ideas he espouses allows him to deliver a pedagogy that is student-centered.

Gorgias and hooks provide roadmaps for close readings of Umbridge, "Moody," and Lupin. Linking rhetoric with magic and *eros* with successful pedagogy not only encourages a new take on DADA instruction in *Harry Potter* but also provides a new concept of teaching composition. Umbridge, "Moody," and Lupin craft identities of instructors that utilize the power of rhetoric as a magical tool and a mark of their teaching pleasure in varying ways. The archetypes they create can then pivot towards composition instruction to encourage a revitalization of trickery, world-collapsing, and shared pleasure in the classroom. A close reading of these three DADA instructors demonstrates how their pedagogical personas can inform composition instruction in our rhetorical—magical—world.

Umbridge, Theory-Only Teaching and Harmful Ignorance

Professor Dolores Umbridge begins her teaching career at Hogwarts in Harry's fifth year. She is a squat, unpleasant woman, frequently described as "toad-like." While her embodiment does not necessarily have a relationship with her pedagogy, Rowling makes it clear to her audience that Umbridge is physically un-appealing and intimidating. The description of her physical appearance indicates a character that the audience is intended to distrust and disagree with. This is obviously problematic, given Rowling's similar characterization of Snape throughout the series as untrustworthy and unappealing through his physical appearance, but Snape's double-agent work complicates this interpretation of the emotional response to physical descriptions by Rowling. Umbridge's strict presence in the castle and her extreme refusal to acknowledge Voldemort's return quickly cause her to receive intense ire from Harry. Eventually, she becomes a powerful figure within the school, becoming one of the most formidable villains in the series. Her pedagogical presence is the nexus of her entry into the students' lives and serves as the opportunity to present her highly controversial views of the Dark Arts and education in the defense against them.

On her first day in the classroom with Harry and the other fifth-years from Gryffindor, Umbridge begins her assault on the ideas of magic that have been taught to them so far. She starts class by explaining that the students "have been introduced to spells that have been complex, inappropriate to your age group, and potentially lethal. You have been frightened into believing that you are likely to meet dark attacks every other day" (*OotP* 243). She is, of course, speaking of two of her predecessors: Crouch-as-Moody and Lupin. To Umbridge, these two instructors erroneously scared the students into believing that the Dark Arts are an immediate threat to them. As a result, Harry was introduced to "inappropriate" magic for his age—the Patronus charm, in particular—and the students were scarred with exposure to the Unforgivable Curses and rumors of Voldemort and his followers returning to wreak havoc on the Wizarding world. Simply put, Umbridge barely acknowledges that the Dark Arts exist, and if they do, they are most certainly not a real, credible, modern threat.

Her pedagogical approach, then, reflects this purposeful blindness to danger. She instructs the students to put away their wands—a key difference from Lupin—and to open their textbooks to the first page to begin silently reading. She introduces her course aims as focusing on "a carefully structured, theory-centered, Ministry-approved course of defensive magic this year" (*OotP* 239). Her presentation of anemic course aims prompts a fierce argument with the class, beginning with Hermione, about the lack of practical instruction and magic use in the classroom. This argument comes to a head when Parvati Patil incredulously asks if the students are expected to take their Ordinary Wizarding Level exams (O.W.L.s)—which include a practical portion—having never cast a counter-curse before. Umbridge blithely shrugs her question off, stating that anyone can cast defensive magic in a testing setting if they have studied the theory thoroughly. Umbridge, as a representative of the Ministry of Magic, is attempting to remove from the course the practical aims and methods that could make students dangerous. While she claims that students can successfully prove DADA skills in a testing environment with just theoretical readings, her actual goal is much more sinister. She hopes to prevent the students from arming themselves with magic that could awaken their consciousness to the dangers that she knows for a fact exist in the "real world." She hopes to silence the students politically to maintain the *status quo* that the Ministry so desperately longs to hold onto.

This approach does not sit well with any of the students, as they have just recently experienced first-hand what unprepared students face: death at the hands of Lord Voldemort. Umbridge argues with several students' questions and concerns before Harry explodes, asking "what good's theory going to be in the real world" (*OotP* 244). Obviously, Harry has a particular, vested interest in the people around him being equipped to deal with the very-real dark threat that he knows exists. Having personally witnessed Voldemort coming back to power and his willingness to kill without a second thought, Harry is diametrically opposed to the *status quo*. The real world will not hesitate to take advantage of ignorance anymore, and Harry cannot allow his friends and colleagues to be harmed, epistemologically or physically, because of an instructor's unwillingness to teach "reality." This conflict, of course, results in Umbridge's infamous, cruel punishment for Harry: forcing him to write "I must not tell lies" with his own blood, forming a scar on his hand.

There is an important parallel here to the teaching of composition instruction in modern university settings. Whether because of fear or ignorance, a prevailing theme among many composition instructors is that teaching students theory and abstract concepts from textbooks prepares them for a testing environment in which they can perform the necessary rhetorical skills to pass the course. This, of course, ignores the "real world" as Harry so angrily puts it. Teaching only theory in the classroom does not prepare students to perform magic/rhetoric in the real world. Critics of composition classes could apply this example to argue that such classes do not prepare students for writing outside of academia, but the point is broader in scale. What Umbridge is attempting to create is an apolitical classroom, one devoid of engagement in the current social and cultural situation, to avoid arming her students as agents in the societal revolution that is threatening to occur.

So, too, do composition instructors declaw their students in the university classroom. A decision to teach only theory and skills in the composition classroom, basing assignments only on textbooks and discussions only on rhetorical concepts, reveals a desire to create an apolitical classroom. However, both with Umbridge and with compositional pedagogy, an apolitical classroom is a political classroom. The politics of the classroom breed fear and ignorance, in an attempt to avoid difficult dialogues and engagement with nuanced, potentially "scary" topics. This issue of apolitical classrooms is taken up in Frankie Condon and Vershawn Ashanti Young's *Performing Antiracist Pedagogy in Rhetoric, Writing, and Communication*. They note that it is the responsibility of the instructor to engage critically with nuanced topics such as race/racism in their classrooms (Condon and Young xiv). Rather than engaging, Umbridge attempts to silence discussion. For Umbridge and instructors like her, magic/rhetoric is not a tool or a voice. It is a vice, an unfortunate, necessary evil that can be toothless when restricted to the right environments. Classrooms that are compositionally engaged, then, resist this endeavor: they purposefully tackle the "real world" by acknowledging the inherent power and politic in magic/rhetoric.

Unfortunately, Umbridge's pedagogical approach also comes with political baggage unrelated to the way she teaches: bigotry. Her descriptions of "Moody" and Lupin are condescending, offensive, and discriminatory, playing on oppressive attitudes present in the Wizarding and Muggle worlds. She utilizes this bigotry to show a lack of respect towards alternative pedagogical approaches, claiming that the past DADA teachers have been too political. In particular, she implies that Lupin's teaching methods were inappropriate directly due to his "condition" and that "Moody" exposed them to dangerous magic unnecessarily due to his overt paranoia (*OotP* 243). Her actions suggest that she believes that she can save the classroom and the students from this unnecessary practical work. Teaching the subject as easy, lifeless, void of intention and lacking practical application, doubles down on her critiques of the previous instructors. Umbridge uses her privilege as the instructor to prove to the students that the politicization of magic is unnecessary and unwarranted and to discredit previous instructors who believe differently. The dark subliminal workings of composition classrooms that do not acknowledge privilege unfortunately result in similar "apolitical" pedagogies and student experiences.

Umbridge is privileged, narrow-minded, and cruel, but more importantly, she is woefully unwilling to teach the students about the realities of dark magic, instead choosing to rely on theory and abstract concepts to further the political agenda of "apolitical" classrooms. Rhetoric as magic suffers from the same mistreatment as composition classrooms when privileged instructors refuse to engage in the very real oppression and sociocultural milieu of their students' lives. Condon and Young argue with respect to the composition classroom that "it is our job to help students 'think critically,' so when we are confronted with a student's ignorance or racism, we feel we must name it, critique it, and ask the student to rethink, restate in more acceptable ways (to the teacher), or at least avoid the discussion because it's not okay in this classroom" (xiv). Applying this argument to DADA classrooms, we can see that avoidance of problematic rhetoric/dark magic gives it power. On the extreme opposite side of the spectrum, however, is "Moody."

"Moody," Practice-Only Teaching and Harmful Knowledge

It is important to acknowledge that "Moody," the DADA instructor, was not actually Alastor Moody but Barty Crouch, Jr., under the guise of Polyjuice Potion. However, his DADA pedagogical approach still deserves critical analysis in this essay, even though the complications regarding his identity are beyond the scope of this argument. As the instructor during Harry's fourth year in *Goblet of Fire*, "Moody" is anxious, gruff, and paranoid. He is brought on the teaching staff after the departure of Lupin, supposedly as a one-year favor to Dumbledore before returning to his retirement (*GoF* 211). The students are wary of him, especially after he turns Draco Malfoy into a ferret as punishment. On the first day of his course, "Moody" describes his course goals much as Umbridge will later do. However, his goals could not be further from hers.

"Moody" defines the Dark Arts as powerful, worthy of respect, and with significant potential for abuse: "How are you supposed to defend yourself against something you've never seen? A wizard who's about to put an illegal curse on you isn't going to tell you what he's about to do. He's not going to do it nice and polite to your face. You need to be prepared. You need to be alert and watchful" (*GoF* 212). "Moody" sees the Dark Arts as a force that not only exists, but actively acts upon people even when they are not engaging with it themselves. He sees the Dark Arts as a concept that one cannot opt out of, contrary to what Umbridge seems to think. While he actually gives due credit to Lupin for his exceptional teaching of dark creatures and how to deal with them practically, he believes that the students are far behind on dealing with dark magic itself.

"Moody" is human-centered in his classroom in a unique way. His pedagogical approach is keyed in to the dark magic of fellow wizards: "you're behind—very behind—on dealing with curses ... so I'm here to bring you up to scratch on what wizards can do to each other" (*GoF* 211). He then spends the rest of the class time quizzing them about the three Unforgivable Curses—*Imperio*, *Crucio*, and *Avada Kedavra*—and showing them the effects of these curses on a spider. This is the inappropriate magic Umbridge refers to later on; these spells are the ultimate sins in the Wizarding world. He sums up his pedagogical stance near the end of class with his infamous catchphrase: "you need preparing. You need arming. But most of all, you need to practice *constant, never-ceasing vigilance*" (*GoF* 217; emphasis original). This end phrase is of paramount importance for "Moody" and his characterization throughout the series. He is labeled as paranoid by many other characters but is also known for his uncanny awareness of his surroundings. In this first class, he attempts to impart this awareness as essential to DADA. In sharp contrast to the blinders Umbridge wants to impress on students, "Moody" wants to impose hyper-awareness. There is no space for discomfort for "Moody" since discomfort would impede vigilance.

"Moody's" pedagogical approach is the foil to Umbridge's. He displays brutal honesty and acute awareness of socio-cultural situations, and he shares overt political tones with his students regardless of their maturity status. When he discusses the Killing Curse, *Avada Kedavra*, he explains that it is worth seeing regardless of the lack of a counter-curse "*because you've got to know.* You've got to appreciate what the worst is. You don't want to find yourself in a situation where you're facing it" (*GoF* 217; emphasis original). He sees knowledge itself as the ultimate weapon, because the Dark Arts exist in powerful and evil quantities and denying them is simply asking for pain and suffering.

Rhetoric is approached with similar fear and respect in the ancient texts from Gorgias, Plato, and Socrates. Some modern composition instructors implement this by showing the realities of Dark Arts in rhetorical modes: racism, sexism, and oppression of variously marginalized groups, all through rhetorical means (Martinez). They use accessible methods to illuminate the darkest part of society. This promotes an aura of respect for the craft itself and prepares students to face it. "Moody" and composition instructors like him see students as fellow soldiers, in a sense—as adults who have an inherent right to knowledge and preparation. Students deserve access to information about the political war raging around them with powerful magical rhetorics.

"Moody's" approach is most noted in his treatment of students as equals and co-conspirators to fight the good fight. However, this also comes with its own pedagogical baggage: trauma. His constant insistence that students "have got to know" about the depths of human cruelty through this powerful dark magic has significant emotional and mental effects on both Neville and Harry since their parents were subjected to *Crucio* and *Avada Kedavra*. The justification of exposing students to trauma is problematic, especially when applied to the real issues tackled in composition classrooms, like oppression and various acts of epistemic violence. He offers a superficial trigger warning prior to his lesson, telling students that he is not supposed to show them the Unforgivable Curses until their sixth year, but that "Professor Dumbledore's got a higher opinion of your nerves" (*GoF* 211) than the Ministry of Magic does. This attempt at acknowledging the danger and trauma in his lesson is just a formality for him; he clearly considers the students seeing the curses more important than their mental health.

"Moody's" lack of nuance and finesse when exposing his students to these Dark Arts is reflected in an overtly violent classroom, one that believes the students' right to know outweighs the possible harm it may do to students to see such graphic content. He does show care towards Neville and Harry after class, asking how they felt after seeing the Unforgivable Curses that their parents had suffered, but this does not excuse the trauma he had already dealt upon them. His material-centered approach can be drawn towards rhetoric, too. When the rhetorical power is always more important than students' "comfort," sometimes students' health can be compromised. This moment highlights where a properly theorized composition classroom would employ content warnings and nuanced discussion of the relationship between power, trauma, and actors. As Emily J.M. Knox discusses in *Trigger Warnings*, students should be made aware of the rhetorical reality, but in a space that allows for their emotional and mental wellbeing. Fortunately, a more nuanced approach is given by "Moody's" predecessor, Lupin.

Lupin, Complex Teaching and Helpful Honesty

Remus Lupin is the most well-rounded of the instructors under consideration. He becomes the DADA teacher in Harry's third year. Initially received with suspicion and derision due to his shabby appearance, Lupin becomes known as a beloved student advocate and brilliant scholar. His entrance into the school is marked by the reported escape of assumed mass murderer Sirius Black from Azkaban prison, and thus, a heightened awareness of the Dark Arts' potential for harm.

His introduction into the classroom occurs in a particularly uncommon way. Rather than having the type of "syllabus day" that both Umbridge and "Moody" have, Lupin opts instead to immediately take the students with him on a mission to deal with the boggart in the teacher's lounge. His lack of a clear speech in which he gives his opinions about Dark Arts and pedagogical goals is notable in and of itself. But, his description of the Dark Arts can be gleaned from a conversation he has with Harry sometime later. When Harry asks Lupin why he did not allow him to attack the boggart, Lupin responds, "I didn't think it a good idea for Lord Voldemort to materialize in the staffroom. I imagined people would panic" (*PoA* 155). Lupin reveals many aspects of his opinions about Dark Arts here. He respects the Dark Arts and the power they have over people—his concern about panic is notable—but he does not fear the Dark Arts. He is one of the few characters in the books who is willing to use Voldemort's name.

Lupin respects the fear the Darks Arts cause, but refuses to fear them as a source of darkness. This could be due to the existence of Dark Arts within him. As a werewolf, dark magic courses through his veins. He cannot afford to be fearful of something that exists within him. But, he can approach the subject with respect to others' opinions. Lupin's method of dealing with his werewolf transformations also provides a parallel to how he deals with DADA pedagogically. He works closely with Snape, a questionable ally to say the least, to create a potion that renders his transformation non-violent. These key notions—working with a questionable ally to render the darkness non-violent—are of utmost importance in his pedagogical practices. He works with the dark creatures themselves to teach his students to render them, and thus dark magic, non-violent and under their control. Lupin's intimate relationship with dark magic prompts his unique understanding of DADA pedagogy: one must respect the Dark Arts and work alongside them to conquer and understand them.

This key idea of Dark Arts as a source of fear, but not a worthy one, is evident in his pedagogical approach. When the students enter his class, he instructs them to follow him out of the classroom. Their surprise is met with an explanation: "today's will be a practical lesson. You will need only your wands" (*PoA* 130). In stark contrast to Umbridge, Lupin desires to show the students the potential of their actions against dark magic and creatures. He labels the lesson as "practical," a telling word related to accessibility, relevance to the sociocultural surroundings, and intentionality of lesson. Lupin focuses his pedagogical approach around practical ways to deal with dark creatures. His idea of appropriate lesson material centers on creatures rather than fellow humans or abstract concepts. He even exhibits this in his private lessons with Harry to teach him the Patronus charm. Though he expresses a hesitancy due to the advanced nature of the charm, Lupin acknowledges the usefulness of the charm to Harry due to his exposure to the Dementors and his sensitivity to their dark power. Again, his pedagogy is attached to the Dark Arts within the creature, not to theory or to fear of fellow humans.

The overarching attraction of Lupin is that he teaches with actions instead of words. His lack of a pedagogical introduction to his class speaks volumes. He prefers to expose students to situations and allow them to gradually build confidence in dealing with the Dark Arts themselves. His pedagogical approach is akin to hooks': education is a liberating experience for the students. He also learns alongside his students, treating them more like co-laborers, reasoning out solutions and tactics together. Simply put, Lupin is student-centered, rather than material-centered like "Moody" or teacher-centered like Umbridge. This has been proven to be an effective and attractive model for the composition classroom as well. As Paulo Freire argues in *Pedagogy of the Oppressed*, student-centeredness results in a freedom-giving education and a focus on the concepts most important to the students. Lupin's ultimate goal is also the student-centered goal of the composition classroom:

magic/rhetoric is powerful when it is given power. There is no inherent power derived from the Dark Arts. The vigilance Lupin teaches is more about the force of mind that is necessary to do magic, and thus rhetoric, rather than the evil force itself. Lupin is dedicated to an age-appropriate, yet honest, depiction of the Dark Arts, and this shows in his pedagogy.

In addition, Lupin's approach opens itself to feminist and intersectional frameworks. AnaLouise Keating defines feminist work in composition theory as the practice of dismantling hierarchies in the classroom, including that between teacher and student. Intersectional work seeks understanding of commonalities and difference in varying identity formations, with a similar focus on determining which identities have and lack power and using them to inform the ways students and teachers respond to one another and to the world around them (Condon and Young). Lupin's willingness to decenter his ideology in favor of prompting students to create their own power within the DADA course is a sharing of the instructor space seen often in feminist composition scholarship. He is sensitive to the various traumas and triumphs students are bringing to the classroom with regards to the power of dark magic and encourages them to feel those realities. Ultimately, Lupin seeks to provide an empowering space for varying intersections of experience with dark magic. He wants his students to know the intricacy of dark magic but also know the intricacy of working with it to defeat it.

Quirrell, Lockhart and Snape: Brief Departures

Umbridge, "Moody," and Lupin embody three variations of DADA/composition pedagogy: theory/teacher-centered, material-centered, and student-centered, respectively. That does not mean, however, that the other three DADA instructors do not have corollary themes in their pedagogies. In fact, Quirrell, Lockhart, and Snape each roughly correspond to at least one of the three variations in their own ways, but their pedagogies are more influenced by external stimuli and factors than Umbridge, "Moody," and Lupin. For example, Quirrell is quite literally under the influence of Voldemort himself, prompting his frequent fear, milquetoast course material, and inability to teach effectively. However, his behavior resonates with a concept of Umbridge's pedagogy: his fear of, and her refusal to engage with, actual dark magic manifesting in real time. They both attempt a teacher-centered pedagogy, wanting to push an agenda of ignorance and un-knowing onto their students to avoid difficult conversations and confrontations with powerful magic/rhetoric.

Lockhart is forced to reckon with the mysterious Chamber of Secrets and its deadly contents during his tenure at Hogwarts. He, too, falls into the teacher-centered pedagogy. More self-centered than any other instructor, his only concern is ensuring his fame and façade remain untarnished. Lockhart wants to push un-knowing onto his students if for no other purpose than to allow him to continue to live in ignorance, himself. This un-knowing is harshly countered by Snape in *Half-Blood Prince*, as he becomes the DADA instructor and ushers in actual curriculum. While the argument that Snape and Lupin are similar teachers may strike some as odd or blasphemous, in this argument, it rings true: Snape has student-centered teaching practices to an extent. He genuinely wants to teach the course material, effectively and truthfully. Of course, he is malicious, condescending, and cruel, like Umbridge before him, and like his Potions master days, but his course aims ring closest to Lupin's.

I offer this brief report about the other three DADA instructors to call upon their pedagogical realities. Quirrell, Lockhart, and Snape all occupy significantly different spaces in the canon and the classroom, pushing them beyond the main scope of this argument. However, they offer an interesting look at varying manifestations of the pedagogical aims I illuminate from Umbridge, "Moody," and Lupin. The rhetorical foundations for the understanding of magic/rhetoric are similar for all six, but the relevant work of Gorgias and bell hooks relate closest to Umbridge, "Moody," and Lupin.

Composition Pedagogy and Magic

The crossover to composition is one of focus: student-centeredness results in liberation. Composition pedagogy within, around, and of *Harry Potter* sees rhetoric as magic. This magic, however, is only given power with agents: spellcasters, wizards and witches, who have the fortitude necessary to cast it. Thus, teaching must respect constellations of power in and outside the classroom. Composition instructors can implement this truth of power, action, and rhetoric. Who is creating and who is being created with dark magic? With dark rhetoric? The narrow-mindedness of both Umbridge and "Moody" are stark in this regard. Neither instructor properly considers the effect of the dark magic on power structures that affect their students. Theory is not enough. Fear is not enough. Rather, Lupin's key traits provide a roadmap for composition pedagogy: care, defiance, reaching students where they are, and respecting the craft, while not fearing it and its effects. Student-centeredness is essential to allowing students to see rhetoric for its magic and utilize that magic on their own.

Cultural artifacts like the *Harry Potter* series can give fresh ways of teaching and knowing, exposing new and exciting connections between rhetoric and "real life" topics people are passionate about. Connecting rhetoric and real life in the classroom can unlock the rhetorician inside of a student when no other pedagogical approach will reach them. Worlds can be created and destroyed with words, both in fiction and in the increasingly fractured world in which we live. The power of words has come to the forefront of societal consciousness with conversations about intent, motivation, reception, and dissemination swirling around topics of ever-increasing importance. The societal reality is fractured around epistemological, political, and methodological frames, all of which have potential to do violence. DADA pedagogy gives us two key concepts in this regard: persuasion and self-care. Persuasion speaks to the rhetorician in every student: what power can be unlocked by teaching about the power of the voice students possess? Self-care, though, speaks to the health and wellness of that rhetorician: how can that body be supported to continue to dismantle dark magic and understand the fight more clearly? These concepts are the cornerstones we should carry into the composition classroom, allowing our students' "houses," their natural intersections, skills, and nuances, to bring about communal understanding and defiance towards harmful norms.

To conclude, there are several concrete suggestions I have for introducing DADA concepts into the composition classroom. I would recommend having an activity much like Lupin's on the first day of class, wherein a rhetorical artifact is brought to the class and analyzed together to promote shared understandings of rhetorical power and tools—maybe even an excerpt from *Harry Potter* itself. Instructors can also be intentional about expanding the definition of rhetoric in the composition classroom to be actor and results-centered: that is, explicitly defining rhetoric as a tool that is wielded by various actors, for good and for ill, and defining students' ability to analyze and argue rhetorically as the skill aims for the course. Lastly, composition instructors can utilize *eros* in their classrooms by incorporating rhetorical artifacts that they and their students are passionate about (like weaving together *Harry Potter* and rhetorical awareness), to cross the boundaries of "academic life" and "real life" and encourage the realization that magic/rhetoric surrounds us.

DADA is defiance. But what the defiance is directed towards, matters. What dark magic is being understood, fought against, ignored? Composition pedagogy, then, is defiant. What rhetoric are we defying? Are we teaching the magic of rhetoric responsibly? Are we weaving new pedagogies of and with pop culture, deriving new methods from fictional classrooms and allowing these classrooms to meld with our own? Are we finally reintroducing *eros* into our teaching identities, and inviting our students to join our passions? The "Dark Arts" will always be there, and it is up to the composition instructor to teach wizards of all kinds to defy it.

WORKS CITED

Condon, Frankie, and Vershawn Ashanti Young. *Performing Antiracist Pedagogy in Rhetoric, Writing, and Communication.* UP of Colorado, 2016.

Freire, Paulo. *Pedagogy of the Oppressed.* Translated by Myra Bergman Ramos, 50th Anniversary ed., Bloomsbury, 2018.

Gorgias. *Encomium of Helen.* Translated by Brian Donovan, 1999. http://caseyboyle.net/3860/readings/encomium.html.

hooks, bell. *Teaching to Transgress: Education as the Practice of Freedom.* Routledge, 1994.

Keating, AnaLouise. *Teaching Transformation: Transcultural Classroom Dialogues.* Palgrave Macmillan, 2007.

Knox, Emily J.M. *Trigger Warnings: History, Theory, Context.* Rowman and Littlefield, 2017.

Martinez, Aja. "The Responsibility of Privilege: A Critical Race Counterstory Conversation." *Peitho,* vol. 21, no. 1, 2018, pp. 212–233.

Rowling, J.K. *Harry Potter and the Goblet of Fire.* Scholastic, 2000.

_____. *Harry Potter and the Order of the Phoenix.* Scholastic, 2003.

_____. *Harry Potter and the Prisoner of Azkaban.* Scholastic, 1999.

Active Learning Pedagogy at Hogwarts

JESSICA L. TINKLENBERG

Since so much of their instruction is focused on the development and practice of particular wizarding skills, the faculty of Hogwarts School of Witchcraft and Wizardry regularly employ active and activity-based learning throughout their instruction and across disciplines. This might come as no surprise to the reader. What might be a bit more surprising, though, is that those faculty exhibit a wide range of understandings of active learning, and each finds varying degrees of success with their own version of the pedagogy. Active Learning (AL) is an established K–12 and higher education pedagogy based on the constructivist principles of Jean Piaget, Lev Vygotsky, and others. AL pedagogy is most often characterized by classroom activities that promote iterative skill development, metacognition, peer teaching and learning, reflection, self-assessment, and collaboration. These activities align with transparent and clearly defined student learning outcomes. AL pedagogy has been shown in numerous studies to improve outcomes for first-generation and other underrepresented students in higher education, particularly pertaining to their sense of group belonging and persistence to graduation (see for example Braxton, et al.; Schettino; Snyder, et al.).

This essay explores the ways AL pedagogy is exhibited throughout the seven-book series. In particular, I note the critical nature of iterative learning, peer teaching, and collaboration that Rowling portrays as among the most formative of Harry, Ron, and Hermione's educational experiences. I also analyze Rowling's thoughtful critiques of the nature of teaching or misimplementing AL in the classroom. Specifically, I examine: (1) those who see AL pedagogy as a fad or "non-traditional" form of learning that does not contribute to quality education; (2) occasions in which the AL activity moves too far beyond Vygotsky's "Zones of Proximal Development"; and (3) instances in which active learning is confused with edutainment or activity-for-activity's-sake. Ultimately, I argue that Rowling offers a nuanced critique of the pedagogy that aligns with current scholarly and practical studies. In so doing, she provides insights on quality teaching and learning available to a wider audience.

What Is Active Learning?

Active Learning is at once a pedagogy, a practice, and an ethical framework for teaching that relies on the constructivist principles promoted by Piaget, Vygotsky, and others. Constructivism, broadly defined using these theorists, is an understanding of learning in which knowledge is co-created and re-created by learners as they experience and reflect upon experiences in community. That is, knowledge is not a "thing" that exists "out there" to be implanted in our students' brains; instead, it is a process of active discovery and meaning-making that requires students to both draw on previous knowledge and engage with and reflect on new ideas to create and make sense of their worlds.

Piaget is rightly credited with the move to constructivism as a way of thinking about child development and student learning. Piaget posited that child learners develop cognitive schema (structures or units of knowledge) that are then tested, revised, and adjusted based on encounters with new information. As a child grows, the schemata become increasingly complex through this process of assimilating the new with the previously understood. For AL practitioners, this becomes a foundational principle: our knowledge is constructed via a process of connecting past knowledge with current experience in a way that aims to "makes sense" of it all. Moreover, peer interaction is, for Piaget, a critical practice by which this assimilation and construction of new knowledge takes place in learners. In the course of interactions with peers, learners are confronted with a variety of ideas and perspectives, presented in language that makes sense to them at their developmental stage. These conversations invite learners to reflect on and revise previous schemata and to see both similarity and difference with one's peers. Through peer interactions, then, learners develop the skill of "perspective taking" or differentiating between one's own perspective and that of others. Scholars have indicated that perspective taking is critical for socialization, communication, and the development of altruism (LeMare and Rubin 306). In an AL environment, peer interaction most often comes in the form of peer teaching or peer review of student work.

While his theories on learning remain foundational to constructivism and AL pedagogy, one critique of Piaget's work has been that he conceives of cognitive development as discrete, universal stages *internal* to the learner. Piaget's contemporary Lev Vygotsky, while agreeing that knowledge is a process of construction, argued that this process is instead both *on-going* and *social.* Vygotsky, particularly, noted the critical role of community in structuring learning. Mentors guide learners toward greater understanding by providing language, tools, and context. These people are known as "More Knowledgeable Others," and for Vygotsky they are necessary to the process of cognitive development. Because learning is a social task that happens in communities and depends on communities, Vygotsky's version of constructivist pedagogy is often called *social constructivism* or *social learning* theory. This essay explores Vygotsky's ideas further by analyzing how certain communities of learners at Hogwarts, such as Dumbledore's Army (the D.A.), become the most formative educational experiences of Harry, Ron, and Hermione's lives. I also discuss Professor Lupin's role as a model AL practitioner, and how his classes and exams become Rowling's exemplar of Vygotsky's understanding of cognitive development. Finally, I examine Dumbledore's private lessons with Harry in his sixth year as an example of the powerful role of the More Knowledgeable Other (MKO) in deep learning.

One of the critical features of social constructivist pedagogy for this study is the concept of "Zones of Proximal Development," or ZPD.[1] Basically, ZPD are ranges of possible learning as indicated by a student's development, age, prior learning, and social interactions with the MKO and with other peers. If a teacher employs active learning techniques (or really, any learning techniques) that are either too advanced or too basic for their students, it is unlikely that learning will occur because it falls outside the learners' ZPD. The constructivist teacher will therefore consider prior knowledge, learning that needs to be introduced, and gains that are expected through activities and reflection to create a cogent plan that both supports students and offers opportunities for more challenging student learning. Often, the teacher will offer *task scaffolding* as a way to bridge the difference between current knowledge and challenging learning goals. Scaffolding is an iterative learning process by which assignments are broken down into smaller, more manageable learning tasks to encourage progressive learning within and toward the edge of the ZPD. When introducing academic writing, for example, a social constructivist teacher might have multiple assignments in which each part of an academic article (introduction, methods, results, discussion, etc.) is created and peer-reviewed separately such that the learner receives iterative feedback to gradually improve toward desired learning outcomes. Understanding the ZPD of the young witches and wizards of Hogwarts is key to both Harry's success with the D.A. and Hagrid's failure with Care of Magical Creatures in Harry's third year.

Constructivist theories, whether in the mold of Piaget or Vygotsky or others, share an emphasis on metacognition as critical to cognitive development. Metacognition is often understood as "thinking about our thinking." While this is partly true, Pina Tarricone notes that metacognition also includes planning and monitoring one's own learning (also known as the process of self-regulation), reflection on experience, and metamemory. In AL classrooms, metacognition is a skill commonly practiced through reflection and self-assessment activities. Using the writing example above, a teacher might ask students to write a short note to accompany each draft or section in which they describe their responses to feedback, writing process, improvements, and desires for the next draft. Another emphasis in AL pedagogy is the focus on transferable skills, rather than static disciplinary knowledge, as critical to student learning and growth. Among the most important of these transferable skills are higher order thinking skills. In their foundational work, Bronwell and Eison note that, in active learning, "less emphasis is placed on transmitting information and more on developing students' skills," particularly analysis, application, synthesis, and evaluation (2). Additionally, AL pedagogy encourages the development of ethical reasoning and communication skills as critical aspects of student learning and meaning-making.

As a pedagogy, then, active learning is tied to constructivist and social constructivist conceptions of how learning works and what knowledge is. As a practice, it is marked by iterative skill development, metacognition, peer teaching and learning, reflection, self-assessment, and collaboration. When these two elements (pedagogy and practice) are meaningfully and thoughtfully combined, active learning "works" in that it provides better educational outcomes for a wide variety of students. In fact, several stand-alone studies and meta analyses have indicated that AL is impactful in diverse contexts, with students of varying levels of preparation, and that it functions particularly well to support learning for historically underrepresented students in higher education.[2] Finally, it is important to note that AL is also understood as an ethical framework for teaching. AL educators see learners as critical co-creators of knowledge who ought to inspire our respect and mutuality, and who certainly need to be seen as whole humans bringing context, values, and ideas from their respective backgrounds to the learning moment. Unfortunately, valuing students' diverse backgrounds and experiences is often at odds with educational systems that normalize one type of student experience (by race, gender, or previous educational experience, for example); thus, AL pedagogy requires a moral commitment to attending to structural inequalities and promoting equity.

This analysis highlights some highly successful AL practitioners at Hogwarts, but it will also detail many of the ways AL can be misapplied, misunderstood, or misused in classroom contexts by examining ineffective uses of AL by certain professors. Professor Lockhart, for example, misapplies AL as simply a form of classroom "edutainment" that is meant to impress, not educate. His use of AL as "edutainment," instead of a pedagogy that deepens learning, feeds into real-world criticism of AL. Many Muggle-world faculty rail against Active Learning as a "craze" or "vogue" that only exists for entertainment or playing into the customer-service mentalities of our students (Worthen SR1). AL is also often misunderstood as simply "doing activities" in class without regard to outcomes, reflection, ethical considerations, or even student safety. In the Muggle world, just "doing activities" without considering the implications for our students has been shown to increase anxiety, reinforce systemic inequalities, and even damage long term mental health (Cooper et al., Browne and Roll). At Hogwarts, Hagrid is perhaps most often guilty of this type of misunderstanding, as indicated by the fact that his activities regularly result in injury to his students. However, many other Hogwarts faculty fail to engage in reflective practices that might inform why or when they choose to use AL in their courses.

Iterative Learning, Peer Teaching and Collaboration: Successful AL at Hogwarts

In the educational world of Hogwarts School of Witchcraft and Wizardry, we see many ways in which AL pedagogy and techniques are used successfully in the education of young witches and wizards. In particular, lessons in which Harry, Ron, Hermione, and their classmates experience iterative learning, peer teaching, metacognition, reflection, and collaboration are highlighted as among the most formative educational experiences of their lives. Remus Lupin's Defense Against the Dark Arts (DADA) lessons, Harry's leadership in the DA, and Dumbledore's private lessons with Harry in his sixth year all bear the hallmarks of successful applications of AL, and in these positive examples, Rowling provides a roadmap to guide readers toward a more robust understanding of quality teaching and learning.

In Harry's third year, the students at Hogwarts meet Professor Remus J. Lupin, DADA professor. Harry's two previous DADA instructors had been abysmal. His first teacher, Professor Quirinus Quirrell, had been possessed by Lord Voldemort. His second instructor, Professor Gilderoy Lockhart, had been a celebrity-seeking egomaniac without any real defense skills. Lupin, however, proves on the first day that he is made of better stuff than these teachers with what he calls "a practical lesson" (*PoA* 133) involving no books and only wands. The students are intrigued, as this is something that had almost never happened in a DADA class before (*PoA* 133). The lesson is on boggarts and how to defeat them. Boggarts are shapeshifters that hide in small places and become whatever a person fears most. Lupin first confirms to the students that the thing wobbling and bouncing in the staff room wardrobe is a boggart, then describes what its qualities and attributes are, and then discusses with the students what they might do so that no one person is forced to defend against it alone. Once this foundational knowledge is firmly grasped, Lupin notes that since laughter is what destroys a boggart, they must all force the boggart to transform into something funny. He teaches them a spell—*Ridikkulus*—that they practice together without wands. Inviting Neville Longbottom to assist him, Lupin guides each student to think of something that frightens him (Professor Snape, in Neville's case) and a way of turning that fear into something funny (Snape in Neville's grandmother's clothes). Once Neville is prepared, they open the wardrobe together. The other students, following Neville's example, also reflect on what scares them and how to make that thing funny. After Neville's initial success, each student takes a turn against the boggart until it is confused and eventually defeated by their laughter.

At the conclusion of the boggart lesson, Ron exclaims, "That was the best defense against the dark arts lesson we've ever had, wasn't it?" (*PoA* 140). In part, of course, his enthusiasm is related to his own success against the boggart-spider, but even this is indicative of the success of the class as a whole. In the boggart lesson, Lupin gives students a chance to be successful and to feel good about their success. This opportunity bolsters even students like Neville, who had just been demeaned by Professor Snape as hopeless in his previous class. The perception that the class is great is certainly shared by the other students who talk excitedly about the lesson on their way back to the classroom. Hermione even confirms that Lupin is a very good teacher, and within a few weeks, DADA is everyone's favorite class. Student reactions like these seem to indicate that Rowling is using this "practical lesson," with all the hallmarks of great active learning pedagogy, as an exemplar of the very best kind of teaching, especially given the detail, care, and enthusiasm with which the entire episode is related to the reader.

This lesson has all the hallmarks of great active learning pedagogy. Lupin's socially constructivist approach, particularly, stands out as aligned with AL pedagogies. By inviting students into the process of coming up with a strategy and participating in the actual defeat of the boggart, Lupin shows that he views learning as a community process in which everybody brings something to the task (even Neville, who is often demeaned by other professors). Students' reflection on their own ideas about what is scary and what is funny play a crucial role in the boggart's demise, and the students have to draw on this knowledge as well as act responsively in the group to complete the task. As is common in relational problem-based learning—a common type of AL technique in which students must work together to solve or better understand a difficult issue—this lesson results in a sense of satisfaction, group belonging, and a sense of accomplishment for the students. And, throughout the lesson, Lupin mentors the group with foundational knowledge, questions, and information that guides the students toward their own success.

Another indicator that Lupin is an AL practitioner is his choice of final exam in Harry's third year. After their boggart lesson, the students studied grindylows, Red Caps, and hinkypunks over the course of the year. In the final exam, the students performed "a sort of obstacle course outside in the sun, where they had to wade across a deep paddling pool containing a grindylow, cross a series of potholes full of Red Caps, squish their way across a patch of marsh while ignoring misleading directions from a hinkypunk, then climb into an old trunk and battle with a new boggart" (*PoA* 318). This final exam emphasized transferable, higher-order thinking skills including application and analysis as well as problem-based learning and reflection on previous work. It also shows Lupin's understanding of scaffolding and iterative learning, since these skills had been introduced separately in previous lessons that built on each other, and then drawn together in a new way to show student learning.

Perhaps because of his experiences with Lupin (but also because his teacher that year was his worst yet), Harry takes on the role of unsanctioned DADA teacher in his fifth year at Hogwarts. In that year, Harry and his classmates are presented with Dolores Umbridge, the Ministry of Magic Undersecretary and Hogwarts "High Inquisitor," as their official instructor for the course. Umbridge, as a representative of the Ministry, has a vested interest in *not* teaching students defensive magic. With Voldemort returned to full strength, and with their Ordinary Wizarding Level (O.W.L.) exams on the horizon, Harry's classmates form a secret organization called Dumbledore's Army (or the D.A.) to learn defensive magic. Harry, who has survived being killed by Voldemort twice, is elected to lead.

Harry's method of teaching defensive magic is quite similar to Lupin's method. Beginning with the first lesson, Harry places a good deal of emphasis on skill development, group work, and iterative learning within what he, as the More Knowledgeable Other, perceives as his classmates' Zones of Proximal Development. For example, the very first spell they practice in the D.A. is *Expelliarmus* (the disarming charm), which Harry notes is "pretty basic" (*OotP* 391) but essential for self-defense. After watching them all practice in pairs, Harry moves about the room offering suggestions and corrections to improve their technique. He then encourages them to practice again. At the end of the hour, both Ron and Hermione agree that it was a very good lesson, and many in the room want Harry to teach them again, as soon as possible (*OotP* 396).

Using this basic strategy of introducing, practicing, correcting, and revising together as peers over the course of many lessons, Harry moves the group from very basic to quite advanced magic. Shortly after the winter holiday, in fact, the D.A. members are so advanced that they can reliably stun, immobilize, and shield themselves from an attacker, and several of the members have produced Patronuses, which Lupin had previously noted requires "highly advanced magic ... well beyond Ordinary Wizarding Level" (*PoA* 237). Nowhere is this advancement as evident as in Neville, who "was improving so fast it was quite unnerving" (*OotP* 553). Neville is, of course, motivated by the mass breakout from Azkaban that freed his parents' attacker, Bellatrix Lestrange, but Rowling clearly wants the reader to understand here and elsewhere that it is Harry's approach to teaching that allows Neville to turn his fear and anger into a passion for successful mastery of skills. Thus, it seems that the D.A. is only one, but perhaps the clearest, example in the series of the benefits of AL practice and peer instruction for meaningful learning.

AL pedagogies and practices are also useful for creating group cohesion, empathy, and persistence, and it is clear from the later books that the D.A. served just that function for Neville, Luna Lovegood, Ginny Weasley, and the other members. Neville, Ginny, and Luna are alongside the trio when they break into the Department of Mysteries to save Sirius Black (Harry's godfather) at the end of their fifth year, and they battle Death Eaters with the skills they have built in the D.A. Two years after this battle, Hermione, Ron, and Harry visit Luna's house to speak to her father. Upon entering Luna's bedroom, Harry notices that "Luna had decorated her bedroom ceiling with five beautifully painted faces: Harry, Ron, Hermione, Ginny, and Neville. [...] Harry realized the chains [that wove around their faces] were actually one word, repeated a thousand times in golden ink: *friends ... friends ... friends...*" (*DH* 417). And, when the trio finally returns to Hogwarts at the end of that year, they learn that Ginny, Neville, and Luna have been leading the resistance inside the school. They use the fake gold coins the D.A. originally made to pass messages to each other, and "sneak out at night and put graffiti on the walls: *Dumbledore's Army, Still Recruiting*," in spite of being tortured by the Carrows, sibling Death Eaters, for their leadership (*DH* 575). They even returned to the Room of Requirement, which they first used for those clandestine D.A. meetings, when times were tough at Hogwarts. Neville summarizes the powerful impact of peer learning: "We're his army [...] Dumbledore's Army. We were all in it together, we've been keeping it going while you three have been off on your own—[...] Everyone in this room's been fighting" (*DH* 581). Clearly, peer learning, iterative teaching, and transferable skills Harry taught the D.A. were critical to long-lasting group cohesion, empathy, and persistence among its membership.

While Lupin displays collaboration, reflection, and mentorship in his DADA classes and Harry does so in D.A. lessons, it is really Dumbledore who exemplifies the mentorship style of the More Knowledgeable Other. In his sixth year, Dumbledore invites Harry to attend what he calls "private lessons" with the headmaster (*HBP* 78). These lessons, which are opportunities for Dumbledore to teach Harry key aspects of Voldemort's past, also demonstrate a critical component of AL pedagogy: reflective learning through mentorship with an MKO. During his private lessons, Harry and Dumbledore use the Pensieve, a basin that allows wizards to enter stored memories and relive the experiences in those memories as invisible observers. In the Pensieve, the two watch Tom Marvolo Riddle grow up and rise to power, eventually becoming Lord Voldemort. The memories are those Dumbledore has collected from himself and others during his lifetime, and he provides the structure and background for each. Before and after each new memory is relived, Dumbledore asks Harry questions about his recollections and observations and provides any theories the headmaster has about the meaning of each. Harry is also permitted to interrogate the memories and build a synthetic picture of the young Lord Voldemort from what they witness. Together, with Dumbledore serving as an MKO, Harry is able to build a cogent picture of Voldemort's motivations for building Horcruxes (magical containers that hold a piece of the wizard's soul) and an understanding of how he, Harry, might destroy them. The emphasis on connection making, learning through observing social interaction, reflection, and higher-order thinking all indicate that Dumbledore is serving as a model MKO in Harry's quest to understand and destroy the Horcruxes.

There are many other positive examples of AL pedagogy, practice, and ethics that could be mentioned here from Harry's time at Hogwarts. Professor Grubbly-Plank's Care of Magical Creatures lessons, which—unlike Hagrid's—feature creatures appropriate to the students' Zones of Proximal Development, would qualify. Certainly, the way in which Professor McGonagall describes her approach to teaching and learning as requiring "serious application, practice, and study," mirrors the AL principles of iterative learning and transferable metacognitive skills (*OotP* 257). However, Hogwarts also contains many misapplications or misappropriations of AL. Examining these negative examples will help clearly elucidate the principles, practices, and ethics of an active learning framework.

When AL Goes Awry: Misapplication and Misunderstandings of AL at Hogwarts

As is true at many educational institutions, not all Hogwarts professors use AL as a framework for their teaching. Professor Binns, a ghost who teaches History of Magic, and Dolores Umbridge, Harry's fifth year DADA instructor, both rely on "traditional" teaching methods for very different reasons. Professor Binns is described thusly in the first book: "Professor Binns had been very old indeed when he had fallen asleep in front of the staff room fire and got up the next morning to teach, leaving his body behind him. Binns droned on and on while they scribbled down names and dates and got Emeric the Evil and Uric the Oddball mixed up" (*PS* 133). Before Hermione queries him about the legend of the Chamber of Secrets in their second year, Binns "opened his notes and began to read in a flat drone ... a deadly dull lecture" (*CoS* 148–149). These two descriptions of the professor indicate that Binns is uninterested in the engagement, interaction, community-based learning, or higher-order thinking activities generally associated with AL. Instead, he values rote memorization (names and dates) and seems unconcerned with relating as a mentor to the students in his class. Rowling herself has confided that the character of Binns was based on a professor she had in college who was incredibly smart but made no effort to connect with students. According to Rowling's disclosures, "The inspiration for Professor Binns was an old professor at my university, who gave every lecture with his eyes closed, rocking backwards and forwards slightly on his toes. While he was a brilliant man, who disgorged an immense amount of valuable information at every lecture, his disconnect with his students was total" (*Pottermore*). As was true of her own professor, Rowling seems to indicate that Professor Binns' lack of engagement with students in ways that align with our active learning framework is due to advanced age, an unwillingness to change or adapt, and a commitment to lecturing without pausing for interaction with the students. However, she also indicates that this type of pedagogical practice has consequences for student learning; apparently, only Hermione receives an O.W.L in the subject, and even she discontinues studying it after her fifth year.

Professor Umbridge, on the other hand, is more intentional and straightforward regarding her reasons for choosing non–AL pedagogies. At the first DADA lesson of their fifth year, Hermione asks why the course aims written on the board contain no mention of actually practicing defensive spells. Umbridge replies, "it is the view of the ministry that a theoretical knowledge will be more than sufficient to get you through your examination, which, after all, is what school is all about" (*OotP* 243). Here, Umbridge makes clear her preference for disconnected theoretical knowledge and clarifies her understanding of education broadly as oriented on succeeding at examinations, rather than student cognitive growth or community formation. Again, this sentiment is quite opposed to an AL ethical framework. AL pedagogies and practices generally favor transferable skills and practical application, rather than teaching to a test. These pedagogies certainly see the goals of education as more than getting successfully though an exam.

In this first lesson, Umbridge also assigns a essay for the students to read with the admonition "there will be no need to talk" (*OotP* 240), a statement that seems to indicate her belief that knowledge comes out of books with little need for discussion or community construction. Readers of the series will note that Umbridge's teaching strictly adheres to this theoretical approach, which she gestures towards in her speech at the Sorting on the first night of Harry's fifth year (*OotP* 213). Through her many speeches and classes, it becomes clear that Umbridge avoids AL practices like application, practical problem-solving, and group interaction (talking) particularly because the theoretical approach discourages students from gaining and building on the practical skills necessary to fight back against dark forces.

While Professor Binns and Umbridge both hold to a "traditional" approach to teaching that is oriented on book knowledge and disengaged lecturing, other professors at Hogwarts attempt to engage in AL, but misapply the principles, practices, and ethics to disastrous effect. Professor Lockhart, Harry's second year DADA teacher, is perhaps the most egregious offender in this category. One common misunderstanding of AL pedagogy is that it is the same as "doing activities" in a classroom setting. However, activity alone does not attend to the metacognitive, reflective, and ethical dimensions that are integral to AL pedagogy and often fails to structure, scaffold, and organize course materials in a way that a More Knowledgeable Other should do. In fact, several studies have shown that when activities are done only for the sake of activity the potential exists to do harm to learners, rather than improve their learning outcomes. In one study of college students, Katelyn Cooper and colleagues found that some class activities, like cold calling, group work, and clicker questions have the potential to increase anxiety and fears of failure in science courses. In these high-anxiety situations, students are less likely to engage, putting both their college success and mental health at risk (2–3).[3] Lockhart's first lesson is an example of a misapplication of AL that causes anxiety rather than learning.

Lockhart seems to have wholeheartedly accepted the misunderstanding of AL as merely activities, and all the accompanying harm to students inevitably follows. In their first lesson, Lockhart releases a cage full of Cornish pixies into the classroom with only the instruction "Let's see what you make of them!" (*CoS* 102). His own spell (*Peskipiksi Pesternomi!*) has no effect, and he abandons Harry, Ron, and Hermione to the task of returning them to their cage. Despite Hermione's insistence that leaving them to round up the pixies is his way of giving them hands-on experience, it is clear to the students that Lockhart has neither understanding of the Dark Arts nor expertise in teaching about them. From the standpoint of AL pedagogy, Lockhart's pixie lesson is a failure in many ways: he does not scaffold the task, does not have the understanding or mentorship to be an MKO for the students, elicits no reflection or metacognition, and confuses doing activities with active learning.

And, of most concern, it ends with students "sheltering under the desks and Neville Longbottom hanging from the iron chandelier in the ceiling" (*CoS* 102). Unlike Lupin's boggart lesson, which exemplifies the very best of active learning, Lockhart's first lesson is an AL failure in every way.

Sadly, Lockhart learns little from this failure. While he stops bringing live creatures to class, Lockhart continues to misuse activities in the place of active learning throughout Harry's second year. For example, he spends several lessons forcing Harry and other students to reenact episodes from his books (*CoS* 161). Unfortunately, Lockhart's reenactments and the homework he assigns following them lack an opportunity for critical reflection on the event or any awareness of student experience of the simulation (*CoS* 162). Without these metacognitive elements that are critical to AL pedagogy, Lockhart's simulations alienate students and make them disengaged observers in their education.

While Lockhart may be the clearest example of mistaking activities for AL, Hagrid shows the reader what happens when teaching happens outside the students' ZPD. Hagrid, Hogwarts Keeper of Keys and Grounds, becomes the Care of Magical Creatures teacher in Harry's third year. For their first lesson, Hagrid chooses to introduce them to Hippogriffs, which are half horse and half eagle, with "cruel, steel-colored beaks and large, brilliantly orange eyes. The talons on their front legs were half a foot long and deadly looking" (*PoA* 114). While Hagrid is more effective at scaffolding the meeting with the Hippogriffs than Lockhart had been with the pixies, the creatures are clearly much too advanced for new students to master. Most struggle to properly complete the task, and Draco Malfoy is injured by his hippogriff, Buckbeak— an injury that imperils both Draco and the hippogriff. Obviously, harm to students is one of the most common indicators of failed AL practice.

After this injury and Buckbeak's subsequent trial as a dangerous creature, Hagrid errs too far the other way on the students' ZPD by choosing the most unengaging creature he could find. By October, the reader learns, "[n]obody really liked Care of Magical Creatures, which after the action packed first class, had become extremely dull. Hagrid seemed to have lost his confidence. They were now spending lesson after lesson learning how to look after flobberworms, which had to be some of the most boring creatures in existence" (*PoA* 142). This change in approach suggests that Hagrid lacks a clear sense of the appropriate zone for his students' optimal learning. First, he exposes students to situations that could harm them without proper scaffolding or a path to success, and then he abandons any challenge or encouragement toward successfully completing more difficult tasks, which suggests that he no longer values their learning. It seems that the students also recognize Hagrid's failure to operate in the ZPD since even Harry—reflecting on two years' worth of Care of Magical Creatures classes with Hagrid—is forced to admit that his lessons swung wildly between unengaging and downright scary, rather than encouraging an iterative process of skill development as he experienced with his other professors (*OotP* 258).

Throughout the series, Rowling constructs a complex academic world, including a nuanced view of how learning happens and what makes it work. Through characters like Professor Lupin, we see that she clearly values an iterative and community-oriented approach to student learning. In Dumbledore's Army, we see that she recognizes the power of peer-teaching. Characters like Professor Binns offer counter examples that further reinforce her view of powerful learning; his boring drone is clearly shown as ineffective for both student engagement and student learning. However, she does not simply limit her cast of instructors to the binary of "good" teachers and "bad." Instead, she shows clearly how well-intentioned teachers (like Hagrid) can misappropriate active learning in ways that do more harm than good, and the ways in which inept teachers (like Lockhart) can misunderstand active learning as simply class activities.

What is remarkable, in each of these instances of teaching and learning throughout the series, is how closely they correspond with our academic understanding of AL as a pedagogy, practice, and ethic. When Harry and his classmates form the D.A., we not only see peer-teaching work, but we see the expected impacts that have been shown in scholarly literature: particularly, rapid skill development and the creation of a community that sustains its members in the long term. When faculty move beyond the ZPD of their students or do not allow adequate time for reflection or iterative practice, we see the expected downturn in meaningful student learning. Such a careful articulation of what makes teaching and learning powerful, nuanced through a wide variety of examples, allows Rowling to make insights on quality education available to a much wider audience than might read scholarship on AL pedagogies. She shows us all what great active learning can be, and that is just one more kind of magic to be found in the pages of these books.

NOTES

1. The ZPD is most fully developed in Vygotzky's work *Mind in Society: The Development of Higher Psychological Processes*. Harvard University Press, 1978.

2. AL also seems to have outsized benefits for students' "soft skill" development and produces many desirable outcomes beyond classroom learning, such as student retention, persistence to graduation, feelings of belonging, and general well-being (see Michael; Prince; Braxton, et al.; Snyder; Schettino).

3. Similarly, in their research on poverty simulation "games" Browne and Roll note that without proper attention to critical reflection on social inequality, simulation activities are likely to further reinforce systemic inequalities rather than encourage commitments to justice and equity (265).

Works Cited

Bathgate, Meghan E., Judith Sims-Knight and Christian D. Schunn. "Thoughts on Thinking: Engaging Novice Music Students in Metacognition." *Applied Cognitive Psychology*, vol. 26, 2012, pp. 403–409. *Wiley Online Library,* doi:10.1002/acp.1842.

Bonwell, Charles C., and James A. Eison. *Active Learning: Creating Excitement in the Classroom*. Jossey-Bass, 2005.

Braxton, John, et al. "The Role of Active Learning in College Student Persistence." *New Directions for Teaching and Learning*, 2008, pp. 71–83. *Wiley Online Library,* doi:10.1002/tl.326.

Browne, Laurie P., and Susan Roll. "Toward a More Just Approach to Poverty Simulations." *Journal of Experiential Education*, vol. 39, no. 3, Sept. 2016, pp. 254–268. *ERIC,* doi:10. 1177/1053825916643832.

Cooper, Katelyn M., et al. "The Influence of Active Learning Practices on Student Anxiety in Large-enrollment College Science Classrooms." *International Journal of STEM Education*, vol. 5, no. 23, pp. 1–18. *NCBI,* doi:10.1186/s40594-018-0123-6.

Lindenman, Heather, et al. "Revision and Reflection: A Study of (Dis)Connections Between Writing Knowledge and Writing Practice." *College Composition and Communication*, vol. 69, no. 4, June 2018, pp. 581–611.

Michael, Joel. "Where's the Evidence That Active Learning Works?" *Advances in Physiology Education*, vol. 30, no. 4, 2006, pp. 159–167.

Prince, Michael. "Does Active Learning Work? a Review of the Research." *Journal of Engineering Education*, vol. 93, no. 3, 2004, pp. 223–231. *Wiley Online Library,* doi:10.1002/j.2168-9830.2004.tb00809.x.

"Professor Binns." *Pottermore,* www.pottermore.com/explore-the-story/professor-binns.

Rowling, J.K. *Harry Potter and the Chamber of Secrets*. Scholastic Press, 1999.

_____. *Harry Potter and the Deathly Hallows*. Scholastic Press, 2007.

_____. *Harry Potter and the Goblet of Fire*. Scholastic Press, 2000.

_____. *Harry Potter and the Half-Blood Prince*. Scholastic Press, 2005.

_____. *Harry Potter and the Order of the Phoenix*. Scholastic Press, 2003.

_____. *Harry Potter and the Prisoner of Azkaban*. Scholastic Press, 1999.

_____. *Harry Potter and the Sorcerer's Stone*. Scholastic Press, 1997.

Schettino, Carmel, "A Framework for Problem-Based Learning: Teaching Mathematics with a Relational Problem-Based Pedagogy." *Interdisciplinary Journal of Problem-Based Learning*, vol. 10, no. 2, Sept. 2016, pp. 42–67. *EBSCOhost,* doi:10.7771/1541–5015.1602.

Snyder, Julia J., et al. "Peer-Led Team Learning Helps Minority Students Succeed." *PLoS Biology*, vol. 14, no. 3, 2016. *NCBI,* doi:10.1371/journal.pbio.1002398.

Tarricone, Pina. *The Taxonomy of Metacognition*. Psychology Press, 2011.

Vygotsky, L.S. *Mind in Society: The Development of Higher Psychological Processes*. Harvard UP, 1978.

Sorted on the First Day

A Hogwarts Guide to Extinguishing Growth Mindset and Instilling Fixed Ideas of the Self

Tara Moore

Since Rowling's novels became popular, a host of blockbuster young-adult (YA) narratives have adapted her iconic Sorting process as part of a dystopian trope. In subsequent series, narratives villainize the new versions of Sortings or lotteries because they define a child's identity without giving agency to the child. Such novels or series include: *The Hunger Games, Divergent, Matched*, and *Legend*. Protagonists like Katniss, Tris Pryor, Cassia, and Day eventually recognize that their Sorting confines their opportunities and self-expression. All four of these protagonists react against the injustice involved in their society's Sorting or lottery. Each one becomes involved in a resistance movement that works to destabilize the society that enforces the Sorting (Moore 30). While rebellions undermine these obviously evil Sortings, the Hogwarts Sorting remains beloved in its fictional world. The non-fiction world embraces it, too, and the prevalence of House-based swag attests to fans' deep reverence for Rowling's Sorting of society. Other YA Sortings determine a dystopian character's whole future, but at Hogwarts, the Sorting mainly influences students' social status for seven years of schooling. While there is evidence that the Sorting sticks with Hogwarts alumni, readers also know that students have relative freedom to choose their future lots in life. This fundamental difference of the Hogwarts Sorting—its temporary influence—prevents it from being worthy of the teen rebellion found in other Sorting dystopias.

Nonetheless, critics might question the wisdom of setting up an institution that labels children, especially when the Sorting assigns one fourth of the children to a House that has traditionally produced bigots and megalomaniacs. In the non-fiction world, we tend to discontinue such practices, and even the Sorting Hat itself questions its function in the song for year five. Dumbledore, the man who oversees the system, also expresses some distrust of it when he voices his opinion that Severus Snape may have been sorted too soon (*DH* 680). Nonetheless, the Sorting Hat labels students in a public, irrevocable way during the child's first moments on campus. This institutional ritual, the Sorting, embodies the school's dedication to the fixed mindset, a belief that the learner does not change. The teaching habits of Hogwarts professors align with the institution's devotion to Sorting by nurturing a fixed mindset.

Adding Growth Mindset to the Reading List

Rowling's school exists within a previously determined framework of literary tradition—school story tradition made popular by Victorian novels for children. This category of literature regularly pits students against unsympathetic teachers. The development of witch school stories in the mid–20th century continued this and other Victorian boarding school practices (Pesold 2). As such, Hogwarts's educational practices function along prescribed tropes that hearken backward, not forward. While we cannot hold Hogwarts to current educational standards, readers can assess how this fictional icon sometimes teaches by negative example, including its approach to mindset.

The now-popular concept of growth mindset had not yet filtered into teacher training when Rowling penned her first *Harry Potter* novel. However, educators and students naturally vacillate between growth and fixed mindsets. Growth mindset advocates offer evidence in favor of "direct[ing] each person to believe in their own ability [...]—*to become better at being themselves*" (Hochheiser). Now that researchers have made arguments in favor of growth mindset, there is plenty of evidence to suggest that supporting effort and process, not success and intelligence, results in more enlightened, more engaged, and more strategic students.

In the most general terms, growth mindset is "the belief that intelligence can be developed through effort" (Education Week Research Center 16). This concept originated from the work of psychologist Carol Dweck and various co-authors dating back to the 1980s and 1990s and was made accessible through Dweck's widely circulated 2006 book, *Mindset: The New Psychology of Success*. According to Dweck, her motivating ideas all grew from an early study she performed with ten-year-olds faced with perplexing puzzles. Some of the children resented the challenges Dweck's puzzles posed; others enjoyed and even desired puzzles they could not solve (Dweck, *Mindset* 3). This second set of children, according to Dweck, exhibited growth mindset. Dweck supplies examples of tenacious schoolchildren, famous athletes, entertainers, and scientists, all people who delight in overcoming obstacles and respond well to trials.

On the other side of the equation are learners with fixed mindset, people who believe that success comes from an innate ability, something you either have or don't have from the start (Dweck, *Mindset* 191–92). A fixed mindset limits learners' ability to push through snags, since such students can easily blame failure on their lack of innate ability. They feel helpless in the face of learning challenges because they believe they do not possess ability in that area. Students with fixed mindset prefer to avoid learning encounters that might end in mistakes, and they are less likely to take advantage of remedial assistance because they feel that it cannot make a difference in their innate ability (Hong, Ying-yi, Dweck, Lin, and Wan 597). In contrast, students with growth mindset believe that success arises from a student's ability to try and grow: "A successful student is one whose primary goal is to expand their knowledge and their ways of thinking and investigating the world" (Dweck, *Mindset* 192). These students value not just the final grade, but the process of gaining knowledge.

More importantly, educators are able to share motivating, scientific data with students to encourage them to transform their mindset. A 2007 study introduced one group of elementary school children to concepts of brain science, including the idea that "mental activity results in measurable physical changes in the brain" (Blackwell, Trzesniewski, and Dweck 262). The children who were taught that "learning makes you smarter" later demonstrated increased math scores compared to the control group which was not given this information (Blackwell, Trzesniewski, and Dweck 262). Thus, when learners see their brains as muscles that they can exercise and grow, they will place increased value on intellectual challenges rather than give up or feel helpless.

As a sign of growth mindset's impact on K–12 education, educators who are inspired to live out a growth mindset have switched from telling students they are "good at" something to encouraging students to work hard at everything, even after they may fail at it the first time. The demands of schooling with terms, final grades, and standardized tests make a pure growth mindset challenging to enact—even though schools may be encouraging it. Despite the challenges associated with a growth mindset, educators now see the potential danger of the fixed mindset, since that outlook means that students (and teachers) might infer, "If at first you don't succeed, you probably don't have the ability" (Dweck, *Mindset* 9–10). The fixed mindset now reviled in K–12 education is frequently enacted in Hogwarts classrooms. It is the subtext, for example, of Snape's public critique of Ron: "I would expect nothing more sophisticated from you, Ronald Weasley, the boy so solid he cannot Apparate half an inch across a room" (*H-BP* 460). Ron's reaction demonstrates the danger of fixed mindset: he takes the criticism to heart and considers giving up on his efforts and the upcoming Apparition test.

In fairness, Rowling was under no obligation to depict a Hogwarts influenced by growth mindset when she began publishing the series in 1997, a decade before Dweck's trade paperback appeared and long before mindset ideas hit institutional education by storm. Instead, Rowling recreated a common plot structure in books for young people. Children's literature shows that the more challenging the obstacles the protagonist faces, the more satisfying his or her eventual independent victory will be for readers. Fans and literary critics, however, can work to make sense of how pedagogical ideas reveal themselves in what must be one of the most well-known portrayals of an educational setting of the 21st century. The Sorting and the fixed mindset habits of Hogwarts professors label and limit students from reaching greater learning potentials.

The Sorting Hat's Lessons in Fixed Mindset

At Hogwarts, teachers and students both make assumptions about others based on how they are Sorted. Malfoy taunts Neville based on the Gryffindor's apparent lack of bravery: "'There's no need to tell me I'm not brave enough to be in Gryffindor, Malfoy's already done that,' Neville choked" (*SS* 218). Here the sorting expectations are weaponized to attack a student's insecurities. Similarly, a Ravenclaw classmate, Terry Boot, questions Hermione's house in *Order of the Phoenix* when she shows excellence with a Protean Charm, asking why she's not in Ravenclaw (*OotP* 399). Hermione has to defend her Gryffindor identity. The exchange shows that, to students, the Sorting really does matter. The taunting/questioning students feel that they know something about Neville and Hermione's identities based on their public House identity.

Terry Boot's question, though intended to show respect for impressive Charms work, is the equivalent of social policing. It points out what appears to be an error, and it does so in a way that is not designed to make the recipient feel established and supported in his or her role. This resembles a microaggression, such as voicing an assumed infraction about a person of a particular ethnicity or culture and forcing them to then defend their right to their identity. Given the stress that Harry and Neville feel when they doubt their Sorting, it seems that basing groupings on an assumption about innate abilities can make students vulnerable and self-conscious.

The use of houses also engenders competitive hostilities between the students (Lavoie 37). Readers learn that "Gryffindor and Slytherin students loathed each other on principle" (*H-BP* 143). Although Professor Slughorn gathers children from various houses for his Slug Club, house identities prevent them from using the experience to break down barriers. Children from different houses do take classes together, and occasionally they date; however, with the notable exception of the Gryffindors' friendship with Luna Lovegood, the friend groups represented in the novels are primarily comprised of children from the same house (Draco Malfoy's Slytherins, Ernie Macmillan's Hufflepuffs, Harry Potter's Gryffindors, and James Potter's Gryffindors).

Moreover, the Sorting labels the children for life. Several adult characters are identified by their childhood Sorting, so we know that the identity never entirely leaves a person. With no apparent process for transitioning to a different house or trying out new "qualities," the Sorting removes a great deal of agency from the child's process of self-creation. Rather than nurturing a growth mindset through ongoing experimentation and inquiry, this first day of school experience "settles" the child's abilities (cleverness, courage, cunning or—in the case of Hufflepuff—the lack of these distinct qualities) and opens his or her education with a public lesson in fixed mindset. The Sorting locks the child into a mold very early during his or her time at Hogwarts. In Harry's fifth year, the Sorting Hat's song blatantly informs Hufflepuff students that they are categorized based on a lack of strengths rather than any overriding character trait: "Good Hufflepuff, she took the rest" (*OotP* 205). Good Hufflepuff can easily be read as inclusive, but the quote also opens the house up to claims that it absorbs the leftovers.

Moreover, the Sorting Hat serves as a magical algorithm that not only identifies wishes and dominant qualities (or lack thereof), but also seems able to parcel out first years evenly between the four houses. The narrator makes no mention of a shortage of Slytherin or Hufflepuffs, for example, in a given year. One would imagine that, in a real school setting, much would be made of the number of new children allocated to each house. In one song, the Hat admits to "quarter[ing]" the incoming students each year (OotP 206). Either the house characteristics are evenly distributed in the magical population or the number of beds in each house dormitory also plays a role in the Sorting.

Sorting causes students to ignore or under-appreciate other qualities that they possess, qualities that do not fit into the rigid boxes of the Sorting Hat's songs. Instead of telling a student they have innate cleverness and belong to Ravenclaw, imagine the modern Hogwarts instructor saying something like, "I like how you worked hard to be cunning in that situation even though it didn't come naturally to you" or "You couldn't create a horoscope the standard way the first time around, but you found a new strategy of collaborating to solve the problem. That's fantastic!" The growth mindset so rarely seen at

Hogwarts would encourage students to avoid resting on their laurels and instead, enjoy the challenge of learning. Dweck's research has popularized the phrase "Not yet" as in "I'm not good at Potions yet." Since housing placements at Hogwarts lack fluidity, the system trains children to see their aptitudes and abilities as set in stone—suggesting they have as much courage as they will ever have—rather than as qualities that are "not yet" fully realized. No one counsels students to wait to see how their focal qualities will unfold later. Instead, if they see no evidence immediately, they may, like Neville, feel like a failure. A fixed mindset approach believes the student's abilities are already determined, and, if they fail to show strengths, it is because their abilities are weak and will remain weak.

Fixed Mindset in the Hogwarts's Classrooms

Sorting has its own ethical problems, but it also represents only part of the fixed mindset problem at Hogwarts. Other than Professor Lupin and perhaps Professor Dumbledore, Hogwarts professors rely on insult, nepotism, and preconceived ideas about the students rather than modeling growth mindset and allowing the students a chance to learn and grow in a safe space. Growth mindset is infiltrating 21st-century culture and takes some of the sting out of failure; in contrast, the hard-core emphasis on instantaneous, untaught perfection required by most Hogwarts teachers comes across as stultifying. For instance, in their very first Potions lessons, the first-year students find themselves immersed in a fixed mindset classroom. Professor Snape arrogantly assures them, "I can teach you how to bottle fame, brew glory, even stopper death—if you aren't as big a bunch of dunderheads as I usually have to teach" (*SS* 137). Snape does not encourage students to feel like they can find strategies in a safe, supported environment; rather, he quickly expresses that they will need to work out of fear of his vindictive authority. Instead of learning to value the struggle—which would be a characteristic of growth mindset—students here learn that signs of struggle will mark them as "dunderheads" and failures. During this first meeting, Snape publicly quizzes Harry on several difficult potions questions, a practice that merely serves to belittle Harry as a learner. The quizzing also emphasizes Harry's lack of previous knowledge, and it suggests that this, rather than an assessment of his efforts and engagement, is an evaluation of how well he will do in the class.

Neville Longbottom provides a particularly relevant case study when it comes to the effects of the fixed mindset at Hogwarts. When Neville "managed to melt Seamus's cauldron into a twisted blob" releasing a toxic potion (*SS* 139), Snape does not react to this as a process toward a more successful result. Instead he snarls, "Idiot boy!" and caustically identifies the problem with Neville's recipe himself rather than allowing the student the opportunity to strategize about what he could have done differently (*SS* 139). Based on the teacher's wrathful reaction, the entire class has learned that Snape values the success of the final product, not the process of exploration and learning.

Neville's trials continue throughout the series. In the second year, just as Professor Lockhart is about to give Neville a chance to shine in dueling practice, Snape cuts in, belittling Neville's abilities: "Longbottom causes devastation with the simplest spells" (*CoS* 193). Showing his fixed mindset, Snape teaches Neville and his peers that a student who has performed poorly is incapable of making an effort to bring about a better outcome. Snape refuses to even allow Neville an opportunity to experiment and evaluate strategies. The next year, Snape again attacks Neville's identity in a way that goes far beyond any useful discussion of his learning: "Tell me, boy, does anything penetrate that thick skull of yours? [...] What do I have to do to make you understand, Longbottom?" (*PoA* 126). According to Dweck, students and educators can retreat into a fixed mindset when they are feeling threatened: "These [threats] can be challenges, mistakes, failures, or criticisms that threaten our sense of our abilities" (Dweck, "Recognizing"). It seems that Neville receives mostly criticisms. This constant harassment greatly affects Neville's ability to learn: "Neville regularly went to pieces in Potions lessons; it was his worst subject, and his great fear of Professor Snape made things ten time worse" (*PoA* 125). Snape shows disdain, not respect, for his students. We can contrast Snape's teaching style with the Prensky Partnering system, a growth-mindset style of teaching. Prensky challenges educators to respect students, identify their passions, and partner with them in their learning (2–3). Snape instead chooses to set himself up as such an authority that his students fear him, and some cannot even learn in his presence.

The faculty's complaints against Neville are well known to his peers and to Rowling's readers. Consider Professor McGonagall's harsh instructions: "Longbottom, kindly do not reveal that you can't even perform a simple Switching Spell in front of anyone from Durmstrang!" (*GoF* 237). This teacher feedback appears "at the end of one particularly difficult lesson," but McGonagall here focuses on the failure, not the attempt to find a path through the struggle (*GoF* 237). Due to a fixed mindset, she allows only a finite chance to show success. Fans of the series find it unsurprising to learn that it takes five years for Neville to receive a kind word from his long-time teacher. When it finally happens, the narrator shares that "Professor McGonagall had never paid [Neville] a compliment before" (*H-BP* 174). While Dweck warns against over-praising students, teachers can certainly recognize some aspect of strength or effort when students dedicate themselves to the struggle of learning.

Neville also demonstrates how a fixed mindset influences a child's self-perception and future goals. When his Defense Against the Dark Arts teacher gives Neville a special book, Neville explains it is because "Professor Sprout told Professor Moody I'm really good at Herbology" (*GoF* 220). While this compliment seems like a sweet relief from the harsh words Neville has come to accept, it also serves to label Neville as having an innate ability for something. These interactions are a direct result of a fixed mindset in the teachers—McGonagall, Sprout, and "Moody"—which has now caused the student to parrot that mindset as part of his sense of self. Eventually, Neville becomes a Herbology professor. He chooses this career path despite his remarkable dedication to learning Defense Against the Dark Arts and his demonstrated mastery of this subject by surviving the Battle of Hogwarts and killing the living Horcrux Nagini. Neville eventually becomes adept at many skills, but his career choice must partly be tied to how his teachers labeled him when he was only thirteen.

As a student, Neville would have found the fixed mindset at work in his other Hogwarts courses as well. Professor Trelawney believes that Divination is "a Gift granted to few," suggesting you either have it or you do not (*PoA* 103). Professor Umbridge's pedagogy, which seems to have more to do with fascist censoring and control than actual learning, demonstrates an extremely fixed mindset. She shuts down student-led conversations about learning when she refuses to engage with Hermione who wants to talk about the efficacy of jinxes (*OotP* 317). According to Dweck, students with growth mindset take charge of their own learning, as Hermione is attempting to do here when she seeks to make meaning out of her reading (Dweck, *Mindset* 61). In contrast to Umbridge's reaction, a teacher modeling growth mindset would make time to support student inquiry and gently guide students toward learning (O'Brien et al. 475). The following year, Slughorn attributes Harry's strengths to heredity—"you've inherited your mother's talent" (*H-BP* 191)—and "natural ability" (*H-BP* 319). In all instances, the professors shut down further opportunities for learning. Umbridge blocks student questioning and discovery, and Slughorn and Trelawney attribute success to innate attributes. In the non-fiction world, in contrast, "[t]he majority of teachers report praising students for their efforts on a daily basis or encouraging them to continue improving in areas of strength or to try new strategies when they are struggling" (Education Week Research Center 3). Hogwarts' students might only attempt "new strategies" as acts of rebellion against their teachers.

Harry ironically stumbles upon a possible growth strategy for self-improvement while trying to survive in a fixed mindset classroom. By relying on the Half-blood Prince's Potions notes, Harry earns Slughorn's respect but Hermione's resentment. Harry's Potions risk-taking is comparable with data that readers glean about other learning going on in the Potions classroom.

Potions class shows active learning and some foundational theory but no chance for revision or learning from mistakes. Students mostly open books and follow recipes. Harry struggles to make successful potions during his first five years because he cannot or does not focus on following detailed instructions. In his sixth year, the new notes captivate his interest, and he adheres to them perfectly. It is as though he is learning a literary classic by reading and enjoying a graphic novel or an audiobook adaptation. He is still achieving the same end through augmented means. If the goal of the class is to have students pay careful attention to detail while mixing what amount to recipes, then using the slightly renegade alternative recipes appears to help Harry finally reach the objective.

When Harry has to apply theory rather than obey a recipe, as he does on an antidote project in Potions, he fails. He realizes "that his reputation as the best potion-maker in the class was crashing around his ears" (*H-BP* 376). He has no renegade notes for this scenario. His work on the project shows that while previous lessons have taught him to follow directions carefully, he has not learned to apply theory. His failure follows a breakdown in Slughorn's scaffolding. Harry is being asked to move from one level of Bloom's Taxonomy (Knowledge) to another (Applying) without being given what he needs to make that transition successfully. Every indication from the Potions lessons narrated in the book suggests that teachers ask students to perform tasks like following a recipe without fully understanding why it works. According to the text, "Nobody apart from Hermione seemed to be following what Slughorn said next either" (*H-BP* 375). So, it appears that the jump in Bloom's Taxonomy levels has been unsupported, and that the students' failures are due to pedagogical incompetence, not a lack of engagement on their part.

In addition to the lack of scaffolding, students at Hogwarts also face physical threats. Even everyday lessons have high stakes consequences that emphasize success on the first try (fixed mindset) rather than applauding inquiry and exploration (growth mindset). Neville breaks his wrist during his first flying lesson in year one, and Malfoy is wounded by Buckbeak in the first Magical Creatures class in year three. That same year, Snape tests Neville's fraught potion on Neville's own pet, stating that a failed potion will poison the toad (*PoA* 128). Later, in the fourth year, Snape "had hinted that he might be poisoning one of them before Christmas" to test their antidote research (*GoF* 234). That same year, "Moody" (the Death Eater Barty Crouch, Jr., who is impersonating Mad-Eye Moody) claims to have Dumbledore's approval for directing illegal curses at the fourteen- and fifteen-year-olds in Harry's class. There is often a chance that an engaged lesson like Care of Magical Creatures, Herbology, or Potions will result in a painful wound, embarrassing transformation, or illegal, and possibly traumatic, curse. These high stakes lessons do not generally include opportunities for revision or trying again after learning from mistakes, and they underscore the school's fixed mindset approach to learning.

Harry's "Chosen One" status, a common fantasy trope, spotlights the fixed mindset prevalent in the wizarding world. The narrative emphasizes its protagonist's natural abilities that make him stand out above his peers. Harry's flying talents suggest that, like other famous protagonists, he has special innate abilities: "The boy's a natural. I've never seen anything like it. Was that your first time on a broomstick, Potter?" (*SS* 151). Like Anakin Skywalker and his midichlorian-powered podracing, Harry is perceived to have innate gifts that propel him to prominence. Excellent flying comes to him "naturally." In a place like Hogwarts, natural abilities are celebrated and unquestioned.

Practicing Growth Mindset on the Sly

Dickinson has observed that real learning at Hogwarts comes from "self-teaching," and that students pursue learning when it suits their personal goals (242). Hermione dedicates herself to her studies, and readers might wonder if this is because she has perfectionist tendencies or if it is a sign of a more enlightened growth mindset. During her interaction with the boggart in *Prisoner of Azkaban*, Hermione reveals that her greatest fear is "fail[ing] everything" (*PoA* 319). This detail weakens the argument for the force of her growth mindset. However, Hermione also seems convinced that hard work, practice, and careful reading will help her solve the problems in her classes. She applies the same tactics to hacking wizarding world politics, as evidenced by her careful study of *The Daily Prophet*, her instigation of Dumbledore's Army, and her leadership and problem solving in the Horcrux quest. Hermione believes that effort, not inherent abilities, are needed to succeed at Hogwarts.

Hermione demonstrates a growth mindset, though this characteristic goes un-nurtured by her classroom instructors. When Harry asks how she completes all her lessons, she says by "working hard" (*PoA* 251). When she has an assignment on something like Animagi, she takes the time to dig deeper and to find the Ministry of Magic list of registered Animagi. Harry can only admire her tenacity: "Harry had barely had time to marvel inwardly at the effort Hermione put into her homework…" (*PoA* 351). Hermione puts in the time and relies on books because she realizes that, due to her school's pedagogical weaknesses, she must teach herself (Clark 87). For example, as the trio contemplates tracking the person trying to steal the Sorcerer's Stone, Hermione flips through her notebooks, hoping to find some helpful charms that might save them when they face their adult enemy. Hermione is still very young when she learns that her skills may just be needed to save her world.

The student-initiated Defense Against the Darks Arts club, Dumbledore's Army (the D.A.) forms the greatest example of growth mindset depicted in a classroom setting. Hermione suggests the plan, arguing that the students need to learn this content to survive, and she argues that they will need to teach themselves (*OotP* 325). Shortly thereafter, Harry and his students begin work in the Room of Requirement. Although Harry's teachers have mostly modeled fixed mindsets in the classroom, Harry does not teach like them. Instead, he applies growth mindset both during D.A. lessons and when captaining his Quidditch team. Perhaps Harry appreciates a growth approach because he knows that it is lacking from his current lessons. When he teaches, he focuses on progress and encouragement (*OotP* 454–5). For example, Harry encourages Neville, who other teachers constantly belittle, and he recognizes improvements in the various D.A. students.

At each narrated lesson of the D.A., the narrator points out the specific ways in which the members are improving. Harry does not award empty praise except, once, to Cho. Moreover, he vocalizes his encouragement while maintaining high standards pushed higher by his fear of the deadly threat of Voldemort (*OotP* 394). In this environment, Neville blossoms: "Neville had improved beyond all recognition" (*OotP* 454). Neville works tirelessly, partly inspired by his own family narrative and hatred for Bellatrix LeStrange and partly because he is surrounded by supporters who do not pretend to have all the answers but struggle alongside him to improve their abilities (*OotP* 553). Unlike the faculty, Neville's peers do not treat him like his abilities are fixed. Due to the supportive, nonjudgmental environment, Neville can imagine himself tapping into his potential. Just like in a growth mindset classroom, repetition, trial, and effort characterize Harry's lessons.

The official wizarding teachers occasionally show glimmers of growth mindset. When students are praised or rewarded for their effective strategies—not merely for their success—they are being encouraged to aim high regardless of the outcome. McGonagall introduces unexpected growth mindset as she encourages the fifth years: "I see no reason why everybody in this class should not achieve an O.W.L. in Transfiguration as long as they put in the work" (*OotP* 257). Growth mindset appears briefly, but delightfully, in the plot of the first book when Dumbledore awards Neville points for trying to stop his friends from doing what he believes to be wrong. This lesson in ethics recognizes Neville's growth rather than the success of his attempt. Neville's well-intentioned efforts to stop his peers failed, and in fact, they seem misguided when set against the celebration of the trio's successful quest. However, growth mindset overlooks the outcome and instead values the student's efforts and willingness to try something new. In Neville's case, the willingness to stand up for what he believes to be right is a sign of growth.

Ironically, "Moody" shows some moments of growth mindset in the way he encourages Harry through his terrible Imperius Curse lesson, a lesson that, at the same time, represents what can only be seen as an abuse of the schoolchildren. Harry resists the Unforgivable Curse, and "Moody" celebrates the effort: "Look at that, you lot.... Potter fought! He fought it, and he damn near beat it! We'll try that again, Potter [...] very good indeed!" (*GoF* 232). "Moody" models growth mindset by teaching the class that they should "accept the positive inclusion of failure in the larger picture of learning, rather than the immediate need for instant academic success" (Pueschel and Tucker 2). Here the instructor reacts to a good effort as something to be praised even if the student failed to achieve the target goal. This teacher feedback must strike the students as unusual in their Hogwarts experience.

"Moody's" lesson's aside, Clark has already charted how the "best teaching seems to be done outside the classroom by Remus Lupin and Albus Dumbledore [...] who were willing to demonstrate and explain magic, evaluate Harry's performance, and admit fault" (86). When teaching Harry how to repel Dementors, Lupin does not expect Harry to perfect the task at one go, but rather coaches Harry through the process, listening to Harry's narration of his strategies along the way. Lupin certainly sees the accomplishment of the Patronus as a process. He praises Harry for the small steps he has taken in forming a cloudy Patronus after several attempts: "Excellent Harry! That was definitely a start!" (*PoA* 242). Lupin allows Harry to try and fail and then coaches Harry's improvement from that point of failure (Clark 86). This mentorship relationship shapes the inquiry experience on the individual student's need. Lupin applies the same tactic in coaching Neville through the lesson on boggarts. His respectful language and pedagogical inquiry into meeting the student where he is allows Neville to shine here. Trained as they are to see Neville as a classroom failure, readers can use the litmus test of Neville's success to judge Lupin's growth mindset teaching style.

In close agreement with Clark, Dickinson identifies Dumbledore as the ultimate teacher at Hogwarts because he models inquiry and stages of learning and synthesis so well in the sixth book through his private lessons with Harry (244). The film *Fantastic Beasts: The Crimes of Grindelwald* highlights the effectiveness of Lupin's boggarts lesson, establishing it as the icon of good teaching at Hogwarts by replicating it to depict the teaching savvy of a younger Dumbledore. The young Dumbledore's lesson takes place in 1927, so, technically, it predates and possibly informs Lupin's lesson set in 1993. Yet, fans familiar with Lupin's boggarts lesson from *Prisoner of Azkaban* (published in 1999) come to the 2018 film greatly informed by the context of Hogwarts: professors are generally strict and autocratic, so when the rare professor cheers on students as they tackle their greatest fears, students and viewers alike find them approachable and charming.

In the novels, Dumbledore is mostly removed from the classroom setting.

He does eventually develop a kind of independent-study course for Harry in which he models growth mindset. However, these lessons, ones which could be titled "Studies in Voldemort," are an anomaly. Overall, Dumbledore's teaching is woefully inconsistent. The Trio feel that Dumbledore allows them just enough room to test out their abilities, to try and fail, for example, by giving Harry the Invisibility Cloak in their first year. So, yes, if we overlook the fact that the headmaster allows eleven-year-olds to strategize through their failure while facing a murderous sociopath, we might applaud this demonstration of a growth mindset. But Dumbledore finally chooses to work with Harry on "Voldemort lessons" after years of failing to support Harry's special learning needs, including his confusion about his connection to Voldemort, his lack of a nurturing family, and his oftentimes trying celebrity status.

The headmaster's crimes also include sabotaging the learning of the Hogwarts student body. Jenny McDougal has rightly traced the headmaster's "manipulation and deceit" through the series, highlighting the ways that Dumbledore steals agency from Harry along the way (162). Moreover, from an educational standpoint, Dumbledore has the sole responsibility of hiring all of the professors except Umbridge. Despite being a hero of the wizarding world, Dumbledore's staffing choices are terrible and impart lasting emotional and educational damage to the students under his control. Slughorn had taught before he returns to teach in Harry's sixth year, but there is no evidence that the other last minute, long-term substitutes have teaching experience or teacher training. Hagrid transitions from wizarding world pariah to game-keeper to instructor with no time for teacher training in between. Similarly, the choice to bring Firenze into the castle in *Order of the Phoenix* does not involve discussion of his resume nor does organized teacher training seem to fit into his background narrative. The same is true of Snape, who joins the school staff within three years of his own Hogwarts graduation. Snape's loyalty and secret politics seem to have been the greatest recommendation for being employed at Hogwart. The piecemeal hiring demonstrates Hogwarts's lack of an institutional vision statement. Kelly E. Collinsworth has called it a place "where discipline was inconsistent and the rules unknowable" (15). Dumbledore alone has control over building the staff and the teaching personality of Hogwarts, but his decisions seem more tied to offering refuge for those seeking shelter than building the most constructive teaching body.

Just as Dumbledore's focus on what McDougal calls his "endgame" caused him to make unethical choices (162), his fight with Voldemort becomes an obsession that jeopardizes the education and mental health of several generations of Hogwarts students. The headmaster selects faculty based on his "witness protection" plan, which puts a hateful Snape in the path of hundreds of children. The administration in charge of Hogwarts does not value teachers for their pedagogy or their ability to engage and support students. Instead, it values knowledge of a discipline. For example, Hagrid has an uncanny way with animals, but even Hermione feels his lessons on Magical Creatures are weak and uninspiring. Genius in a subject does not guarantee that the teacher possesses the ability to gently and efficiently transfer knowledge to vulnerable boarding school students. Readers witness how the trio and a few of their peers find ways to achieve learning despite their circumstances, which contributes to the underdog narrative that makes the series so popular. However, we have no evidence to prove that the rest of the student body is as resilient and independent as the trio.

The teachers of Hogwarts mishandle classroom management and their students' learning. Megan L. Birch has called them "ineffective and disconnected" with teaching strategies that show "passion without application" (107). Some teachers may merely be inept, but others threaten child wellness. This instruction could only be possible at a boarding school where the children have no parental advocates to protect them from abusive teachers and systems. Even those adults who the students respect or tolerate with affection show deep flaws as educators. While the Harry Potter fandom reveres Professor McGonagall, she also has flaws as an educator. She belittles students and maintains her place on a pedestal of learning without building a ladder to meet her students part way. Of all the teachers to which readers are introduced, only Lupin appears to consistently care about his students' sense of self, their safety in the classroom, and their process of learning.

The "tenured" professors at Hogwarts, those who remain in place for years, demonstrate a rampant, ingrained devotion to fixed mindset. Their keenness for fixed mindset-informed teaching offers a clue to the great failures of the wizarding world as a society. Outside of Hogwarts and Ministry leadership, Rowling presents adult wizards as eccentric and impractical. In the first year, as Hermione faces Snape's potions challenge, she explains to Harry that "[a] lot of the greatest wizards haven't got an ounce of logic, they'd be stuck in here forever" (*SS* 285). We see evidence of adult foolishness throughout the series, from the failure to blend in with Muggle culture even when wizards wish to, to the obstinate refusal to engage with the facts about Voldemort's return. If readers accept this portrayal of a faulty adult population at face value, we have to consider that a Hogwarts's education has failed generations of students, failed them because the school does not teach civics and higher orders of thinking nor does it teach growth through failure. The culture of design thinking celebrates trial and error; in contrast, most wizarding adults fear to test alternate theories and solutions. Like the fixed mindset students Dweck first identified, the Hogwarts-educated, Sorting Hat-labeled British wizarding population prefers to avoid tricky challenges; they forsake outside-the-box approaches to tackling problems because they loathe a challenge. The wizarding world needs the series' courageous children to come to their rescue because the adult community is a product of Hogwarts's fixed mindset. Fortunately, the self-taught children rise to the occasion.

Works Cited

Birch, Megan L. "Schooling Harry Potter: Teachers and Learning, Power and Knowledge." *Critical Perspectives on Harry Potter.* 2nd ed. edited by Elizabeth E. Heilman, Routledge, 2009, pp. 103–120.

Blackwell, Lisa S., et al. "Implicit Theories of Intelligence Predict Achievement Across an Adolescent Transition: A Longitudinal Study and an Intervention." *Child Development,* vol. 78, 2007, pp. 246–263.

Clark, Elizabeth Morrow. "Teaching Harry Potter: How the Wizarding World Has Transformed Higher Education." *From Here to Hogwarts: Essays on Harry Potter Fandom and Fiction,* edited by Chris Bell, McFarland Press, 2016, pp. 78–98.

Collinsworth, Kelly E. "'I Will Have Order': A Potterish Examination of Authoritarian School Disciplinary Trends and Reactions." *From Here to Hogwarts: Essays on Harry Potter Fandom and Fiction,* edited by Chris Bell, McFarland Press, 2016, pp. 7–27.

Dickinson, Renee. "Harry Potter Pedagogy: What We Learn About Teaching and Learning from J.K. Rowling." *The Clearing House,* vol. 79, no. 6, 2006, pp. 240–244.

Dweck, Carol. *Mindset: The New Psychology of Success.* Ballantine Books, 2006.

_____. "Recognizing and Overcoming False Growth Mindset." *Edutopia,* 11 Jan. 2016, www.edutopia.org/blog/recognizing-overcoming-false-growth-mindset-carol-dweck.

Education Week Research Center. *Mindset in the Classroom: A National Study of K–12 Teachers. Education Week.* Editorial Projects in Education, Inc., 2016. secure.edweek.org/media/ewrc_mindsetintheclassroom_sept2016.pdf.

Hochheiser, David. "Growth Mindset: A Driving Philosophy, Not Just a Tool." *Edutopia,* 16 Sept. 2014, www.edutopia.org/blog/growth-mindset-driving-philosophy-david-hochheiser.

Hong, Ying-yi, et al. "Implicit Theories, Attributions and Coping: A Meaning System Approach." *Journal of Personality and Social Psychology,* vol. 77, no. 3, 1999, pp. 599–599.

Lavoie, Chantel. "Safe as Houses: Sorting and School Houses at Hogwarts." *Reading Harry Potter: Critical Essays,* edited by Giselle Liza Anatole, Praeger, 2003, pp. 25–49.

McDougal, Jenny. "Doubting Dumbledore." *A Wizard of Their Age: Critical Essays from the Harry Potter Generation,* edited by Cecilia Konchar Farr, State University of New York Press, 2015, pp. 159–180.

Moore, Tara. "Lotteries, Sortings, and Choosings: Rebelling Against the Dystopian Lot in Young Adult Literature." *SIGNAL Journal,* vol. 43, no. 1, Fall 2018/Winter 2019, pp 30–35.

O'Brien, Mia, et al. "How Inquiry Pedagogy Enables Teachers to Facilitate Growth Mindset in Mathematics Classrooms." *38th Annual Meeting of the Mathematics Education Research Group of Australasia (MERGA), Sunshine Coast, Queensland, Australia, 2015.* MERGA, 2015.

Pesold, Ulrike. *The Other in the School Stories: A Phenomenon in Children's Literature.* Brill-Rodopi, 2017.

Prensky, Marc. *Teaching Digital Natives: Partnering for Real Learning.* Corwin, 2010.

Pueschel, Andrew, and Mary L. Tucker. "Achieving Grit Through the Growth Mindset." *Journal of Instructional Pedagogies,* vol. 20, 2018, pp. 1–10.

Rowling, J.K. *Harry Potter and the Chamber of Secrets,* Scholastic, 1998.

_____. *Harry Potter and the Deathly Hallows,* Scholastic, 2007.

_____. *Harry Potter And the Goblet of Fire.* Scholastic, 2000.

_____. *Harry Potter and the Half-Blood Prince.* Scholastic, 2005.

_____. *Harry Potter and the Order of the Phoenix.* Scholastic, 2003.

_____. *Harry Potter and the Prisoner of Azkaban.* Scholastic, 1999.

_____. *Harry Potter and the Sorcerer's Stone.* Scholastic, 1997.

Fascism in the Classroom in *Harry Potter and the Order of the Phoenix*

LAURIE JOHNSON *and* CARL NIEKERK

"Progress for progress's sake must be discouraged," says Ministry official and new Hogwarts teacher Dolores Jane Umbridge by way of introducing herself to the students in *Harry Potter and the Order of the Phoenix* (*OotP* 213). Obsessed with the desire to deny that Lord Voldemort has returned, the Minister of Magic has installed Umbridge at Hogwarts to undermine head-master Albus Dumbledore and Harry Potter himself, who battled Voldemort at the end of the previous school year. Umbridge gradually creates a regime with traits that could be called fascist, first in her classroom, and then throughout the school as Headmistress and High Inquisitor of Hogwarts— a title that evokes resonances with totalitarianism in Europe's past. Umbridge's methods are those of a classically intolerant and repressive regime: she teaches the students nothing but obedience; she manipulates Hogwarts rules in order to torture students legally; and she demonizes the opposition while lying continually. And yet, Harry's godfather Sirius Black maintains, Umbridge is not a follower of Voldemort (*OotP* 302). Umbridge seems to believe that she is doing the right thing, but her actions demonstrate how easily an atmos-phere of joyful learning and harmless socializing among students of different backgrounds can devolve into one of sadism and repression.

This essay examines the pedagogical strategies employed in *Order of the Phoenix* in order to explore the ways in which the text illuminates power relations and the political implications of pedagogy. In our view, pedagogical practice, rather than theory, changes Hogwarts from a place of seemingly free and creative learning to that of a penal colony run by an authoritarian leader. But, what makes a Hogwarts student into either a willing victim or

121

someone prepared to break the rules in order to resist Umbridge's repressive regime? To explore that question, we situate the *Harry Potter* series in the context of historical thinking about pedagogy. The *Harry Potter* books are compelling because they document "the everyday struggles of growing through childhood to adolescence and adulthood" and include characters that "confront real-world issues such as racism, class status, war, political corruption, and ethnic cleansing" (Belcher and Stephenson 4). In *Order of the Phoenix* "rebellion" is a major topic (Bealer, Alkestrand), but on what principles is this rebellion based? The text does not provide us with easy answers, but the questions it asks remain relevant.

Dolores Umbridge's "Dark Arts" and the Power of Writing

Soon after Umbridge's arrival at Hogwarts, Harry gets into serious trouble. He mentions Lord Voldemort by name in Umbridge's class and contradicts her when she claims he is lying about Voldemort's return (*OotP* 244–45). As punishment, he must come to her office later that day and repeatedly write a line without ink on a magical piece of parchment: "*I must not tell lies.*" The words appear on the parchment in what appears to be red ink but is actually blood, and they simultaneously appear on the back of his right hand, cut into his skin (*OotP* 266–67). Umbridge insists this procedure is for Harry's own good. She wants her "message to *sink in*" (*OotP* 266). The image used here has a distinct literary genealogy in Franz Kafka's novella "In the Penal Colony" (1919). Kafka's text describes a machine using a set of needles to inscribe the law that a prisoner of the penal colony supposedly has broken directly into his skin. Many read Kafka's story as a premonition of the torture techniques of the Third Reich. But it can also be understood in the context of new technical media of Kafka's own time, including gramophones, films, and typewriters (Kittler 296, 316). Kafka was interested in the ways in which humans' thinking was shaped materially through the production of language as a material process and with the help of available media and technology. Using writing and the written text to shape young people's minds is central to Umbridge's pedagogy as well.

Umbridge enjoys a steeply upward career trajectory due to her connections at the Ministry of Magic and not because of her competence as an educator. Soon after her appointment, she can call herself by ministerial decree "Hogwarts High Inquisitor" (*OotP* 306–07).[1] The title gives Umbridge "supreme authority over all punishments, sanctions, and removal of privileges pertaining to the students of Hogwarts" (*OotP* 416). Later, after Dumbledore's exile from Hogwarts, Umbridge becomes Headmistress and employs an "Inquisitorial Squad" composed mostly of students from Slytherin House.

Fascism and the History of Pedagogy

Throughout the series, Rowling alludes to events that happened during (or just after) the reign of fascism in Germany (for instance, Dumbledore defeated Grindelwald in 1945, and Grindelwald was then imprisoned in "Nurmengard"), and she has mentioned National Socialism as a term of comparison when discussing *Harry Potter* (Reagin 128 and 148; Castro). The term "fascism" refers to historically specific phenomena that involved unprecedented levels of violence and intolerance, including visions of national glory and racial purity. Totalitarian regimes often target educational institutions (Castro 123). But how can a seemingly idyllic community like Hogwarts transform so quickly and relatively imperceptibly into something resembling a fascist state?

To answer this question, we need to consider the history of pedagogy. There is something inherently paradoxical about modern approaches to teaching that are student-centered and presume that students learn better if they are creative and take initiative. At the same time, that creativity and initiative are partly "coerced" in the unnatural setting of the classroom, and the desire to transmit "desirable" content is central. The roots of this modern pedagogy are situated in the 18th century, where they find their perhaps most famous expression in Jean-Jacques Rousseau's *Émile, or on Education* [*Émile, ou de l'Éducation*] (1762) (see Rutschky xl). In *Émile*, Rousseau prescribes what he calls an "inactive education": the teacher interferes as little as possible in the learning process, and pupils must be free essentially to teach themselves (146). The educator should take each student's character as a point of departure (113–19). Rousseau thus foregrounds the autonomy of the student who engages with the real world and discovers what is most valuable in life. Rousseau was adamantly against learning from books and advocated a practice-oriented pedagogy (238).

However, in spite of such ideals of freedom and individual development, teaching after Rousseau remained a form of disciplining—not only because it involved the communication of a (to an extent necessarily uniform) body of knowledge, but also because it was—and arguably still is—about mediating rules of behavior. In other words, the history of modern pedagogy can also be read as a history of implementing discipline or as a history of "poisonous pedagogy" (a term often used to translate the title of Katharina Rutschky's *Schwarze Pädagogik*) more inclined to regulate behavior than to let it develop freely. In addition, educational priorities mirror those set by society as a whole and may exhibit irrational tendencies toward control and domination (Rutschky xxvi).

In the 20th century, the French philosopher Michel Foucault showed the connection between the invention of modern subjectivity and new forms of disciplining and punishing. In Foucault's reading, the primary goal of educational institutions was not to repress certain behavior, but rather to encourage desirable behavior. This presupposes a certain order and regularity (179), both of which are ubiquitous at Hogwarts even pre–Umbridge. Punishment is administered at Hogwarts as part of a system that enables gratification and increases student desire for gratification, for instance by gaining points for their house. Exams are another example of a pedagogical strategy combining gratification (passing the exam and gaining access to new and more interesting courses) and possible punishment (not passing); this "makes it possible to qualify, to classify and to punish" the student in question (Foucault 184).

The idea of selecting "from among the best pupils a whole series of 'officers'—intendants, observers, monitors, tutors" is an invention of modern pedagogy (Foucault 175). The method deploys the students' own sense of responsibility in the interest of a disciplinary apparatus. This applies not only in Umbridge's regime, but under Dumbledore's leadership as well: Ron and Hermione are made prefects and must school and discipline younger students. The badges prefects wear are distant cousins of the military attire that accompanied such positions in the 19th century. Umbridge acts according to a similar principle later in *Order of the Phoenix* when she appoints some of her favorite students "who are supportive of the Ministry of Magic" to her "Inquisitorial Squad" (*OotP* 626). The fact that Umbridge and her Squad use disciplinary measures to divide students against one another, often quite arbitrarily, demonstrates the vulnerability of the method of turning students into monitors.

A Change of Regime at Hogwarts

This paradox of empowerment and disempowerment, or of elevating certain students only to punish others, is apparent in Umbridge's attitude upon arriving at Hogwarts. She announces the goal of making teaching at Hogwarts more efficient and uses phrases that, had they been spoken by Dumbledore, would seem welcoming. She expresses a desire to better know the students and affirms that it is the task of the teacher to ensure that the "rare gifts with which you were born" are "nurtured" (*OotP* 212). Here, Umbridge adopts the rhetoric of modern pedagogical reform in which students are central to the process of learning as a cooperative and collegial project with their teachers.

However, in part due to her own previous education at Hogwarts, Hermione spots the punitive and authoritarian aspects of Umbridge's "modern" mission right away. At the year-opening feast in the Great Hall where Umbridge is introduced to the students, the Sorting Hat speaks (or rather, sings) first and warns that the very dividing it must do, of the students into four houses, could weaken Hogwarts and make it more vulnerable to enemies from without. The Hat's ballad, with its varied vocabulary organized into an *abcb* rhyming scheme, contrasts vividly with Umbridge's later speech, with its trite use of alliteration that condescends to the students even while inviting them to be part of her mission.

Before the Hat sings, Harry informs Ron and Hermione that Umbridge, whom they see sitting at the teachers' table, was present at his earlier hearing at the Ministry of Magic, where he was charged with using magic improperly outside of school. Harry's statement alerts his friends to Umbridge's possible ill intents. But it is her own rhetoric, which cloaks the language of modern pedagogy in a highly contrived and artificial style, that confirms the danger ahead. Harry and Ron find the speech pointless, but Hermione echoes Dumbledore's description of the dull and stilted speech as "illuminating" (*OotP* 214). Hermione, Ron, and Harry intuit that Umbridge represents a transition at Hogwarts from a disciplined and regulated, yet also fundamentally free, institution to a repressive regime.

Once Umbridge becomes High Inquisitor, her methods turn ever more openly sadistic while remaining supposedly inside the limits of official bureaucratic regulation. Indeed, the Ministry of Magic, desperate to deny the reality of Voldemort's return, has simply shifted the boundaries of what is legal at Hogwarts. When Umbridge wishes to punish Fred and George Weasley, whose civil disobedience is becoming ever more disruptive, she dispatches Hogwarts caretaker Argus Filch to her office to search for forms labeled "Approval for Whipping" (*OotP* 673). She only apologizes when she is witnessed behaving in a way that the Ministry has not yet sanctioned: when she shakes Marietta Edgecombe, a student who is unwilling to report on the activities of Dumbledore's Army, she counters, "I forgot myself" (*OotP* 617). This too shows that Umbridge recognizes, at least in principle, that current pedagogy discourages physical coercion. But her behavior also makes clear that the new pedagogy's relationship to its repressive past is ambiguous— there is the danger of a relapse.

Ultimately, however, for Harry, Hermione, and Ron, Umbridge's use of corporal punishment and of what Rutschky terms "education as a rationalization of sadism" (376) is not as damning as the fact that they do not learn anything valuable in her class. Their revolt against Umbridge begins as a protest against her pedagogical practice (Bealer 182). Harry objects that learning only defensive theory is not going to be of much use in the "real world," prompting Umbridge to give an unintentionally funny answer: "This is school, Mr. Potter, not the real world" (*OotP* 244). Here Umbridge defies one of the most basic principles of modern pedagogy since Rousseau: the conviction that learning should establish a connection between the student and the world. And yet, in general she uses a student-focused vocabulary to legitimate her view of pedagogy. As much as readers may dislike Umbridge and her methods, she is neither a Death Eater nor a deliberate supporter of Voldemort. Rather, she has copied the beliefs and attitudes of the incompetent Cornelius Fudge, Minister of Magic. Umbridge is, perhaps unwittingly, part of a "Ministry-sponsored misinformation campaign against Harry and Dumbledore" (Bealer 176).

Hogwarts and the Absent Parent

Hogwarts resembles traditional British boarding schools in many respects, including the division of students into houses, the process of examinations at certain levels, and the hierarchies within the staff and the student body. The separation and different treatment of male and female students is also quite old-fashioned: boys are not allowed to visit the girls' dormitories, although girls are permitted in the boys' dormitories. Hogwarts builds on structures students already know from their families. Historically, schooling young people in classrooms (instead of through individual apprenticeships) emerged together with a new conceptualization of the family. At least since the Enlightenment, the family has been conceptualized as a disciplining force that is simultaneously subject to societal and cultural discipline itself (Foucault 215–16; Ariès 369–70). Parents send children to school because they expect them to be looked after professionally, in an environment that, to some extent, parents choose and can control.

Attitudes acquired at home shape students' behavior at school (although students may also consciously decide to break with those attitudes). This impact of the home environment is clear in the opening pages of *Order of the Phoenix*. After his previous experiences with the Dursleys, Harry has become quite immune to any pedagogical impulses his adoptive parents may exhibit. The fact that their son Dudley is utterly different from Harry—he is a lazy bully who enjoys spending summer evenings terrorizing younger children—has much to do with his parents' attitudes toward learning. Mr. Dursley is proud of Dudley's ignorance of the wider world. In Mr. Dursley's view, this ignorance makes his son "normal" (*OotP* 2). Harry, who in contrast is desperate for news about how Voldemort's return may be affecting the Muggle and wizarding worlds, hides outside near the window so he can overhear the television (*OotP* 6).

Harry's rebellion against the Dursleys helps define him as an independent thinker and a strong individual. At Hogwarts, however, he wishes to fit in. This desire intensifies when Harry faces rejection from classmates who have been told at home to discredit Harry and Dumbledore's insistence that

Voldemort has returned. Still other parents go further by actively encouraging their children to side with Umbridge and the Ministry. Marietta Edgecombe, for example, serves as an informant on the secret meetings Harry, Ron, Hermione, and a group of friends have been holding in order to practice spells; she does so because her mother works for Minister of Magic Cornelius Fudge (*OotP* 611–12). Such examples raise the question of how students can behave ethically if they cannot rely on the word and advice of familial authority figures.

What is new in *Order of the Phoenix* is the absence of figures that, until this volume, had functioned as parental substitutes for Harry. Harry's godfather Sirius Black, who perhaps comes closest to a father-figure for Harry, exhibits adolescent behavior early in the book because he is unhappy with being told by the resistance group to stay inside headquarters for his own safety. Harry thus has to learn not to rely on Sirius as an idealized father—that is, as a figure whose symbolic authority belies the fact that he is a human being with strengths and weaknesses. Because he does not trust Sirius as a responsible adult, Harry mistakenly chooses not to use a two-way mirror to communicate with Sirius about what's happening at Hogwarts. Consequently, he forgets about this means of communication until the very end of the book, when he finds it while rummaging through his possessions after Sirius's death (*OotP* 857–58). This signals that a good relationship between adults and adolescents has more to do with good and timely communication rather than with the adults telling the adolescents what to do.

Another parental figure, Albus Dumbledore, is nearly absent in *Order of the Phoenix*. To Harry's surprise and dismay, Dumbledore assiduously avoids contact with him all year. We only discover why near the book's conclusion when Dumbledore explains what he should have told Harry earlier: a prophecy had been made that predicted a final confrontation between Harry and Voldemort that must be fatal to one or the other. Dumbledore feared that his contact with Harry would make Voldemort more eager to intrude upon Harry's mind. He acknowledges that Sirius might not have died had Harry known that Voldemort would likely use Sirius as bait to compel Harry to the Department of Mysteries (*OotP* 825–26). Here too, an important point is made about communication between adults and adolescents; Dumbledore comes to the realization that he could have done a better job communicating what he knew to Harry.

Dumbledore's confession hints at one of his greatest dilemmas, a dilemma he shares with philosophers and practitioners of various pedagogies: whether children, particularly adolescents, should be treated as capable of making their own decisions or instead should be considered dependent on the guidance and support of the adults surrounding them. Enlightenment and post–Enlightenment pedagogy advocated treating children and adolescents not as inferior adults, but rather as beings with their own needs, interests, and rights (Ariès 43, 46–47; Rutschky xlvii). Only when childhood and adolescence are conceptualized as specific life stages does the possibility of treating young people more appropriately to their actual abilities and knowledge arise—as does the chance to underestimate and infantilize them. From this perspective, the absence of a parental figure offers a chance, but also poses a risk. Within the *Harry Potter* cycle, *Order of the Phoenix* illustrates the point that the absence of a parental figure is not incidental but rather fundamental for the protagonist's learning experience. At the end of this process, they must be autonomous, able to act without deferring to authority.

Bad Teaching at Hogwarts

While Dumbledore and Sirius are no longer reliable "parents" for Harry in much of the volume, other authority figures, in particular teachers, do play major roles. None of them are unquestionably dependable sources of support and knowledge, as evidenced from their often-flawed teaching (to the extent that the reader gets the impression that much teaching at Hogwarts is substandard). Focusing on this bad teaching is helpful because, paradoxically, it can have two effects: intentionally or not, bad teaching can foster students' autonomy and inventiveness, or in contrast, it can be instrumentalized to suppress these qualities and be used instead to facilitate acceptance of a fascist-style regime. *Order of the Phoenix* offers examples of both effects.

Hagrid is an effective example of how bad teaching can promote autonomy. Hogwarts' students are already well-acquainted with Hagrid as a good character but a really bad teacher. Luna Lovegood, known for her eccentricity, is oddly on-point as she dares to criticize loveable Hagrid, saying he "isn't a very good teacher, is he?" (*OotP* 200). Hermione, who clearly agrees, only grudgingly contradicts Luna after Harry and Ron come to Hagrid's defense. While he defends Hagrid vigorously, Harry knows that many students prefer Professor Grubbly-Plank as teacher of the subject Care of Magical Creatures because her classes are physically safer (*OotP* 442). Harry is not blinded by his loyalty to Hagrid, although he does insist that Hagrid's unorthodox methods may teach the students something valuable. And, Grubbly-Plank herself acknowledges that Hagrid's overview of magical creatures has been quite thorough (*OotP* 323), and above all, it has taught the students real-life skills.

Among the bad teachers at Hogwarts, however, Dolores Umbridge stands out for her use of bad teaching to facilitate acceptance of her fascist-style regime. Her teaching is centered on the use of a textbook entitled *Defensive Magical Theory*, which the students are instructed to read during class. This demonstrates her belief in the written word's ability to shape the students' minds. This approach is not at all appreciated by the students: "All we do is read the stupid textbook," Ron complains (303), quite in line with a model of pedagogy that, following Rousseau, emphasized practical experience over book learning. Practice, however, takes on another form for Umbridge. If a student refuses to follow her directions, she resorts to corporal punishment. Umbridge views the human mind itself as something upon which commands can be inscribed and tries to use her classroom to suppress student's autonomy. However, this plan backfires and leads the students to revolt.

Anti-Pedagogy, Alternative Pedagogies and Resistance

The abundance of bad teaching at Hogwarts could be construed as an argument against any form of pedagogy, and some characters in *Order of the Phoenix* indeed opt for an anti-pedagogical stance. Twins Fred and George Weasley conclude they have "outgrown full-time education" (*OotP* 674). They embark on a successful career in the wizard economy as owners of the joke shop Weasleys' Wizard Wheezes. Before they leave Hogwarts, they engage in a series of disruptive pranks. Yet, despite their rejection of formal schooling, education pays off for them. The "quality of their mischief is the clear result of hard work and application" at Hogwarts, and this hard work helps them to be successful in Diagon Alley (Matthews 140).

Rather than rejecting education, Harry, Ron, and Hermione respond to Umbridge's bad teaching by creating Dumbledore's Army (the D.A.), not only to resist Umbridge and her regime, but also to learn real skills. Hermione recognizes that Harry has the potential to be a very good teacher, and at her urging, he forms the D.A. to teach his fellow resisters how to defend themselves against the Dark Arts. The students create an alternative pedagogy demonstrated by their organized resistance and civil disobedience. In spite or because of the bad teaching at Hogwarts, Harry and his friends have learned basic ethics: the awareness of right and wrong, the importance of perseverance and of making conscious choices, and the insight that ethics is always a way of acting (Kern 19). This exposure to bad teaching emboldens Harry, Ron, Hermione, Luna, Neville, and Ginny to act against the Death Eaters and Voldemort himself.

Order of the Phoenix does give examples of responsible pedagogy, for instance, by examining the importance of pedagogy for magical creatures that are outsiders—such as Grawp, Kreacher, and Firenze—who help breed a pro-resistance mindset among the students. Hagrid is hiding Grawp, his giant half-brother, in the Forbidden Forest after abducting him from a colony of giants where his future would have been dim. Hermione, Harry, and eventually Ron are skeptical about Hagrid's attempts to educate Grawp. Hagrid's educational efforts mostly limit themselves to keeping Grawp from harming others and teaching him some basic English. Hagrid refuses to acknowledge that his educational experiment might be a failure, insisting that Grawp is "getting better" (*OotP* 693). Indeed, the fact that Grawp actually does learn something about relationships is crucial to the novel's plot, as he saves Harry and Hermione after they have led Umbridge into the Forbidden Forest and are threatened by centaurs. Grawp expresses that he misses Hagrid and then saves the children when he recognizes Hermione (*OotP* 758). It is precisely because Hagrid never gave up on teaching Grawp that he becomes a helpful ally.

Grawp's storyline in *Order of the Phoenix* is a counterpoint to that of Kreacher, the Black family's house-elf who is resistant to education and change. Like giants, house-elves are magical creatures that wizards often treat as inferior. While Hagrid believes tirelessly in Grawp's ability to learn, Sirius Black has no faith in Kreacher, and this has fatal consequences. Kreacher has served the Black family for generations and has subscribed completely to the family's "pureblood" elitism and disdain for Muggles and "half-bloods." When Sirius, who disagrees vehemently with the rest of his (absent) family, takes up residence at Grimmauld Place with members of the Order, Kreacher bows and scrapes to the resistance while continuously and passive-aggressively muttering his real thoughts about the "blood traitors" who have moved into his home (*OotP* 108). Although Kreacher is obviously hostile, no one is particularly concerned. Kreacher resists attempts by the Order to change his views because they lack a connection with him.

Kreacher's only potential ally is Hermione, whose advocacy on behalf of house-elf rights is treated with skepticism by her friends. But even Hermione does not see that Kreacher's allegiance to the Black family is a form of nostalgia: the elf lives predominantly in the past and holds on to mementos in a way that is reminiscent of Umbridge's emphasis on tradition as a counterweight to innovation, which she stressed in her initial speech in the Great Hall at Hogwarts (*OotP* 213). Dumbledore explains, however, that Kreacher is bound not so much by allegiance to the Black family's philosophies as to the fact that they (except for Sirius) treated him well. Ultimately, then, Bellatrix Lestrange and Narcissa Malfoy can make use of Kreacher to endanger the members of the Order who have disregarded him and failed to teach him their values.

The Order of the Phoenix assumes that as a house-elf Kreacher has no will of his own, since he must obey the master of Grimmauld Place: Sirius. But Kreacher can interpret Sirius's orders creatively. When Sirius tells him to "get out," he interprets this as permission to leave Grimmauld Place, even though this is not Sirius's intent (*OotP* 830). And he can lie to Harry, telling him Sirius is not at home when Harry attempts to find out whether Sirius is at the Ministry (*OotP* 829). As Dumbledore notes, all these actions are logical consequences of Kreacher's education (or lack thereof): "Kreacher is what he has been made by wizards" (*OotP* 832). Had Kreacher been treated as a "being with feelings as acute as a human's," Dumbledore remarks, he might have behaved differently (*OotP* 832). In other words, all creatures deserve an education and the accompanying attention and care. Pedagogy functions here as a kind of equalizer: it can help prevent exclusion and an "us-versus-them" mentality.

Centaurs, also magical creatures who are disdained, underestimated, or romanticized by wizards, ultimately play a role in resisting Umbridge and the Ministry's coercive pedagogies. They defend Harry, Ron, and Hermione from Umbridge in the Forbidden Forest and effectively remove her from power. But the centaur Firenze also demonstrates a form of anti-pedagogy that makes an impression on Harry. Centaurs are arrogant, but their disregard for "human nonsense" relativizes human authority and authoritarianism (*OotP* 603). Firenze models a form of resistance to the Hogwarts students when he reminds them that centaurs "are not the servants or playthings of humans" (*OotP* 602). He praises half-giant Hagrid, saying he has earned his "respect for the care he shows all living creatures" (*OotP* 605). When Firenze has his Divination class lie on the floor and contemplate a magically star-filled ceiling, he emphasizes that the meaning of the stars' movements remains mysterious. Centaur knowledge is contingent and incomplete. Firenze's pedagogical goal is to emphasize that no one has all the answers and no knowledge is absolute (*OotP* 604). Firenze's skeptical pedagogy acknowledges the vulnerability of any teaching endeavor while maintaining its significance. Good pedagogy is not about theoretical knowledge but about practices that impart relativity and contingency and thus foreground the importance of our choices.

However, the most organized and ultimately effective form of resistance in *Order of the Phoenix* is the D.A. Hermione encourages Harry to form the group in order to teach Hogwarts students how to use defensive spells, and students from all houses except Slytherin join. Initially, these students come for different reasons: Luna and Ron, for instance, want to defeat Umbridge and support Harry, while Zacharias Smith is interested primarily in learning the details of Cedric Diggory's death. Eventually, the group unifies behind Harry as the teacher who astutely builds his students' confidence by having them gain experience with some simple, but useful, spells. When the group practices *Expelliarmus*, normally clumsy Neville Longbottom experiences a rare moment of proud accomplishment (*OotP* 393). Here, too, we see the importance of practice over theory and attitude over knowledge. Supported by Hermione, Ron, and others, Harry seems naturally to develop a student-centered and practice-based pedagogy. This brings him more into line with

Rousseau's ideal (and modern pedagogy) than any other instructor at Hogwarts. Harry's teaching is based on his belief that his fellow pupils are not only competent and capable of defending themselves but also able to perform even advanced and difficult moves such as the Patronus Charm.

Rethinking Pedagogy

Harry teaches the members of Dumbledore's Army how to work defensive spells successfully, but he also makes mistakes throughout the novel, including a lack of trust. Most notably, Harry refuses to trust Snape, although Dumbledore insistently trusts him (*OotP* 555). Harry is also too convinced that his experience is unique. Deceased Slytherin and former Hogwarts Headmaster Phineas Nigellus chastises Harry and "all young people" for their audacity in believing that they alone have all the answers (*OotP* 496). This could certainly be interpreted as adolescent sense of uniqueness and certainty, but it is also part of a learning process that involves the acceptance of the complex nature of his relationship with the people surrounding him. Throughout *Order of the Phoenix* and the entire series, Harry repeatedly faces decisions that (as the editors of *Teaching Harry Potter* put it) are "not delineated in 'either/or' terms" (Belcher and Stephenson 4). Moral categories of good and bad are fundamental to the world views of Harry and his friends, but as they "*think* through their problems, usually in a group process," they must continually adjust to the fact that those around them are neither all good nor all bad, and that the motives and actions often fall on a spectrum of ethical behavior (Belcher and Stephenson 5). They must try to resolve this issue collectively (Kern 233–35). Sirius's statement that "the world isn't split into good people and Death Eaters" (*OotP* 302) makes clear that Umbridge is not an overt supporter of Voldemort but also addresses a broader philosophical point about our capability to make good or bad choices.

Dolores Umbridge's pedagogy fails largely because she is more interested in discipline and conformity than in teaching skills. Together with the aforementioned forms of resistance, this misplaced aim makes the reign of her authoritarian-style pedagogy at Hogwarts short-lived. But Umbridge's regime demonstrates how easily pedagogy can turn into its opposite: a medium for the mediation of false information, including false ideals of purity at the cost of marginalizing those who are "impure." The opposite of this repressive pedagogy, however, is also fragile: a notion of education without clear principles or rules other than aspiring to center students' wishes and identities.

Order of the Phoenix portrays all pedagogy as fallible. Even Harry leads his pupils in Dumbledore's Army into great danger in his misguided attempt to rescue Sirius. Dumbledore's confession of his own pedagogical errors near the end of *Order of the Phoenix* might at first lead readers to agree with scholars who argue that the novel ultimately re-establishes a comforting "status quo" in which "the inherently good adults take care of the adolescents" (Alkestrand 119). But instead, it illustrates that Dumbledore, too, is learning. In this way, Dumbledore and Harry enact Rousseau's model of teacher and student learning together (Rousseau 55, 261). Even in his explicatory final speech to Harry, a speech in which he admits he should have entrusted Harry with more information, Dumbledore refrains from telling his favorite student everything. Like Harry, readers will not learn the whole truth about the relationship between Harry and Voldemort, as well as the truths Dumbledore knows about Severus Snape, until the series' final volume.

Along with Firenze, Snape presents perhaps the most complicated and open-ended view of knowledge in the novel. While teaching Harry Occlumency, Snape explains that the "mind is not a book, to be opened at will and examined at leisure. Thoughts are not etched on the inside of skulls" (*OotP* 530). Implicitly this is a criticism of Umbridge's attempt to torturously rewrite Harry's sense of ethics via the magical quill (not unlike the writing machine in Kafka's "Penal Colony"). But Snape also teaches Harry that the complete contents of another person's mind (as well as of our own) resist legibility (or in the language of the novel, "legilimency," related to the Latin *legere*, "to read").

As part of this criticism of the written word, *Order of the Phoenix* also contains a critique of written media: the official newspaper *The Daily Prophet* is used for government propaganda and spreads lies, while the tabloid-like *Quibbler* prints an interview with Harry that allows him to tell his side of the story. In his explicatory confession to Harry near the end of the novel, Dumbledore forgoes written testimony and relies on the Pensieve instead, a magical memory instrument that relays information about the past in images and sound rather than text. This ability to rely on authentic images and sounds has its advantages. But even the Pensieve is constrained by being the representation of only one person's memories. The irony of these cautionary messages about the limits of text and representation being conveyed within a novel perhaps indicates Rowling's acknowledgment of the limits of her own methods.

Voldemort is fixated on obtaining the prophecy's record, its text, but he overlooks the role of choice, not fate, implied by the original spoken prophecy itself: it could have applied to one of two different boys. Voldemort decides to attack Harry who, as a "half-blood," resembles Voldemort himself more closely than does the other boy, the "pureblood" Neville Longbottom. This decision "marks" Harry "as his equal," thus inadvertently making Harry far more dangerous. Harry doubtless learns about the vexed intertwining of contingency and determinism from Dumbledore's tale of Trelawney's true prophecy. However, Trelawney's blatantly false sideshow-psychic predictions about dire illnesses or other catastrophes indirectly help teach Harry how *un*predictable the multidirectional consequences of each of our choices are. Voldemort, in contrast, conceives of the future as a prophecy—as a text that can no longer be changed.

Love and Pedagogy

The most powerful force in *Order of the Phoenix* and the entire *Harry Potter* series cannot be contained within textual boundaries or expressed fully in text. That force, love, is even more necessary for the resolution of the main conflicts in the *Harry Potter* cycle than is knowledge. But this love is often potentially linked to violence and proximate to death. *Order of the Phoenix* is the volume in which it becomes clearest that Voldemort and Harry are connected and in fact, that there is something of Voldemort actually within Harry (*OotP* 531). The text reveals that, like the centaurs, we may never fully understand the complete truth about the connections between past and future, between choice and contingency, and between hatred and love.

Even Dumbledore's mistakes, including his unwillingness to treat Harry as capable of knowing the full truth, are motivated out of love. In the language of a parent, he explains that he put Harry's emotional well-being over his need to know essential information (*OotP* 838). Dumbledore defends this action by declaring, "I defy anyone who has watched you as I have—and I have watched you more closely than you can have imagined—not to want to save you more pain than you had already suffered" (*OotP* 839). There are reasons to be skeptical of Dumbledore's words. His reference to watching Harry certainly indicates his own direct observation. But it also evokes his use of Fawkes, the Phoenix, as a form of surveillance technology. The name of the resistance group The Order of the Phoenix implies that order, or organization and discipline, are necessary for resistance to be effective. Fawkes maintains order by surveilling Umbridge for Dumbledore (*OotP* 474), but in *Chamber of Secrets* Dumbledore has Fawkes watch Harry, enabling the phoenix to save Harry in the Chamber. This is reminiscent of Foucault's link in *Discipline and Punish* between surveillance and the development of modern subjectivity. Surveillance, for Foucault, represents a shift from an overtly punishing, threatening "sovereign" form of power (arguably more typical of pre-modern societies) to an all-monitoring "disciplinary" form of power, which manipulates the subject into conforming to behavioral norms. Despite the prevalence of fascist behavior at Hogwarts, resistance (via love) is victorious.

Nevertheless, Dumbledore's speech evokes love as a power that can resist pedagogy, even as it emerges from within a pedagogical relationship (Dumbledore's to Harry) and environment (Hogwarts). In *Order of the Phoenix*, resistance to fascist and other poisonous pedagogy is an act of love for one's friends and fellow students and even teachers. But this love grows and even flourishes in an atmosphere of bad teaching. And although Dumbledore will soon leave Harry to learn more about love and about death without him, at the end of *Order of the Phoenix* love is a living, accessible, experiential power within Harry, his friends, and some of his teachers. It is also in part inaccessible: locked, as Dumbledore reveals, in a room in the Department of Mysteries (*OotP* 843–44), where it cannot be written, read, or taught.

NOTE

1. The term "inquisitor" is associated with the Spanish Inquisition and its persecution of anyone not following the Catholic faith. "High inquisitor" is also a title used in *Star Wars* for those fighting on the dark side (starwars.wikia.com/wiki/High_Inquisitor), as well as a figure in *World of Warcraft*. It may also be an allusion to Dostoyevsky's *The Brothers Karamazov* (see Bealer 188fn15).

WORKS CITED

Alkestrand, Malik. "Righteous Rebellion in Fantasy and Science Fiction: The Example of Harry Potter." *Hype: Bestsellers and Literary Culture*, edited by Jon Helgason, Sara Kärrholm, and Ann Steiner, Nordic Academic Press, 2014, pp. 109–26.

Ariès, Philippe. *Centuries of Childhood: A Social History of Family Life*. Translated by Robert Baldick, Knopf, 1962.

Bealer, Tracy L. "(Dis)Order and the Phoenix: Love and Political Resistance in Harry Potter." *Reading Harry Potter Again: New Critical Essays*, edited by Gizelle Liza Anatol, Praeger, 2009, pp.175–90.

Belcher, Catherine L., and Becky Herr Stephenson. "Introduction: Why Harry?" *Teaching Harry Potter: The Power of Imagination in Multicultural Classrooms*, edited by Catherine L. Belcher and Becky Herr Stephenson, Palgrave Macmillan, 2011, pp. 1–14.

Castro, Adam-Troy. "From Azkaban to Abu Ghraib: Fear and Fascism in Harry Potter and the Order of the Phoenix." *Mapping the World of Harry Potter*, edited by Mercedes Lackey and Leah Wilson, Bebella, 2006.

Foucault, Michel. *Discipline and Punish: The Birth of the Prison*. Translated by Alan Sheridan, Vintage, 1995.

Kafka, Franz. "In the Penal Colony." *The Metamorphosis and Other Stories*, edited by Ritchie Robertson, Translated by Joyce Crick, Oxford UP, 2009, pp. 75–99.

Kern, Edmund M. *The Wisdom of Harry Potter: What Our Favorite Hero Teaches Us About Moral Choices*. Prometheus, 2003.

Kittler, Friedrich A. *Discourse Networks 1800/1900*. Translated by Michael Metteer and Christ Cullens, Stanford UP, 1990.

Matthews, Susan R. "Ich Bin Ein Hufflepuff: Strategies for Variable Skill Management in J.K. Rowling's Harry Potter Novels." *Mapping the World of Harry Potter*, edited by Mercedes Lackey and Leah Wilson, Bebella, 2006, pp. 133–44.

Reagin, Nancy R. "Was Voldemort a Nazi? Death Eater Ideology and National Socialism." *Harry Potter and History*, edited by Nancy R. Reagin, Wiley, 2011, pp. 127–52.

Rousseau, Jean-Jacques. *Émile Ou De L'Éducation*. Garnier-Flammarion, 1966.

Rowling, J.K. *Harry Potter and the Order of the Phoenix*. Scholastic, 2003.

Rutschky, Katharina. "Einleitung." *Schwarze Pädagogik*. Quellen zur Naturgeschichte der bürgerlichen Erziehung. Ullstein, 1977, pp. xvii–lxxiv.

Fantastic Mentors and Where (Not) to Find Them

Defending Against the Dark Arts

Harry's Path from Pupil to Professor
in The Order of the Phoenix

LEE ANNA MAYNARD

Though the entire *Harry Potter* series is explicitly and implicitly concerned with education, J.K. Rowling's fifth book, *The Order of the Phoenix*, most pointedly reflects upon and interrogates the nature of teaching and learning. With the insertion of Dolores Umbridge into Hogwarts, Harry's beloved school is unyoked from the benevolent if distant supervision of the accepting and inclusive Albus Dumbledore and instead shackled to more-familiar preoccupations of the educational establishment: teaching to the test, standardization of curricula, and the monitoring and regulation of teachers and teaching styles. In the face of Umbridge's intrusive agenda in *Order of the Phoenix*, Harry becomes not just a consumer of education but also a producer, navigating the stumbling blocks and dangers of both Umbridge's style of education and her larger political plans while determining pathways to attain his and his friends' own goals.

With Umbridge's authority and agenda first and foremost in their minds, Harry and Hermione develop ongoing (and evolving) analyses of what content and presentation really mean to the educational experience throughout the novel. Harry, historically an indifferent pupil, suddenly cares deeply about teaching methods, largely because of his own elevation from student to educator. Umbridge's inspections of her fellow teachers provide Harry with a more analytical lens through which to view and assess the styles and choices of his teachers. As he tries to mold himself into an effective educator, Harry surveys the variants available at Hogwarts in much closer and more critical detail, sorting through what aspects of what classes and teachers provide useful models.

Once Harry takes on the mantle of teacher, leading Dumbledore's Army (the D.A.) in their secret Defense Against the Dark Arts (DADA) educational mission, the book generates pointed contrasts between student-centered experiential learning and the passive method Umbridge insists upon in her own courses, as well as her punitive and repressive classroom environment. Harry will become a measurably successful educator—as revealed first by his students' Ordinary Wizardly Level (O.W.L.) exam results but ultimately demonstrated by the survival of many of his peers-turned-students during the final Battle of Hogwarts. Harry's growth as a teacher manages to affirm what Rowling perhaps argues for throughout her novel-long pedagogical critique: the best teachers shape their content and style to their individual students' needs and learning styles, are motivated by a desire for student growth, and utilize a combination of the abstract and concrete in instruction.

Dolores Umbridge, She-Whose-Teaching-Practices-Must-Not-Be-Emulated

Student growth is demonstrably low on Dolores Umbridge's list of priorities. Umbridge is a central character for this educationally focused analysis and the central antagonist and generator of conflict for Rowling's entire novel. Despite abiding fears of Voldemort and the active threats and dangers he generates, it is truly Umbridge's particular brand of villainy that dominates the novel. She is a duly appointed and ostensibly legitimate instructor at the school; furthermore, she has the additional validity implied by her association with the Ministry and the Minister himself, Cornelius Fudge. Umbridge's power and ever-extending purview make her nearly unassailable, and her legitimacy is used to erode Harry's.

Unlike previous antipathetic professors in the series, Umbridge operates in the open, imposing scarring punishments, writing and enforcing restrictions, denying privileges, undermining previous support structures, and fostering an environment of surveillance and denouncements. Umbridge's *bona fides* come from within the institution and from without (and, she would argue, *above*). Umbridge's centrality to the novel's tensions and conflicts more deeply emanates from her performance of pedagogy and the pedagogical expectations she requires of other Hogwarts professors in her role as High Inquisitor. Umbridge's classroom is ground zero for the new Hogwarts she wishes to build.

In her usual protective coloration of fuzzy pink cardigan and black velvet bow, Umbridge opens her first DADA class for fifth-year students in what will become her characteristic style, demanding the students chant, in unison, "Good afternoon, Professor Umbridge" (*OotP* 239). The students are initially concerned by this infantilizing expectation but soon thoroughly disenchanted by her directive "Wands away and quills out, please" (*OotP* 239). Umbridge lays out her plan to pursue "a carefully structured, theory-centered, Ministry-approved course of defensive magic" (*OotP* 240) with course objectives that focus entirely on theory. Umbridge attempts to forestall and thwart any discussion of the objectives, first by ignoring Hermione's raised hand and then by diminishing the validity of her voice and perspective since the girl lacks Ministry credentials and pedagogical authority (*OotP* 242).

Umbridge's reliance on hierarchical authority and presumed expertise align her with two particular manifestations of the five teaching styles delineated, influentially, by psychologist Anthony F. Grasha in the 1990s. In "A Matter of Style," Grasha describes the Expert, the Formal Authority, the Personal Model, the Facilitator, and the Delegator. Grasha claims that the most-effective teacher will combine these styles and adapt them to context and subject matter; in Umbridge, we can find manifestations only of the Expert and the Formal Authority. In the classroom, the Expert prioritizes maintaining her status as an expert, while the Formal Authority is critically "concerned with the 'correct, acceptable, and standard ways to do things'" (143). Though she tracks with these elements of the Expert and the Formal Authority, Umbridge lacks some of the other primary qualities of these two types of teachers, which include demonstrable subject-matter expertise and a desire to provide useful feedback to students. Umbridge unerringly finds the least-educational elements of these teaching styles and deploys them in her rigidly passive, nearly silent classroom.

Umbridge disingenuously tries to reframe and recontextualize DADA as a theory class, one that involves no practical application because there is no classroom or real-life context for practical application. In addition to minimizing the prospective impact of Dumbledore-friendly trained wizards, the Ministry wants to utilize Umbridge's position of educational authority to promote their propaganda talking points: Voldemort has not returned, the Death Eaters have not reconvened, and thus students are not in harm's way outside Hogwarts. Inside the classroom, Umbridge first attempts to laugh off the idea of needing to protect oneself during a DADA class meeting, and then, when that gambit appears to fail, she embraces the notion that the students have indeed been endangered during previous iterations of the DADA class in earlier years with their exposure to "some very irresponsible wizards" (*OotP* 243). As more students voice questions and concerns, Umbridge reveals the core of her educational philosophy as theoretical and test-based. Umbridge, and thus the Ministry, claims to believe that school's purpose is—and students' goals should be—merely to pass tests, not to actively learn (*OotP* 243).

Rather than desiring her students' mastery of subject-matter content in any sort of deep, lasting, and meaningful way, Umbridge's philosophical statements and pedagogical approach reveal she is instead invested in a power dynamic that solidifies her dominance and total authority. She avoids discussion, rejects student engagement, and fosters an atmosphere hostile to questions and critical thinking. In what will become almost a mantra for the class, the students are told to read from their books silently, and the class settles into an atmosphere of disengagement (*OotP* 240). The stultifying "torpor" is jarred by Hermione, who alerts her classmates to the real thrust of Umbridge's policies, questioning the absence of application of defensive spells in the course. In future lessons, as is her wont, Umbridge continues to assign reading to be done silently during class, with wands safely stowed away, and any questions stymied.

When Hermione attempts again to engage both with the assigned text and Umbridge, the professor dismisses her opinion. Umbridge then affirms her concept of her teaching post and its approach: "I am here to teach you using a Ministry-approved method that does not include inviting students to give their opinions on matters about which they understand very little" (*OotP* 317). Instead of engaging students by proposing real-world applications of the course content, Umbridge makes a point of divorcing theory and praxis (*OotP* 244). The Ministry-approved pedagogical approach, and Umbridge's ideal, is a silent class, where the instructor tasks the students and eventually assesses their attainment of the assigned material, either through homework completed outside of class or a test completed (again, silently) during class. Students are expected to memorize what they read and to accept its legitimacy without comment. The memorization does not serve as the foundation for synthesis, application, or execution; instead, students in Umbridge's class are to remain safely on the bottom tier of Bloom's taxonomy, far from evaluation or analysis. They are merely what Eric Gill, in his analysis of teaching styles and philosophies, would identify as "empty vessels," with their minds needing to be filled by the expert—in this case, Slinkhard's textbook.

Between Hermione's questions and the students' voicing a fairly uniform desire for practical application and opportunities for practice, an astute educator with a focus on higher-level learning would identify her class's need for a different pedagogical model. Instead of solely conforming to key aspects of Grasha's Expert and Formal Authority approaches, an effective DADA instructor would incorporate elements of his Personal Model, Facilitator, and Delegator roles. The Personal Model encourages students to observe the instructor and then emulate, while a Facilitator develops students' abilities to analytically approach the material and fosters their ability to act independently (Grasha 143). The Delegator clusters students into groups or has individuals work on projects, with an emphasis on independent learning (Grasha

143). Especially in a class like DADA that has historically wed theory, content, and practical application, the advantages of an environment that asks students to assess context and situation, analyze options, and correctly apply the best approach are clear. Umbridge, of course, does not desire a truly effective learning environment.

It is Umbridge's philosophical and pedagogical approach to the DADA course that mobilizes Hermione, who then goes on to recruit Harry for his new role as unofficial professor. While Harry rages against Umbridge's unjust policies and Ron just shrugs his shoulders and accepts that they are stuck with her because of her ministry connections, Hermione proposes a solution, at least to part of their problem (*OotP* 325). She floats the idea that they should learn DADA themselves with "a teacher, a proper one, who can show us how to use the spells and correct us if we're going wrong" (*OotP* 325). Ron's awareness and seeming acceptance of the confluence of the Ministry and Hogwarts, as embodied in Dolores Umbridge, resonates with Roni Natov's argument in "Harry Potter and the Extraordinariness of the Ordinary" that the entire *Harry Potter* series highlights the "rigidity and fraudulence embedded in our institutions, particularly the school" (327). Hermione is not content to accept the fraud, however. As the boys mull over her proposal, Hermione launches her suggestion of the right person to be the "proper," non–Umbridge teacher: Harry.

Floored by the prospect, Harry lists all the reasons he is an inappropriate choice: that he is not a teacher; that Hermione is better at everything, academically; and that his survival and success have depended on luck and timely intervention, not actual skill. Hermione and Ron counterargue, noting that Harry is the best at Defense Against the Dark Arts both in terms of test results and what Harry has accomplished, such as saving the Sorcerer's Stone, killing the basilisk, fighting off dementors, and surviving Voldemort's attempts on his life (*OotP* 327). Harry initially reacts angrily to his friends' praise, but as the idea marinates, he begins to seriously entertain it, even considering curriculum (*OotP* 331). Harry, though initially discounting himself, begins to realize that he does have experience and knowledge the other students both lack and need; thus, we can identify him as equipped to function as Grasha's Expert, one with valid claims to expertise (Grasha 143) as opposed to Umbridge.

When Hermione organizes the exploratory meeting at the Hog's Head, Harry hears from a range of his classmates of his perceived fitness to teach based on real-world application of DADA theory. Susan Bones and the Weasley twins attest to his Patronus-producing skill, Neville notes his saving of the Sorcerer's Stone, and Cho cites his performance in the Triwizard Tournament (*OotP* 342). These testimonials show that Harry also qualifies as Grasha's Formal Authority, one who can base instructional fitness on the status he holds among his prospective students (Grasha 143). In contrast, Hermione classifies Umbridge's instruction as "rubbish" (*OotP* 339), and Ernie Macmillan echoes the ineffectiveness of Umbridge's pedagogical approach, finding it especially frustrating in the face of all the other professors' insistence on the importance of performing well on O.W.L.s.

Harry's Alternative Pedagogical Models

As Harry contemplates his move from learner to teacher, he has years of experiences in Hogwarts classrooms to sift through for examples of what he finds engaging, instructive, and effective from his student perspective. His own triumphs and failures in the classroom will direct his teaching, and he considers how they relate in each case to such variables as his own effort, his desire for success, his perception of the possibility of success, and his sense of the relevance of the subject/content, as well as the instructor's manner of teaching. Models of what to do and what not to do abound, but a heightened attention to and awareness of pedagogical philosophies and practice is efficiently generated in *Order of the Phoenix* through Dolores Umbridge's insertion (and often intrusion) into classroom contexts where previously, familiarity with the teachers and their styles had blunted Harry's evaluation and conscious assessment. Umbridge's queries, reactions, and pronouncements help shape Harry's own critical lens, sometimes through comparison but often through contrast. Her inspections will highlight both what she claims are the significant facets of educational effectiveness and what Harry and Hermione, present for many of her inspections, determine to be the important qualities in a teacher and a learning environment, thus helping shape Harry's pedagogical approaches as he teaches his clandestine DADA class. Umbridge inspects Care of Magical Creatures classes taught by both Grubbly-Plank and Hagrid, Snape's Potions class, McGonagall's Transfiguration class, and Trelawney's Divination class, all with Harry and/or Hermione as unauthorized secondary observers.

Sybill Trelawney's Divination class offers Harry's first opportunity to witness an Umbridge inspection, and his sympathies reside with neither the inspector nor the inspected. Trelawney's history of predicting Harry's imminent demise, as well as her historically frustrating approach to assessing his abilities, have not endeared her to him. Umbridge takes a prominent seat near Trelawney's desk initially and then follows her around the classroom, taking notes on her clipboard while listening to Trelawney's conversations with students and posing her own questions. Umbridge questions the Divination teacher about her experience, the tenure of her employment, and her heritage (*OotP* 314). Umbridge also demands a demonstration of expertise, requiring Trelawney to make a prediction, which the Divination professor weakly attempts (*OotP* 315). Hermione has long given up Divination as a worthless course, partly because it seems to offer no concrete basis for assessment and evaluation. While some scholars, such as Mary S. Black and Marilyn J. Eisenwine offer a more charitable interpretation of Trelawney, Hermione labels her "an absolutely appalling teacher" (*OotP* 365). Harry struggles with the course's vagueness, too; Harry and Ron both consider Trelawney "an old fraud" (*OotP* 366), and their disdain stems from Trelawney's pedagogical choices as well as the nature of the subject matter itself.

On her observation day, Trelawney, who usually tries to embody a mystic presence in her clothing and tones, instructs students to use their copies of *The Dream Oracle*, one of their textbooks, to aid in interpreting dreams they recorded outside of class in their dream diaries. The students work in small groups or pairs, with Trelawney circulating to probe or offer guidance. This seems a reasonable plan, on the face of it, for Divination instruction, as Trelawney has students utilize real-world and personally significant content, their own dreams, as the source material for an in-class hands-on exploration of the concepts and techniques outlined in the course's instructional texts. Theoretically, this approach should allow for student engagement and active learning. However, few of the students find the class interesting or instructive, so things go off the rails, pedagogically. First, the course material is, by definition, more accessible to some students than others—after all, as Trelawney and Umbridge's exchange seems to establish, you are born with prophetic sight or you are not. Secondly, the content students are expected to generate, both in terms of the raw material of dreams and the analytical element of dream interpretation, is intangible, vague, and unreliably produced. Many students are forced to falsify their dreams, thus debasing the potential validity of the entire interpretive process. Finally, the instructor's questions and guidance, rather than detecting the falsehood, signify she is unaware of the students' creative license, thereby undercutting her own expertise in the subject matter.

Harry can learn much from his heightened attention to Trelawney's teaching: in his own DADA class, it will be important not only to demonstrate expertise in the subject matter but also to reinforce the content's significance and attainability. He emphasizes that students both need to learn it and actually can learn it. Umbridge's inspection results both in Trelawney's probation and in future lessons conducted under the High Inquisitor's watchful eye. In the probationary period, when Trelawney has the supposed opportunity to demonstrate improvement, Umbridge contributes to the Divination teacher's further pedagogical unspooling, peppering Trelawney with complicated questions in the midst of her lectures and insisting Trelawney "predict students' answers before they gave them" (*OotP* 552). Even a confident and competent teacher would find these interruptions distracting, and Umbridge's active and public eroding of Trelawney's supposed Expert status shakes Trelawney to the core.

Umbridge next inspects Transfiguration teacher Minerva McGonagall, and Harry and Ron eagerly anticipate Umbridge's comeuppance, as McGonagall is a formidable presence in the classroom (*OotP* 319). McGonagall's classroom management skills and confidence are immediately observable, as she tasks one student with returning graded papers and another with handing out the mice to be used in the day's hands-on lesson, while the other students quickly hush and prepare to work. The High Inquisitor does not follow the students' cues, though, insistently interrupting Professor McGonagall with tiny faux coughs ("hem, hem") until McGonagall corrects her: "I wonder … how you expect to gain an idea of my usual teaching methods if you continue to interrupt me? You see, I do not generally permit people to talk when I am talking" (*OotP* 320). She refuses to allow Umbridge to dominate her class, relegating her to furious scribbling in a corner as the Transfiguration professor conducts her class as usual.

McGonagall explains how this day's lesson is scaffolded onto the previous class meeting's content, with an amplification of the concept, an increase in difficulty in the attempted task, and additional practice time. She circulates to correct students, guide their practice, and keep them on-track and on-task in what is typically a "busy" classroom as they attempt to vanish their mammalian subjects. Transfiguration students learn concepts, explore them through out-of-class essays, and practice executing them during class and under her watchful eye before being released to practice the spells on their own after class. McGonagall's field, unlike Trelawney's, does produce concrete results that are visibly right or wrong, which certainly is a pedagogical advantage. However, her credibility is also enhanced by students' appreciation that she has a history of being tough but fair. She is not overly positive in her commentary to students, but she does encourage those who, like Neville, lack confidence. McGonagall suggests that focused practice and conscientious application should always result in skill attainment, whereas Trelawney's shifting evaluations and either-you've-got-it-or-you-don't subject matter cannot offer students the same assurance. Harry can learn much from McGonagall, with her insistence on students' individual focus, their hands-on practice, and their ability to tackle increasingly difficult content, and he will incorporate these elements into his own classroom.

Care of Magical Creatures is the next course on Umbridge's inspection list, and she first observes it as instructed by substitute teacher Professor Grubbly-Plank. "Well, *you* seem to know what you're doing, at any rate," Umbridge opines at the end of the class (*OotP* 323). Grubbly-Plank's inspected lesson appears to be of a piece with the first lesson Harry and friends have with her. In that lesson on bowtruckles, Grubbly-Plank first identifies the existing level of student knowledge about the subject, then provides positive feedback for the student (Hermione, of course) who correctly answers her questions, expounds upon the information, and warns students of potential dangers posed by bowtruckles. She then assigns them to observe, sketch, and identify the anatomy of the creatures, offering techniques and materials for placating the creatures during the students' observation to generate a safer learning environment. Though Harry is injured during the lesson, he acknowledges it is the effect of his not following Grubbly-Plank's instructions carefully enough. Though his loyalty to Hagrid prevents his expressing it, Harry is "fully aware that he had just experienced an exemplary Care of Magical Creatures lesson" (*OotP* 261). Harry notes practices and qualities he would be wise to incorporate into his own teaching, such as generating a responsive environment driven by the content the teacher needs to convey, a desire for the students' safety, and an awareness of the students' rate of acquisition.

Harry's displeasure stems from his unarticulated anxiety that a competently taught Care of Magical Creatures class generates a negative comparison to Hagrid's typical class. Umbridge's observation of Grubbly-Plank's lesson establishes a baseline performance Harry fears Hagrid will not be able to match. Hagrid's instructional history has been fraught, but Harry, Ron, and, usually, Hermione, are among Hagrid's greatest supporters. Harry often steps up during Care of Magical Creatures classes to interact with the creatures, to be the first to follow through on Hagrid's instructions, and to attempt to diminish or defuse student complaints.

Though Hagrid's expertise in the subject is clear—he has an extensive knowledge of magical creatures and many years of experience with their management under a wide variety of circumstances—this core credibility is often clouded by other pedagogical factors. Consistently, Hagrid inaccurately gauges student knowledge, interest, and ability, assigning off-putting texts and requiring behaviors the students consider dangerous, disgusting, or pointless. Hagrid's textbook of choice in Harry's third year, *The Monster Book of Monsters*, is emblematic of the disconnect between the instructor's values and aims and student perception. Whereas Hagrid finds the text informative and easily managed, students such as Harry encounter a text that seems openly antagonistic, snarling and snapping when they attempt to open or read it. Hagrid's instructional life seems plagued by this gap between professor-perspective and student-perspective, where his skill with and admiration for magical creatures consistently clouds his ability to envision a student motivated only by a desire to pass the class and remain relatively uninjured. Andrea Bixler characterizes Hagrid's assigning of *The Monster Book of Monsters* as a "practical pre-test," a good pedagogical move by Hagrid in theory, but a bad one in practice, as "an assessment that every student fails is not an ideal way" to begin the term (76). This task moves beyond challenging to impossible, considering the "students' level of knowledge, interest, and skills" (Bixler 76). In this example from Harry's third year, Hagrid is surprised and disappointed that no students have completed their assigned readings, as they have had to strap the book shut out of fear and desperation. To Hagrid, making the book cooperate is simple and intuitive: one must merely stroke its spine.

Hagrid's classes are typically light on information and clearly stated goals and heavy on hands-on activity. Hagrid is unable to view magical creatures other than through his own lens of appreciation and connoisseurship, while students react to the creatures' frightening or disgusting appearances, defensive mechanisms, and care and feeding requirements quite differently. Blast-Ended Skrewts offer a relevant example of these divergent perspectives. While almost all of the courses students can take at Hogwarts generate risk, students typically seem unconcerned for their safety, which implies other professors are able to create learning environments that are interpreted by the students as fairly safe, regulated, and protected. The exchange of "gloomy looks" and the shaking of heads by his classmates when Hagrid returns indicates what Harry fears, that "many of them preferred Professor Grubbly-Plank's lessons, and the worst of it was that a very small, unbiased part of him knew that they had good reason" (*OotP* 442). Harry worries for Hagrid's job because he knows, from a pedagogical standpoint, Grubbly-Plank is a more effective teacher who creates a safer and more instructive environment than Hagrid, whose intoxication with the creatures he introduces prevents his communicating to students the purpose of their learning or a sense of their safety when taking his class.

Based on their experiences of Hagrid's teaching methods and of Umbridge's inspections, Harry and Hermione attempt to steer him toward less threatening waters, pedagogically. They encourage him to introduce less-dangerous creatures and generally play it safe: Hermione argues that Hagrid should teach to the test, but Hagrid rejects her approach as boring and claims "I wouldn' give yeh anything' dangerous! I mean, all righ', they can look after themselves" (*OotP* 439). The gulf between Hagrid's assessment of appropriate creatures and anyone else's classification of them appears almost unbridgeable.

When Umbridge inspects Hagrid's version of Care of Magical Creatures, he has taken his fifth-year students into the Forbidden Forest to encounter creatures invisible to most of them. Hagrid involves the students, asking who can see the creatures and then determining base-level knowledge by asking for more information once he names them as thestrals. Next, he explains the creatures' utility, tries to dispel some prejudice and misinformation, and begins to detail their rarity. What he planned for any active learning is unknown, as Umbridge's inspection quickly becomes insulting, intrusive, and derailing. She hijacks Hagrid's class and soon enlists student co-conspirators. She interrupts him mid-thought, employs a "loud, slow voice" when speaking to Hagrid, and pretends to be unable to discern his communications in response to her (*OotP* 447). Malfoy, Pansy Parkinson, and other Slytherins pile on, telling Umbridge, for her report, that Hagrid's lecture "sounds ... like grunting a lot of the time" (*OotP* 448). Enraged, Hermione complains that without Umbridge's interference, this had promised to be an effective and appropriate lesson (*OotP* 450). As Hermione observes, this Care of Magical Creatures lesson was especially competent, and Harry could look to at least the first part of it for a positive model for his own teaching, as Hagrid demonstrated the relevance of the day's content, established parameters for safety, and planned some sort of hands-on learning for the students.

Umbridge's negative evaluation of Hagrid is a forgone conclusion, but her inspection of Snape is less predictable. Snape's educational credentials are in order. His Death Eater history seems a strike against him, but he has fourteen years of teaching experience. Pedagogically, Snape's observed lesson is a continuation of a previous day's content, the second half of a modified version of the process of gradual release of responsibility, whereby "cognitive work should shift ... from teacher modeling, to joint responsibility between teacher and students, to independent practice and application by the learner" (Frey and Fisher). Snape's compressed version of gradual release—a not-so-gradual release—involves briefly explaining the effects and properties of the potion under study (often on the heels of a familiarizing homework assignment), producing detailed instructions for the potion's composition, circulating around the dungeon to provide needs-based additional guidance, and then providing commentary and assessment of each student's finished product. Students who do not meet expectations during class are often instructed to reproduce the product on their own for homework or otherwise remediate through reading or essay-writing assignments. Snape's credibility, in terms of his subject-matter expertise, is high with his students, and they take seriously his displeasure or concerns.

However, some students find it difficult or impossible to succeed in Snape's course, despite the tangible and concrete nature of their skill development and active learning. Harry and Neville Longbottom are among the most notable examples. In one characteristic class meeting, Snape publicly "taunt[s]" Harry by asking if he can read, makes Harry loudly state to the class that he has not adequately followed instructions, labels his potion an "utterly worthless" "mess," and vanishes what Harry has been laboring over for the last forty-five minutes (*OotP* 234). Melissa Johnson usefully clarifies the difference between how Snape's ostensibly "active" learning methods might sound, on paper, and how they are executed: Snape's students are required to "practice" potion-making but "are not actually given instruction or advice ... in doing so" (83). Andrea Bixler agrees, clearly thinking of Snape when characterizing a typical Hogwarts classroom as a place where "students practice skills more than they strive to understand theory ... [which is] obvious time and again when professors tell them nothing other than to follow instructions printed on the board" (75). Snape's observation of students' progress and choices and his circulation around the classroom while they work seem focused on noting and criticizing deviations from the prescribed steps rather than encouraging their critical thinking or deeper understanding. Snape's clear favoritism for Slytherin students, his noted antipathy towards Gryffindors, and his scathing commentary about underperforming students further undermine what would have appeared, in lesson-plan form, to be an effective pedagogical approach.

Unfortunately for Harry, his exposure to Snape's brand of persecutional pedagogy is not limited to Potions classes: Dumbledore tasks Snape with teaching Harry Occlumency in private lessons. To add insult to injury, Harry must call these "remedial Potions" lessons to preserve secrecy. At Harry's first private lesson, Snape does, under intense questioning from Harry, answer basic informative and conceptual questions about Occlumency, Legilimency, and the real-life conditions and applications that warrant Harry's developing a skill set in this field. Also, he takes the logical next step, which is determining Harry's baseline resistance to the mind-probing of Legilimency. However, his approach here destabilizes the entire rest of the proposed pedagogical project. Harry feels unprepared and besieged: "Snape had struck before Harry was ready, before Harry had even begun to summon any force of resistance" (OotP 534). He knows the painful memories Snape uncovers bring Snape pleasure and might easily feed future scornful (public) attacks in Potions class. Snape does label Harry's first attempt at resistance "not as poor as it might have been," but he proceeds to renew his efforts despite Harry's plea for additional guidance (OotP 535). Every word out of Snape's mouth, every insult and abstract instruction, contributes to Harry's sense that these lessons amount to little more than torture at Snape's hands, not a legitimate educational experience. After this initial lesson, rather than appearing to be shored up against theoretical assaults from Voldemort, Harry is instead "shivery," "almost feverish," and looking "very white," with pain shooting through his scar. Future Occlumency lessons make Harry feel weaker, less able to protect his mind and memories, and Ron broaches the concern perhaps on readers' minds at this point in the series: is Snape actually trying to help Harry? In other words, is Snape a teacher invested in Harry's success or in his failure? When Harry works with his D.A. peers, he will carefully avoid the appearance of persecuting students, enjoying their failures, or reveling in his own superiority. His actions are calculated to help his students feel he wants them to learn.

Harry's Teaching: A Best-Practices Amalgam

As Harry approaches taking on the mantle of instructor for the D.A., he is aware, thanks to his own recent and current experiences as a student, of the importance of a teacher who does not merely make subject-matter content available to students but who is invested in their success. Harry identifies teacher characteristics and pedagogical approaches he wishes to emulate as well as those he determines to jettison. To Harry's mind, important elements to include in his class are concept and execution explanations, discussion of real-world applications, teacher modeling, and teacher-guided student practice. He is invested in generating a classroom environment that emphasizes safety and encourages progress through positive feedback. He rejects all characteristics and practices associated with Umbridge's classroom—an authoritarian structure, passive memorization, and minimal teacher involvement—as well as the more-negative aspects of Trelawney's, Hagrid's, and Snape's classrooms environments, including unclear goals and aims, a sense of clear and present endangerment, insufficient teacher-led instruction, hypercritical teacher feedback, and insufficient differentiation.

Of his current teachers, Professor McGonagall offers the closest facsimile to the learning environment Harry aims to engender. Like McGonagall, he embodies expertise in the subject matter and offers his own demonstrations of spells done correctly; he convinces students he is invested in their progress; and he attempts to provide strong theoretical and practical foundations for the active learning he will encourage. Unlike McGonagall, Harry strikes a more consistently positive and encouraging tone and wisely approaches his students more as a peer coach and facilitator than a professor. His total rejection of anything approaching Professor Umbridge's authoritarian model or even McGonagall's authoritative model is signaled by his egalitarian election to be leader of the D.A., as well as by his generally being able to rely on other students to offer attitude or behavior corrections rather than having to administer them himself. Harry is solely responsible for the curricular direction of the class, and he starts the first lesson with *Expelliarmus*, the Disarming Charm. He first offers, neatly in one package, a demonstration of his fitness to teach and a real-world application of the spell, noting, "It saved my life last June" when facing Voldemort (*OotP* 392). Harry then circulates, offering corrections and encouragement. After completing a class-wide circuit, Harry gets their attention as a group, briefly re-instructs, and urges them to try again. Throughout the D.A. meetings, he uses most of his allotted time for students' active learning, letting them familiarize themselves with not only the effects of casting spells but also of being on the receiving end of some of them.

To remedy the deficits or stumbling blocks to learning he has discerned in other professors' classes, Harry works to generate a safe space for learning—both physically and psychologically—and to differentiate between student ability levels and learning needs. While Hagrid's students fear for their physical safety and Snape's must guard their self-concept and self-esteem, Harry wants to create a place where these barriers to understanding and execution are removed. In addition to having books to aid their theory and padding to break their falls in the Room of Requirement, Harry's safe space features Harry's tone, one more encouraging than many of his classmates are educationally accustomed to. When Neville disarms Harry under unfair conditions, rather than diminishing his friend's accomplishment, Harry proclaims "Good one!" (*OotP* 393). Harry regularly tells the class they have made good progress, and he feels proud as he watches his students practice (*OotP* 454). At the final meeting of the D.A. before their discovery by Umbridge, Harry endeavors to contextualize their achievements without dampening their pleasure and enthusiasm at their own progress. He emphasizes the difference between the safety of the classroom and the real-world factors that would make the spell harder to execute (*OotP* 606). Harry's expertise and experience continually temper his teaching, as he knows on-the-ground, real-world applications of DADA practices are complicated by timing, fight-or-flight responses, and other factors, and he thus does his best to suggest realistic applications to his students.

Beyond his practices of affirmation, differentiation is important in Harry's classroom, too. Initially, Harry works most with Neville, who is usually the least-impressive student in a class (except Herbology). Johnson aptly labels Neville a barometer of "the impact course climate can have on learning" (84). His seemingly natural aptitude with Herbology, for example, is perhaps just as much a result of the nurturing and supportive environment Professor Sprout creates. With the mass breakout from Azkaban, Neville finds a new level of intensity with his D.A. training, and Harry recognizes and instructionally accommodates the shifting of gears Neville undergoes. When some students, like Cho Chang, are disconcerted by his watching their performance, he makes certain to assess their progress from across the room when they are unaware to determine what needs remediation versus what is merely a product of discomfort or performance anxiety. Harry is especially attuned to this not only from his own Potions experiences but also from the extracurricular struggles Ron has faced in this novel with his Quidditch performance. Though Harry assigns all students the same ultimate goals, he adjusts who is working with whom and what they need to focus on based on his observation of their facility with any given spell.

Harry's short-term pedagogical goal is helping the D.A. prepare for the practical component of the DADA O.W.L. His longer-term goal is helping the D.A. members protect themselves in a climate growing ever darker and more dangerous. Both of those aims are largely achieved. Despite the D.A.'s exposure to Dolores Umbridge, Harry has the satisfaction of performing defensive spells to the applause of the official examiners right in front of her during his O.W.L. practical portion, and he learns later that many of his students performed admirably on their DADA practical tests. In the ultimate test, in *Deathly Hallows*, not all of his original D.A. members survive the climactic Battle of Hogwarts (Fred Weasley and Lavender Brown are notable examples of those who do not), but many do. Not long after the O.W.L. for DADA, Luna Lovegood, Neville Longbottom, and Ginny Weasley accompany Harry, Hermione, and Ron on a rescue mission to the Ministry of Magic. These rescuers are, to an extent, rescued themselves when adult members of the Order of the Phoenix arrive to extricate them from Voldemort's trap, but overall, they make an admirable showing of both ability and preparedness in the face of an unpredictable and deeply dangerous setting for utilizing their DADA training, another feather in Harry's cap as an instructor.

Renee Dickinson rates Harry the third-best instructor in all the *Harry Potter* series, coming in only behind Dumbledore and Lupin, primarily because of his skill set gleaned from life experiences with the subject matter but also because of his educational exposure to the aforementioned professors. Some readers might disagree with this ranking, but Harry's move from pupil to instructor is undoubtedly successful. His transition is fueled by a desire to help his students learn, grow, and survive, and it is shaped by his jettisoning of that which he disapproves in his own professors in *Order of the Phoenix*: ineffective pedagogical techniques, abrasive or inhibiting styles, and restrictive, non-nurturing classroom environments.

By all reasonable metrics for the subject matter, Harry proves himself to have been an effective educator. His students not only academically survive major examinations but actively survive real-life Dark Arts situations, thanks to their preparation. Harry's classroom, thus, is a space where real learning takes place, not merely the temporary acquisition of content for an assessment. After his term of instruction ends, students can recall their course content, even under highly stressful and uncontrolled circumstances, and they can deploy it fluidly and creatively. Harry is able to view the array of pedagogical approaches at Hogwarts anew his fifth year, under the lens of Umbridge's observational microscope, and he thereby brings a heightened awareness and analysis to how teachers' choices and decisions affect student engagement and learning outcomes. Thanks to Harry (and Hermione's) utter rejection of Umbridge's pedagogy and teaching philosophy, a vibrant—if secret—learning community is born amidst the ideological and educational wasteland the High Inquisitor wishes to engender at the new and ostensibly improved Hogwarts.

WORKS CITED

Bixler, Andrea. "What We Muggles Can Learn About Teaching from Hogwarts." *The Clearing House*, vol. 84, no. 2, 2011, pp. 75–79. *Academic Search Complete*, doi: 10.1080/00098655. 2010.507825.

Black, Mary S., and Marilyn J. Eisenwine. "Education of the Young Harry Potter: Socialization and Schooling for Wizards." *The Educational Forum*, vol. 66, no. 1, 2001, pp. 32–37. *Taylor and Francis Journals Complete*, doi: 10.1080/00131720108984797.

Dickinson, Renee. "Harry Potter Pedagogy: What We Learn About Teaching and Learning from J.K. Rowling." *The Clearing House*, vol. 79, no. 6, 2006, pp. 240–244. *JSTOR*, www-jstor-org.ezproxy.augusta.edu/stable/30182136.

Frey, Nancy, and Douglas Fisher. "Gradual Release of Responsibility Instructional Framework." *Formative Assessment and the Common Core Standards: English Language Arts/Literacy.* pdo.ascd.org/lmscourses/pd13oc005/media/ formativeassessmentandcc swithelaliteracymod_3-reading3.pdf.

Gill, Eric. "What Is Your Teaching Style? Five Effective Teaching Methods for Your Classroom." *Room 241*, Concordia University–Portland, 21 Aug. 2018, education.cu-portland. edu/blog/classroom-resources/5-types-of-classroom-teaching-styles/.

Grasha, Anthony F. "A Matter of Style: The Teacher as Expert, Formal Authority, Personal Model, Facilitator, and Delegator." *College Teaching*, vol. 42, no. 4, Fall 1994, pp. 142–149. *JSTOR*, www.jstor.org/stable/27558675.

Johnson, Melissa. "Wands or Quills? Lessons in Pedagogy from Harry Potter." *The CEA Forum*, vol. 44, no. 2, Summer-Fall 2015, pp. 75–91, journals.tdl.org/ceaforum/index. php/ceaforum/article/view/7061.

Natov, Roni. "Harry Potter and the Extraordinariness of the Ordinary." *The Lion and the Unicorn*, vol. 25, no. 2, 2001, pp. 310–327. *Project Muse*, muse.jhu.edu/ezproxy.augusta. edu/article/35514.

Rowling, J.K. *Harry Potter and the Chamber of Secrets.* Levine, 1999.

———. *Harry Potter and the Deathly Hallows.* Levine, 2007.

———. *Harry Potter and the Goblet of Fire.* Levine, 2000.

———. *Harry Potter and the Order of the Phoenix.* Levine, 2003.

———. *Harry Potter and the Prisoner of Azkaban.* Levine, 1999.

———. *Harry Potter and the Sorcerer's Stone.* Levine, 1997.

Harry Potter's Pedagogical Paradigm

Multiple Mentors Maketh the Man

MARY REDING

Every year, as Wizard and Muggle parents alike wave their magical prog-
eny off from Platform 9¾, a new term at Hogwarts School for Witchcraft
and Wizardry begins, and with it, a new adventure for Harry Potter and his
friends. At its core, the *Harry Potter* story is a serialized school days novel,
and Harry himself a schoolboy hero. Of course, the student-as-hero archetype
has long been considered a pillar of the *bildungsroman* tradition, instituted
centuries before J.K. Rowling would invent her magical young pupil. However,
the creation of Harry—and the scope and breadth of his namesake saga—
has also created an opportunity for expansion within this narrative tradition.
Unbounded by the confines of limited text, Harry enjoys the benefits of modern publishing, namely space and time (thousands of pages and nearly a
decade, respectively), which allow his school days tales to progress far beyond
the manifestations of previous generations. In perhaps no other aspect is this
evolution more conspicuous than the multitude of mentors Rowling provides
to guide Harry throughout his hero's journey.

Harry's heroics and ability to cross the thresholds of the Wizarding world,
traveling deeper within it with increasing proficiency, are facilitated by a diverse
cast of witches and wizards either much older, more experienced, or more
knowledgeable than himself. The frequency with which Rowling pairs Harry
with such figures signifies the boy's hero status and presages his eventual triumph. In each case, the facilitating character becomes a mentor to Harry: initiating him to magical modes and methods and bringing him deeper into the
heart of their realm. This recurring process of initiation, guidance, movement,
and mastery may be viewed not only as a classic example of the student-as-

155

hero-model, but also as a prototype for pedagogical success. Within the framework of these combined structures, Rowling applies the multiple mentor model to meaningful effect, furnishing Harry with an array of aides and supporters, the most significant of whom serve to guide him through the Wizarding World—beyond new thresholds and across the increasingly complex liminal spaces between them.

A Hero Needs a Mentor

According to structuralist theories of heroics pioneered throughout the 20th century by the likes of psychoanalyst Carl Jung, mythologist Joseph Campbell, and folklorist Vladimir Propp, the presence of a guide or mentor figure is essential to the development and success of a hero. The story is a universal one: hero meets mentor, then mentor guides hero through a series of trials from which hero emerges victorious. Medievalist Susan Yager affirms that "Harry's extended *bildungsroman* is an ideal example of the hero's journey monomyth described in Joseph Campbell's *Hero with a Thousand Faces*" (214). Indeed, the *Harry Potter* stories both exemplify the archetypal pairing of student and teacher as the preferred pedagogical paradigm of the hero narrative and manage to move beyond it. Achilles has Chiron, Arthur has Merlin, Bilbo and Frodo have Gandalf, and Luke Skywalker has Yoda. Harry has a horde.

While the typical hero is provisioned with one mentor to see him or her through, Rowling equips Harry with a generous assortment. More common definitions of mentorship—tutor, counselor, teacher, supporter, or wise friend—leave readers with a plethora of suitable characters from which to choose. Anyone who teaches Harry anything or looks out for him in any way could be considered a candidate. By this broad characterization the list of those qualified would be a long one, including the likes of Remus Lupin, Sirius Black, Barty Crouch, Jr., Alastor Moody, or Severus Snape, to name a few. How to narrow them to only the most critical, then? Here, Campbell's definition is most valuable. At the "First Threshold" to the "Otherworld" the hero is met with "a protective figure ... who provides the adventurer with amulets against the dragon forces he is about to pass" (Campbell 57–59). This characterization offers a simple yet specific set of parameters with which to work. According to the hero's journey paradigm a true mentor must (1) equip the hero with new knowledge or skills that (2) help the hero cross a new threshold/boundary and (3) move them beyond some difficulty or danger, deeper into the Otherworld. The transferal of the "amulets" of skills and knowledge from mentor to Harry must occur in order for Harry to "pass the dragon forces," moving ever deeper into the perilous realm of the wizarding world.

In these instances, the mentor figure serves not only to teach Harry, but also often to accompany and protect him. The mentor guards Harry against danger while he learns the knowledge or skill the mentor offers and then uses it to cross thresholds by performing magic and overcoming obstacles that he would be unlikely to manage if left to his own devices. Once Harry masters whatever skills the mentor is intended to teach and traverses whatever space the mentor guides him across, the mentor withdraws, and Harry is left either to the auspices of another mentor or to carry on alone, as every hero eventually must.

The Multiple Mentor Model

Harry's journey is long, limited to not only one, but a series of heroic cycles involving movement across progressively challenging spaces and the performance of increasingly complex magic. His quest to avenge the deaths of his parents, ultimately killing Lord Voldemort and becoming master of the Muggle and Wizarding worlds, is a monumental one. The roster of magical skills at which Harry must become adept in order to succeed often seems unending. The quantity and variety of these skills make it unlikely that Harry would be able to acquire them with the help of one mentor alone. Rowling anticipates and overcomes this concern by embedding the multiple mentor model into Harry's hero's journey cycle.

In his seminal work on the subject, psychologist Larry D. Burlew explores the multiple mentor model as a framework for the individual's success within an organization, arguing that the model is meant to function over time throughout the individual's evolving organizational life. During this period, Burlew contends, mentorship occurs as a series of events or interactions with mentors of different types—each able to offer specialized skills and knowledge—at various levels within the organizational structure (220). The purpose of the mentor, he explains, is to provide the protégé with guidance, support, and opportunities: "The relationship exists because one person is helping another person progress through life" (Burlew 214). Applied to fiction, this may be translated as one character helping another progress along his or her narrative arc. In Harry's case, the ongoing and repetitive nature of his arc supports what Burlew describes as the protégé's need for several mentors and phases of mentoring (214).

Focusing only upon those mentors that move Harry forward in his hero's journey, helping him to cross thresholds and the liminal spaces between them, the corresponding phases of mentoring become clear. Harry's progression as a protégé begins with mentor patterns that often require direct assistance and ends with, as historian Edmund Kern argues, a more hands-off approach: a dynamic which provides insight into how children balance their own dependence and independence (103). The first and most elementary phase occurs with gamekeeper Rubeus Hagrid, Harry's "Training Mentor." The second involves several members of the Weasley family who function as "Education Mentors." Finally, Hogwarts Headmaster Albus Dumbledore completes the cycle, serving as Harry's most sophisticated "Development Mentor." Through all, the social position and attitudes of these mentors shape Harry's own. It is no accident that each character occupies, in his or her way, socially liminal space. The mentor's situation as both insider and outsider in the wizarding community eases mobility within and without. Unlike more neutral or antagonistic characters, the supernatural guides lead the hero and the reader toward an easier movement between, and eventual transcendence of, the magical and non-magical worlds.

In Harry's case, the "organization" described by Burlew may be understood as not only the wider wizarding world, but also Hogwarts School, specifically. Located in a remote northern wilderness, Britain's premier school for magic is a natural setting for Harry's supernatural education. Built upon centuries of wizarding tradition, filled with arcane objects and quirky-yet-powerful professors, Hogwarts offers an exemplary situation for a schoolboy hero in need of magical tutelage. Philosopher Gregory Bassham argues that within the *Harry Potter* novels, magic is portrayed as a hard-to-acquire skill set, the acquisition of which involves students and teachers in an "apprentice-like" relationship. According to Bassham, this relationship unfolds in the following way: the "(1) demonstration of a magical technique by a skilled teacher, (2) practice of the technique by the students, (3) individualized coaching by the instructor to correct faults, and (4) continued practice by the students until the technique is mastered" (214). Scholars Charles and Emma Kalish agree, asserting that the prevailing instructional model at Hogwarts is one of apprentice and master (61). This process bears all the hallmarks of a Campbellian mentor-hero training sequence.

Rubeus Hagrid: Training Mentor

With the introduction of half-giant Rubeus Hagrid, Rowling provides Harry with one of his first and most influential mentors. Not only does Hagrid transport and protect Harry, he also cares for Harry emotionally. As Deborah De Rosa claims, "Hagrid continues to physically nurture Harry throughout the series" (167). Indeed, Hagrid often performs the functions of a surrogate parent: baking Harry a birthday cake, buying him gifts for holidays, keeping tabs on him so he does not get into too much trouble, and guiding him through Wizarding rites of passage such as buying a wand, a magical pet, and wizard's robes. In this sense, Hagrid exemplifies what Burlew terms the "Training Mentor" (216), acclimating Harry to his new environment and supporting him until he feels capable of functioning within it.

Living as a gamekeeper in a hut on the fringe of the Hogwarts grounds, it is easy to identify Hagrid as "the supernatural helper [who] is masculine in form ... some little fellow of the wood, some wizard, hermit, shepherd, or smith, who appears, to supply the amulets and advice that the hero will require" (Campbell 59). In physical appearance, as well as occupation and dwelling-place, Rowling positions Hagrid as a "fellow of the wood" and a natural mentor for Harry. Of Hagrid's physical stature, Rowling writes, "He was almost twice as tall as a normal man and at least five times as wide. He looked simply too big to be allowed, and so wild—long tangles of bushy black hair and beard hid most of his face, he had hands the size of trash can lids, and his feet in their leather boots were like baby dolphins" (*SS* 14). This striking depiction marks the half-giant as an outsider in the Muggle world, where his size and wildness seem "too big to be allowed" in comparison with a "normal man." However, in this passage Rowling also implies that despite the magical penchant for eccentricity, Hagrid's dimensions, half-blood status, and association with other giants are beyond the norm in the Wizarding world as well. At the moment of introduction, the author uses each descriptive element to firmly root Hagrid in the tradition of supernatural guide figures. Hagrid's readiness, however, does not mean he is without flaw.

Expelled from Hogwarts, his wand snapped in half for crimes he did not commit, Hagrid is capable of performing magic only with the remnants, secreted in a pink umbrella. As "Harry's initial helper ... the supernatural 'protective figure,' the shaggy, bumbling, half-giant Hagrid is no angel, but he is more than adequate to get Harry started on his hero's journey into the Wizarding world" (Black 243). By his own admission Hagrid was expelled, prevented from completing his own Hogwarts education and therefore "not supposed ter do magic, strictly speakin'" (*SS* 59). Despite this fact, he not only performs magic on a regular basis, but eventually becomes a Hogwarts professor in charge of teaching the Care of Magical Creatures course. Hagrid's credentials as a mentor only qualify him to assist Harry in the most elementary of modes: guiding the hero across the outermost of the initiatory thresholds from the Muggle world and the care of the Dursleys inward, toward Hogwarts.

He begins in the derelict courtyard beyond the Leaky Cauldron. To activate the magic that reveals the hidden portal to the world beyond, a wizard or witch must use his or her wand to perform a complicated tapping pattern. Though the snapping of his wand should significantly compromise, or at least complicate Hagrid's performance of this magic, scholar Nicholas Sheltrown affirms that the possession and operation of a wand represents identification with and membership within the magical community. Subsequently, he argues that the ability to use a wand to pass through the brick portal is equivalent to the possession of a "passport to qualified status in wizarding society" (49–51). In short, knowledge of the threshold or portal's existence, possession of a wand with which to activate the portal, and the ability to perform the magic that will actually open it, are all indicative of Hagrid's inclusion in wizarding society. These assertions corroborate the theory that this space between worlds, the boundaries of the Leaky Cauldron and the brick wall beyond, function in the *Harry Potter* story as the first threshold of initiation.

The second threshold and liminal crossing-between-worlds with which Hagrid is involved is the flight of the magical motorbike. Harry's parallel trips between the Muggle and Wizarding realms on Hagrid's borrowed bike follow the Campbellian hero cycle—separation, initiation, acquisition of power, and return—with remarkable precision. As an infant in the beginning stage of his hero cycle Harry is vulnerable and unskilled: completely dependent upon Hagrid as he crosses liminal space and is deposited on a literal threshold in the Muggle world, the Dursleys' front doorstep. Sixteen years later, Harry departs from that threshold with Hagrid once again, but as a fully trained wizard and of his own volition. Rowling makes the transferal of power in this mentorship instance explicit when Hagrid loses control of the bike, and the pair must rely on Harry's quick spellwork to in order to get to safety.

With such moments, Rowling illustrates Hagrid's limitations as a mentor, foreshadowing Harry's eventual outgrowing of Hagrid's assistance. Often, Hagrid brings Harry to the threshold of one world or the other, leaving Harry to fend for himself at the crucial moment. For example, Hagrid provides Harry with a ticket for the Hogwarts Express in his first year but fails to include the necessary instructions as to how to actually *reach* the train. A young wizard as yet uninitiated to this particular threshold, Harry has no idea how to find the correct platform, hidden beyond the invisible barrier between Platforms 9 and 10. Stranded and at a loss, Harry muses that "Hagrid must have forgotten to tell him something [he] had to do, like tapping the third brick on the left to get into Diagon Alley" (*SS* 91). Thus, Harry recognizes early on that his friend is not infallible. The pattern of Harry and Hagrid's mentor relationship follows what Gayle S. Baugh and Terri A. Scandurra explain as a common pattern: when the protégé has grown enough to stand on his or her own two feet, the mentor-protégé relationship becomes more akin to one between peers (516). Hagrid's ability to help Harry complete his hero's journey has limitations, which must eventually be compensated for either by Harry himself or by another, more capable and sophisticated mentor.

The Weasley Family: Education Mentors

Next in Harry's multiple mentor model sequence are the lively, red-headed Weasleys. Known in the wizarding world as a "pure-blood" family, the seven Weasley children have been raised fully immersed in wizarding culture: enjoying the kind of practical, everyday experiences of magic that Harry's Muggle upbringing did not afford him. The Weasley family represents for Harry a source of relational awareness, including him in their family dynamic and demonstrating for him typical wizarding behaviors and social cues. Together, the Weasleys form what Burlew describes as the "Education Mentor," showing Harry what it means to be a part of wizard society: allowing him to observe and participate in a typical wizarding lifestyle, providing him with support, and helping him to make decisions about his future within the community (216).

To begin, the Weasley children, specifically those boys closest in age to Harry—Fred, George, and Ron—initiate Harry into the realm of wizarding childhood: fun, mischief, and rebellion. Equivalent in age to Harry, the youngest Weasley son, Ron, is a natural friend and foil. It is Ron who first introduces Harry to the liminal travel mode of riding aboard the Hogwarts Express. The steam engine provides the most literal, geographical form of movement between worlds, carrying Harry from the threshold of King's Cross in the Muggle world to Hogwarts School. For many Muggle-born students, the Hogwarts Express is one of their first immersion experiences into the culture of wizarding children. Wizards like Ron, who have grown up in the magical world, initiate those like Harry who have not. Comfortably ensconced in their cabin on the train, Ron explains childlike concerns such as chocolate frog cards, the dangers of Bertie Botts Every Flavour Beans, and Quidditch trivia. In turn, Harry tells Ron about his life in the Muggle world with the Dursleys. At this moment, "both boys marvel at the technical novelty of the other's world" (Sheltrown 57), while simultaneously acknowledging the metaphorical liminal space between their childhood environments as they traverse the corresponding physical liminal space.

Having already accompanied Harry across the space between the Muggle world and Hogwarts by more conventional wizarding means in year one, the Weasley boys step things up a notch for year two, staging a rescue under cover of darkness in their father's (illegal) flying Ford Anglia. This time, Ron is joined by his twin brothers Fred and George, who help break Harry out of Number Four Privet Drive, where Harry's uncle, Vernon Dursley, has imprisoned Harry in his room "round the clock," vowing that Harry will never be allowed to go back to school (*CoS* 21). Pulling the bars from Harry's bedroom window during the heady, airborne escape to the Burrow, the Weasley boys ensure that Harry will be able to continue his quest and join them for another year at Hogwarts. With the flight of the Ford Anglia, the youthful mentors help the hero to cross yet another barrier—this one Muggle-made—and initiate him to a new mode of travel between worlds. In the case of the Weasley boys, moments of guidance such as this often involve harmless rule-breaking, the relationship moving between peer and mentor roles with ease.

As their children initiate Harry into what it means to be a rebellious teenaged wizard, Molly and Arthur Weasley act in many ways as surrogate parents, caring for him as one of their own. Like Hagrid, the couple protects and nurtures Harry in the Campbellian sense consistent with an aide or mentor figure, welcoming him to stay at their home and taking pains to include him in the family dynamic. Molly knits Harry a "Weasley Sweater" (*SS* 202) and insists that Harry is "as good as" a son (*OotP* 124). On Harry's seventeenth birthday, she and Arthur give Harry a "traditional" wizard's watch—a family heirloom once belonging to Molly's brother Fabian—to celebrate his coming-of-age (*DH* 114). It is Molly who helps Harry cross the second threshold of his hero's journey: the barrier to Platform 9¾, at which Hagrid has left Harry, stranded without instruction. Like the brick wall separating the Leaky Cauldron courtyard from Diagon Alley, the threshold at Kings Cross is a quite literal portal: a solid-yet-permeable barrier between the Muggle and wizarding worlds. The platform is more symbolic as an initiatory boundary in the sense that every young witch or wizard who wishes to attend Hogwarts School must learn to cross it. As with the brick wall, movement through the platform (without the direct assistance of an adult) is an initiatory test which must be passed in order for the young wizard or witch to signify that he or she is indeed of age and ready to begin attending the magical school. Harry repeats Molly's advice in his mind as he makes his own (successful) attempt. In this moment, Molly empowers Harry to enter the wizarding world entirely of his own volition, his ability to do so indicative of a deeper degree of heroic entrée earned.

Later, Molly also teaches Harry how to travel via "Floo powder." The connections of this transportation mode to notions of hearth and home are undeniable, as are the advantages to the busy mother of a large family. As Margaret Oakes argues, Floo powder is the wizarding equivalent of a Muggle minivan. "The solutions here," she explains, "fit the situations: Floo powder, the fireplace-to-fireplace mode, is quick, direct, and well suited to family groups" (120–122). It is fitting then, that Mrs. Weasley uses this mode to run family errands, travelling from the Burrow to Diagon Alley in order to buy her children and Harry school supplies. As with the platform, Molly does not actually physically transport Harry across the Floo powder threshold, but instead, stands back and provides verbal guidance, allowing Harry to make the attempt on his own. In both cases, Molly allows Harry to cross the necessary thresholds independently, encouraging him to participate in a process of learning and making mistakes. And make a mistake Harry does, immediately landing himself in dodgy Knockturn Alley by accident. The method Molly uses to mentor Harry, guiding him across thresholds, ensures Harry's self-sufficiency. Much later in the series, Harry demonstrates this autonomy when he communicates with his godfather via Floo powder. The evolution of Harry's skill operating the Floo Network indicates his mastery— an increasingly controlled dexterity—of movement beyond barriers and between worlds.

Similarly, Molly's husband Arthur includes Harry on a family trip to the Quidditch World Cup and later delivers Harry to the Ministry of Magic to a trial for charges of underage sorcery. In both instances, Arthur introduces Harry to new portals between the magical and non-magical realms. Yet Arthur's significance in regard to the connection between wizarding and Muggle worlds extends beyond initiation into the methods of passage between them. As Ron explains, his father "works in the most boring department [of the Ministry] ... [in] the Misuse of Muggle Artifacts Office" (*CoS* 30). In spite of his job, or more likely because of it, Arthur cherishes an overwhelming fascination with Muggle culture and technology. His pastime must be enjoyed clandestinely, however, as it combines elements of the Muggle and wizarding worlds in a way that is considered illegal and potentially dangerous. In addition, Arthur and his family do not concern themselves with wizarding ethnic purity. On the contrary, they often endure scorn for their acquaintance with "Mudbloods" like Hermione Granger and "half-breeds" like Remus Lupin and Rubeus Hagrid. Wizards such as Lucius Malfoy fear the co-mingling of the magical and non-magical worlds that wizards such as "Muggle-loving fool Arthur Weasley" (*CoS* 51) encourage. Arthur's attitude of acceptance and inclusion, and subsequently that of his family, exposes Harry to a point of view conducive to the blending of wizard and Muggle culture. In this way, the Weasleys are ideal mentors for Harry: their position in socially liminal space corresponds with their movement across the physically liminal.

When travelling to the Quidditch World Cup, this movement is achieved by means of a magical object called a portkey. Arthur explains to Harry that portkeys are "objects that are used to transport wizards from one spot to another at a prearranged time ... [that] they can be anything ... unobtrusive things, obviously, so Muggles don't go picking them up and playing with them" (*GoF* 70). On their way to the World Cup, Arthur and his motley crew catch a portkey—in this case, a "manky old boot" (*GoF* 71)—that will transport them to their campsite. In theory, the inexhaustible supply and mobility of portkeys make them a convenient option for wizard travel. This convenience is deceptive, though, as the corresponding initiation sequence is more complex. Not only must the wizard or witch already be aware of the existence and basic function of portkeys, he or she must also know ahead of time exactly what form the particular portkey will take and when it will be activated. The increased level of sophistication necessary to locate and operate a portkey *correctly* (they can be discovered or used by accident) parallels Harry's growing agency. It is important to note that with all of the magical enchantments placed around Hogwarts, a portkey is also one of the limited magical methods a witch or wizard may use to travel in and out of the school. Harry moves in and out of Hogwarts via portkeys such as the Triwizard Cup, the head of a golden statue, and a blackened kettle. By introducing Harry to this transportation mode, Arthur serves his protégé several times over, augmenting Harry's ability to pass more deeply into the wizarding world.

Arthur continues to facilitate this expansion of Harry's mobility throughout the interior strata of his new world with a trip to the Ministry of Magic, hidden beneath the heart of London. Summoned for the crime of misusing underage sorcery, Harry must stand trial before the full Wizengamot (wizard court). Descending by means of a defunct telephone booth, Arthur and Harry's entrance to the Ministry of Magic is highly reminiscent of "the passage of the magical threshold [as] a transit into a sphere of rebirth ... symbolized in the worldwide womb image of the belly of the whale" (Campbell 74). After navigating a maze of dark stone hallways, Harry faces very real danger in the Department of Mysteries, namely wand-snapping and expulsion. In this instance, however, he has Arthur to guide him.

Later, in yet another tidy narrative parallel, Harry returns to the Ministry of Magic on his own. This time he passes the Ministry threshold independently, applying the knowledge and power his mentor has bestowed. Harry himself then becomes the guide, leading his friends as they break into the Ministry on two separate occasions. On the first, Harry mimics the steps that Arthur taught him, cramming himself and his friends through the visitor's telephone booth. Together, Harry and his friends enter the Department of Mysteries, exploring several of the Department's most secret rooms. By penetrating the Ministry to such depths—rooms which most qualified adult wizards will never be allowed to enter—Harry proves that he is in the process of achieving a level of mastery within the wizarding world that few will ever realize.

Dumbledore: Development Mentor

Finally, in Headmaster Albus Dumbledore, Rowling delivers a philosophical leader capable of guiding Harry through the deepest realms of magical knowledge and spiritual awareness. Under Dumbledore's tutelage, Harry is able to achieve true mastery of movement beyond boundaries. This qualifies

Dumbledore to fulfill the most sophisticated and complex role of Development Mentor to Harry. The Development Mentor, Burlew clarifies:

> Is a unique person who must be a futurist; at least enough to help the protégé perform activities that would benefit the future of the organization or the protégé him/herself ... the Development Mentor helps a worker grow as a person and perhaps even strive for personal/professional self-actualization [217].

First by broomstick, then Apparition, and finally metacognition, Dumbledore prepares Harry for the day Harry will be on his own, divested of his mentors and forced to go on alone. The modes to which Dumbledore initiates Harry enable the hero's eventual transcendence of boundaries and spaces, culminating in his enlightenment: the ultimate archetypal form of "personal/professional self-actualization" (Burlew 217).

In many ways, Dumbledore fits the archetypal ideal of the mentor figure, a case which Christina Vourcos argues in-depth in her essay "Mentoring in the Wizarding World: Dumbledore and His Literary Ancestors." And indeed, the Headmaster's similarity to preceding prototypes such as Geoffrey of Monmouth's Merlin (and subsequent variations) is undeniable. Scholar Lisa Hopkins agrees, emphasizing the similarities between Merlin and Dumbledore as she explains, "Both are much older and wiser mentor figures who guide the young hero toward fulfilling his potential; both can perform formidable magic; and Dumbledore, like Merlin, is involved in arranging the young hero's fosterage" (63). Not only does Dumbledore physically resemble Merlin—with pointed hat, billowing robes, long white beard, and preternatural age—the Headmaster also arranges for Harry's fosterage and safety in early childhood, as Merlin does for Arthur. In orchestrating Harry's removal to the Dursleys home, Dumbledore facilitates Harry's first crossing of the threshold between worlds, knowing that in the end, Harry must one day return.

Dumbledore's preeminence in the wizarding community is such that he is elected Chief Warlock of the Wizengamot, appointed Headmaster of Hogwarts School, and offered the position of Minister of Magic several times. He is also the only person in the world that "Lord Voldemort was ever afraid of" (*SS* 56). Dumbledore is among the outstanding witches and wizards who appear on chocolate frog cards. His own card informs readers that Dumbledore is "Considered by many to be the greatest wizard of modern times" (*SS* 92). It seems only natural that Rowling positions the "greatest wizard of modern times" as Harry's most influential mentor, capable of initiating Harry into the most sophisticated realms of magic.

Dumbledore's influence, however, is not without controversy. Though his superior magical ability and position as Headmaster of Hogwarts School situate him as a figurehead of protagonistic forces for good, Dumbledore is often depicted as a man apart. As the "spiritual centre" of Hogwarts, Dumbledore models what Rowling seems to consider ideal social standards and corresponding behaviors which often deviate from the wizarding norm (Hennequin 69). Throughout the series, Dumbledore is often at odds with or targeted by the Ministry of Magic, the Hogwarts Board of Governors, and the *Daily Prophet*. These conflicts occur in response to Dumbledore's continual challenging of standards of inequality and oppression in the wizarding world: his support of magical minorities and outspoken opposition to not only the violent extremism of Voldemort and his followers but also the prejudices and classism of wizard-kind. This additional function of Dumbledore's character is consistent with what Richard Schwartz and Kemp Williams describe as the mentor's occasional role as philosopher-king, "a benevolent dictator who creates and shapes the ideal community in which all citizens aspire to their greatest fulfillment" (104). Dumbledore's efforts throughout the series to unite the teachers, creatures, and students of Hogwarts—urging them to overcome differences and work together—mimic this shaping of an ideal society. Eventually, Dumbledore's influence ripples outward from Hogwarts School to the wider wizarding world.

Similarly, Dumbledore begins to expand Harry's ability to maneuver throughout and beyond Hogwarts by expanding his options for liminal travel. The Headmaster begins by "bending the rules" that restrict first-year Hogwarts students from owning and operating a broomstick while at school (*SS* 152). After his latent potential for flying is discovered by Professor McGonagall, Harry receives a parcel containing a new Nimbus 2000 racing broom courtesy of the Headmaster's special permission (*SS* 152). Though he does not directly teach Harry how to operate a broomstick, by bending his own school rules and allowing Harry the broom, Dumbledore allows Harry's flying skills to flourish and provides a mode of travel that is one of the most convenient and consistently useful. It is important to note that early on, Harry's broomstick travel is limited to the Quidditch pitch or Hogwarts grounds. Only when he has become a highly proficient flyer is Harry able to use a broomstick to travel between worlds.

Like a broomstick, the mode of Apparition provides a convenient means of individual travel. The magical ability to disappear and reappear at will, Apparition is the most elite transportation method used in the wizarding world and consequently, is highly regulated by the Ministry of Magic. Requiring specialized training from a Ministry official, the process of learning to Apparate is viewed by the wizarding community as a formal rite of passage. However, for those who have not yet come of age, Apparition is still possible with the aid of a fully qualified wizard, using the "Side-Along-Apparition" technique (*H-BP* 57–8). It is this technique which Dumbledore uses at the beginning of *Half-Blood Prince* to introduce under-aged Harry to the transportation mode. When Harry expresses concern about possible attack, Dumbledore responds, "I do not think you need to worry about being attacked tonight.... You are with me" (*HB-P* 57–8). Near the end of the book—in what is clearly Rowling's preferred method of indicating that Harry's abilities have advanced far enough to come full circle—Harry then uses Side-Along-Apparition to transport a desperately weakened Dumbledore from a remote seaside cave. In this moment, Dumbledore reverses his earlier sentiment, assuring "I am not worried, Harry.... I am with you" (*HB-P* 578). At this point the Headmaster knows he will soon be killed and so passes the metaphorical wand to Harry, trusting that the transfer of skills and knowledge has been sufficient, and that Harry will be able to carry on alone in his quest.

After Dumbledore is gone, Harry must figure out how to defeat Lord Voldemort and cross the final threshold unaided. At the crucial moment, Harry invokes the memory of his greatest mentor as a model for his actions. Preparing for his own death, Harry makes contingency plans as he believes Dumbledore would do. Marching toward his fate, Harry tells himself that "he must be like Dumbledore, keep a cool head, make sure there were back-ups, others to carry on" (*DH* 696). In order to fulfill his destiny—protecting his friends and allies, avenging the deaths of his parents, and triumphing over Voldemort—Harry resolves that he must sacrifice his own life. The protégé adopts the methods modeled for him by the mentor, and so Harry follows Dumbledore's example as a means to achieve the desired ends (Scholz 136). Harry's diligence is quickly rewarded when he finds Dumbledore on the "other side."

Instead of the usual debriefing in the Headmaster's office, Harry's meeting with Dumbledore in the final installment occurs in a nameless region beyond death, understood as a potential limbo or World Navel. At this point, Harry no longer needs to use tangible, formalized magic; he is able to transcend worlds with the power of his mind. Successful transition to this pseudo-divine cognitive space signifies Harry's ultimate achievement of heroic enlightenment. Yet even in this moment of preeminence, Harry comprehends that he possesses the power to navigate back across or beyond this final threshold only after Dumbledore explains, "I think that if you decided not to go back, you would be able to ... let's say ... board a train" (*DH* 722). Though Harry has now proven himself both physically and psychologically capable of independent movement across liminal spaces and worldly boundaries, he is still not above seeking help from his trusted mentor.

Harry's growth and development as a hero depends upon his ability to navigate between the Muggle and Wizarding worlds with increasing fluidity and skill. However, the length and scope of the *Potter* series and subsequent repetition of the hero cycle increases the number and manner of thresholds and spaces that Harry must learn to cross. The trajectory of his pedagogical paradigm parallels that of his hero's journey, requiring assistance from multiple guide figures in order to progress. To meet this need, Rowling supplies Harry with a diverse group of mentors including Rubeus Hagrid, the Weasley family, and Headmaster Albus Dumbledore, who together are able to initiate Harry to all necessary modes of travel. With the cumulative guidance of his multiple mentors, all physical and metaphorical thresholds are passed and liminal spaces crossed, distinguishing Harry as a Master of Two Worlds in true Campbellian fashion.

WORKS CITED

Bachelard, Gaston. *The Poetics of Space*. Beacon Press, 1964.

Bassham, Gregory. "A Hogwarts Education: The Good, the Bad, and the Ugly." *The Ultimate Harry Potter and Philosophy: Hogwarts for Muggles*, edited by Gregory Bassham, John Wiley & Sons Inc., 2010, pp. 212–226.

Baugh, S. Gayle, and Terri A. Scandurra. "The Effect of Multiple Mentors on Protégé Attitudes Toward the Work Setting." *Journal of Social Behavior & Personality*, vol. 14, no. 4, Dec. 1999, pp. 503–521.

Black, Sharon. "The Magic of Harry Potter: Symbols and Heroes of Fantasy." *Children's Literature in Education*, vol. 34, no. 3, 2003, pp. 237–47.

Burlew, Larry. "Multiple Mentor Model: A Conceptual Framework." *Journal of Career Development*, vol. 17, no. 3, Spring 1991, pp. 213–221.

Campbell, Joseph. *The Hero with a Thousand Faces*. 3rd ed., New World Library, 2008.

De Rosa, Deborah. "Wizardly Challenges to and Affirmations of the Initiation Paradigm in Harry Potter." *Harry Potter's World: Multidisciplinary Critical Perspectives*, edited by Elizabeth E. Heilman, Routledge, 2003, pp. 163–184.

Hennequin, Wendy M. "Harry Potter and the Legends of Saints." *Journal of Religion and Pop Culture*, vol. 25, no. 1, 2013, pp. 67–81.

Hopkins, Lisa. "Harry Potter and Narratives of Destiny." *Reading Harry Potter Again: New Critical Essays*, edited by Giselle Liza Anatol, Praeger, 2009, pp. 63–76.

Jung, C.G. "The Archetypes and the Collective Unconscious." *The Collective Works of C.G. Jung*. Translated by R.F.C. Hull, 2nd ed., vol. 9, Princeton UP, 1981.

Kalish, Charles W., and Emma C. Kalish. "Hogwarts Academy: Common Sense and School Magic." *The Psychology of Harry Potter: An Unauthorized Examination of the Boy Who Lived*, edited by Neil Mulholland, Benbella Books Inc., 2006, pp. 135–152.

Kern, Edmund M. "Imagination, History, Legend, and Myth." *The Wisdom of Harry Potter*. Prometheus Books, 2003, pp. 179–222.

Nikolajeva, Maria. "Harry Potter—A Return to the Romantic Hero." *Harry Potter's World: Multidisciplinary Critical Perspectives*, edited by Elizabeth E. Heilman, Routledge, 2003, pp. 125–140.

Oakes, Margaret J. "Flying Cars, Floo Powder, and Flaming Torches: The Hi-Tech, Low- Tech World of Wizardry." *Reading Harry Potter: Critical Essays*, edited by Giselle Liza Anatol, Praeger, 2003, pp. 117–130.

Propp, Vladimir. *Morphology of a Folktale*. Translated by Laurence Scott, University of Texas Press, 1968.

Reding, Mary D. "Concentric Mastery Model: Harry Potter's Hero Journey." 2018. *Unpublished Manuscript*.

_____. "Harry Potter's Heroics: Crossing the Thresholds of Home, Away, and the Spaces In-between." *Graduate Theses and Dissertations*, 15068, Iowa State University, 2016, doi:10.31274/etd-180810–4671.

Rowling, J.K. *Harry Potter and the Chamber of Secrets*. Scholastic, 1999.

_____. *Harry Potter and the Deathly Hallows*. Scholastic, 2007.

_____. *Harry Potter and the Goblet of Fire*. Scholastic, 2000.

_____. *Harry Potter and the Half-Blood Prince*. Scholastic, 2005.

_____. *Harry Potter and the Order of the Phoenix.* Scholastic, 2003.

_____. *Harry Potter and the Prisoner of Azkaban.* Scholastic, 1999.

_____. *Harry Potter and the Sorcerer's Stone.* Scholastic, 1998.

Scholz, Victoria Lynne. "Other Muggles' Children: Power and Oppression in Harry Potter." *Midwest Quarterly*, vol. 59, no. 2, Winter 2018, pp. 123–144.

Schwartz, Richard A., and Kemp Williams. "Metaphors We Teach By: The Mentor Teacher and the Hero Student." *The Journal of Aesthetic Education*, vol. 289, no. 2, University of Illinois Press, Summer 1995, pp. 103–110.

Sheltrown, Nicholas. "Harry Potter's World as a Morality Tale of Technology and Media." *Critical Perspectives of Harry Potter,* edited by Elizabeth E. Heilman, 2nd ed., Routledge, 2009, pp. 47–64.

Vourcos, Christina. "Mentoring in the Wizarding World: Dumbledore and His Literary Ancestors." *Critical Insights: The Harry Potter Series*, edited by M. Katherine Grimes and Lana A. Whited, Salem Press, 2015, pp. 163–179.

Yager, Susan. "'Something He Could Do Without Being Taught': Honors, Play and Harry Potter." *Honors in Practice: A Publication of the National Collegiate Honors Council*, vol. 11, 2015, pp. 213–222.

The Good, the Bad, the Toxic

*Using Muggle-Borns as a Lens
for the First-Generation-Student
Experience with Mentorship*

JAMIE L.H. GOODALL *and* KERRY SPENCER

Educators are generally expected to mentor students and/or junior colleagues as part of their role at a university. In the academic world, "mentoring" and "advising" are often used interchangeably. Yet, there is a fundamental difference between the two: mentoring, more than advising, is "a personal, as well as, professional relationship" (NAS 1). While an advisor may be a mentor, they are not automatically one, and their focus is usually on academic success alone. A mentor, on the other hand, generally supports a mentee beyond simple academic performance: providing career advice, offering personal support, and acting as a sounding board for problems. While mentorship has important positive influences, the mentor/mentee relationship can also cross into toxic territory. Mentor/mentee relationships "may have constituted emotionally intense arenas in which we have successfully resolved our struggles with some of our deepest personal issues," yet they also hold the potential to be incredibly destructive (McClelland 61). Because mentorship is inherently relational, it can be possible for the relationship to change or to move from appropriate to inappropriate. Deviating from appropriate mentorship boundaries and protocol can have serious consequences not only for those involved in the mentoring relationship, but also for the broader academic field of research or the institution.

First-generation students are in a particularly vulnerable position when it comes to mentorship. In this essay, we use Victor Saenz and Doug Barrera's definition of first-generation as those "whose parents have had no college or post secondary experiences" (1). Without the cultural fluency to protect and inform their mentorship choices, first-generation students can become entangled in insufficient or ineffective mentorship relationships, and sometimes even destructive ones. First-generation students are also less likely than their peers to seek mentorship. A 2016 study by the National Center for Education statistics found that first-generation students made up approximately 44 percent (and rising) of college students (Nadworny and Depenbrock). It seems particularly important to recognize how we fail these first-generation students by not equipping them and their potential mentors with the tools to develop or recognize appropriate mentoring relationships.

The experience of Muggle-born students provides us a lens with which to examine mentorship from the viewpoint of the first-generation student. Both sets of students are lacking in cultural fluency and both are vulnerable to potentially destructive mentorships. Because the salient question is about cultural fluency, we expand the notion of Muggle-born students to include students, like Harry, who though born of magical parentage were raised in a wizarding-naive environment. Having no shared knowledge to draw from and no prior knowledge of conventions/practices, such students are in a position to greatly benefit from good mentoring relationships. Yet, their lack of cultural vocabulary and inability to identify toxic behavior can leave them vulnerable to destructive ones. Additionally, first-generation students, much like Muggle-born students, may find themselves overlooked when it comes to mentoring relationships due to subconscious (or even conscious) biases about their abilities.

In this essay, we look at the good, bad, and toxic mentoring relationships that Muggle-born/wizarding-naive students of *Harry Potter* are asked to navigate. While there are some characteristics of effective mentorships that may be the same regardless of a student's status, first-generation students often lack the support system to help them recognize these characteristics and seek out appropriate mentorships. By examining the experiences of Muggle-born/wizarding-naive students in *Harry Potter*, we provide insight into the way first-generation students may experience mentorship and demonstrate how this can be applied to real-world first-generation mentorships. Knowledge of such experiences is helpful to both mentors and mentees; it can help mentors better provide for first-generation student needs while also protecting them from destructive/exploitative relationships. It can also help mentees recognize good/bad/toxic behavior.

Muggle-Borns as a Lens
for First-Generation Students

The experience of being a first-generation student can be overwhelming. While other students may have grown up with stories about what to expect at college or may have witnessed older siblings navigating the world of higher education, first-generation students have no such way to establish expectations. They may not know who to ask if they have questions; more importantly, they may not even know what questions to ask. First-generation students are, too often uninformed about the "hidden curriculum" or what Mikhail Zinshteyn calls the "mix of bureaucratic know-how and sound study skills that can make or break a student's first year in college." These include things like knowing about office hours, finding the right classes, managing time, and using library or university resources.

These issues are reflected in the experiences of Muggle-born and wizarding-naive students at Hogwarts. Harry has to be told not just how to find his school supplies, but what supplies he will need at all. His lack of cultural awareness ranges from the insignificant—just what *are* Bertie Bott's Every Flavor Beans and why should you be very, very careful when eating them?—to the more profound: who is Voldemort and why are people afraid to speak his name? Dealing with so many unfamiliar cultural factors is difficult. And while some Muggle-borns like Hermione are able to use their incredible work ethic and research skills to overcome the challenges, the additional labor of mastering cultural fluency is one that traditional students do not have to encounter.

This new cultural fluency can also cause difficulties with balancing a student's identity as a Muggle-born witch or wizard, especially in connection with their parents. Hermione's parents, when first seen in the wizarding world, are described as "standing nervously at the counter" of Gringotts bank (*CS* 56). The next time we see them, they are "shaking with fright" (*CS* 63). Having witnessed a feud between Lucius Malfoy and Arthur Weasley, they are clearly desperate to return to the relative safety of the Muggle world. The longer Hermione remains at Hogwarts, the more distant she becomes from her parents. It becomes apparent in *Order of the Phoenix* how little Hermione's parents understand about her accomplishments or the culture at Hogwarts. Hermione is elated to learn that she has been made a prefect, a position at school that has an equivalent in the Muggle-world, remarking that her parents will be proud because "prefect is something they can understand" (*OotP* 165). While being made a prefect is something that Hermione is proud of, the reality becomes painfully clear for her in this moment: it may be the only accomplishment at Hogwarts with a direct Muggle-world parallel that her parents can understand. Thus, while her parents may be proud of her wizarding accomplishments, Hermione realizes that they cannot truly understand them.

In these ways, we witness Hermione facing many of the same struggles as first-generation students. Their families often lack the institutional knowledge to connect with the college student over accomplishments like Dean's/ President's List or honors like *magna, summa, cum laude.* Having parents who did not attend college may lead to mixed messages of support. On the one hand, parents may encourage their students to be diligent with their studies. On the other hand, they may not understand the additional demands like heavy homework loads, extracurricular clubs, work as a research assistant, or internships, which may conflict with familial expectations like jobs and household responsibilities. Parents might view these as unnecessary or as a waste of time or money. They might "express both pride that their child will excel and fear that they'll evolve into someone the family no longer recognize" (Tugend). First-generation students may therefore find themselves straddling two identities, two worlds, much like Muggle-borns. Other family members may view going to college as foolish or view the first-generation student as "stuck up." First-generation students who choose to attend school far from home may face parents who do not understand why they want the distance, being unaware of the "hierarchy and prestige of different universities" or taking the choice as a personal rejection (Tugend). First-generation parents may not be able to help their children spot potentially problematic relationships with mentors. They, like their students, might think a professor paying inappropriate attention to a mentee is flattering or normal.

Because they cannot rely on family to help them master cultural fluency, first-generation/Muggle-born students have a greater need for mentors. However, their status can lead to implicit biases that limit their opportunities for mentorships. There are often lower expectations or assumptions of knowledge made about first-generation/Muggle-born students. When they first meet, Professor Slughorn remarks to Harry, "Your mother was Muggle-born, of course. Couldn't believe it when I found out. Thought she must have been pure-blood, she was so good" (*H-BP* 70). When Harry reminds Slughorn that "one of my best friends is Muggle-born ... and she's the best in our year," Slughorn further demonstrates his bias by remarking "Funny how that sometimes happens, isn't it?" (*HB-P* 70). Such expectations may result in fewer mentorship opportunities for first generation/Muggle-born students. In this way, Muggle-born students become not only a lens for first-generation students, but for any students who are at all marginalized or initially judged as lesser. Women, students of color, and queer students all may find resonance in the experience of lowered expectations and lack of mentorship opportunities.

Although they are perhaps the population for which mentorships are most beneficial, first-generation/Muggle-born students may not realize they are expected to seek out mentors. A potential mentor may not realize who *is not* seeking them out or understand that they, as a mentor, may need to take the first step in developing a mentoring relationship with a student. If a mentor is not first-generation themselves, they may believe that all students know how to pursue mentoring relationships and be unable to recognize first-generation students who need their help. Having a better understanding of the first-generation experience can help faculty members better tailor their approach to mentorship.

First-Generation/Muggle-Born Students and Mentoring Relationships

The critical problem for first-generation students in seeking out good mentoring experiences is that, without academic cultural fluency, they do not always know how to spot a good mentor versus a bad or a toxic one. The experience of Muggle-born students with good, bad, and toxic mentors can give first-generation students insight into what each kind of relationship might look like. While much of our essay focuses on basic mentoring types and qualities, which can be applied to any mentoring relationship, first-generation students face a unique challenge because they do not have family members with experience to rely on to teach them the importance, purpose, and typical experience of mentorship.

A good mentor can be hard to define. A mentorship is, primarily, a *relationship*. And relationships, even the best ones, can be messy and variable, can involve differing levels of emotional investment, and can turn from good to bad without warning. David Perlmutter says, while ideals of mentorship are something akin to "a Karate Kid seeking a Mr. Miyagi who will train his acolyte to be a skilled warrior in the art of research, teaching, and service and impart pithy life lessons along the way," the reality of mentorship is far more mundane. We may not find that one master who can impart all knowledge and direct our careers, but we may find "several mentors who, while not well-versed in all aspects of academic life, will offer good advice in one or another area" (Perlmutter). And while a mentor might be good for one individual, any number of reasons—such as personality or goals—might make them a bad mentor for another.

But there are some ways faculty can universally demonstrate good mentorship, especially by being approachable and available (NAS 4). According to Cho, et al., a good mentor has experience with the work and challenges that their mentees may face, has admirable personal traits (such as "enthusiasm, compassion, and selflessness"), and supports the personal/professional balance of their mentees (456–8). When a mentee faces challenges or difficulties, a good mentor should be an advocate, supporting them with resources and helping them network in academic and/or professional opportunities (Blixen et al. 88). A good mentor helps their students navigate academic and professional cultures, including ethical considerations, institutional language, communication skills, and proper socialization. And a good mentor should be concerned with the well-being of their mentee, both within and outside the academic setting (NAS 2). A mentoring relationship, particularly a good one, takes time to develop, "during which a student's needs and the nature of the relationship tend to change" (NAS 1). A good mentor is aware of these changing needs and adapts their mentoring strategy to fit the evolving relationship. Students need tools to recognize a potentially good mentoring match, and they should take an active role in finding a mentor.

When it comes to professional mentorships, *Harry Potter* is rich with examples. Among these, however, are largely examples of ineffective and downright toxic relationships. Mentors and mentees are people, and no mentoring relationship is perfect. Mentorships involve emotional connections and considerable personal investment. But while such personal investment is mandatory in a good mentoring relationship, it is also part of what enables it to cross into toxic. Indeed, there is a great deal of overlap between the two.

One of the most salient features of mentorship between faculty and students is that they typically involve a power differential. First-generation students, in particular, are vulnerable to exploitation within such relationships because they might not always recognize the ways in which the power-differential is limiting their ability to make choices freely. Their inexperience/naivety may lead them to believe exploitative relationships are typical university experiences. The professor/student power differential is a particularly strong one; it persists long past the time when a student is enrolled at university. It may never fully dissolve (NAS 4). Navigating this power differential within the bounds of an emotionally complex relationship is, perhaps, the most difficult aspect of mentorship and the aspect for which first-generation students need the most guidance.

And yet mentoring relationships can be particularly important to the success or failure of Muggle-born/first-generation students. Harry is able to navigate his experience at Hogwarts largely through the help of mentoring relationships. Hagrid shows him how to access Diagon Alley and how to purchase and pay for his supplies. He introduces him to the people he needs to know. Harry is not alone in struggling in his first year; "Lots of people had come from Muggle families and, like him, hadn't had any idea they were witches and wizards" (*SS* 134). Having a good mentor can be the difference between a first-generation student thriving and flailing at the university. A mentor can help a first-generation student with issues ranging from appropriate professor/student conduct to where to get help with registration or counseling services. But how does a first-generation student know if the relationships they are working to cultivate are productive or destructive ones? The experience of the Muggle-born students at Hogwarts elucidates the defining characteristics of good, bad, and toxic mentors.

Good Mentor: Minerva McGonagall

Though *Harry Potter* is not particularly filled with examples of truly effective mentorship, Professor McGonagall provides our best example of an experienced educator. She provides supportive mentorship and offers resources to her students, both pureblood and Muggle-born, beyond their academic studies. According to J.K. Rowling, McGonagall is a half-blood, born to a Muggle father (the Rev. Robert McGonagall) and a witch mother (Isobel Ross), which provides her a unique opportunity to connect with Muggle-born and wizarding-naive students like Hermione and Harry (*Pottermore*). She is perceptive, recognizing the gifts of her students, like when she catches Harry disobeying Madam Hooch during flying lessons (*SS* 149). Although she is deeply concerned for Harry's safety and upset at his insubordination, she acknowledges his natural talent on a broom. She brings him immediately to the captain of the Gryffindor Quidditch team, Oliver Wood, remarking, "I've found you a seeker…. The boy's a natural. I've never seen anything like it" (*SS* 151). She even puts herself on the line for Harry, getting Dumbledore to bend "the first-year rule," which typically bars first year students from having their own brooms. She sets clear expectations for Harry: "I want to hear you're training hard, Potter, or I may change my mind about punishing you" (*SS* 152), but she also smiles, letting Harry know that his father would have been proud. In doing so, not only does McGonagall demonstrate good mentorship generally—creating a meaningful connection with a student—she addresses Harry's first-generation experience by being the one to initiate a mentoring relationship.

One of the important approaches a good mentor can take is to both challenge and support their mentees. We see McGonagall demonstrate this quality several times throughout the series. Rowling acknowledges "Professor McGonagall's classes were always hard work" (*CS* 94–5), but she lays out her expectations for all her students on the first day of Transfiguration class (*SS* 134). One of the most consequential examples of McGonagall challenging yet supporting her students comes with Hermione and the Time Turner. Hermione speaks of McGonagall's support in obtaining the device: "Professor McGonagall made me swear I wouldn't tell anyone. She had to write all sorts of letters to the Ministry of Magic so I could have one. She had to tell them that I was a model student, and that I'd never, ever use it for anything except my studies" (*PoA* 395–6). McGonagall clearly believes in Hermione—to the extent that she vouched for her with the Ministry of Magic—and she makes her expectations clear. Hermione, knowing this, knowing the *importance* of this, is more capable of seeing herself as someone deeply competent, deeply trusted. Her Muggle-born status becomes a non-issue in the face of McGonagall's belief in her. McGonagall does not expect Hermione to fail, even though Hermione has no known wizarding genealogy, no wizarding history, and no specific knowledge about what the traditional/expected outcomes *should* be. The stakes are high, for both Hermione and McGonagall, were she to use the Time Turner for trivial means. Good mentors hold high expectations for students, but make sure they believe in their ability to meet those high expectations. In a first-generation student's experiences, they may be more likely to apply for a competitive scholarship or write a difficult paper because mentors tell them that their ideas, that *they*, are worthy.

Another important characteristic of a good mentor is knowing the boundary between support and favoritism. Despite all the evident ways that McGonagall supports her students—particularly the trio—she does not display favoritism to her house, Gryffindor. Harry even remarks in *Sorcerer's Stone* that he wished she favored them, noting that even though she was head of Gryffindor "it hadn't stopped her from giving them a huge pile of homework the day before" (*SS* 135). She is not afraid to take points from her house should the students behave inappropriately. She takes five points from Gryffindor in *Sorcerer's Stone* when she believes Hermione had attempted to take on a troll by herself (although she does give Ron and Harry points for coming to save her). And she gives her own house the largest single deduction of points in the series. When she catches Hermione, Harry, and Neville wandering the halls at one in the morning, she takes one hundred and fifty points from Gryffindor (fifty points each), putting Gryffindor in the last place for the House Cup. She reprimands them by stating, "I've never been more ashamed of Gryffindor students," (*SS* 243–4) a sentiment that conveys her high expectations, even as it conveys her disappointment in their failure to meet them.

As a mentor, McGonagall often challenges her students, but she never does so without a great deal of emotional investment. The longer she spends with the students in the series, the more we see her develop a strong mentoring bond. In *Chamber of Secrets*, McGonagall becomes visibly emotional when discussing students who have been petrified in a series of mysterious events, including Hermione. Harry recalls seeing her with "a tear glistening" and "distinctly heard Professor McGonagall blow her nose," as he and Ron made their way to see Hermione at the infirmary (*CoS* 288–9). McGonagall again shows distress when she learns that a student was "taken by the monster.

Right into the Chamber itself" (*CoS* 293). Despite her praise of Harry for succeeding in his first task of the Triwizard Tournament in his fourth year, McGonagall is also clearly concerned for his well-being after seeing his injuries. Harry notices "her hand shook as she pointed at his shoulder," and she ushers him to the first aid tent quickly (*GoF* 357). When Dolores Umbridge attempts to punish Harry for supposedly breaking Educational Decree Number 24 via the formation of an "illegal society" the following year, McGonagall is quick to rush to Harry's aid, demanding evidence of her accusations (*OotP* 613–4) and warning Harry to keep quiet while Dumbledore hatches a plan to protect him (*OotP* 619). These examples highlight McGonagall's qualities of good mentorship and underscore that she is particularly good for first-generation students by never falling prey to the lowered expectations of implicit bias, providing them with emotional support, and challenging and believing in her students—pure-blood and Muggle-born alike.

Bad Mentor: Severus Snape

Professor Severus Snape provides our best example of a clearly bad mentor, particularly ill-suited toward mentoring Muggle-born students. He largely refrains from having any sort of emotional connection to his students that is not fueled by his own history or emotional agenda. Even as his love for Harry's mother leads him to do everything he can to protect Harry, his hatred of Harry's father causes him to torment and antagonize him. This is particularly evident when Snape is tasked with mentoring Harry in Occlumency, at which Snape fails miserably. He is unable to form meaningful emotional relationships with his students; in fact, it is this lack of true emotional connection with his students that prevents him from crossing into toxic territory.

Snape's primary modes of teaching/mentoring are based on intimidation and bullying. Such methods are particularly ineffective for non-traditional or first-generation students. Rob Smith argues such students do best under a style that "amounts to nurture and has a communicative dimension—in other words involves supportive contact with staff who can respond to their individual needs" (692). He cites Read, et al., who argue that traditional sink-or-swim type academic practices alienate non-traditional students and that such practice "both reflects and reinforces the dominant discourse of the student as white, middle-class and male" (690). When educators maintain such a stereotype of the student population and engage in ineffective academic practices, first-generation students are particularly vulnerable to "sinking" and being left out of the dominant discourse, something that could be mediated with good mentorship and worsened by the bullying-style of education/mentorship typified in Snape.

Good mentorship requires an emotional connection with mentees, but Snape seems to largely avoid non-problematic emotional ties to Muggle-born/wizarding-naive students. Without healthy emotional attachment, his mentoring cannot ever be particularly effective, but he seems incapable of forming these bonds. His lack of emotional attachment, especially with respect to Muggle-born students, may be a result of his own wizarding history; born to a pure-blood witch and an abusive Muggle father, he was largely neglected by both parents. He, himself, demonstrates a semi-first-generation-esque naivety in his oversimplified childhood assumption that Slytherin House was for the brightest students—perhaps unaware of its complex past and reputation of producing a large number of dark wizards. And he lacked the tools to deal with the bullying he experienced in school by purebloods like James Potter and Sirius Black. This experience may be a source for his inability or refusal to connect with and mentor Muggle-born students as he tries to distance himself from his Muggle heritage, further impacting his ability to be a nurturing and effective mentor.

Although Snape may have some redeeming personal qualities, in terms of mentorship, he is just plain bad. He is emotionally disturbed and operates out of a twisted love for Lily, rather than any true desire to mentor, and he transfers his hatred for James to Harry. He bullies and belittles his students. He does not encourage or support them, but rather intimidates them and causes them to question their abilities. Johnson and Nelson argue that bad mentorship can take several forms: (1) incompetence, (2) inappropriate/exploitative relationships, and (3) unequal access to mentoring. Snape exemplifies the latter. He clearly favors more "traditional" wizarding students, and his reliance on bullying makes his mentoring relationships fraught, inappropriate, and ultimately, ineffective, particularly for Muggle-born students.

Toxic Mentor: Albus Dumbledore

While it is relatively easy to discern the qualities of a *bad* mentor, like Snape, the mentorships that are the *most* destructive share many qualities with the mentorships that are the most productive. Such effective mentorships can inevitably become messy due to deep emotional investment. A bad mentor is bad, but toxic mentors are toxic because they have a level of good emotional connection: they are able to hurt us in a way that someone without that connection could not. A questionable/toxic mentor is one that is both good *and* bad. Much like other personal relationships, people tend to prioritize the good and explain away the bad in order to maintain the relationship. When a relationship has failed, the opposite tends to be true: people tend to villainize the other, whether or not such vilification is completely warranted.

So how do we know what is truly toxic behavior and what is human incompetence/misunderstanding/hurt?

A first-generation student is particularly vulnerable to becoming entangled in toxic mentorships because they may not have sufficient knowledge about what a good mentorship looks like to be able to spot the red flags in the relationship. They might feel flattered or honored to have a mentor single them out as special or center an unusual amount of attention on them. And even if they become aware that the relationship has become problematic, they may have come to rely on their mentor for simple survival in the unfamiliar academic environment and may not know how to function without their guidance. Thus, they may feel unable to extricate themselves from the relationship. The experience of Hogwarts students provides us with a way to illustrate what this kind of problematic relationship might look like.

In the texts, the best example we have of students becoming entangled with a toxic mentor is in the relationship between Dumbledore and his chosen favorites. Dumbledore exemplifies the requisite aspects of good mentorship along with the destructive elements that turn these relationships toxic. He cultivates and nurtures emotional connections with his mentees: Harry is devoted to him, and Snape is blindly loyal to him. His students approach him with adulation. He is revered with something like unto worship, as we see when Hagrid loses his temper when Harry's uncle Vernon insults Dumbledore (*SS* 58–9). Dumbledore does some wonderful things as a mentor, yet none of this can erase the emotional manipulation of his mentees, especially those who are Muggle-born or wizarding naive, and the downright dangerous and compromising positions in which he places them.

Dumbledore is a toxic mentor because he uses students for his own purposes, cloaked in the "greater good." He uses the power he has over people and the sheer intensity of their devotion to him to get them to do things that are unacceptable. It is not appropriate for a man of his experience and stature—let alone age—to ask a literal child to delve into his memories when the entire wizarding world is at stake. Yet Dumbledore does exactly that. Whether Dumbledore is simply trying to provide Harry the knowledge he needs to move forward or needs Harry's help sorting through those memories, it is a manipulative move on Dumbledore's part as he again fails to provide straightforward expectations and context. He only provides Harry the memories that he believes will encourage Harry to do whatever Dumbledore asks of him.

Dumbledore asks his mentees to take on too great of an emotional burden. This is evident when he asks Harry to pour poison down his throat in the cave where they have found a Horcrux (*H-BP* 569). He tells Harry that the potion must be drunk and says, "it might paralyze me, cause me to forget what I am here for, create so much pain I am distracted, or render me incapable in some other way" (*H-BP* 569). He tells Harry that it is his job, as a boy of sixteen, to make sure Dumbledore keeps drinking even if Harry must force-feed it to him, reminding Harry that he promised Dumbledore he would follow any command Dumbledore gave him (*H-BP* 569–70). Harry is deeply traumatized by this task, he does as he is told, "hating himself, repulsed by what he was doing" (*H-BP* 571). Again, Dumbledore uses his emotional connection to Harry in a manipulative fashion in order to get Harry to do what he asks.

When it comes to all mentoring relationships—Dumbledore and Harry's relationship included—a power differential exists between mentor and mentee. Sometimes this power differential is more obvious, as between an undergraduate student and a faculty mentor. But there are often areas where that power differential can become less obvious. We might see a gray area between an undergraduate student and a graduate mentor, a graduate student and their faculty mentor, or between a former-student-turned-colleague and their mentor. The power a mentor holds over their mentee can range from helpful to hurtful to harmful. And a mentee may be less willing to challenge a mentor out of fear that they will damage their mentoring relationship (Hudson 32). While it is up to a mentor to wield this power professionally, it is important for mentees to recognize this power differential and how it can be abused by their mentor. This is especially true for first-generation students who, again, may be naive to the abuse happening, may find the additional attention flattering or encouraging, or may not know what to do if they are concerned their mentor is abusing this power.

Textual incidences of Dumbledore abusing his power differential are copious. An illustrative one occurs in *Half-Blood Prince* when he uses Harry to retrieve something he needs and cannot get for himself: a memory from Professor Slughorn. It starts with Dumbledore using Harry's mere presence to lure Slughorn into returning to Hogwarts to be the Defense Against the Dark Arts teacher, knowing Slughorn will not be able to resist trying to "collect" Harry (*H-BP* 69–70; 75). Once Slughorn is back at Hogwarts, Dumbledore reveals to Harry a memory that has been tampered with, featuring Slughorn speaking to Tom Riddle (aka Voldemort) about Horcruxes when Riddle was still a student. Slughorn has altered the memory so that it shows him telling Riddle that he would not tell him anything about Horcruxes and to never ask again. Dumbledore tasks Harry with persuading Slughorn "to divulge the real memory, which will undoubtedly be our most crucial piece of information of all" (*H-BP* 372). While the memory reveals that Slughorn *did* talk to Riddle about Horcruxes, it is incredibly inappropriate to ask a mentee to try to manipulate another professor.

Furthermore, it is not appropriate for a mentor to ask a mentee to *kill him*, and yet, this is precisely what Dumbledore does with Snape. We learn from Snape's memory that Snape was summoned to Dumbledore's office after Dumbledore placed a cursed ring on his finger. While Snape was able to trap the curse in Dumbledore's hand, it was a temporary solution. The curse would claim Dumbledore's life within the year (*DH* 681). Dumbledore finds the news of his impending demise a blessing, knowing that Voldemort had ordered Draco Malfoy to kill him but that the boy would be incapable of completing the task and would be killed. If Dumbledore was going to die within the year, he believed he could at least save Draco. He tells Snape: "*You* must kill me" (*DH* 682). Snape completes the impossible task asked of him "with revulsion and hatred etched in the harsh lines of his face," no doubt internally conflicted over what he had to do (*H-BP* 595). The power dynamics of a mentor/mentee relationship among professors and students simply do not go away after the passage of time. They persist. They can persist long into adulthood, when the two are ostensibly "peers." It was not appropriate for Dumbledore to ask Snape to do something Snape could not, within the bounds of such a power disconnect, easily deny. Harry and Snape never stood a chance against the master gamesman. He manipulated them both effortlessly and so completely that even when his machinations were revealed, his mentees still obeyed.

And here is the crux of toxic mentorship: asking a mentee to do something outside the bounds of an acceptable professor-student relationship, something they cannot refuse *because* of the power the mentor has over them, is a clear abuse of that power. Encouraging students to do things that help their careers—helping them apply for scholarships, jobs, suggesting they take difficult classes—that is what a good mentor does. What a good mentor does *not* do is abuse their power. While having an emotional relationship is a natural outcome of a mentorship, good mentors do not ask their mentees to do emotional labor for them. We do not fully agree with E. Scott Warren's recommendations for ethical mentorships: we do not believe that the personal should be eschewed for the professional, that engagements outside the professional settings should be avoided, that group meetings should *always* be favored over individual meetings, or that mentees should be discouraged from discussing their non-professional lives (Warren 145). We argue the personal cannot be excised in a mentoring relationship—nor should it be. But neither do we agree with the other end of the spectrum. When Christopher James Ryan argues that "power differentials are universal in society" and thus, insufficient to proscribe sexual relationships (389), we adamantly disagree. A good mentoring relationship is somewhere in between these two extremes. And equipping first-generation students to navigate this complexity is part of good mentoring.

While a mentorship is a human relationship with human flaws and complexities, there are certain actions that, clearly, cross the line. In the *Harry Potter* series, this manifests when Dumbledore asks his mentee to kill him.

In the non-fictional world, this often manifests in the form of sexual relationships. In a student/teacher relationship, all sexual relationships, even ones ostensibly "consensual," are inherently exploitative. When the APA prohibited sexual relationships for practicing psychologists with not just *current* clients, but *all* clients—including former clients *in perpetuity*, even after "a decent interval" has passed (Vasquez 49), all of the reasons they give are also found in the student/teacher relationship: title, authority, power differential, harm to clients (students), harm to colleagues, harm to the profession. While Blevins-Knabe argues that because "the central issue in setting this boundary is power," such relationships may become permissible when "the power of the professor diminishes" (162), we believe that the permissible relationship is the exception, and we agree with Vasquez that "exceptional cases should not be codified and [...] they should never prevent professional organizations from establishing principles that prevent harm" (49). Most former students will never be able to fully extricate themselves from the power differential. Any sexual relationship they find themselves in is likely to be one in which they feel disempowered to speak their concerns, they feel unable to refuse advances, and they may still, possibly without realizing it, be seeking approval from their mentor. We see these same characteristics effected in what Dumbledore asks of Snape.

The fact that the former mentor may be completely unaware of the power differential at play does not stop it from causing harm. Though Dumbledore does not, in the text, seek out a sexual relationship with any of his students, he does abuse the power differential. Snape is still clearly under his thrawl, subject to the power differential that is the result of having been Dumbledore's student. And so, Dumbledore's asking Snape to kill him becomes an abuse of power because Snape is not able to easily say no. While asking a mentee to kill you is probably on the extreme end of toxic mentorship, there are some other, less extreme ways that Dumbledore demonstrates toxic mentoring qualities. From giving a cloak of invisibility to an emotionally immature young boy to manipulating Hermione to use her time-turner, the incidences in which Dumbledore manipulate, exploits, and uses his emotional connections for his own purposes are as copious as references to his sexuality are absent.

Application in the Muggle World

The experiences and struggles of the Muggle-born students at Hogwarts are fraught, complex, and emotionally resonant, particularly for first-generation students. First-generation students may not know how to find a mentor or recognize that a mentor is bad or toxic. So how can we help them better find meaningful mentoring relationships while also recognizing that all mentors come with baggage? We cannot help but be influenced by our backgrounds, by how and why we come to be in the position we are. We have all been influenced by the (often deeply meaningful, even when deeply problematic) relationships we have had with our own mentors. What do we expect from mentors, if it is unreasonable to expect them to come in without baggage?

We maintain that neither extreme—"no personal info" and "it is ok to sleep with students"—is appropriate. The ideal mentorship exists between these two ends of the mentorship spectrum. Good mentorships are emotional, personal, and may extend outside the classroom. But mentorships that abuse or fail to recognize the power differential, relationships that are sexual, and relationships that ignore all emotional connections are inappropriate and ineffectual. If we want first-generation students to succeed, if we want to retain them through graduation, mentors have to recognize the unique challenges first-generation students face and how their lack of academic cultural fluency makes them particularly vulnerable to the absence of mentorship, bad mentorship, or even toxic mentorship. If a mentor has no experience as a first-generation student themselves, then institutions need to offer training and support so that mentors can be sensitive to first-generation experiences. The experiences of the Muggle-born students at Hogwarts is a good place to start.

WORKS CITED

Bettinger, Eric P., and Rachel Baker. "The Effects of Student Coaching in College: An Evaluation of a Randomized Experiment in Student Mentoring." March 7, 2011, ed.stanford.edu/sites/default/files/bettinger_baker_030711.pdf.

Blevins-Knabe, Belinda. "The Ethics of Dual Relationships in Higher Education." *Ethics and Behavior*, vol. 2, no. 3, 1992, pp. 151–63.

Blixen, Carol E. "Developing a Mentorship Program for Clinical Researchers." *Journal of Continuing Education in the Health Professions*, vol. 27, no. 2, Spring 2007, pp. 86–93.

Cho, Christine S., et al. "Defining the Ideal Qualities of Mentorship: A Qualitative Analysis of the Characteristics of Outstanding Mentors." *The American Journal of Medicine*, vol. 124, no. 5, May 2011, pp. 453–58.

Hudson, Peter. "Forming the Mentor-Mentee Relationship." *Journal of Mentoring and Tutoring* vol. 24, no. 1, 2016, pp. 30–43.

Johnson, Brad W., and Nancy Nelson. "Mentor-Protege Relationships in Graduate Training: Some Ethical Concerns." *Ethics and Behavior*, vol. 9, no. 3, 1999, pp. 189–210.

McClelland, Richard T. "The Dark Side of Mentoring: Explaining Mentor on Mentee Aggression." *International Journal of Applied Philosophy*, vol. 23, no. 1, Jan. 2009, pp. 61–86.

Nadworny, Elissa, and Julie Depenbock. "Today's College Students Aren't Who You Think They Are." *NPR*, 4 Sept. 2018, www.npr.org/sections/ed/2018/09/04/638561407/todays-college-students-arent-who-you-think-they-are.

National Academy of Sciences (NAS), et al. *Adviser, Teacher, Role Model, Friend: On Being A Mentor to Students in Science and Engineering*. The National Academies Press, 1997. doi.org/10.17226/5789.

Perlmutter, David D. "Do You Have a Bad Mentor?" *Chronicle of Higher Education*, 19 May 2008, www.chronicle.com/article/Do-You-Have-a-Bad-Mentor-/45819/.

Pope, K.S., et al. "Sexual Intimacy in Psychology Training: Results and Implications of a National Survey." *American Psychologist*, vol. 34, no. 8, Aug. 1979, pp. 682–89.

Rowling, J.K. *Harry Potter and the Chamber of Secrets*. Scholastic, 1999.

———. *Harry Potter and the Deathly Hallows*. Scholastic, 2007.

———. *Harry Potter and the Goblet of Fire*. Scholastic, 2000.

———. *Harry Potter and the Half-Blood Prince*. Scholastic, 2005.

———. *Harry Potter and the Order of the Phoenix*. Scholastic, 2003.

———. *Harry Potter and the Prisoner of Azkaban*. Scholastic, 1999.

———. *Harry Potter and the Sorcerer's Stone*. Scholastic, 1998.

Ryan, Christopher James. "Sex, Lies and Training Programs: The Ethics of Consensual Sexual Relationships in Mentorship." *Australian and New Zealand Journal of Psychiatry*, vol. 32, no. 3, June 1998, pp. 387–91.

Saenz, Victor, and Doug Barerra. "What We Can Learn from UCLA's 'First in My Family' Data." *Retention in Higher Education*, vol. 21, no. 9, 2007, p. 1–3.

Smith, Rob. "An Overview of Research on Student Support: Helping Students to Achieve or Achieving Institutional Targets? Nurture or De-nature?" *Teaching in Higher Education*, vol. 12, no. 56, October/December 2007, pp. 683–95.

Tugend, Alina. "The Struggle to Be First: First-Gen Students May Be Torn Between College and Home." *California Magazine*, Spring 2015, alumni.berkeley.edu/california-maga zine/spring-2015-dropouts-and-drop-ins/struggle-be-first-first-gen-students-may-be.

Vasquez, Melba. "Sexual Intimacies with Clients After Termination: Should a Prohibition Be Explicit?" *Ethics and Behavior*, vol. 1, no. 1, 1991, pp. 45–61.

Warren, E. Scott. "Future Colleague or Convenient Friend: The Ethics of Mentorship." *Counseling and Values*, vol. 49, no. 2, Jan. 2005, pp. 141–46.

Weil, V., and R. Arzbaecher. "Ethics and Relationships in Laboratories and Research Communities." *Professional Ethics*, vol. 4, nos. 3–4, Spring-Summer 1995, pp. 83–125.

Zinshteyn, Mikhail. "How to Help First-Generation Students Succeed." *The Atlantic*, 13 Mar. 2016, www.theatlantic.com/education/archive/2016/03/how-to-help-first-generation-students-succeed/473502/.

The Fractured Pedagogy of Care

How Hogwarts' Teachers (Don't)
Demonstrate Self-Care

JEN MCCONNEL

Caring in schools can sometimes feel like a struggle. Standards-based accountability, coupled with teachers and school personnel who are often spread too thin, make it challenging to develop authentic caring relationships between teachers and students (and teachers and colleagues). An added component of these challenges stems from a "universal dilemma" in the caring professions: the tension between care for others and care for self (Skovholt and Trotter-Mathison 3). What, then, does it look like to cultivate a pedagogy of care in our schools? Nel Noddings articulates care as relational, rooted in the relationship between the carer and the cared-for. By her explanation, care requires participation from both parties: the responsibilities of the carer include connection through listening, seeing, and feeling "what the other tries to convey," while it is up to the cared-for to exhibit "reception, recognition, and response" (*Challenge to Care* 16). A true pedagogy of care is reciprocal and synergetic, requiring connection and engagement from both parties. However, as Thomas M. Skovholt and Michelle Trotter-Mathison note in their book *The Resilient Practitioner*, burnout in the caring professions often stems from an overabundance of care for others without a professional and personal emphasis on strategies that can foster resilience and self-care. This struggle to balance care for others with care for oneself extends to the world of fiction, as well.

A wide variety of pedagogies and personalities shape the learning of students at Hogwarts, and an exploration of various characters' forms of caring is necessary to understand what a pedagogy of care looks like in the wizarding world. This essay centers on the ways Remus Lupin, "Moody" (Barty Crouch, Jr., during his impersonation of Mad-Eye Moody), Rubeus Hagrid, and Minerva McGonagall demonstrate care throughout the series. These four teachers cultivate caring relationships with students beyond Harry, allowing the reader to interpret their care as care for students in general, rather than simply the mentorship of "the boy who lived." However, there is a darker side to the pedagogy of care practiced within the walls of Rowling's castle. Teachers who care for their students without also caring for themselves and their careers are subject to ministry intervention, burnout, and bodily harm. This essay will explore the ways in which Professors Lupin, "Moody," Hagrid, and McGonagall enact various forms of care in their teaching. I will draw on the works of Noddings for her framework of care in teaching and on *The Resilient Practitioner* to consider the ways in which these Hogwarts teachers (except for McGonagall) make common mistakes that can lead to professional and personal burnout in the caring professions.

Rooted in Care: Professor Lupin

When Harry, Ron, and Hermione meet Professor Lupin on the Hogwarts' Express, it is in the context of their first encounter with a dementor. After thwarting the attack and defending the children with his Patronus, Lupin is on hand with chocolate to ease the symptoms. The students still do not warm to him, and Lupin, recognizing this, takes himself out of the compartment with the flimsy excuse of going to speak with the engineer, leaving them to unpack their terrifying (and for Harry, moderately embarrassing) experience in peace (*PoA* 87–88). This instance makes it clear that Lupin cares about his students even before he knows them, something that is further demonstrated during their first Defense Against the Dark Arts (DADA) class together. Rather than hovering over them or being heavy handed in his advice or instruction, Lupin fosters a sense of curiosity and problem solving in the classroom, all while expertly scaffolding safety precautions, as exemplified in his first lesson with the boggart.

This lesson allows Lupin's caring to shine. It is their first class, and yet he is already calling each of the students by name. Additionally, he uses the lesson as a confidence builder for everyone—especially Neville, who has, until this point in the series, not had a teacher step in to stop the bullying he endures. In fact, Neville is bullied by Professor Snape before the Boggart lesson begins. Lupin, instead of mirroring Snape's behavior, singles Neville out to start the lesson, giving him control and a huge burst of confidence (while, it must be noted, also making Professor Snape look foolish and giving the third-year Gryffindors a good laugh). The lesson is both silly and empowering as the students face their fears with laughter. When the boggart is weak, instead of defeating it himself, Lupin hands the victory to Neville: "'Forward, Neville, and finish him off!' said Lupin, as the Boggart landed on the floor as a cockroach. *Crack!* Snape was back. This time, Neville charged forward looking determined" (*PoA* 146). In a single lesson, Lupin has not only given the students a more deliberate, scaffolded experience than they have had in the course up until that point, but he has also made clear that his care for his students does not require them to be the bravest or the brightest. By singling out Neville, Lupin shows the students that each of them can be the hero of the day. Contrary to the experiences the cohort has had at Hogwarts thus far, Lupin does not allow Harry to take center stage. For Neville, the experience is transformative; he begins to grow in confidence from this point forward.

The students respond to Lupin's care for them and his subject area reciprocally; he quickly becomes a favorite teacher, with only Draco finding anything unpleasant to say. However, after the first lesson, Harry feels uncertain about Lupin's feelings toward him. When Harry is unable to attend the first Hogsmeade trip of the year and Lupin spots him wandering around the castle, he invites Harry back to his office for a chat and a cup of tea. Their conversation reveals that Lupin's actions during the boggart lesson possessed another layer of care for the students in his class: Lupin tells Harry that he "assumed that if the boggart faced [Harry], it would assume the shape of Lord Voldemort.... I didn't think it a good idea for Lord Voldemort to materialize in the staff room. I imagined that people would panic" (*PoA* 163). Lupin is able to think on his feet and consider a variety of possibilities in the midst of teaching, indicating that he cares a great deal for his work as well as for his relationships with the students.

Harry leaves that conversation feeling much better, and his relationship with Lupin continues to develop, helped along by Lupin's somewhat questionable choice to take the Marauder's Map and lie to Professor Snape in order to keep both Harry and himself out of trouble (*PoA* 307–308). However, despite their deepening relationship, Lupin does not reveal the connection he has to Harry's father until their first Patronus tutorial session, and then he refuses to elaborate on what appears to be an unintentional statement where he admits to knowing Harry's father and Sirius Black (*PoA* 255, 257). It would seem that Lupin wants to establish a relationship with Harry that is not overtly influenced by his previous relationship with James Potter, perhaps because he wants to build his relationships with all his students based on the present rather than family history or unpleasant events in the past.

Lupin's attentiveness to the present is also seen in his willingness to let go of past grudges, as evidenced in his professional relationship with Professor Snape. Lupin takes the potion Snape prepares for him every month, giving

Snape a great deal of power over him (*PoA* 164–165). In fact, other than the boggart's manifestation as Snape in Neville's grandmother's hat, the interchanges between Lupin and Snape until the climax of the book are, if not friendly, at least coldly professional. Lupin, it would appear, is a teacher rooted in a pedagogy of care, and the students begin to thrive under his tutelage.

It might be easy to read Lupin's care as specific to Harry, given Lupin's relationship with James, but in the limited opportunities where we watch him interact with the other students, he appears just as nurturing toward them. One particular example I have already mentioned is the boggart lesson. Lupin carefully coaches Neville (and the rest of the class) on the best way to fight fear: with laughter. He gives everyone time to prepare for the shape the boggart may take when they face it, engaging the class in a deliberately metacognitive activity that seems lacking from most of the pedagogy at Hogwarts, and then he allows Neville the first crack at facing his fears, which Neville pulls off beautifully. This is a welcome change from countless other class interactions over the years where the reader is told how badly Neville has bungled this or that charm or potion. True, Neville's fear of Professor Snape allows Lupin to tacitly encourage that the students humiliate the professor, so his motives may not be entirely altruistic; however, the fact remains that Neville, bullied by teachers and students, is given his first chance to shine and demonstrate his worth.

Despite the expansive compassion Lupin shows his students, he carries the pedagogy of care too far, ultimately endangering not only his teaching career, but his life and the lives of the students in his care. As noted by Skovholt and Trotter-Mathison, one of the factors that contribute to professional drain and burn-out is the presence of "professional boundaries that allow for *excessive other-care and too little self-care*" (192; emphasis added). When Lupin runs off to the Shrieking Shack in pursuit of Peter Pettigrew, he is so caught up with simultaneously saving Harry, Ron, and Hermione and solving a decade-old mystery that he forgets that the moon is full and that Professor Snape has not yet brought him the potion that will mitigate his monthly werewolf transformation. He forgets the potion, prompting Snape to pursue him, which sets off a chain reaction: Pettigrew's escape, Sirius's recapture and near death, and Lupin's deadly transformation (unchecked, on school grounds, and in front of three students). In caring so much for Harry and his friends, Professor Lupin neglects to care for himself—with disastrous effect.

To his credit, Lupin recognizes the danger of his self-neglect right away and resigns; not because of any complaints (although he acknowledges that they are likely forthcoming from the parents of the students at the school) but because, as he says, "after last night, I see their point. I could have bitten any of you … *that must never happen again*" (*PoA* 450; emphasis added). Once again, Lupin's care for his students supersedes his personal feelings and his desire for professional stability. He is a gifted teacher, but his lack of attention to his own needs effectively ends his teaching career.

Seeming to Care: Professor "Moody"

Next, we will examine the peculiar case of the false Professor Moody, who certainly does not intend to care for Harry and his friends in the same way as Lupin. However, as Noddings establishes in *The Challenge to Care in Schools*, caring is not isolated to care for others. Although "Moody" certainly pretends to care for others, particularly Harry and Neville, it is actually the deep connection he has toward an ideal—namely, helping Voldemort rise to power—that is the catalyst for his caring. While such an ideal should be abhorrent to any reader of the series, Rowling carefully manipulates readers into trusting and connecting with "Moody," primarily because Harry does. It is interesting to note that some of the same tricks she uses to establish Professor Lupin's deeply caring character are employed in the service of "Moody," particularly when it comes to Neville. After his first Defense Against the Dark Arts (DADA) lesson demonstrating the three Unforgivable Curses (which has particularly upset Neville, given the fate of his parents), "Moody" takes Neville back to his office to give him time to get his emotions under control (*GoF* 184). This action, coupled with a compliment "Moody" heard from Professor Sprout and shares with Neville in the hearing of his peers, prompts the narrator to remark that such a gesture "was the sort of thing Professor Lupin would have done" (*GoF* 186), thereby linking "Moody" and Lupin in the mind of Harry and the reader.

Although "Moody's" motives in seeming to care for the students at Hogwarts are self-serving and decidedly dark, the result of his performance is that he fosters feelings of trust and care in the students. In serving the ideals of Voldemort, "Moody" paradoxically becomes a trusted mentor and professional role model. Noddings posits occupational care as a way in which a pedagogy of care can manifest in schools, particularly if teachers recognize that "in addition to finding out what kind of people they are and want to become, our children will also have to choose occupations" (*Challenge to Care* 50). "Moody's" persona as a skilled (if paranoid) auror inspires Harry and Ron to consider following in his footsteps in their own careers, perhaps especially because of the hands-on, dangerous training "Moody" provides in his course that serves to start students thinking about the reality of DADA. "Moody" also boosts Neville's self-esteem, continuing the work Professor Lupin began in book three, which ironically, will prove the seeds of the ultimate destruction of Voldemort. So, although he did not intend it, "Moody's" care-based actions ultimately help defeat the very figure he cares most about.

"Moody" is an interesting case, given his dual identity. The students we hear speaking of him appear to respect him, even when he places an Unforgivable Curse on each of them under the guise of teaching them how to resist such curses. It is likely that "Moody" enjoys tormenting the children, but he keeps a relatively tight rein on himself, and the scene reads as a benign experiential exercise, presumably sanctioned by Dumbledore, until knowledge of "Moody's" identity is revealed at the end of the novel. It is "Moody's" excess of care for the return of Lord Voldemort that ultimately proves his undoing: he gets so caught up that he neglects, like Lupin, to take a necessary potion (in this case, the Polyjuice that allows him to continue his charade). As Dumbledore points out after the disaster of the final task, "in the excitement of tonight, our fake Moody might have forgotten to take it as frequently as he should have done … on the hour … every hour" (*GoF* 574). Perhaps "Moody" is hindered at this point in the story by his "inability to accept any ambiguous professional loss or normative failure" (Skovholt and Trotter-Mathison 192), another common factor that leads professionals in the caring fields to become depleted. He cannot conceive that his plan will fail, and so he neglects to take the necessary steps to preserve himself in the height of the moment. Ultimately, "Moody's" care for his master supersedes his ability to act as Moody, leading to his own destruction.

"Moody" puts on a good show of caring for the students, and even after the big reveal, he has a lasting influence at Hogwarts. Harry continues to pursue the goal of one day becoming an auror, something first inspired by "Moody," and the students who learned from his questionable methods develop confidence when faced with dark wizards, as in the climactic battle at the Ministry of Magic during *Order of the Phoenix*, when not only Harry, but Neville, Ron, Hermione, Luna, and Ginny take on real threats and for the most part, remember their training. "Moody" casts a long shadow of sinister care, but unfortunately for his cause, his care is thwarted by the act he puts on. Seeming to care, it would seem, can offer disastrous consequences for the carer.

Overabundance of Care: Professor Hagrid

Hagrid's teaching is reminiscent of many beginning teachers' careers. He approaches the work with enthusiasm and care for his students, but he soon reveals that he is not as well prepared as he should be. Hagrid is, at best, an unprepared teacher, and at worst, a dangerous role model for the students in his care. When he is promoted from groundskeeper to Care of Magical Creatures instructor, most of the students respond with delight (*PoA* 98). However, from his choice of a potentially harmful textbook, *The Monster*

Book of Monsters, to his first lesson with the hippogriff, Hagrid demonstrates that the reciprocal relationship he has with his students is not enough to make him a good teacher. Initially, the students are willing to overlook the potential danger of Hagrid's class. When the students discover that Hagrid is to teach their Care of Magical Creatures Class, Ron, who is cheering as loud as anybody, declares fondly, "We should have known.... Who else would have set us a biting book?" (*PoA* 99). However, as Hagrid's pedagogical decisions remain questionable and the safety of the students in his course becomes less certain, the students gradually cool to the idea of Hagrid as a teacher. Even Harry, Ron, and Hermione begin to have trouble getting excited about learning from Hagrid, and it is only their relationship with him that keeps them from openly criticizing his teaching.

Early career teachers face a host of difficulties and challenges, but an equally varied number of factors such as peer support, reflection, and self-care can help these teachers develop or strengthen their resilience to both survive and thrive through the long haul of a teaching career, according to a review of studies on teacher resilience conducted by Beltman, Mansfield, and Price in 2011. For Hagrid, as for many early career teachers, the empathetic connection he forges with his students serves as a boost to his resilience, even in the face of minor classroom disasters. However, Hagrid (as with the Hogwarts teaching staff, in general) appears to be lacking any formalized mentorship or support, beyond the confidence Dumbledore has in each of his teachers. Without support, any teacher may falter, no matter how much they care about and are cared for by their students. We see this faltering at various points throughout the series when Hagrid comes close to giving up. His lack of "long-term professional development" (Skovholt and Trotter-Mathison 192) is another common factor that contributes to professional fatigue. Because he does not appear to take a long view of his career, it is hard for Hagrid to build a sustainable teaching practice. Outright hostilities from certain students (*PoA*), the negative press he receives for being half-giant (*GoF*), and Dolores Umbridge's attempts to remove him from his post (*OotP*), each nearly end his teaching career. His willingness to give up forces Harry and his friends to, time and again, remind Hagrid that they believe in his teaching (even if, as the years wear on, it becomes more difficult for the characters to pretend that Hagrid is an excellent teacher). As time passes, it becomes clear that Harry and his friends are acting out of a reciprocal sense of care for Hagrid, not out of any devotion to his teaching; in *Goblet of Fire* they proceed with the lessons solely out of "deep affection for Hagrid" (*GoF* 166). A caring relationship in the classroom is powerful, but no student should feel that their relationship with their instructor precludes their desire to learn.

Through an overabundance of care for others, Hagrid's career is both saved and endangered, again and again throughout the series. However, even as the students lose confidence in his teaching abilities, they are reminded that Hagrid is a deeply caring individual and that certain members of the wizarding world value his expansive care. When, during the reign of Dolores Umbridge, Firenze the centaur is brought into the castle to teach Divination, he pulls Harry aside after the first lesson to deliver a cryptic message meant for Hagrid. Firenze tells Harry that he respects Hagrid "for the care he shows all living creatures" (*OotP* 558), but he adds, Hagrid must stop caring for Grawp, his giant half-brother. Even the centaurs, who hold themselves generally aloof from the rest of the wizarding world, acknowledge that Hagrid's capacity to care is vast. Yet, they can also see that Hagrid fails to consider the consequences of his care. Despite Hagrid's record of loving monsters who never cease to be dangerous, his care of Grawp ultimately proves not to be misplaced, and the giant becomes more empathetic throughout the series, eventually proving to be a powerful ally during the Battle of Hogwarts. Perhaps the example of Grawp is meant to show readers the potential of care to transform, but Hagrid's choices up to that point do not paint an encouraging picture. The carelessness for his and other's well-being that Hagrid demonstrates in caring for Grawp (and other creatures over the course of the series) is often extreme and unnecessary, putting himself and others at frequent risk.

Hagrid's compassionate carelessness, while problematic, is not something that only emerges through his teaching. From the first chapter of *Philosopher's Stone*, the reader does not just meet a heroic Hagrid on Sirius Black's motorcycle, safely delivering Harry to his relatives. Moments before his arrival, we instead encounter the perception others have of him as helpful but perhaps unreliable: "'You think it—wise—to trust Hagrid with something as important as this?' 'I would trust Hagrid with my life,' said Dumbledore. 'I'm not saying his heart isn't in the right place,' said Professor McGonagall grudgingly, 'but you can't pretend he's not careless'" (*PS* 14). In the same book, Hagrid betrays Dumbledore's trust about the hiding place and security measures protecting the Philosopher's Stone with little more incentive than a night of free drinks and the promise of a dragon egg. And yet, when Hagrid perceives something as a genuine threat, he is fiercely protective of the students in his care, including Draco Malfoy. When Harry, Draco, Hermione, and Neville are serving detention in the Forbidden Forest with Hagrid to search for the wounded unicorn, Hagrid's lovingly bumbling demeanor is completely gone, replaced by a gruff, crossbow-wielding man who will brook no nonsense and gives the children explicit instructions related to safety (*PS*).

Perhaps, at the heart of these contradictions, Hagrid's compassion prevents him from experiencing some situations as threatening or dangerous, even if others in the wizarding world would approach the same situations with fear. His love of monsters goes back to his own childhood where he was expelled and risked Azkaban for keeping an acromantula (a gigantic spider) inside the castle during the initial opening of the Chamber of Secrets (*CoS* 249). His introduction of creatures like hippogriffs and blast-ended skrewts to his students may actually be rooted in Hagrid's deep ethic of care. It is not just the students that he seeks to mother and mentor. Any living thing, other than the truly evil, is deserving of Hagrid's loving attention. I use the word "mother" here deliberately; the ethic of care is often conceptualized as being a feminine ethic, linked to motherhood and women in general (Noddings, *Caring: A Feminine Approach* and Noddings, *Challenge to Care*).

In moments of high emotion, Hagrid identifies himself not as the father of the creatures he adores, but as their mother. During his brief ownership of Norbert the Norwegian Ridgeback dragon, Hagrid refers to himself as Norbert's "mummy" three times in the span of five pages. When the egg hatches and the dragon snaps at Hagrid, his joyful response is, "Bless him, look, he knows his mummy!" (*PS* 234). When Harry, Ron, and Hermione visit again, Hagrid tries to convince them, "He really knows me know, watch. Norbert! Norbert! Where's Mummy?" (*PS* 235). And, when the friends finally convince Hagrid to part with the dragon, his tear-filled goodbye ends with, "Mummy will never forget you!" (*PS* 239). Perhaps the evident patriarchy of the wizarding world has led Hagrid to identify his capacity to care with feminine identity, which is particularly interesting, given his abandonment by his own mother. In many ways, his unquestioning mothering and his tendency to adopt the least loved creatures he encounters mirror the care enacted by Molly Weasley throughout the series, leaving Hagrid as a stand-in mother for Harry and the other children during the school year.

Hagrid's care manifests in other traditionally feminine ways: his willingness to show emotion, the way he insists on nurturing the wild animals he encounters, and perhaps most memorably, the bookends of his relationship with Harry in the first book of the series, where he bakes him a pink birthday cake for their initial meeting and presents him with the carefully crafted photo album of Harry's parents when they part at the end of the school year. Yes, Hagrid can be careless, but it is also clear that he cares a great deal for the creatures (both animal and human) around him.

A Counter Example: Professor McGonagall

As mentioned previously, the caring professions have long been places of "women's work," something Noddings returns to throughout her work. Teaching, although it was once male-dominated, has come to be associated more and more with women, as has the ethic of care. It is interesting, then, to note that the three teachers profiled here who each exhibit a great deal of care for their subjects and their students, while neglecting to care for themselves, are all male. That is not to say that female teachers at Hogwarts are lacking in care; let us consider for a moment the example of Professor Minerva McGonagall. Her care is infinitely practical, and I would argue, more powerful than the care exerted by the men discussed in this essay. More salient for my point, her care does not endanger her career or her students.

Interestingly, McGonagall is the first character we meet when the series opens, watching the Dursely's house intently in her feline form, and yet her care of the school and the students is often implied rather than stated explicitly, functioning quietly in the background of the series. McGonagall's long-term importance to the students at Hogwarts far exceeds Lupin's limited direct impact, despite his continued relationship with Harry. Her decades of teaching, coupled with her ability to approach every student according to her personal belief in fairness, allow her to help students far beyond the circle of Harry and his friends, or even those in her house. Hagrid's potential for impact comes closest to McGonagall's, but his is limited by the biases he does not completely hide in his interactions with the students and the antagonism the Slytherins display toward him over the course of the series.

There is no question that McGonagall cares deeply for the school and the children in her care; her thirty-nine years at Hogwarts (*OotP* 321) coupled with her strong sense of right and wrong make her a formidable school matriarch who is willing, on numerous occasions, to risk physical and professional harm in the protection of Hogwarts and its students. However, unlike Hagrid, Lupin, and "Moody," McGonagall never seems to act without thought for the consequences. When she puts herself at risk, the reader understands that she is in control of her decisions, which are rooted in an ideal that she believes is worth dying for: the continuation of Hogwarts. And, more importantly, she does not endanger her students. Even at the Battle of Hogwarts, she performs the magic necessary to animate the castle in order to fight, but she does not require that any of the students join her, and she actively tries to prevent the underage students from participating in the battle.

She also exhibits a great deal of care tempered by commitment to Hogwarts when she shelters Professor Trelawney after Dolores Umbridge has stripped her of her teaching post: "Professor McGonagall ... marched straight up to Professor Trelawney and was patting her firmly on the back while withdrawing a large handkerchief from her robes. 'There, there, Sybill ... calm down ... blow your nose on this ... it's not as bad as you think...'" (*OotP* 550). This example is particularly interesting, since earlier in the series (*PoA*), McGonagall and Trelawney have been unfriendly to each other, and McGonagall gives the impression she thinks Trelawney's teaching methods are unnecessarily theatrical. Professional differences aside, however, McGonagall is the first witness to Trelawney's dramatic near-expulsion from the school to offer care to the divination teacher, even though Professors Sprout and Flitwick jump in once Dumbledore has overruled Umbridge and insisted that Tre-lawney should remain at Hogwarts.

McGonagall presents a steely demeanor to her students and is more than willing to take points from her own house, but her "fairness" is infused with caring. Unlike the three male teachers we have been discussing, one does not have the sense that McGonagall's care comes regularly at her own uninten-tional expense. However, there are exceptions—such as when she is willing to draw her wand against the Minister of Magic during the confrontation in which Dumbledore flees Hogwarts (*OotP* 573) and when she goes to Hagrid's defense and ends up badly injured (*OotP* 666). McGonagall eventually recov-ers from her injuries with no lasting harm done to her person or her career. She also avoids what Noddings has pointed out about the misrepresentation of care as "touchy-feely" (*Critical Lessons* 230), particularly when applied to women in power (she is always deputy headmistress over the summers while Dumbledore is off questing, and the letters from Hogwarts come from her). Yet, she offers biscuits, tough-love advice, and support to Harry when he is first confronting Umbridge over Voldemort's return (*OotP*).

McGonagall appears to be a solid example of what bell hooks argues will happen when teachers approach their work with love: "combining care, commitment, knowledge, responsibility, respect, and trust, we [teachers] are often able to enter the classroom and go straight to the heart of the matter" (hooks 134). From her "finely tuned professional boundaries" and her sharp "sense of humor and playfulness" (Skovholt and Trotter-Mathison 192), McGonagall seems to have taken the necessary steps to support her students and thrive in her chosen profession, unlike the men discussed in this essay. McGonagall may not appear to care with the warmth and emotion offered by Hagrid and Lupin, but she is a force of power, tough love, and grit that quietly supports the students while maintaining her career and, as near as readers can tell, her health and well-being.

The Cautionary Tales from Hogwarts

Noddings's pedagogy of care is one in which relationships and curiosity take center stage, rather than content or memorization, and Noddings includes many purposes of care, including: care for others, care for ideas, care for objects, and care for living creatures. Each of the professors discussed in this essay embody a different type of caring. Lupin's dedication stems from the direct relationship he has with the Hogwarts students. He teaches practical spells based on listening and responding to the notes left by the previous two DADA teachers and the students themselves, highlighting the relational aspect of a pedagogy of care. "Moody," on the other hand, presents his caring in the form of care for ideas and professional work. He bases his teaching on the real Moody's work as an auror and offers lessons that are brutal yet necessary introductions to the "real world" of the Dark Arts. Hagrid, a loving and long-term presence at the school, embodies care for all living creatures, from the frightened first years to the monsters in the Forbidden Forest. And as for Professor McGonagall, the depth of the care she holds for the institution and everyone in it is visible multiple times throughout the narrative.

When it comes to Lupin's care for both his subject and his students, I would argue very few of the teachers at Hogwarts ever comes close. Certainly, none of the DADA teachers over the course of the series can rival the care with which Lupin instructs his students. And no one, not even Minerva McGonagall, can question that Hagrid's heart is in the right place: he wears it on his sleeve, and it is vast enough to encompass just about everyone he's ever encountered, unless he has reason to mistrust them. Hagrid is deeply loving, rooted in care and compassion, and yet the very trait that may attract the students to him in the first place may also limit his ability to effectively teach in the wizarding world. Care must be tempered with thought, and Lupin's and Hagrid's disregard for the consequences of their loving actions leads to the endangerment of both their students and their longed-for teaching careers. "Moody," plays a major role in fostering student confidence when it comes to facing dark wizards, and this confidence affects the way the students are able and willing to fight during the Battle of Hogwarts. Ironically, the false care with which "Moody" teaches proves vital in the destruction of the thing he cares about most, offering us a cautionary tale of the negative effects of pretending to care.

Although care is in abundance at Hogwarts, from teacher-student relationships to the care that arises between peers, it is worth considering the ways in which Hogwarts' teachers demonstrate a pedagogy of care that fails to take into account the needs of the teachers themselves, with the notable exception of the care exemplified by Professor McGonagall. This is, perhaps, not a surprise: even though Noddings devotes a chapter to "Caring for Self" in *The Challenge to Care*, her examples are all oriented toward ways in which students can be taught to care for themselves, rather than providing practical advice for the carers. At the end of the chapter, she does acknowledge that "to convey such messages authentically, we must ... show by our examples that life is both consummatory—to be enjoyed from moment to moment— and instrumental preparation for further activity, enjoyment, and fulfillment" (90), but she does not offer any concrete suggestions for how a caring teacher can authentically integrate the self-care they are expected to model to their students. The strategies presented in *The Resilient Practitioner*, such as incorporating reflective writing to decompress from teaching challenges and embracing opportunities to reinvent ourselves and our teaching practice, provide a starting place for teachers and other carers to begin to develop the resilience that will help them sustain their teaching careers, particularly if we can internalize the statement that "self-care is always important" (Skovholt and Trotter-Mathison 162).

As Nel Noddings and others who have considered the implications for a teaching practice built around a pedagogy of care have argued, "caring is the very bedrock of all successful education" (Noddings, *Challenge to Care* 27). However, I struggle with the ways in which care in the classroom often ignores the self-care a teacher must practice in order to continue to successfully care for their students. The examples of Professors Hagrid, Lupin, and "Moody" demonstrate some of the pitfalls of a pedagogy of care that neglects self-care, while Professor McGonagall offers an alternative conception of care for others that does not neglect care of self. The magical world has much to teach us about Muggle relationships, particularly in the classroom, and the lessons of care presented here may offer cautionary tales and guideposts for teachers as they navigate their caring careers. Cultivating reciprocal care for our students is an important part of teaching, but we must remember not to neglect care of ourselves as well: we must attend to our health, seek mentorship and support throughout our careers, and keep our caring authentic. Perhaps then we will be able to sustain a career that is as long and vibrant as that which Professor McGonagall has enjoyed.

WORKS CITED

Beltman, Susan, et al. "Thriving Not Just Surviving: A Review of Research on Teacher Resilience." *Educational Research Review*, vol. 6, no. 3, 2011, pp. 185–207. *Scholars Portal Journals*, doi:10.1016/j.edurev.2011.09.001.

hooks, bell. *Teaching Community: A Pedagogy of Hope*. Routledge, 2003.

Noddings, Nel. *Caring: A Feminine Approach to Ethics & Moral Education*. U of California P, 1984.

———. *The Challenge to Care in Schools: An Alternative Approach to Education*. 2nd ed., Teachers College Press, 2005.

———. *Critical Lessons: What Our Schools Should Teach*. Cambridge UP, 2006.

Rowling, J.K. *Harry Potter and the Chamber of Secrets*. Anniversary ed., Bloomsbury, 2014.

———. *Harry Potter and the Goblet of Fire*. Anniversary ed., Bloomsbury, 2014.

———. *Harry Potter and the Order of the Phoenix*. Anniversary ed., Bloomsbury, 2014.

———. *Harry Potter and the Philosopher's Stone*. Anniversary ed., Bloomsbury, 2014.

———. *Harry Potter and the Prisoner of Azkaban*. Anniversary ed., Bloomsbury, 2014.

Skovholt, Thomas M., and Michelle Trotter-Mathison. *The Resilient Practitioner: Burnout and Compassion Fatigue Prevention and Self-Care Strategies for the Helping Professions*. Routledge, 2016.

About the Contributors

Emma Louise **Barlow** is a Ph.D. candidate in Italian studies at the University of Sydney (Australia). Her doctoral research proposes a study of the liminal geography of suicide in Dante's *Commedia* and of the ways in which this conception of suicide was shaped by Dante's experience of exile and by the contemporaneous intellectual and literary landscape. Her research interests include medieval and Renaissance Italian literature, palaeography, the history of emotions, and pedagogical practices in tertiary education.

Samantha **Bise**, MLIS, is the Reference & Instruction Librarian and an English instructor at Central Penn College. She is enrolled in a doctoral program in language, culture, and literacy education, and her research interests include correctional and critical pedagogy, critical information literacy instruction methods, and ethnolinguistics. She serves in various volunteer positions in her community and is passionate about teaching and creating equitable educational opportunities for adult learners.

Brynn **Fitzsimmons** teaches first-year writing courses at the University of Missouri–Kansas City as part of her graduate teaching assistantship and master's program. She is completing a master's in English with an emphasis in manuscript, print culture, and editing, and intends to pursue further study in the field of rhetoric and composition with a focus on using storytelling and narrative theory concepts to effectively guide students toward being more conscious creators and consumers of stories—creative, academic, and otherwise.

Jamie L.H. **Goodall**, Ph.D., is an assistant professor of history in the Public History Department at Stevenson University in Baltimore, Maryland. Her publications include "Tippling Houses, Rum Shops, & Taverns" in the *Journal of Maritime History* as well as several forthcoming publications including *Selling the Seven Seas: Piracy, Taste-Making, & Consumption in the Early Modern Caribbean World (1650–1790)* and *Pirates of the Chesapeake Bay: A Brief History of Piracy in Maryland and Virginia.*

Laurie **Johnson** is a professor of German at the University of Illinois at Urbana-Champaign, with affiliations in comparative and world literature and in the Unit for Criticism and Interpretive Theory. She is the author of *Forgotten Dreams: Revisiting*

Romanticism in the Cinema of Werner Herzog (2016), *Aesthetic Anxiety* (2010), and *The Art of Recollection in Jena Romanticism* (2002), as well as numerous articles. She regularly teaches a course at Illinois entitled "Harry Potter and Western Culture."

Rachelle A.C. **Joplin** is a rhetoric, composition, and pedagogy doctoral student at the University of Houston. Her scholarly projects center around the rhetorical implications of allyship, especially in the academy. She is interested in the application of affect theory and intersectional feminism to the teaching of rhetoric and composition and the study of pop culture. She is also the editorial assistant for *Peitho*, the journal of the Coalition of Feminist Scholars in the History of Rhetoric and Composition.

Alice **Loda** holds a Ph.D. in Italian studies from the University of Sydney (Australia). Her doctoral dissertation, "Exophonic Poetics in Contemporary Italy" (2017) engages with migration and translingual poetic writing in contemporary Italy. She is a lecturer in Italian studies at the University of Technology Sydney. Her research interests include rhetoric and stylistics, contemporary poetry, comparative literature, translation studies, and migration literature.

Addison **Lucchi**, MS, MBA, serves as an assistant professor and Instructional & Research Librarian at MidAmerica Nazarene University. He is pursuing a Ph.D. from the University of Missouri–Kansas City. His publications include a book chapter, "The Writerly Librarian" in *Creativity for Library Career Advancement* (2019) and an article in Brick and Click's conference proceedings, "Know What You Write: Teaching Research to Creative Writers" (2018).

Lee Anna **Maynard**, Ph.D., is an assistant professor of English at Augusta University, where she teaches *Harry Potter* texts in courses ranging from college composition to children's literature and adolescent literature. Her book, *Beautiful Boredom: Idleness and Feminine Self-Realization in the Victorian Novel*, explores the manifestations of women's boredom(s) in 19th-century literature and art.

Jen **McConnel**, MS, MA, is a Ph.D. candidate and a long-time teacher. She holds an MS in library science from Clarion University of Pennsylvania and an MA in children's literature from Hollins University. She teaches literacy, technology, and professional courses to teacher candidates at Queen's University in Kingston, Ontario. Her research focuses on literacy across contexts.

Tara **Moore**, Ph.D., has written two books about Christmas culture, *Victorian Christmas in Print* (2009) and *Christmas: The Sacred to Santa* (2014), and edited a book of Victorian Christmas ghost stories. She has also published about focalization in *Harry Potter and the Cursed Child,* adoption in the wizarding world, and violent girl warriors in fantasy YA. She teaches workplace writing courses and young adult literature at Elizabethtown College in Lancaster County, Pennsylvania.

Carl **Niekerk** is a professor of German at the University of Illinois at Urbana-Champaign, with affiliations in French and Italian, comparative and world literature, Jewish studies, and European studies. He is the author of *Reading Mahler: German Culture and Jewish Identity in Fin-de-siècle Vienna* (2010/2013), *Zwischen*

Naturgeschichte und Anthropologie (2005), and *Bildungskrisen* (1995), as well as numerous articles. He is the editor-in-chief of *The German Quarterly and The Lessing Yearbook*.

Mary **Reding**, MA, serves as the Writing Center Director and is a lecturer of English at Upper Iowa University, Fayette, Iowa. Her research concerns the intersection between hero studies and academic success, which was also the focus of her thesis, "Harry Potter's Heroics: Crossing the Thresholds of Home, Away, and the Spaces In-Between" (2016).

Marcie Panutsos **Rovan**, Ph.D., is an assistant professor of English and director of First-Year Writing. She has a doctorate in literature from Duquesne University with a specialization in children's literature and literary modernism. Her publications include "The 'Broken Mirror': Casualties of Nation-Building in Train to Pakistan," in *Impressions* and a book chapter, "What to Do with Supergirl? Fairy Tale Tropes, Female Power and Conflicted Feminist Discourse" in *Girl of Steel: Essays on Television's* Supergirl *and Fourth-Wave Feminism* (2020).

Kerry **Spencer**, Ph.D., teaches writing in the sciences at Stevenson University in Baltimore, Maryland. Her publications include creative works, book chapters in edited collections, and peer-reviewed journal articles, including "Research Methods in Creative Writing" (2015) and "Marketing and Sales in the US YA Fiction Market" (2017). Her novel won an award from the Utah Fine Arts Council for Young Adult fiction, and she has received a seed grant to study the marketing of young adult fiction in the US.

Jessica L. **Tinklenberg**, Ph.D., is the program director of the Claremont Colleges Center for Teaching and Learning (California), where her work emphasizes the importance of transparency, equity, and engagement to improve learning outcomes for all students. She has a Ph.D. in religions of Western antiquity from Florida State University and has spent the previous ten years incorporating and assessing active learning (AL) pedagogy in her religious studies classes at Morningside College (Sioux City, Iowa).

Melissa **Wehler**, Ph.D., a professor of interdisciplinary studies, has published essays in a variety of edited collections where she discusses topics including the gothic, feminism, performance, and popular culture. She has published on Neil Gaiman's *Coraline*, PBS' *Downton Abbey*, Netflix's *Jessica Jones*, and Disney's *Maleficent*. She is the coeditor, with Tim Rayborn, of *Girl of Steel: Essays on Television's* Supergirl *and Fourth-Wave Feminism* (2020).

Index

active learning 42–43, 45, 56n1, 61, 63–64, 66, 69, 92–7, 100–104, 114, 145, 148–149, 151, 201
Azkaban 32, 36, 71, 86, 99, 115, 152, 193

Battle of Hogwarts 34–35, 54, 113, 140, 153, 193, 195, 197
Binns, Cuthbert 2–3, 5, 62, 66, 100–102, 104
Black, Sirius 37, 62, 86, 99, 121, 127–128, 130, 132, 156, 179, 188–189, 193
Bloom's Taxonomy 2, 114, 142
boggart 48, 64–5, 71, 86, 96–98, 103, 115, 117, 187–189
bullying 35–36, 49, 51–52, 126, 178–179, 187
Burbage, Charity 5

Campbell, Joseph *see* hero's journey
Care of Magical Creatures 27, 42, 63, 94, 100, 103, 114, 128, 144, 146–149, 159, 191, 192
The Carrows 6, 99
Chamber of Secrets 16, 19, 65–66, 68, 88, 101, 134, 177, 194
Chang, Cho 32–33, 62, 116, 143, 152, 174
charms 42, 44, 55, 109, 115; course 62; *see also Expelliarmus*; Patronus
critical thinking 2, 142, 150
Crouch, Barty 3, 5–6, 51, 69, 78, 81, 84, 114, 156, 187; *see also* Moody, Alastor

The Daily Prophet 13, 19, 115, 133, 166
Dark Arts 34, 39, 81, 84–88, 97, 102, 129, 197; *see also* Defense Against the Darks Arts (DADA)
Dark Lord *see* Voldemort
death eaters 32, 34, 38–39, 54, 63, 99, 129, 132, 141
Defense Against the Dark Arts (DADA) 4–5, 14, 27, 36, 38, 44, 48, 52, 60, 63, 68, 71, 77–80, 82–90, 96–102, 113, 140–145, 152–153, 181, 187, 190, 196–197; *see also* Dark Arts
Dementors 35, 61, 87, 117, 143
Diggory, Cedric 33, 131
Dobby 31

Dumbledore, Albus 3, 5–6, 13, 15, 19, 24, 31, 34, 64, 72, 84, 99–100, 107, 111, 116–118, 121, 123–124, 126–128, 130–135, 139, 141, 150, 153, 158, 164–168, 176, 178–183, 191–193, 196
Dumbledore's Army 5, 27–30, 30–39, 52–54, 94, 98–99, 104, 115–116, 125, 129, 131–132, 140, 150–153
The Dursleys 50, 126, 161, 180
Dweck, Carol 107–108, 112–113, 119

Expelliarmus 36, 68, 131, 151

feedback 2, 5, 43, 45, 53, 55, 69, 70, 94–95, 112, 117, 141, 147, 151
Filch, Argus 125
fixed mindset *see* mindset
Flitwick, Filius 66, 65, 195
Foucault, Michele 123–124, 126, 134
Fudge, Cornelius 13, 126–127, 140

goal-oriented learning 63, 65–67, 117
Granger, Hermione 15, 19, 21–23, 31, 34, 36–38, 44–47, 49, 54, 62, 65–66, 69, 81, 96–99, 101–102, 109, 113–116, 119, 124–125, 127–131, 139, 142, 143–145, 147–149, 153, 163, 172–173, 176–177, 183, 153, 163, 172–173, 176–177, 183, 187, 189, 191–194
growth mindset *see* mindset
Grubbly-Plank, Wilhelmina 6, 65–66, 128, 144, 146–8
Gryffindor 31, 49–50, 59–67, 69, 71, 81, 109–110, 176–177

Hagrid, Rubeus 3, 5–6, 21, 23, 43, 65, 69, 96, 103–104, 118–119, 128, 130–131, 144, 147–149, 158–160, 162–163, 168, 175, 180, 187, 181–198
half-blood 133, 159, 176; *see also* pure-blood
Half-Blood Prince *see* Snape, Severus
Harry Potter and Half-Blood Prince 49, 65, 89, 166, 181; *see also* Snape, Severus
Harry Potter and the Chamber of Secrets 16, 65, 68, 134; *see also* Chamber of Secrets

203